The More I Owe You

The More I Owe You

· Michael Sledge ·

COUNTERPOINT

BERKELEY

Excerpts from "Arrival at Santos" and "Song for the Rainy Season" from THE COM-
PLETE POEMS 1927–1979 by Elizabeth Bishop. Copyright © 1979, 1983 by Alice
Helen Methfessel. Reprinted by permission of Farrar, Straus and Giroux, LLC.

Excerpts from "Sammy" and "Aubade and Elegy" from EDGAR ALLAN POE & THE
JUKE-BOX by Elizabeth Bishop, edited and annotated by Alice Quinn. Copyright ©
2006 by Alice Helen Methfessel. Reprinted by permission of Farrar,
Straus and Giroux, LLC.

This is a work of fiction. Names, characters, places, and incidents are the product of
the author's imagination or are used fictitiously. Any resemblance to actual persons,
living or dead, is entirely coincidental.

Library of Congress Cataloging-in-Publication Data
Sledge, Michael, 1962–
The more I owe you : a novel / by Michael Sledge.
p. cm.
ISBN 978-1-58243-576-3
1. Bishop, Elizabeth, 1911-1979—Fiction. 2. Poets, American—20th century—
Fiction. 3. Women poets, American—Fiction. 4. Soares, Lota de Macedo, 1910-
1967—Fiction. 5. Architects—Brazil—Fiction. 6. Women architects—Fiction.
7. Lesbian couples—Fiction. 8. Rio de Janeiro (Brazil)—Fiction. I. Title.

PS3619.L43M67 2010
813'.6—dc22
2010003258

Cover design by Ann Weinstock
Interior Design by Elyse Strongin, Neuwirth & Associates, Inc.

Printed in the United States of America

COUNTERPOINT
BERKELEY

Counterpoint
2117 Fourth Street
Suite D
Berkeley, CA 94710

www.counterpointpress.com

Distributed by Publishers Group West

10 9 8 7 6 5 4 3 2 1

FOR RAUL CABRA ESTRELLA

. . . O dar-vos quanto tenho e quanto posso,
Que quanto mais vos pago, mais vos devo.

—Camões

rrival at Santos

. . .

[NOVEMBER 1951 – JANUARY 1952]

Here is a coast; here is a harbor;
here, after a meager diet of horizon, is some scenery:
impractically shaped and—who knows?—self-pitying mountains,
sad and harsh beneath their frivolous greenery,

with a little church on top of one. And warehouses,
some of them painted a feeble pink, or blue,
and some tall, uncertain palms. Oh, tourist,
is this how this country is going to answer you

and your immodest demands for a different world,
and a better life, and complete comprehension
of both at last, and immediately,
after eighteen days of suspension?

Finish your breakfast.

· I ·

THE SHIP CROSSED the equator sometime in the night. Elizabeth sat on deck among the crates of cargo bound for South America, taking shelter from the damp wind. The sky was vast, with half a moon and masses of soft, oily-looking stars.

She was middle-aged. It was her first trip to the Southern Hemisphere.

Storms and rolling seas had followed them ever since they'd left New York. Each morning when she came up from her cabin, gray rain-squalls surrounded the freighter. They seemed to tease the ship, coming close on either side, then retreating, ahead, then behind. Among the black waves appeared glittering silver sheets where the sun broke through the clouds, roving across the water's surface like searchlights. The captain, a reticent Norwegian, had said it was the roughest trip he'd made in years, but it was certainly not so rough as to dissuade her from lounging on deck long past midnight. Better still, not so rough that it had prevented her from working. At last she'd finished those reviews that had weighed on her mind for months.

Miss Lytton, however, had not fared as well. Seasick in her cabin most of the time, she emerged from below only at meals to attempt a few spoonfuls of broth. Poor thing, though she really was too stupid for words.

All of them, so immeasurably stupid. Miss Lytton and Mr. Richling, absolute torture to be stuck on a ship with those two. Just this evening at dinner, the petty boastings of the Uruguayan consul could not have been borne with good grace for five minutes more. The even-tempered captain had retired from table with the most brusque of good evenings. One simply couldn't compete. The only passenger Mr. Richling didn't successfully brutalize with narrations on the superiority of his intellect or physical courage or haberdashery was the thoroughly green and nauseated Miss Lytton. She managed to hold her own in spite of her debility, luring Mr. Richling away from the subject of himself with her own tantalizing accounts of the latest society-page improprieties, or, when she'd exhausted that topic, of the lowbrow scandals of common folk. Elizabeth supposed she should be happy the two of them had found one another. Savaging people who were not currently onboard the SS *Bowplate* kept them occupied and, for the most part, out of the private lives of the people who were. Tomorrow, there was to be a shipboard Thanksgiving dinner for the lot of them. The thought of that communal meal, rather than the constantly rolling ship, was enough to make Elizabeth grow nauseated herself.

I ran away into shifting weather, swaying walls. Squalls day after day.

Still, in spite of her fellow passengers, Elizabeth could imagine no more pleasurable way to travel than by sea. She could gaze at the ocean for hours and never grow tired of it. No looking forward or back, no thoughts of what you've taken leave of, what you hope to find when you arrive. Just this perfect suspension.

At the railing not twenty feet from her deck chair, a figure appeared out of the dark.

Recognizing the tall, angular form, Elizabeth was instantly upon her feet. When the shifting deck caused her to lose balance, she held fast to the cargo of tractors and combines. Fortunately, the hulking farm equipment was lashed down and crated, unlike the miniature vehicles constantly rolling about underfoot, endangering passengers and crew alike. The missionary had managed to teach his three young boys to speak a foreign language; was there some impediment to teaching them to put away their toys? It really could be hazardous, one's dealings with humankind, to body and to mind.

So as not to startle her, Elizabeth softly called the elderly woman's name.

"Elizabeth," Miss Breen answered. The scarf she'd tied over her head was unable to contain the nimbus of white hair that floated ethereally around her angelic expression. "Why am I not surprised to find you here?"

"You're up too, I see."

"I've never been able to sleep much past four o'clock."

"And I've never been able to sleep much at all."

Miss Breen smiled in her hazy, enigmatic way. *Why Brazil*, Elizabeth had asked early on in the trip, *why'd you decide on Brazil?* and Miss Breen had answered simply, *You of all people asking me that.* What Elizabeth hadn't admitted was how haphazard her own choice had been. When she'd gone to the shipping agent, intent on booking a passage to Europe, there'd been only one ship sailing on the day she hoped to depart, the *Bowplate* bound for Argentina, making a stop at Santos harbor near São Paulo, and so that was the voyage she'd booked instead.

"We've just passed over the equator, I think," Elizabeth said. "I came on deck to see if there was any notable change."

"And how does this hemisphere look?"

"Much the same. The fact is, one is stuck with oneself wherever one goes. Understanding myself or the world any better will not come as easily as the price of a freighter ticket."

"No," Miss Breen said mysteriously. "But it will come."

"Is that the voice of experience?"

"Not at all, of hope for myself!" She added, "But then, Ida always tells me I'm a Pollyanna."

The freighter dipped roughly to the side; Elizabeth held the railing with both hands as a laugh escaped her, of surprise and physical pleasure. She faced the warm ocean wind, inhaled the equatorial air.

Where the ship split the sea, a froth of luminescence. She felt nearly a child beside the towering Miss Breen, who was willowy but not stout, probably just short of seventy, with hair so fine and billowy you wanted to pet it. Knobs of bone stuck out from her elbows. Her eyes were large and expressive, of the bluest blue. They seemed to have no age at all. One felt certain there was quite a bit more going through Miss Breen's head than she let on to the immediate company. The few personal details Elizabeth knew—that she'd been a police lieutenant, now recently retired from directing a women's prison in Detroit for over twenty years, and that she'd even played a part in solving a number of murders—had been extracted during the voyage bit by bit, after much pressing by Miss Lytton & Co. When asked the most rude and intrusive questions, Miss Breen consistently refused to lose her patience. She was extremely kind to everyone onboard, and so gentle that Elizabeth found it difficult to imagine her overseeing a stable of criminal women. A number of times, Miss Breen had referred to her friend Ida, but Elizabeth noticed it was only when the two of them were alone that she spoke of Ida as her roommate.

"Do you suppose Reverend Brown will teach his children to sing hymns on a Buenos Aires street corner?" Elizabeth asked.

"They all will sing, I imagine. Isn't that why they've come?"

"Yesterday his wife asked me to read to her about Argentina from my guidebook. She knows nothing whatsoever about the place they're going to, hasn't read a thing about it. And I thought *I* was traveling in the dark. I almost feel protective of them, they seem so lost and pitiful. Though no doubt she thinks the same of me."

"About both of us," Miss Breen said. "We're fallen women." She turned her gaze upon Elizabeth, as if her blue eyes could see directly into Elizabeth's thoughts.

They had discovered over the days, shyly and slowly, that in their daydreams they'd imagined the same Brazil, the same tapestries of green forest, the colors of birds and flowers.

"They are all more and more annoying," Elizabeth said, with a surge of bitter feeling. "They're more like caricatures of people than real ones—"

"Dear, it doesn't matter."

This hatefulness, this poison. She couldn't escape; it had followed her out to sea. Yes, one certainly stayed what one was—that was the lesson, cross as many latitudes as you liked. Or was it possible, could she hope, that this was no more than the toxic vestiges of the last two years at last getting out of her system, like water from an unused pipe spewing rust before it ran clear? "You're right," Elizabeth said. "It doesn't matter one bit, it really doesn't."

She and Miss Breen looked at one another.

Boldly, Elizabeth asked, "Wouldn't Ida have liked to come with you?"

"I'm sure she would have, but she's had to go to South Korea."

"South Korea! So you're *both* intrepid explorers."

"She's helping to set up a women's police force there."

"And you're both in law enforcement! Your neighbors must feel extremely safe."

"Oh, yes," Miss Breen said, smiling, "everyone feels very safe around me."

THE TINY CABIN was not unpleasant, but in the dark it was reminiscent of other rooms in other places where Elizabeth had felt too keenly her distance from any living being. Attempting to settle on the bunk, she was nearly tossed to the floor each time the ship pitched over a wave. Some sort of strap or bunk belt was called for. She was thankful, at least, that for once her own body, unlike the unfortunate Miss Lytton's, did not betray her.

It was nearly dawn, yet her mind raced along with the ship's engines reverberating through the cabin wall, surging, slowing, surging again. *I'm doing well*, the engines repeated, *I'm doing well, I'm doing well*. It was in still moments such as this that her craft showed itself to be the most useless. Why couldn't her thoughts fill with soothing scraps, with lines and rhymes, or images she'd seen that day, the flying fish and refracted light in the ship's spray, storm clouds, the missionary's children in a row singing a hymn? Why could her imagination not reach, as it had so insistently when she was a child, to capture in words all the world's unfolding marvels? Instead, her brain was in a tempest, like the rainsqualls that tossed the ship, churning in every direction, erupting with incoherent thought. A brainstorm, night after night. That's exactly what had happened at Yaddo last year. Her mind would not alight and rest. Yaddo, the utopian dream of some mad millionairess, where the squalor of the real world was kept briefly at bay so that artists could roam at their leisure, chew their cud, and sculpt, compose, finger paint, what have you, without interruption. Elizabeth, too, had strolled the tranquil grounds, watched chipmunks scamper in the garden, fed buttered bread to the chickadees, blown soap bubbles from her balcony as an afternoon diversion, and gone quietly mad. All of it so perfect; it was only Miss Bishop that was wrong. The nervousness, the dizziness, the little splinter of panic working its way deeper and deeper—one thing alone fended them off. Each afternoon she walked past the scummy ponds and into town, directly to a trustworthy trader, then returned to her room and proceeded to drink herself numb. She slipped the bottles into the trash bin outside the kitchen, but the others knew, of course. So nice and pleasant and young, the whole herd of them, they smiled and said good morning, which was even more sinister than if they'd avoided her glance altogether. Somehow, throughout, she'd managed to keep writing, but it did not matter, not really. The weeks passed.

The night the hurricane struck, Elizabeth watched from her window as a fantastic wind uprooted the great old pines. One came crashing down across the roof of the painting studio next door. The destruction thrilled her. Then came a sharp report like a gunshot, and the wall of Elizabeth's room lifted away from the house. A few strips of lathing stood between her and the wind and lashing rain. In her drunken state, she'd either fallen and hit her head or else been conked on the bean by a wayward piece of plaster. A draft of cold air upon her face brought her back to consciousness. Opening her eyes, Elizabeth looked directly outdoors upon the devastated scenery. It was morning now, a sky of clear blue.

Her head was in terrible pain; her decision, absolute. Elizabeth checked herself into a hospital, stayed there for a time, and that did her good. It was a start. This trip had done her even better. Since leaving New York, she'd felt stronger, saner, more productive, certainly more sober than she had in ages. She was being very good. One drink a day, that was the limit, and if she could manage, not until evening.

Dimly visible on her cabin table was the pot of white chrysanthemums Marianne had given her as a bon voyage present, still keeping after two weeks onboard. The only friend to see her off. She had to laugh thinking of Marianne's gruff *Goodbye, Elizabeth* before the ship left. Elizabeth concentrated on the white flowers, which swayed and trembled with the rolling ship. They looked just like the huge foggy star visible from the ship's deck, on clear nights, in the southwest.

SOUTH OF RIO, they sighted land. An outline of high, jagged mountains, and then, as the ship came near, ruffled green foliage on the slopes and a white knife-edge of beach. Dark clouds hovered over the coast.

After dinner, they entered the port of Santos, navigating among the two dozen big ships in the harbor. It was raining heavily, and Elizabeth went below to prepare her luggage. Before retiring for the night, she stood outside Miss Breen's cabin door, having come with no real purpose, no offering of any sort, like a suitor without flowers.

Miss Breen filled the doorway, appearing rather monumental in the tiny cabin. Behind her stood an open trunk, half-packed, and a small dressing table with her perfumes and toiletries, neatly arranged.

"Your cabin is even smaller than mine," Elizabeth said. "I wish I'd known. I would have asked you to switch."

"But I've liked it," Miss Breen replied. "I've felt as snug as a snail in its shell."

Elizabeth thought she might have offered one of her own books as a gift, but it was such an embarrassing thing, being a poet. *Thank you for living so gracefully*. That's what she would have liked to say, if you could actually say that to a person. *Thank you for showing me it can be done.*

In several days, at the São Paulo railway station, she will kiss the cool, powdery cheek of Miss Breen and bid her goodbye; the two women will never see one another again. But for many years, the image will remain vivid to Elizabeth of Miss Breen in the doorway of her cabin: the kind guard at the gate, inviting her to reenter the world.

BY MORNING, THE rain had ceased. It happened that she and Miss Breen were the only passengers leaving the ship at Santos; the rest would continue stupefying one another all the way to Buenos Aires. Misses Breen and Bishop waited on deck for the immigration officials to board. Under low, gray clouds, the harbor was full of activity, with men hauling big canvas sacks and metal drums along the wharves, and little dinghies crossing the oily water here and there, while a variety of smells assaulted the senses—diesel exhaust, coffee, and something rancid—rotten fruit, perhaps. A shark fin appeared among a pile of floating garbage, but when Elizabeth pointed it out to Miss Breen, the fin submerged in a whirlpool. The warehouses along the water were fanciful colors, pink, yellow, and blue, but the paint was faded and peeling, the buildings unkempt, some of them close to collapse. Rusted tin roofs ascended the hillside, then mountains soared up, how high she couldn't see, their peaks were enshrouded in mist.

The sad industry of a port, a dirty and dispiriting place.

The tender was there; she saw it skirting around a ship toward them, a buoyant, battered little craft bearing the Brazilian flag, piloted by an elderly black man in a white cap.

Elizabeth gripped the railing like a bird on a branch. She wore her usual tan slacks and shirt, while beside her, Miss Breen looked elegant in a black linen dress and a scarf with blue polka dots. Why was it that a seventy-year-old prison director carried herself with greater style than Elizabeth could muster? This morning, she had discovered a scrap of paper on the cabin floor, a receipt from Macy's in New York for $9.32, something she'd bought right before the ship had left, she could no longer remember what. She was about to throw the receipt away when she saw words on the back, in her own chicken-scratch handwriting, a note she'd scribbled in the dark the other night when she couldn't get to sleep. *Beginning of a poem—begins before the beginning—it anticipates the beginning—the act of preparation for what will come, though one doesn't know what will come, the preparation to make a leap of faith.*

Two days in São Paulo with Miss Breen, then on to Rio, where Mary and Pearl would meet her at the train station. In the midst of a thousand strangers, those two would recognize her; each would take her arm. She needn't worry that she'd have no anchor, that she'd lose her bearings, end up in a bar somewhere.

And she would see Lota again.

She and Miss Breen peered over the railing as the customs official climbed the ladder and came aboard, and then again as their luggage was lowered on ropes into the tender.

Elizabeth felt a leap of excitement, followed by a wave of foreboding.

Miss Breen took hold of her hand.

· 2 ·

*P*AULO AND JULINHO returned with their arms full of grass, long yellow-green bundles that brushed the ground like sweeping horsetails. Lota showed the men how they were to load the rocks that she and Mary had chosen from the streambed into the back of the jeep. First a thick layer of grass, then the rocks placed upon it, like prehistoric eggs in a nest. Another bed of greenery, then more rocks. The grass was still green and aromatic from the rainy season. When they were girls, she and Marietta had tried to dry the grass and roll it in cigarette papers they'd stolen from their father and smoke it. They had rattled their bones from coughing. Her sister used to be so devilish, and now—such a bore! That's what happened when you married a brute.

You are very smart, Dona Lota, Julinho said as he watched her arrange the rocks in the grass. Look how you protect the car.

Surprise! It's not the car I'm protecting. Come here, *coraçao*.

He was a youth, his brown neck so delicate it was like a girl's. Lota chose a rock and showed him the ruff of lichen on its underside, the play of grays and soft greens. This is what I'm protecting.

Julinho said nothing, simply turned to her with the look she'd seen so many times on the faces of men that she'd become inured to it. She ignored the look, his and others', except on the occasions it triggered her rage. They might give her the look that said she was crazy, but afterwards they always did what she commanded. Just wait, she told the boy, you'll see what a beautiful wall we will make.

She sent the men to gather more grass while she and Mary carried the rocks they'd selected from the stream up the hill to the car. Mary was a strong worker. She could probably haul a sack of these rocks on her back, though she looked as though she were put together with little twigs and chicken bones you could snap with your finger.

This is the last load for me, Lota, Mary said.

What are you talking about? We've hardly begun.

I have to go to Rio, remember? Don't be obstinate. I know you haven't forgotten that I'm meeting Elizabeth's train.

Oh yes, our American friend. But must you really leave now?

In fact, Lota was excited by Elizabeth's upcoming visit. Of all the people they'd met in New York, she was by far the most perceptive, the most brilliant. In a roomful of people talking, she would stay quiet for half an hour, then make one comment that cut through all the *merde*. But someone had hurt her terribly, that was plain to see. Why else did she act like a mouse scurrying along the wall? She needed to be cared for like a flower; then she would bloom. And what better place for a flower to bloom than here at Samambaia?

Lota could still remember the moment she had first set eyes on Elizabeth, in the Museum of Modern Art in New York. She had gone there with Candido Portinari to meet her new friend Elodie, and the three of them—Lota de Macedo Soares, arm in arm with the preeminent Brazilian painter and the director of Moma's circulating exhibitions—had strolled through the galleries, talking of how they might put together an exhibition of these paintings to send to Brazil. After a time, Lota noticed they were being followed at a discreet distance by a woman who pretended to look at the paintings but was actually eavesdropping on their conversation. The woman was small and very neat, her clothes put together with an excellent eye, everything of *bom desenho*. At last,

Lota addressed her directly. She raised her voice and said, Would you like to come closer so that you can hear me better? The woman turned, and for an endless time they held one another's stare. Her face was a perfect doll's face, her eyes a pale northern blue. Lota smiled—she did not want to scare this little bird away, but she already had. In a fierce voice, the woman said, Oh, no thank you, and hurried off. In the way that fate worked, it was less than a week later when their friend Louise brought someone new to dinner, and Lota recognized her immediately, the woman of *bom desenho*.

At that dinner, Elizabeth claimed to have no recollection of the incident at the museum. It will become a joke between them, a game, to admit or not to admit remembering that first encounter, the jolt it had sent through them both. When did you mark the beginning, the moment the wheels were set in motion? At the first meeting of eyes, the formal introduction with names? Or later, when the inevitability of something more could no longer be denied, when it had to be spoken aloud?

After Mary left, Lota drove the jeep full of rocks up to the house. She arrived just in time. The workmen pouring the floor had begun marking square divisions in the setting concrete, and she had to scream, Leave it smooth, you clowns! This is not a sidewalk!

Yes, Elizabeth would bring a breath of fresh air to their mountain. And more than that: the spark of her genius. Lota could hardly wait to show her all this, all that she had made.

But still, how annoying to be interrupted!

· 3 ·

ER HEAD FELL back against the taxi seat. Out the window, a parade of sights. Skyscrapers, a harbor circled by mountains, ships going back and forth, Christ atop a cliff in a swirl of clouds with his arms spread wide, speeding cars, men chasing after a soccer ball. A cobblestone street with sunlight beaming through the foliage of great big trees. "Here we are," Mary said as the taxi slowed. Tall apartment buildings, and tree limbs laden with vines and flowers. It was like New York a bit, but with orchids growing on the telephone lines.

In the apartment, they settled into chairs, and a maid set a tiny cup of coffee in Elizabeth's hand. Her luggage was shuttled down a back hallway. Then the three ladies were making small talk, just as if she'd popped over for a neighborly visit. The typical back-and-forth rhythms: How was the ship, *oh it was wonderful and dreadful*; and how was the train, *such impractical scenery!*; and how was São Paulo, *total chaos I must have gotten lost a thousand times*. Mary, after all these years in Brazil, still sat as stiffly as if she possessed a steel rod for a spine. No doubt it would be a greater challenge to one's expectations to have discovered otherwise. Lovely woman, though. And Pearl, one of her favorites from Yaddo, so pretty and impetuous, but really too young to be down here on her own, or practically on her own.

Mary expressed surprise to have heard Elizabeth was coming by train; she'd been led to believe the route from São Paulo had been discontinued.

"I did get the impression the service is erratic," Elizabeth said. "My friend Miss Breen knew people in São Paulo who tracked down the information for me." She'd loved traveling by train, the view of lush mounds of mountains with cows perched on their steep slopes. Elizabeth hadn't slept a bit all night, she was utterly exhausted, and yet she felt truly awake and alert. A film of perspiration lay over all her skin, but it made her feel right at home, it was that Key West feeling. "This coffee is delicious," she said.

"Would you like another?"

"Yes, please."

Mary spoke to the maid. Mary of all people, the proper Bostonian, speaking Portuguese in Rio de Janeiro! "You said you were lost in São Paulo?" Mary asked.

"At least twenty times in two days. The city is a labyrinth."

"You were on foot?"

Elizabeth nodded.

"That was brave," Pearl said.

Abruptly she stood. She couldn't sit still a moment longer. She'd been sitting down for the last twelve or fourteen hours. She'd been sitting the last twenty days, perhaps that many years. Across the apartment a wall of glass beckoned, and Elizabeth moved toward it. From there she took in the wide blue planes of sea and sky, exactly as she had on the ship, and down below, a yellow stretch of beach. Behind her, Mary murmured polite questions to Pearl. *How long have you been in Rio? Oh, really, not even a year? You seem so at home already.* Then Mary was standing at Elizabeth's side with her hand upon the window latch. The entire wall slid open, not a window after all but a door, and the sea breathed into Elizabeth's face. The terrace offered an even more impressive view. To the left, a mountain, with another mountain peeking up over it—was that the Sugar Loaf?—and to the right, the great sweep of Copacabana. "This is magnificent," Elizabeth said. "I didn't realize you were quite so in the clouds."

"If you like being in the clouds, wait until you see Samambaia."

"That's your place in the mountains?"

"Yes, it is."

Mary's intent presence seemed to expect further inquiry, but in the face of Elizabeth's silence the other woman returned inside. It was extremely hot. An iron lid of cloud clamped down, steaming them alive. Below, hundreds of men were running around on the beach, kicking and lobbing balls back and forth, on the sand, over nets. How they were able to do so in such weather, Elizabeth couldn't fathom.

"I'd love to explore a bit," she said when she rejoined her friends.

"Yes," Pearl said brightly, with a touch of desperation. "I can't wait to show you around."

Mary reached for her purse. "I'll be heading back to Samambaia, so I can't join you. The apartment is yours while you're here, of course. Lota will come down to Rio in a few days and fetch you back, as we discussed. If you call tomorrow, we'll arrange the time."

"Yes, I'll do that."

"Good, then. Pearl, a pleasure."

As soon as she'd gone, they both fell back in their chairs with relief. "What a dry stick!" Pearl said. "I thought I was going to slap her."

"She's never been anything but gracious to me, but I always feel I have to hold my breath." With Pearl, of course, who'd seen her at her absolute worst, it was the exact opposite.

"You'd think Brazil would have loosened her up. God knows it's loosened me, and I was loose already. You have to wonder why she even came."

"The story is, she met Lota on a ship, trumpets blared, and that was that." In fact, that was as much detail as Elizabeth knew herself. It was too bad you couldn't ask what had really happened, how the first conversation had gone, what had signaled what to whom, how they had known, so quickly, that Mary would move to Brazil. She added, "That was ten years ago. Now they live together quite openly, or so I hear."

Pearl picked up her coffee cup and looked into it, a sour expression on her pretty face. Perhaps, Elizabeth thought, she should have kept that last bit to herself.

"Would you look at this apartment?" she said. "That's an actual Calder hanging there. Lota *knows* him. You've got to meet Lota. She's magnetic, unbelievably sharp and funny. She speaks multiple languages. It's been five years since I spent any time with her in New York, but some people you remember with utter clarity."

"Shall we go out?"

"Yes, of course. Are you able?" At the train station, when Elizabeth had expressed horror at Pearl's swollen, bruised ankle, her friend had explained she'd only twisted it stepping off a curb. But you had to wonder. No one understood at all why she'd come down here to marry Victor Kraft. He was notorious.

"It doesn't feel as bad as it looks. The doctor said I should try to walk on it a little every day."

"Then we'll walk. You can lean on me for a change." She stood and held out her hand. "Maybe we could go someplace close by where I might find just a sip of something."

"Elizabeth!"

"I don't *need* it."

"It's only noon."

"Really, don't worry. I allow myself one a day, and then I'm not afraid of it. Like an inoculation."

ENORMOUS GREEN WAVES crashed on the beach, and swarms of people floated in the water or stood shin-deep in the surf. On the beautiful black-and-white mosaic sidewalk, people of all ages were strolling past and riding bicycles. Every few paces, a kiosk sold drinks and some sort of fried fish, and a number of people sat around these stands in plastic chairs, chatting and drinking beer or sipping from straws stuck into coconuts and wearing practically nothing, even the women. They had dark, thick hair and white teeth and skin a beautiful ochre or even darker, and all the colors of people appeared to intermix freely. In every group she passed, one or two were laughing. The men, in their tiny bathing suits and with their legs splayed out, really left very little to the imagination. Many of them had no shame about staring right at you. They were very curious about her and Pearl, watching them with their glittering black eyes, though not threateningly—more like cows you passed on a country lane. One man, in conversation with his friends, very baldly slipped his hand into his bathing trunks and rearranged himself.

They turned from the beach into Copacabana, where a few blocks in they came upon a street market. The stalls were heaped with pro-duce and fish and meats. It wasn't as if Elizabeth were not a woman of the world; she'd been to the markets of tropical America, she rec-ognized papaya and passion fruit and even the one that looked like a pangolin, the cherimoya, and mango, of course, which she couldn't eat because she was allergic to the skin. But some things did astonish her—figs the size of apples, tiny glossy peppers on little plates, more varieties of fish than she'd ever seen, even when she'd lived in Florida, striped black and silver, vermilion, yellow. There was a grouper as big as a full-grown man, ten varieties of shrimp, piles of octopus, and great big spiny crabs on ice, slowly moving their legs.

"What is that lewd thing?" She pointed to a pyramid of yellow-orange fruits the size of her fist. From the top of each one extruded a green flaccid phallus.

"Cashews," Pearl said. "Too sour for my taste. The green part is the nut, but you can also eat the fruit."

She steered Elizabeth to a derelict little bar that opened onto the street. A few elderly men sat on stools in front, intent on a sports match broadcast over the radio. Pearl spoke a few words of Portuguese to the man behind the counter, and he produced two glasses of clear liquid. Pearl slid one toward Elizabeth. "Here's your inoculation," she said. "You can't have more than one, or you'll become catatonic."

Elizabeth lifted the glass to her nose. Not at all an enticing liquor, she was pleased to discover. "What is it?"

"Cachaça," Pearl said. "The national pastime, after soccer."

The taste was harsh at first, then mellowed. "Pearl, I meant what I told you. I'm doing well. You saw me in terrible shape two years ago, and it got even worse. Last winter, I had to put myself in the hospital again. I wanted badly to stop drinking, but I couldn't do it on my own."

"Yes, you wrote me all that."

"It was a wretched time—" Elizabeth broke off. There was a pressure in her eyes that was as close as she came to tears in the company of another person. "But I'm through it. I've gotten to the other side, I'm not sure how. I could feel it on the ship. I was even productive again. I'm sick of being a fake poet who never writes anything."

"I saw your last poem in the *New Yorker*. Elizabeth, it was very good."

The liquor gave her courage to ask what she'd been dying to know. "So tell me. How are you and Victor?"

Pearl's eyes flicked away, and she smiled. She was happy with Victor, that was apparent. Perhaps she'd hurt herself falling off a curb, after all. "He loves it here."

"And you?"

"It's very *loud*. I'm a bit at loose ends, to be honest. I haven't managed to find any work in six months. But I have become quite a cook."

"I'd take cooking over writing any day. You're brave, I think, getting married. I considered it myself once, but I couldn't do it."

"Victor's not the easiest man in the world. That's no secret. But there's something different about *me* since I've been with him. He can stretch my patience to the breaking point, and still I feel, in some deep part of myself, at peace." She smiled again. "I can see by the look on your face that doesn't make sense."

"Well, I'm not the one who has to live with him."

"So it's true what I heard, that you've broken things off with Tom?"

"Decisively. That's one of the few sane things I've done lately. He's been a true friend, but honestly, I think he's unbalanced. But that's not even the reason. I have no business being with anyone, I have so little to give. I just barely get by on my own. The people I try to love always end up extremely unsatisfied and angry." She took another taste of cachaça. "They end up either wanting to kill me or killing themselves."

"That's completely untrue! You've only driven one man to suicide."

Elizabeth laughed aloud, truly shocked. "You're as horrible as I am. That must be why I like you so much."

Pearl left her there and hobbled across the street to the market. It was Elizabeth's first opportunity since she'd left the *Bowplate* simply to be still, to watch and listen. At least a dozen men lounged under the trees nearby, several of them in bathing trunks, a few without shirts, eyeing the women going past. All of them were quite dark, Elizabeth noted, and two or three were very good-looking. The men at the bar commented to one another about the game on the radio, their Portuguese unlike any language she knew, with no similarity to Spanish or French, a production of somewhat comical sounds from the nose and back of the throat. Across the street at the market, adolescent boys sang out the names of their produce. In the shade, it wasn't too hot, it was just right. The light was strong but was filtered through the leaves of the trees. Elizabeth felt as though she were looking at the world through a green lens.

She finished off her cachaça and noticed that Pearl had left hers virtually untouched. The glass was still warm from Pearl's hand. Elizabeth held it, but she did not raise it to her lips. She was testing her resolve.

Why on earth had she brought up Bob Seaver's suicide? No doubt her recent break from romantic attachment had refreshed that old well of guilt. So many years ago, and yet how clearly, and alarmingly, Bob still came to mind. A lovely, earnest boy, whom she couldn't possibly have married. That would not have done him any favors, though at the time she hadn't been able to explain to him why——she hadn't understood it clearly herself. Of course, he'd believed his polio to be the reason for her rejection, his own infirmity rather than hers; any normal self-loathing person would have. She'd had to be so firm, but she hadn't been firm enough to prevent the second proposal, and refusing that was the absolute worst. And then that awful postcard arriving just days after his death, with the one line scrawled across it. *Go to hell, Elizabeth.* The only request of his she'd been able to comply with. He'd be pleased to know that's exactly where she had gone.

Gone there on multiple occasions, in fact. A repeat visitor, a regular tourist. She'd tried to have a normal life since then, a life of work, friends, love, but something in her was off. And yet the problem was not as easily identifiable—if, fortified by the cachaça, she could be so blunt with herself—as that she simply preferred intimacy with her own sex. Her experience with women was no less marred by disappointment and misunderstanding. Constant, Marjorie's refrain: *All you give is scraps.* She couldn't deny it. That was all she had to give, little scraps with a few words scribbled on them. Sometimes you found them on the floor where they'd fallen, gathering dust.

Well, well, well. Had things really changed so much? Here she was again, a woman drinking alone at a bar and laughing to herself. Thank God Pearl was crossing the street again, greens and fishtails sticking out of her bag, before she ordered another round.

"I'm cooking dinner tonight," Pearl said. "You don't have other plans, do you?"

Even if she had, Elizabeth said, she would cancel them instantly to spend the evening with Pearl and Victor. Then the world took a little slide sideways, as if the public conveyance on which Elizabeth rode had accelerated with a lurch. She said, "I think I'll go home and have a rest first."

·4·

HE AWOKE IN an unfamiliar room, disoriented. Her luggage, three pieces, lay open and rummaged through on the floor. It was some moments before Elizabeth recalled where she was, that she'd arrived the previous day in Rio, had passed the night in a smoke-filled samba club with Pearl and Victor. She had been dreaming of her mother. The two of them were both adults, roughly the same age, chatting over tea, just as she'd done with Mary and Pearl. *It's a good thing you didn't perish in that fire*, her mother said, and poured another cup for herself. She was wearing a purple dress.

Even while dreaming, Elizabeth had been appalled at her mother's nonchalance. *Yes, but you were supposed to have saved me!* she wanted to shout. Now she rose from the bed and wandered into the bright, empty apartment. It was only a few minutes past eight and already hot as blazes. From the kitchen sink, Elizabeth splashed water on her face and the back of her neck. She opened the sliding glass door to the terrace, thinking a bit of sea breeze might cool things down, but outside it was even hotter.

The radio in the maid's room behind the kitchen produced a low buzz. Lucinha? Rocinha? Elizabeth couldn't remember her name, or even if they'd been formally introduced. She knew she ought to put on more clothes rather than drift around the apartment in her slip, in case the maid emerged, but it was simply too hot. Besides, she wouldn't disturb Lucinha, nor Rocinha, for that matter. Preparing a cup of coffee was not outside her range of competence. It came out just as delicious as the cup she'd had yesterday, though honestly it was hard to screw up anything so inherently good. At last she spread out her papers and notes on the table, determined to finish a draft of the last review she was obliged to write.

She worked in her undergarments. It really was impossible any other way.

Before her journey, this review of Marianne Moore's most recent poems had proved intractable. How did you write about the work of someone who had been as close to a mentor and poetical guide as you'd ever had? There was so much Elizabeth admired in her poetry, so much she was indebted to, and, frankly, so much that infuriated her. But the review was for the *Times*, and no one in her right mind said no to the *New York Times*. She'd spent more hours writing apologies to the editor explaining why the review was so late than she had on the review itself.

But now: two hours of good solid work, then it was time for another coffee.

The apartment was wonderful to write in, full of light, with that spectacular view, spare and modern. Lota's hand was so evident, it made Elizabeth impatient to see her in person again. In New York, Lota had been fascinated by everything, books and art and fashion and politics and gardens and sewing. There was no end to what captured her interest; she'd wanted to see and do it all. You had to stand in awe of a woman with so much energy. Such a funny couple: Mary, the tortoise to Lota's hare. The tortoise never won the race, though—that was pure fable.

Sipping her coffee at the window, Elizabeth watched a freighter pass out of the harbor's mouth, heading toward open ocean. The landscape was too ludicrous, these mountains and islands jutting up everywhere, the ocean, the jungle, all those dark men running around on the beach kicking soccer balls, and the women with lovely caramel skin.

Alone in an exotic city, staring at the world from behind glass.

One night, sitting in the dark with Miss Breen on deck, Elizabeth had said, *I lost my way for a while.* She'd seemed to exhale the words, as naturally as breath, and then was unsure she'd spoken them at all. Miss Breen had simply murmured, *Mmm.* This last year or so had been possibly the worst ever, the very worst so far, but she had never contemplated killing herself. Drink, yes, suicide, no. Not as the solution. Even at her lowest, at her most self-despising, she'd been determined to emerge from the wreckage. But she'd gotten a glimpse. She understood now why some people arrived at the decision that all this stupidity, this stupid struggle, must cease.

She returned to the work. Pleased with the draft of the review, Elizabeth began to sketch out the poem she'd been working through in her mind during the train trip. The image of her and Miss Breen standing together on the ship's deck, looking over Santos harbor. The feeling that had come over her as the tender approached, a hope for a new kind of life for herself—wasn't that what travel was for? And the fear that she was not up to the task.

LOTA ANSWERED the phone, her voice husky, unexpectedly alluring. "Elizabeth," she said. Direct, no dancing around with any pleasantries.

"What time tomorrow should I expect you in Rio?" Elizabeth asked, coming straight to the point as well.

"The architect has just arrived. We're waiting for a delivery of materials this afternoon, for the roof." There was a note of irritation in Lota's voice. In the background, the shrieks of children, an adult admonishing them, clatterings and clangings, the life of a household.

"Is this not such a good time to come?" she said brightly, though she felt the collapse of some secret, inner hope.

"You're welcome to come now. I can tell you how to take the bus. It's quite simple."

"I'm happy to postpone until it's more convenient."

"Come if you want. It's up to you."

Elizabeth wrote down the instructions for the bus, but she already knew she wouldn't go to Samambaia. At least not today. She recognized something excessive about her desire to see Lota again, as well as in her disappointment when the prospect dimmed.

Pearl set her straight. "That's a very Brazilian thing to say," she advised when Elizabeth called. "They can be very loosey-goosey about things like this."

Loozey-goozey, Lota will say later, rolling the words around on her tongue, *yes, we Brazilians can be very loozey-goozey*.

"I *did* want to go, and Lota told me I was welcome."

"Then you absolutely should," Pearl said. "They invited you, and they meant it."

"'*It's up to you? Come if you want?*' If she really wanted me to come, she'd have said, '*Darling, you absolutely must get your American behind up here this instant.*' That's what I would have said."

"Elizabeth, just go and call me when you get back."

It was late afternoon by now, too late to depart. Dithering did make one lose opportunities. Action of any sort was the corrective.

Elizabeth left the apartment and began wandering through the streets with no destination in mind, turning here, turning there, whenever something caught her eye, a little park or shop. Shanties ascended the nearly vertical hillside that separated Copacabana from the rest of Rio, so close to the balconies of the apartment buildings that the rich and poor could practically shake hands. It really was a mad sort of place, half jungle—with bromeliads and orchids and tangles of vines in the branches above and ginger and flamboyan trees blooming furiously everywhere, so much green, and native people dancing to drumbeats from their radios—and half twentieth-century megalopolis, with the most modern skyscrapers of glass and steel and buses threatening to run you down every time you stepped off the curb.

That people wore hardly any clothes was beginning to seem sensible. You didn't have to possess a body like a clothespin. The heat was infernal. It was crazy to be bound by the custom of clothing.

The sky began to spit sporadic raindrops, and just as Elizabeth ducked beneath the awning of a fruit-juice bar on a corner, the heavens opened up. She was instantly pressed against the humanity stranded there by the deluge, a businessman on one side, a twenty-year-old beauty in an extremely tight dress on the other. Elizabeth couldn't help but notice that the skin around the girl's eyes was perfectly unlined. It was remarkable. The girl caught Elizabeth staring, and she smiled. The placard over the bar listed the names of mysterious fruits: Abacaxi, Maracuja, Fruta de Conde. When the boy behind the counter spoke to her, she pointed to one and attempted to pronounce it. For a while she sipped the juice—deliciously tart—and watched Copacabana go by. The rain lessened, and her fellow refugees drifted from beneath the awning back into the street. *When in doubt*, Elizabeth thought happily, *take action*. That should be written on her hand in indelible ink. There was a moment after you'd arrived in a new place, after you'd lived there for a time—it didn't matter where, as easily Paris as Mexico City—when the great map of it finally snapped into place in your mind. You no longer remembered the initial period when you hadn't known precisely where you were, how you might be placed in relation to historical landmarks or the apartments of friends, or when it was really fifty-fifty if right or left would bring you to your destination. But Elizabeth loved that early time before the switch, when the place was still outside her grasp. You wandered in a maze, and every turn brought something new, a constant surprise. You didn't know where the streets might lead you, you were constantly lost, but you didn't mind, you had no reason not to feel lost, because of course you *were* lost, how could you not be?

She'd worried over nothing. In the morning, she'd take a bus to Samambaia. It would be an adventure, and what's more, she'd bring an offering, something for the children, too. She'd bake a cake.

The rain ceased, and Elizabeth polished off her *suco de maracuja*. It was time to act like the tourist she was. She dug around in her purse for the Portuguese phrasebook, walked into a pharmacy, and asked, word by mispronounced word, and with many apologies, where was located a seller of dry goods.

It was hell not speaking the language. Later, recounting the episode to Lota, perhaps embellishing a bit to amuse her, Elizabeth will translate what she'd asked the young man at the dry-goods store as something like, *Excuse me, sir, do I have a lighthouse?* Yet somehow he understood the basics of her request, if not the precise quantities, and she walked home along Gustavo Sampaio street with an enormous bag of flour, at least a pound of sugar, a dozen eggs, baking powder, and coconut shavings. The rest she hoped to find at the apartment, and if not, she'd improvise. In the culinary arts, she had no lack of confidence.

The wind was picking up. Turning the corner of Lota's building into a little plaza, she was hit by a wet blast square in the face, the force of it so powerful she felt it might pull off her dress. She got inside the apartment just as another storm broke.

To work in the kitchen while it rained had always been an unparalleled pleasure. The maid, whose name turned out to be Lucia, helped Elizabeth demystify the lighting of the oven, then made coffee for them both. Now she remembered what Mary had said: Lucia was from the north of Brazil, a superior human being. Neither could understand a word the other spoke, so they sipped their coffees and communicated through the ingredients. Skeptical at first, Lucia began to hum in approval as she watched Elizabeth mix the batter. The storm over Copacabana grew stronger, and rain lashed at the windows. After they'd set the cake to bake, Elizabeth was drawn back to the glass by flashes of lightning over the sea. The enormity of blackness pulsed white. As she looked down at the beach, a great gale lifted up a handful of the sturdy plastic chairs from one of the kiosks. Five or six of them came sailing upright into Avenida Atlântica, where there was a momentary break in the traffic. Propelled by the wind, the chairs raced up the empty street, several men in bathing trunks chasing after them.

ELIZABETH ROSE EARLY, planning to take the eleven o'clock bus. Her bag was packed, her dress folded across the chair beside her. She worked on the new poem in her slip. Lucia had prepared coffee and a plate of fruit. In an hour or so, she'd put on the dress and hail a cab.

> *And gingerly now we climb down the ladder backward,*
> *Myself and a fellow passenger named Miss Breen,*
>
> *Descending into the midst of twenty-six freighters*
> *Waiting to be loaded with green coffee beans.*

Miss Breen felt physically close; she seemed to dictate into Elizabeth's ear. Capturing Santos harbor was more difficult. There was so much on which the eye had caught, on land and in the water.

Around ten, as she was pulling her papers together, the door to the apartment flew open with such force that it banged loudly against the wall. Elizabeth yanked her dress from the chair and held it before her. There was Lota in the entranceway, lugging several canvas bags full of what looked to be electrical cables. "If I wanted you to come to Samambaia," she said, grinning, "I guess I had to come get you myself."

· 5 ·

*E*LIZABETH HELD ON tight to the cake in her lap. Lota concentrated on the road, taking corners at high speed and yelling after the pedestrians she'd nearly flattened. The car zigged and zagged up the hillside behind Copacabana, Lota accelerating into the cobblestone curves until the tires cried out, while the force of it pressed Elizabeth's shoulder against the driver's. Only as they crested the mountain did the car pause, balanced momentarily upon the ridge like an eagle surveying its realm. The convolutions of Rio lay before them, the rise and fall of hills populated by slums and apartment buildings, the modern highrises at the center, Christ above, the harbor, the far ring of mountains. Then, launching into air, down they swooped in a rush. Lota's hand, shifting gears, repeatedly brushed Elizabeth's thigh. The contact happened so many times she could not help but feel there was intention behind it. She tried to rearrange her legs, but there was no room at all to maneuver. The car was hardly more than a capsule. Near the bottom of the slope, Lota came to a stop at a crossing where a streetcar passed before them. Decaying nineteenth-century mansions lined the avenue.

"This neighborhood is Santa Teresa," Lota said, apparently oblivious to the fact that her knuckles had come to rest against Elizabeth's skirt. "It was once very rich, as you can see. The aristocrats fled up the mountain to escape yellow fever. Now the buildings are decadent, abandoned to artists and thieves."

Before Elizabeth could respond, off they roared, descending further into the steaming, noxious mess of Rio de Janeiro. The fumes, the heat, the traffic, the blaring horns—it was all more than a little disorienting. No doubt the comments Lota was shouting into her ear pertained to this or that aspect of the city, but they were drowned out by the whine of the engine and the noise that came from every quarter. In such close proximity to Lota, Elizabeth felt acutely the fact that they were strangers to one another. Never mind the many afternoons she'd spent with Lota and Mary in New York, or the letters that had passed between them since. She hadn't set eyes on the woman in at least five years, and even then there'd hardly been a moment shared alone. In fact, she seemed to remember someone altogether different in appearance from this madwoman at the wheel of the convertible. The Rio version of Lota was darker, for one thing, and a bit stouter, her hair was longer and had a vivid streak of white running through it, like a comet. Elizabeth was certain that when they'd first met it had been pure, jet black. One thing she recalled with utter clarity, however, was the voraciousness of Lota's interest in all things, her constant, alert looking. There'd been one afternoon in particular, searching the city with Lota for linens she would take back with her to Rio. Brazilians just don't understand the *art* of stitching, Lota had said, scrutinizing the fabrics. Elizabeth and Mary had followed her from store to store until Lota's eye was finally satisfied.

It could have been that in New York, Lota simply hadn't had the chance to exhibit other colorful qualities, such as her reckless driving. There'd really been no opportunity for them to go flying through the city streets in a red convertible Jaguar.

At last the road opened up and Lota blasted out of Rio's orbit. The wind whipped Elizabeth's hair around her head like Medusa's coils. Still, the highway allowed a respite from the constant gear changing and thigh touching, so she could finally shift her attention from the hand upon her knee to their route. On Rio's outskirts, a settlement of ramshackle houses—if you could even call them houses, these shacks constructed out of cardboard and crates and other discarded materials cobbled together—went right up to the barricade of a petroleum plant, another hellish landscape of billowing gaseous clouds and sulfuric flames leaping out of tall pipes.

"Not the most favorable view of a city," Lota yelled, "its entrance or exit."

Elizabeth nodded. Odd, the things that prompted Lota to speak. Interesting, always, but impersonal.

She turned slightly to study Lota's profile. Even as she drove, Lota grinned, as if dominating the roadway were a source of intense satisfaction. The workman's shirt she wore was rolled up on her forearms. She was a diminutive person, but there was heft to her, strength, and also an ease with that strength. You would not mistake her for a delicate woman, nor one whose habit it was to bend to another's will. Now that she was on Lota's home turf, Elizabeth was desirous to know more, to ask some of the personal questions that came to mind: Where had she grown up, where was her family now—and most of all, what was the real story between her and Mary?

Mountains popped up from the plain, and they began winding steeply upward. Elizabeth had to keep turning in her seat to look at what they'd passed, the unbelievable variety of plants and trees—the mangos, bananas, and papaya, of course, those she'd expected, but also the thousand others she didn't know the names of, so many of them in flower, flowers of every color and size, and great, glorious old trees bearded with exuberant mosses. Underneath them, little roadside stands sold drinks and rugs and purses fashioned out of scraps of brightly colored fabric.

"Look at that," Elizabeth cried. They had slowed enough on the sinuous road that conversation was at last possible. "They're selling old rusted metalwork."

"They'll sell anything," Lota said. "Almost all of it's trash."

Elizabeth had been about to say she found the birdcages charming.

"But I like the bird jails. I bought a very old one for my house. I'm building a house. Did Mary tell you?"

"Yes, she said you were completely obsessed."

"Absolutely! You must be obsessed, or else there's no point. Do you know modernist architecture? Le Corbusier, Oscar Niemeyer?"

"Le Corbusier, I know. I remember now we spoke of him in New York. But I don't know the other one. Is he German? My ignorance is vast."

"Niemeyer is a genius, but of course you Northerners know nothing about him because he is Brazilian and we're just savages! To you, Brazil is coffee and bananas and cannibals and piranhas. Modernism may have started in Europe, but it is pure Brazil. Le Corbusier came here, he influenced our architects, but what they are making now is a uniquely Brazilian form of architecture. Elegant, sophisticated, organic, and slightly insane. It will show the world what Brazil really is."

"Is that what you are? I'm beginning to understand the insane part."

"It's a modernist house I'm building," Lota said proudly.

"I gathered that."

"I hired a young architect. He's very up-and-coming. However, to be honest, the best ideas for the design are my own. It is really like no other house that's been built in this country. Four materials are used: concrete, stone, glass, and metal. All of them are visible. A modernist building does not hide how it's constructed, it prefers to reveal itself to you, it blurs the boundary between inside and outside."

"I've known a few people like that," Elizabeth remarked.

The joke appeared to go right past Lota. Then, smiling, she said, "And those people can be very exciting. Just like my house."

The road climbed higher, up and up. Tendrils of mist began to encircle them, and soon they were driving through dense fog. In the car's cocoon, Elizabeth could see little of their surroundings beyond the latticework of branches over their heads and the screen of thick foliage on either side of the road. She'd have to write a note to Miss Breen. *I've come to the Green Mansions, just as we pictured them.*

Meanwhile, Lota continued her lecture on the subject of Brazil's modernist architecture. No matter what she spoke of, you could not help but be impressed by the expansiveness of this woman's mind. Lota was so passionate about the house she was creating that Elizabeth began to wonder at her failure of passion for her own work. Poetry, when she was young, had seemed to be an open gate into the most lush of landscapes, as lush as that through which they were traveling now; nothing else had compared to the excitement of discovering her growing powers or the reaches of her own imagination. Somehow, that had changed. Poetry had used her up. It had left her desiccated. She'd dedicated her entire adult life to the craft of writing, and yet even with the praise she'd received, the admiration of a number of people she herself had long admired, and the envy of a handful of others, it had given so little back, even less in times of real need. It was like indentured servitude—or no, like faith in some particularly dry, ascetic, self-castigating religious sect. The reward lay in the devotion itself. It did not relieve her of her thirst.

"Do you read much poetry?" Elizabeth interrupted.

"I read everything," Lota said, as if affronted by the insinuation that she might not. "Manuel Bandeira, I love especially. Do you know him?"

"I know the name but not the work, I'm afraid."

"He's one of Brazil's foremost poets. And a friend. Carlos Drummond de Andrade?"

"Nor him." Elizabeth added, "But I enjoy Camões."

"He is not Brazilian, he's European! How can a poet such as yourself not have read the *Brazilian* masters of the Portuguese language?"

"I suppose because I can't read Portuguese."

Lota was quick to beam her beautiful smile. "Then I will introduce you to them."

It was unclear whether Lota meant to the work or to the poets themselves. They continued to gain elevation, Elizabeth could feel it in her ears. The mist, dissipating, transformed into a bright, luminous haze. The sun began to warm her skin. Then she saw that the fog had not simply evaporated but that they had risen above it and were now at such a great height they looked down upon the clouds. Jungled mountain peaks lay all around, the valleys below turned to rivers of pillowy white. A surfeit of feeling bloomed in Elizabeth's chest, a moment of breathless pleasure.

They still had a ways to go, Lota assured her. They were nearing the town of Petropolis. Samambaia was a bit beyond. Just then, they nearly collided with another automobile. A taxi pulled onto the road, and Lota had to brake quickly and swerve into the oncoming lane to avoid it. She screamed something at the taxi driver as she zoomed past, an epithet that Elizabeth, without knowing an ounce of Portuguese, understood to be exceedingly offensive, and immediately resumed her relaxed good nature. "We'll go around the town so we can get to my house more quickly," Lota said.

Elizabeth saw that her thumbs had been digging into the base of the cake. Still shaken by the near accident, she said, "That was a fine how-do-you-do."

For another ten miles or so, Lota kept repeating the phrase and chuckling to herself. *That's a fine how do you do*, she murmured, *ha ha ha*, as she flew along a terrifying stretch of road beside a river, Elizabeth clutching the car seat and still trying not to upend the cake in her lap. Gashes in the hillsides revealed the deep red earth, much of which had washed over the roadway, big splashes of red as though an animal had been obliterated by a truck. They turned into the hills, where eventually the road vanished altogether. They stopped at the bottom of an incline facing a nearly vertical mud track. "Sergio won't drive up here," Lota said, gunning the engine. "He has no balls."

Whoever Sergio might have been, he struck Elizabeth as a man of sound mind. Lota didn't hesitate. Bouncing among the ruts and potholes, she maneuvered the tiny car up the hill from one dry patch to the next like a little wren hopping up a tree trunk.

At the top they reached solid, level ground, and there Lota parked in front of a cement wall. "Come," she cried, leaping out. As Elizabeth struggled to stand from the low seat, Lota was already there to take the cake out of her hands and say, "Leave that for now and come."

SO HERE WAS the famous house. Introduced by a concrete plane that nearly bruised your nose. Lota entered through a hole in the wall, and Elizabeth followed her host through a number of long concrete rooms, one communicating with the next. When they stopped, they'd made a loop back to where they'd begun. As promised, the boundary between inside and outside was blurred beyond recognition. There appeared to be no *inside* at all. The house was open to the sky, and at present it had no external walls, just great gaping holes to the out-of-doors. Thin steel trusses, almost delicate, were being fitted over their heads and would soon, Lota said, support a roof made of aluminum sheets; the trusses called to mind the latticework of tree branches Elizabeth had just seen on the mountain road. Here and there labored dark little men in beaten-up straw hats. One carried stones in a wheelbarrow, a second chipped them with a chisel and mortared them into a wall fifteen feet high. Several more lifted the trusses onto fittings set into the concrete.

"My house is the first in Brazil to incorporate this style of roof," Lota said. "The workers think I'm mad. They've never seen anything like it before. Of course they haven't—it's revolutionary. If I'm not watching them every minute, they build things their own way, as many times as I tell them otherwise. Then they become furious when I have to yell at them to tear down what they've done and start over. We spend the whole day screaming at each other."

She laughed as she reported this, as though the process of altercation and deconstruction were another aspect of the work she heartily enjoyed. As if to prove her point, Lota approached the foreman, and within moments her voice began to rise while a knot of men looked blankly at the ground and shook their heads. At one particularly strident point, the men's voices objected in a chorus. Lota immediately cut them off.

Elizabeth backed away from the argument and stepped outside through one of the enormous holes in the wall. The house was odd, it took some getting used to. She sympathized with the workmen; it was like nothing she'd ever seen before, either. At once solid and light, serious and cheerful, like Lota herself. She squinted her eyes and imagined what Lota had described—a house sheathed in glass, a glass jewel box on the mountainside, inviting nature in from every side—and she glimpsed just how immensely beautiful it would be. From the concrete slab where Elizabeth stood, the view was only the most recent in a series of breathtaking sights. A lush green valley spread before her, forested mountains rising on the other side. Behind the house, a sheer face of black granite shot vertically upward for at least a thousand feet, like something out of Edgar Rice Burroughs. You half expected a pterodactyl to glide across the face of the cliff. Long streaks ran down the black rock, like the tracks of gigantic snails, while clouds cascaded over the lip, creating a waterfall of mist that was constantly evaporating and regenerating. The sun was hot on her skin and head, but before she began to feel she'd had too much, a cloudlet passed over and cooled the air to ease any discomfort. Lota was building a house in paradise.

The argument grew more heated. Elizabeth turned to watch, the men gesticulating while Lota imperiously held her ground. Just as Elizabeth feared they might come to physical blows, they all began laughing and embracing each other. Lota joined Elizabeth outside.

"They are wonderful," Lota told her, "but they're like children. They'd sit here all day scratching themselves if I didn't give them a little push."

"Why is that? If you watch any Brazilian man for five minutes, you'll see him scratching and adjusting himself. It's as if they're constantly arranging flowers in a vase."

"Those aren't flowers," Lota cried. "Those are the jewels of Brazil! If they didn't keep grabbing their balls, they'd forget they were men. That's the problem with this country: The men have to keep reminding themselves they are men, and the women are even worse. They have no balls, either!"

Elizabeth couldn't help laughing, though she was scandalized to hear a woman speak so coarsely. Lota continued to look directly into her eyes, without shyness or embarrassment, like the men who'd watched her from the kiosks at the beach. Only two hours had passed since she'd whisked Elizabeth away from Rio, yet several times already, at different pauses and shifts in the conversation, Elizabeth had found herself thinking, *I'm going a step deeper*. There was a different timbre to their interaction here than in New York. Lota was playful, perhaps even a bit suggestive, but her hostess gave no sign that they were conspiring in anything secretive or untoward. Elizabeth had to suppose that was merely the Brazilian way. There was really nothing more going on here than an interesting, attractive, and high-spirited woman showing an American friend her new house.

"Right where we're standing is one of my favorite places," Lota said. "A patio nearly as many square meters as the house itself. Can you see how the inside, the world of domestic life, what you might call our ordered world, will reach out to greet the natural world, the exuberant world we have no control over?"

"Like a big mouth with its tongue sticking out."

"Or else," Lota said, "like a hand extended." As she spoke, she made the gesture. Her hand, palm up, reached toward Elizabeth.

Stepping back, Elizabeth peered over the edge of the patio. Below lay rubble, rocks, metal scraps. "Are you camping out here? I don't see any furniture. You don't even have a roof."

"We've rented a friend's house down the hill until we can move in. But that will be soon. It's a tradition to have a party when you raise the roof, and I'm planning this party in two weeks' time. You'll be here to celebrate with us."

More a command than an invitation. Elizabeth failed to break from Lota's gaze.

"Mary's down there now," Lota went on. "We're having a lunch today for some friends. My sister will also come. She's a terrible bitch, but she will be polite to you, it's only me she hates. Of course, all of them are eager to meet you."

"*All* of them?" It was absurd, her instantaneous panic, but truly she found it difficult to breathe among such a group of strangers and their expectations of her. At the same time, she was angry that Lota had so quickly snatched away this brief moment of peace.

"You're the guest of honor. I promised to bring them a famous American poet."

"Yes, why don't you go out hunting and shoot one?"

Lota held Elizabeth's eyes with her kind look. "Instead, I think I'll call one from the trees." Gently, she took Elizabeth's arm. "But never mind that now, Elizabeth. Let me show you the rest."

They left the construction site behind. There is the vegetable garden, Lota said, there is the donkey, there is the gardener who once bit the donkey. And here, pass under this bough, let's enter the forest, let me show you all its new and strange pleasures.

Elizabeth watched Lota's solid back as she followed. Climbing the hillside through the trees, Lota pointed out what Elizabeth, even with her trained eye, might otherwise have passed: a lichen that looked like a crater on the moon, an armadillo's burrow, a nearly microscopic bloom. They came upon a stream and followed it back down the slope as it carved out a series of small pools. Lota stopped at an especially lovely one. A waterfall cascaded down, and moss and ferns grew among the rocks. For a while, they sat on a boulder by the water, side by side, in silence. Before today, Elizabeth had never seen Lota outside of the city. Lota had been fixed in her mind as an urban creature, her dynamism necessarily linked to the city's own electricity. The museums, the parties, the galleries, amid the city's great architecture—that was where Lota shone brightly. But here, among these trees and rocks and butterflies, with the city's cacophony a million miles away, Lota was obviously every bit as much at home, if not even more so. She sat as still and quiet, as much in repose, as the stones in the stream.

"I'm going to enlarge this pool," Lota said. "I want to make a bathing place here. It will be a secret place."

"There's no end to your plans."

"That's true. I have many plans."

"They're all perfectly beautiful. Everything you've shown me is beautiful."

"There is even more to show you, Elizabeth."

The noises of construction had faded behind those of the stream and waterfall, the wind, a bird chuckling in the brush. Some minnows nibbled at the debris speckling the pool's surface. The branches hanging low over the pool were covered with bromeliads throwing out scarlet spikes, and all along one branch bloomed small yellow orchids with brown spots; they looked just like a leopard's coat.

"My friend Pearl and I went to the orchid house in the botanical garden," Elizabeth said. "Do you know it?"

"Yes, of course."

"It's funny how they present orchids in a public display, as if they were some overly fussy, Victorian sort of flower, don't you think? Look at those. It's a tough plant, living on the nourishment it derives from nothing more than air. It hardly even has roots. And the leaves, they're almost like a succulent's, something that lives in the desert, without water. Then it produces such an exquisite bloom."

An odd, tight emotion, nearly like anger, strained Elizabeth's voice. Lota was watching her. Before Elizabeth turned away, she thought she may have recognized something of Miss Breen in Lota's eyes, the gentle assurance that Lota could see past her mask and didn't disapprove of what was revealed there, that it wasn't detestable.

"Should we go back?" Elizabeth said, suddenly worried the moment might turn malignant somehow.

"If you'd like."

Elizabeth crouched by the pool and slipped her hand into the water. It was colder than she'd expected. She looked upward into the trees. "Are there parrots here, too?"

"If you'd like," Lota said softly, as if it were a promise.

The two of them fell silent. Elizabeth sensed Lota's eyes on her. She let her hand drift in the cool water, and then she cried out in childish delight, "Look, there's a little fish biting my finger!"

·6·

"CARLOS," LOTA EXPLAINED, "the newspaper editor, he is brilliant, a very old friend, he's going to be president one day, I wish you'd had more of a chance to speak with him. I shouldn't have invited so many people, but really I had to. Rio is a noose that will strangle you. Someone is always becoming extremely offended for any reason, including myself! Sergio, of course, is the architect of my house, though most of the best ideas are my own—even he would have to admit it. He approached me several years ago because he knew I would agree to build something audacious, but I think the house has become too audacious even for Sergio. My sister Marietta, well, I've known her many more years than a person should have to. Did you see how she stayed in the corner the entire afternoon, not talking to anyone? Such a sour woman."

"You do her a disservice, Lota. She's not so bad."

"Morsie, she's terrible, and you know it."

"You are not beyond being terrible yourself," Mary said, with a surprising heat that caused Elizabeth to look down at her hands.

The lunch, in the end, had not been so excruciating. Elizabeth had to confess she'd enjoyed it. Performing the role expected of her, even here, so many thousands of miles from home, was much like lifting a boulder over her head and holding it there for an extended period: Once she'd assumed the pose, it wasn't so difficult to maintain. Now, after many handshakes and a series of kisses upon perfumed, doughy, and bearded cheeks, the three women were alone. The house had fallen beautifully quiet. It was beginning to rain, and as the world outside grew dark, a fire was lit. At the window, a huge moth fluttered like a soft, pink hand. Elizabeth sipped the last of her limoncello, a sweet lemon liqueur one of Lota's friends had brought from Italy, while Lota lay stretched full out upon the rug.

Her hostess continued. "The Polish couple came to Brazil during the war. They used to run the zoo in Warsaw. They showed up here with practically nothing, and now they've set up a business supplying animals to zoos all over the world. We'll pay them a visit tomorrow. You have to see how they live, right among monkeys and lions, like wild beasts themselves. The two brothers, Luiz and Roberto, they are close associates of my dear friend Lina Bo Bardi in São Paulo, very interesting furniture designers. Both have a beautiful heart, very unusual for men. And *both*, if you can imagine, are homosexual. So unlikely."

"Lota, please."

"What now?"

"You know they don't want that to become common knowledge. Not everyone lives as openly as you."

"Well, they should, Morsie. If you don't act ashamed of who you are, then people won't treat you as though you *should* be ashamed."

"It's not that simple."

"I disagree. I think it is very simple."

Again, the private charge of emotion between the two women sent Elizabeth's gaze to the fire. She would have liked to ask for another splash of limoncello, but after Lota had poured her glass, she'd shut away the bottle in a cabinet with a look, not unkind, that clearly indicated, *That's that.* The limit set so firmly, and with so little fuss, really, avoiding any judgment, that Elizabeth felt grateful. That's that, then.

Still, the lunch had been exhausting. She'd performed well, and on the spur of the moment. She'd earned a second glass.

"Dona Fernandes was a friend of my mother's," Lota went on. "She's at least a hundred years old, a devout lady, practically deaf, if you didn't notice. I'm sorry you ended up sitting next to her. That was not where I meant you to be placed."

"She reminded me of my grandmother," Elizabeth said. "Whom I loved. Everyone was so interesting and accomplished. I had no idea they would all speak English. Well, all but Dona Fernandes."

Once she'd discovered she wouldn't have to thrash her way through three hours of monolingual Portuguese, Elizabeth had dipped into the handy pocketful of stories she'd already collected in Brazil with which she might entertain a group of strangers, charming misadventures in which she figured as the well-meaning but hapless tourist. Very quickly she'd found herself doing that embarrassing thing, a performance of herself. She might as well have stood upon a chair and proclaimed, *Look at me, I can hold a boulder over my head*. Once she got going, it was impossible to stop. Yet all the guests appeared to enjoy themselves. Near the end of the afternoon, as the group savored their coffees, she even let fly with the *loosey-goosey* story. How on earth, she asked her audience, had she been supposed to interpret Lota's backhanded invitation? Lota had grinned; it was Mary's flat expression that had finally reined Elizabeth in.

"Your cake, Elizabeth, was *professional*," Lota said. "They loved it. Especially my sister."

"It looks as though your sister is not too discriminating when it comes to cake."

Lota laughed aloud. In the flickering shadows of the firelight, Elizabeth could discern the stamp of disapproval on Mary's face.

SAMAMBAIA TOOK ITS name from a giant fern that grew in the folds of the mountain. *Oh, it goes on for miles*, Lota said when describing the extent of her family's holdings. Exaggeration or literal fact, Elizabeth could not determine; aside from the handful of houses owned by Lota and her friends, there was little sign of human settlement as far as one could see across the gorgeous landscape, certainly as far as one could walk. The surrounding forest felt enchanted, home to so many plants, in an infinity of shapes and sizes, with such a variety of flowers, Elizabeth felt she would need a lifetime to learn them all. Stopping here and there along the paths, she attempted to sketch the wild entanglements of foliage. The plants clung to one another, their leaves and branches intertwined as they climbed toward the light. Buttressed trunks, serrated leaves, fuzzy or horned seed pods—each sculptural, bizarre form was a lesson in adaptation to life's circumstance. Nearly every morning Elizabeth discovered a new bloom: a vermilion crown the size of her fist, a spidery ring of delicate green flowers. The branches of the tall trees overhead were laden with countless puffs of moss, like infants held in their arms. Elizabeth began to feel a funny tenderness, even love, for the vegetation on Lota's mountainside, as though she carefully tended all these plants herself. On her return from these daily wanderings, monkeys scurried along the branches ahead of her, then turned back to give a high little whistle, as if to prevent Elizabeth from losing her way.

HER FIRST MORNING, Elizabeth had woken to the sound of Lota's voice, so commanding it carried down the mountain. Instantly there was a light knock on the door, and the maid brought in a tiny china cup of coffee on a tray, as if she'd been posted in the hall to listen for Elizabeth's first stirrings from sleep. It was not much past dawn when she emerged from her room, yet she found that Lota and Mary had already gone up to the construction site. Over the din of hammering and scraping, Lota continued to make herself heard.

Elizabeth climbed the hillside path and passed through a screen of trees. When Lota caught sight of their visitor, she set down a wheelbarrow full of rocks and, before she'd even said *bom dia*, ordered Elizabeth to carry it around the side of the house.

"But I'm . . ." Elizabeth protested. *Not strong.*

"I'll take it," Mary said brusquely, gripping the wheelbarrow handles.

The smile Elizabeth received was full of amusement rather than rebuke. "We'll toughen you up," Lota said, and placed a hand on Elizabeth's forearm. Her eye returned to the house, but her hand continued stroking Elizabeth's arm affectionately, as though it were a cat. All this touching! The hand placed on the arm, the passing caress, the embraces, the smoothing of the hair, the kiss on the cheek good morning, goodnight, goodbye, hello—was the constant physical contact a Brazilian custom? Or simply a Lota custom?

Elizabeth took a seat under the trees at a worktable littered with tools. She'd brought some of her papers so that she might work alongside the other women. The morning light on the mountains was unbelievably clear and warm, the forest full of sweet aromas. She couldn't imagine a more ideal place to write.

Yet, unable to resist Samambaia's pull, Elizabeth kept looking up from her notebook to the black rock where clouds floated past, to the crimson bird perched at the pinnacle of a tree.

Mary had pushed the wheelbarrow full of stones inside the house. A boy mixed cement in a bucket, and Mary carefully placed each stone onto the leading edge of a wall. Nearly engulfed by her baggy work clothes, her lithe dancer's body was apparently still extremely strong. The men had begun laying down the roof in earnest, bolting the corrugated aluminum panels along the trusses and proceeding so rapidly it appeared that in one day the *idea* of a house might be transformed into an actual shelter. Lota was here, and there, everywhere at once. It became like a game to locate her, to pinpoint the coordinates of the imperious voice. Each time Elizabeth did so, turning her gaze back from mountain or bird, she discovered that Lota was already watching her. Lota didn't act as though there was anything unseemly in these intent, lingering stares, even while Mary labored like a workhorse ten feet away. Elizabeth smiled back at her hostess, and the frantic little engine at the center of her grew calm.

"What on earth will you do with all your time," Elizabeth asked at lunch, "when the house is finally finished?"

"The house will never be finished," Mary said. She opened her mouth as if to voice another thought, then refrained.

"Mary knows exactly how she'll spend her time," Lota said. "She will be busy raising her child."

"Her child?"

"Lota!" Mary protested.

"She's planning to adopt a baby."

"Are you really?" Elizabeth cried, with a surge of affection for her compatriot that caused her to reach out and touch Mary herself. "You'll be such a good mother, I just know it." Mary might not be the sort of maternal vessel that overflowed with love and warmth, but instinctively Elizabeth knew she possessed a quality perhaps even more important: a rootedness that would make a child feel safe in the world, cared for, protected.

"I have been thinking about it," Mary admitted, but she shook her head. "I don't think it will happen. There's too much going on here. I don't have the time to devote to a child. Lota's adopted one, so of course she thinks everyone else should, too."

Elizabeth turned back to Lota in astonishment. "You have a child?"

Lota shrugged. It was Mary who answered. "A crippled boy she found at the mechanic's. He was crawling around on the floor like some old car part they'd discarded."

"That's not true," Lota said. "They did not want to give him up, but they knew I could give Kylso a better life."

"But where is he now?" Elizabeth asked. "Why haven't I seen him?"

"He's grown up and married," Lota said dismissively. "He's already making children of his own."

"What a surprising woman you are," Elizabeth said.

Lota stabbed out her cigarette, looking pleased.

"Yes, she is," Mary agreed. "And in other ways, entirely predictable."

Lota stood. "Let's go. We have much to do."

Late in the day, Sergio the architect stopped by and was subjected immediately to Lota's harangue on how his design of the roof could be improved, even at this late stage. After a number of unsuccessful attempts to interrupt her diatribe, he stormed off, shouting back over his shoulder that he would not return. Five minutes later Sergio reappeared, smiling sheepishly at Elizabeth and giving a shrug, as if to say, *That's just Lota. You have to love her.*

ELIZABETH LOST COUNT of the passing days.

Sitting at the pool, she watched a pair of tiny brown birds chipping a hole in a decayed tree trunk, splinter by splinter, making their nest near the stream. Whenever Elizabeth came here, returning to the spot Lota had shown her their first hour in Samambaia, it was her intention to write a letter to Cal, or to draw a bit. She wanted to leave a record of this place and time. She took out her watercolors, managed a few flowers, her own shoe beside a stone. First her hand and then her mind fell still. If she'd been able to complete any of the letters she meant to write to her dearest friend, usually formidable works detailing every observation of the natural, human, and literary worlds, they would have begun and concluded with a single line.

I'm at peace.

Beside the boulder on which she rested grew a plant with long, feathery leaves. Her finger ran along the vein, and in its path the leaves gently closed. Out of her memory something very old began to unfurl. She recalled looking down, as if from a great height, into a tracery of green, a fern or other plant with leaves similar to these. She was of an age before words, gazing into the leaves while being held in the arms of someone much larger.

That was the entirety of the recollection. An image, and the shadow of a feeling.

The adult holding her could have been her mother. It comforted Elizabeth even this many decades later to imagine she might have once nestled securely enough in her mother's arms to cast an observing eye upon the natural world. More plausibly, the arms had belonged to one of her aunts or to her grandmother.

Good thing you didn't perish in that fire, her mother had said in the dream. She might easily have said it in life.

Her mother had not been *right*. That was a simple fact agreed upon by all parties, with too much evidence to be in dispute. However, the question Elizabeth had never been able to answer to her satisfaction was to what extent her mother's abdication from all responsibility and human connection had been *willed*.

Too clearly, Elizabeth remembered her mother's visits home from the sanatorium, when she, still a small child, joined the worried circle of her aunts and grandmother watching over the skittish, emaciated woman delivered to their house, more like a large, helpless infant than like a mother. How many evening meals had they endured with forced cheer while Gertrude lay on the couch emitting little squeaks and gurgles, one arm over her eyes while the other dangled to the floor, the fingers of her white hand moving as slowly as the claws of a dying crab. On one of those spectral visits, Elizabeth and her mother traveled alone from Great Village to see the widow's in-laws at their summer home in Marblehead. Elizabeth woke in the night, not knowing where she was. Shifting light and shadows played across her bedroom wall. She smelled smoke and heard movement and bustle in the house. Afraid, she called for her mother, yet she heard Gertrude also crying out, and the voices of her paternal grandmother and aunts attempting to calm her.

A long time passed before Aunt Florence appeared in the doorway. Elizabeth tried not to whimper, though she was terribly thirsty.

Is the house on fire? she asked.

Aunt Florence told her that the fire was in a nearby town called Salem; it had spread to engulf many houses, but they were safe. The fire would not reach them here.

A low, inconsolable wail came from across the hall.

Is my mother all right?

Florence slipped into the bed and held Elizabeth close, but the contact made her turn rigid. She closed her eyes and imagined that instead of her aunt, it was her mother holding her, that it was her mother's soft words in her ear, and only after a time of imagining this did she drift into sleep.

At early light, Elizabeth woke alone in the bed and looked out her window to see her mother in a white nightgown, drifting among people wrapped in blankets on the lawn. Gertrude smiled and spoke kind words as she brought them water and coffee, while smoke rose along the horizon.

Why had she been able to offer to strangers what she could not offer to her own child?

As Elizabeth sat beside the stream on Lota's mountain, these memories no longer puzzled or disturbed or enraged her, as they had for most of her life. She sensed a new steadiness in herself, a hopefulness that had remained elusive throughout all her years of itinerancy and searching. This was not merely Samambaia working its magic upon her, she knew, not only the birds and the flowers and the mountain light. It was Lota.

·7·

"WHAT IS THIS marvelous dessert?" Carlos asked, looking down at his plate as if at the most extraordinary occurrence.

"Yes," Lota said, "it's highly unusual."

Elizabeth and Mary exchanged a smile. "It's called apple brown Betty," Elizabeth said.

"Delicious," remarked Carlos.

Lota said proudly, "We've underestimated Elizabeth's talents."

Carlos Lacerda was a bigheaded man with thick, brilliantined black hair, quite a bit too full, Elizabeth felt, of the importance of his own views and the sound of his own voice. She did not warm to Carlos, though Lota obviously worshipped him. Still, she understood Lota's loyalty. She'd be the first to admit not everyone could tolerate the company of Robert Lowell, yet in Elizabeth's eyes Cal could do no wrong.

Once the plates were cleared, it was not long before Lota and Carlos were screaming at one another. Their views were not divergent, Lota had explained; rather, they delivered into the black night a shared, unbridled outrage over the state of their country and the ongoing dictatorship. The first words of Portuguese Elizabeth began to comprehend came clear on these late nights: *ditador*, *inflaçao*, *assassino*. And other words, uttered by Lota, she knew she would not find in any dictionary.

Vargas will be the ruination of Brazil!

Lota's cries reached through the house to the sitting room where Mary and Elizabeth had retired after the meal. Mary was knitting a blanket for one of Lota's nephews, while Elizabeth sat beside a stack of books. These were the volumes produced by Brazil's native sons and daughters that Lota had pressed into her hands—this is an extremely important text, she claimed each time she added another to the pile, to understand the heart of this country—as well as some of Elizabeth's own favorites by Marianne, Cal, Gerard Manley Hopkins, Wallace Stevens. Early Wallace Stevens, that was; these days, she didn't have any idea what he was talking about. Of course, Lota was already familiar with these writers, as there appeared to be no book ever published in any language that she had not devoured, from Renaissance poetry to the most recent theories on composting or septic tank function. But each night they read back and forth to one another, Lota first in Portuguese, then Elizabeth in English, and now Elizabeth was waiting for Carlos to leave so that they could begin.

"You know, Elizabeth," Mary said, without glancing up from her knitting, "I've been meaning to mention how strong your work has become. We do get the *New Yorker* here, even if it doesn't arrive until months late. I always thought your writing very skilled, of course, but there was something slightly too darling about your earliest poems. You've grown tremendously."

"Thank you." The book in her hand was momentarily in jeopardy of being flung into the fire. The sting of *too darling* nullified any compliment. "I was just telling Pearl that sometimes I think I'm only published there because for whatever reason, the boys' club has finally decided to let one woman in."

"Balls to the boys!" Both women looked up to find Lota in the doorway. "You do not wait for an invitation to their club. You smash down the door!"

"Has Carlos gone home already?" Mary asked.

"He has."

"Did you finish plotting Vargas's ouster?"

Lota did not answer but stretched out upon the floor, rested her head on a pillow, and stared at the ceiling while smoking a cigarette. "The problem with this country," she began, "or the *problems* . . ." Then she stopped and did not complete her thought.

These evenings, after the guests had gone and the three of them remained, reading, knitting, discussing the day, were for Elizabeth the greatest luxury during her time at Samambaia. As the night deepened, what made itself evident was the balance Lota had managed to create here, a harmony between the world of action and the world of reflection.

"Besides," Lota said, sitting up abruptly, "you don't need an invitation to the club. You're famous."

"Lota, I'm not famous."

"Of course you are! Among your friends are Robert Lowell and Marianne Moore. *They* are famous poets."

"One isn't famous simply by association."

"Artists have a special status with Lota," Mary said, "if you hadn't realized that already. When we returned from New York, she was determined to create the sort of public arts programs in Rio that we'd seen in the States. There was really nothing like that here before, and now, thanks to Lota, there is." Elizabeth had rarely seen the woman exhibit so much feeling. "Brazilians are extremely proud, but they know almost nothing about their own artists."

"In some ways," Lota said, "we are a very backyard country."

Misuse of the English language had never charmed Elizabeth more.

"Lota knows everyone," Mary went on. "They were all dying to become involved in Lota's plans, even the rich. People flock to you, don't they?"

"It is because I have a great deal to offer."

"Not too modest, our Lota."

"I only say it because it is true."

"She's had no formal training," Mary said, "yet she is a master of every subject. Though sometimes I think she is still trying to find her way."

"Read me another poem from your friend Lowell," Lota demanded.

Mary put away her knitting. "I'm off to bed. The two of you could read all night, I think."

"And all day, too!" answered Lota.

MARY WONDERED HOW long Elizabeth planned to stay at Samambaia. The single instance she'd brought up the subject, Lota had lost her temper. True, as Lota had cuttingly remarked, Mary was not as natural, nor as generous, a host as Lota was, but nor did she desire to be. She greatly preferred the days and nights when they had no visitors. The sounds of the two women reading and laughing in the other room carried back to where Mary now lay in the dark; she knew that she would go to sleep alone and also wake alone. Since Elizabeth's arrival, Lota had not once come to share her bed but had retired each night to her own room. And though Elizabeth had been their guest for only a few days, even the politest, least intrusive of visitors—which, Mary had to admit, Elizabeth was—became a distraction from the construction of the house.

Oddly, Elizabeth's arrival had also brought a flood of memories from the time they'd first come to know one another in New York. Not nostalgia, certainly—Samambaia was Mary's home, she looked neither forward nor back—but recollected rooms and conversations and people that were tinged with fondness and something like longing. At the time, she'd already been living for several years in Brazil, having decided to stay after she retired from dancing, and then, of course, she'd met Lota. It was hardly the city of New York or the life she'd left there that had drawn her back from Rio. Near the end of the war, Mary could no longer resist the duty that called her home to serve in whatever manner she could. She stayed in New York for two years and joined the women's voluntary services, working in a veterans' hospital and occasionally at a children's care center, tending the infants of women who'd taken over the factory jobs left vacant by men who'd joined up to fight. Lota thrived, of course. She turned the whole trip to the States into a grand adventure that, in her mind, had originally been her own idea. In no time, she was bringing her new friends to the apartment: musicians and painters and museum directors and shoe-shine boys and whoever else crossed her path.

That was how Mary first came to know Elizabeth. Louise Crane, an elegant woman whose company she enjoyed, brought Elizabeth to the apartment, and the four of them began spending time together. Louise, sophisticated and certain; Elizabeth, fidgety, uncomfortable in her skin, always making wisecracks instead of speaking from any true feeling. You never had a sense of who she really was. The rumor was that Louise had already left Elizabeth, or that Elizabeth had left Louise, but that was hardly evident in how they related to one another. Louise was still very attentive, and it was understandable why a kindhearted person would be. Elizabeth was like a bird that had flown into the house and was dashing itself against the windows. You rushed to save it, wanted to hold the delicate thing in your hands, even if you might wonder at the same time if it carried some sort of pestilence.

Even then, Mary remembered, she and Elizabeth had not truly spoken to one another. Mary didn't have much to do with literature, though out of duty she read Elizabeth's poems when they appeared. In fact, the two women had almost nothing in common. They had always talked of daily things, just as they did now. Still, she was not incogni-zant of Elizabeth's charm, of her wit and intelligence; she did shine, in her way.

It was a different Elizabeth who'd come to visit them in Samambaia, one with more polish and a greater sense of her effect on others. At those dinners in New York, she'd never noticed Lota watching her, like a sparrow hawk eyeing a morsel, and now she did notice.

During those years back in the States, Mary had given herself one private luxury, a dance class two or three evenings a week. While Lota was out with any one of a hundred new, brilliant acquaintances, Mary had gone to a studio near the hospital where she worked, and there she had pushed her body until it cried out. Sometimes she'd stayed in the studio alone, mastering the slow execution of movement, the extension of line. Her life as a performer had been long past by then. She hadn't been on a stage in over five years, but her body remembered this discipline; it still wanted to be willed into this. Besides, she had always enjoyed the practice more than the performance.

Mary would not deny that Elizabeth subjected herself to her own rigorous discipline; you could see it in the poetry. But Elizabeth, you could also see, enjoyed the performance at least as much as the practice.

ELIZABETH KEPT HER eyes on Mary as she left the room, and then her glance fell to the floor. When she looked up, she found Lota watching her, as Elizabeth knew she would be. Boldly, she held the Brazilian woman's gaze. This was what she'd looked forward to since waking, this stretch of time alone with Lota in the dead of night. Mary's joke was accurate; they really could read and talk until dawn. The comfort and playfulness between them, the unguarded exploration of mind and imagination, and the enjoyment that was so obviously mutual seemed to rise out of a long familiarity and warmth. Only once in her memory—on first meeting Cal, when each had been instantly drawn to the other—had Elizabeth been so aware of her great good fortune in having discovered a like soul. Yet she and Lota were not *like* souls, they were nothing at all alike.

"I'm so envious of what you're making here," Elizabeth said. "You imagine something beautiful, and then you bring it physically into being. But you create something more than a physical place, more than just a house. Somehow it makes possible an interior change as well, an interior space comes alive . . . Oh, I don't know how to explain what I mean."

"Yes, you do!" Lota said, immensely pleased. "We'll make a modernist of you yet."

"I imagine only words. A handful of words, at that."

"But what words."

"Twenty poems in twenty years. Hardly an impressive output. Right now, I'm more excited about cooking."

Lota put a fingertip to the back of Elizabeth's hand. Her eyes commanded Elizabeth to believe. "Poetry, too, is a kind of food. I know that I would starve without it, and I am not the only one."

"Sometimes I think I'd like to do what Mary is considering. To have a child. But I'd make a terrible mother."

"Nonsense," Lota said, "you'd be magnificent."

"I have no idea of mothering." She felt dangerously close to revealing too much, yet she revealed even more. "I never received it myself."

"You had no mother?" Lota said.

Oh, everyone knows my mother went mad, she nearly said, to throw off Lota's concern. But Lota demanded, and deserved, more than easy deflection.

"My father died of a long illness when I was just a few months old. My mother never recovered from his death. That's what they say, but she must have been unbalanced already. Who can really know for sure? I have so few memories of her. She was hospitalized off and on, then permanently when I was five. By that I mean she was institutionalized. I didn't see her after that. She died right when I graduated from college, nearly the same week. Her name was Gertrude Boomer. Imagine—what a name. She was about the age I am now when she died. I lived for a time with my grandparents in Nova Scotia. They were poor, and wonderful. This place reminds me a bit of there, it's funny. Then I lived with my father's parents in Worcester. That's a town in Massachusetts. They were rich but very cold. They had no concept of what to do with a child. And then I went to live with my aunt . . ." Elizabeth trailed off.

"*Coitada*," Lota murmured, putting her hand to Elizabeth's face. "Well, my mother was also institutionalized, but the institution was the Church. They shut her away inside a confessional!" As they both laughed, Elizabeth could hardly bear the hand on the cheek, the compassion in Lota's gaze. The tenderness pained her. Yet her heart moved toward it like a parched woman in the desert to water. Or was it the mirage of water?

THE WEATHER ON the mountainside was extremely changeable. Ominous dark clouds drifted from beyond the black-rock mountain even as sunbeams struck the green expanse across the valley. Fireflies confused the dimming light for dusk. Fireflies an inch long, with lights like beacons. Butterflies as big as hummingbirds, hummingbirds as big as hawks. Caterpillars the size of snakes. A fluorescent green lizard with a red-hot tail. Her notebook and sketchpad lay in a bag at her feet. Every so often while sitting at the pool, Elizabeth was caught in a sudden cloudburst. The rain dripped upon her shelter of leaves, and when it began to drip lightly upon her as well, she did not seek protection indoors. It was only a matter of moving, after the clouds passed, to another rock in a patch of sun, where she would dry out in moments.

ELIZABETH AND MARY drove to the far side of the black rock, to a town called Correia. Correia had none of the grandness of Petropolis, Mary explained, since the mountains had protected it from becoming part of the imperial court established in Petropolis a hundred years earlier. "Petropolis is a town of the rich," she said. "It always has been, and it still is. I prefer simpler places." They drove the rest of the way in silence.

As they wound through the mountains, Elizabeth thought of the party Lota had thrown the previous day to celebrate the installation of the roof. The workmen had all got very drunk on beer, or *choppe*, as they called it, and tried to hoist Lota on their shoulders. "Viva Dona Lota!" they'd shouted. "Viva la *choppe*!" And then, so inebriated they had lost their balance, they'd nearly bashed her head on a rock. Lota had stepped out of their collapsing arms as regally as a queen from a palanquin, gracing the earth with her delicate foot. The afternoon had brought thunderstorms, and as they stood beneath the new roof, admiring the sound of the downpour on the aluminum panels, water had begun to gush down an interior wall. Within minutes, Lota had leapt into the jeep and was speeding down the mountain to Rio for an emergency consult with Sergio. Thinking of Lota now, Elizabeth turned to the car window, hiding her smile from Mary.

She also concealed her disappointment when they reached Correia, which was not exactly dreary but neither was it the charming, unspoiled colonial town she'd imagined. Mary parked in the central square, where the low buildings were a patchwork of new and old materials, plastic upon plaster, and Elizabeth followed her into the church. The painted walls were dingy, nearly blackened by eons of candle smoke. Two people sat in the pews, an old woman in the back and a young one near the front, their mumbled prayers magnified by the emptiness. So quickly that Elizabeth thought she was brushing something off her blouse, Mary crossed herself and dipped in a gesture of genuflection. Something about this made Elizabeth leave the church; she did not know whether to laugh or cry. She honestly wished she liked the other woman more. Mary was surprising, but there was no playfulness to her.

When Mary joined her outside, they strolled around the perimeter of the square. Elizabeth thought, *I will not speak until spoken to.* Lota would have had all sorts of witty things to say about this land of the lost, or else would have known half the people and greeted them by name. A few blocks out from the square, Elizabeth could see the town fading into countryside. She amused herself for a good quarter of an hour with the idea of hanging a left at the next crossing and marching directly into the hills. Then Mary took a seat outside a peculiar little grocery store and ordered coffee for them both.

A birdcage hung from a rope tied to the patio's overhang, in which a dove sat placidly on a stick. Elizabeth sipped the hot coffee. At first glance, the square appeared devoid of activity, but as she continued to observe, the citizenry began to emerge from hiding. A mother holding a baby passed across the square, where she met two girls with jugs balanced upon their heads. A boy exited one storefront carrying a chicken by its feet; he entered another, then came sprinting out, chickenless. A laborer wheeled along a metal cylinder of gas, wearing a straw hat painted green. Stumbling past their table came a toddler with two gold hoops in her ear. She nearly lost her balance and then regained it just as both women's arms went out to catch her fall. Some paces behind came the father, hands behind his back, giving them a smile of golden teeth. Across the square, two young men worked beneath the hood of a car, while managing to keep an eye on the girls filling their water jugs at the fountain. The memory of Great Village rushed upon Elizabeth. On afternoons that had seemed to have no end, she'd sat on the front porch with her grandmother while the townsfolk passed before them. Every person had a story; all the stories interconnected. It struck Elizabeth that her want of drink had never served as more than a distraction from another, more piercing want.

"What a lovely place," she said.

"Yes," Mary replied. "It is."

"Thank you for bringing me here."

Shyly, she met Mary's glance. It was impossible to infer the other woman's emotion. It was as if Mary wanted nothing, as if she were entirely contained, entirely poised.

"I always wondered how you could make your home here," Elizabeth said softly, "how you were able to leave the U.S. utterly behind. Now I'm beginning to understand."

"Brazil can be maddening. It can be extremely difficult to feel comfortable here. For us, I mean, for Northerners. And for all the reasons you'd expect. The poverty is heartbreaking, the inefficiency, the corruption. Sometimes, at their worst, Brazilians seem like parodies of themselves. But the *North* . . ." Mary shook her head. "It gets harder and harder to imagine ever living there again."

Elizabeth became aware of a noise at her back that had been going on for some minutes, a fluttering of wings. She wanted to investigate, but the delicate beginnings of an accord with Mary made her hesitant to move. The waiter who'd served them was talking with the shopkeeper next door. He laughed, spat a big glob onto the ground, and rubbed his crotch. The two women again glanced at one another and smiled.

Once more, she was distracted by the noise, and this time Elizabeth turned. Outside the birdcage, a dove was batting itself against the bars. She thought at first that the dove had gotten loose and was trying to return to its perch. Then she saw that it was a second bird altogether, a wild dove attempting to reach the tame one inside.

"Besides," Mary said, "Lota's very convincing. She wants me here, and she knows how to get her way."

Elizabeth brought her coffee to her lips, but the cup was empty. "Yes, she's very forceful, that's clear."

"But with a gentle touch. You hardly even notice she's maneuvering you. You may have sensed that yourself."

Elizabeth turned again in her seat. The almost violent fluttering of the wild dove against the cage unsettled her.

Mary went on. "She would never say so, but when she adopted Kylso from the mechanic, she saved that boy's life. He would have ended up begging on the street, at best. Lota paid for the operations so that now he can walk. She gave him an education so that now he can work. She has that kind of power and conviction."

"She's an impressive woman, certainly."

"And yet she's not so strong as she acts. She needs absolute loyalty. She requires it. It's not obvious, but Lota has her own fragility. As we all do, of course."

"Yes that's true. We all do."

"I think part of love is like service. It has to be. You have to be able to provide that to each other. You have to reach inside yourself and give to the other even when it seems your own resources are exhausted. Don't you agree?"

"I'm hardly the one to ask," Elizabeth said with a laugh. "My own record is dismal."

"Is it?"

What had she been thinking, that Lota had been so enthralled by her sparkling presence that she was trying to capture her, like a butterfly in her net? Save her from a life of crippledom? "Well, you've both been much too generous to have me for so long," she told Mary. "You'll have to recommend some other places I should visit before I leave Brazil. I've heard Ouro Preto is not to be missed, and I'm dying to see it. I thought I might go there next week."

When she unveiled her smile, Mary could be lovely. If she did that more often, you'd never think, not in a million years, *Dry stick.* "Every Brazilian will tell you Ouro Preto is beautiful, but I've never met a single one who's actually gone there. They're a funny people."

"Yes, they are," Elizabeth agreed, and they shared another laugh over this, simply one more of the many charming quirks of the Brazilian character.

· 8 ·

*L*OTA GRINNED AT the reasons Elizabeth gave for her
abrupt departure; she was pleased even then, Elizabeth could see, by
the determination of her American friend.

Back down the mountainside.

Into the city, choked by smog.

"I'll be leaving Rio soon," she told Pearl, fanning herself with a
newspaper.

They'd ducked out of the afternoon sun into Pearl's dark apartment
in Ipanema. Once, Pearl's place had felt like a closet compared with
Lota's beautiful pied-à-terre; now, it was a refuge from it. Her husband
was nowhere to be seen. Victor rarely was.

"I can't stand it much longer myself," Pearl said. "This hellish heat.
So many people brushing up against you. And the noise is incessant."

"I thought, for a moment, I might stay longer. I thought . . ." Elizabeth shook her head.

"What is it?" Pearl smiled and scooted close. "What's the secret?"

One word was all she could allow. "Lota."

"I don't understand."

Elizabeth tossed the paper to the table. On the front page was a photo of President Vargas, decrying the latest wave of strikes. Then she burst out with it. "I thought something was happening with Lota. I thought for a minute that just maybe this might be more than a place to refuel before I hit the road again."

Pearl moved away; she now looked decidedly unhappy. But Elizabeth went on.

"It's absurd. She's with Mary, of course. But the way she *looks* at me. You should hear what she calls me. *Elizabeechy*." In spite of herself, Elizabeth smiled, hearing her name again in Lota's voice. "She shouldn't play with me like that. I'm too susceptible. *Elizabeechy* . . ."

"Well," Pearl said crisply. She stood and smoothed her dress, then reached for a big woven-straw bag. "I suppose I should do the shopping for dinner."

"Do you think leaving Rio is the right thing to do?"

"Isn't that what you've already decided? I envy you, actually."

Once they were in the street, Elizabeth found that she nearly had to break into a jog to keep up with her friend. Pearl's ankle had apparently healed and possessed greater spring and resilience than ever. That's what it was like to be young; an injury only made you stronger. Pearl flew through the butcher's, the bakery, and the cheese store while Elizabeth remained near the entrance of each establishment, catching her breath. Obviously, she'd disappointed Pearl in some way, yet now that Elizabeth was resolved to leave Brazil, she could at least begin to turn her thoughts to what lay ahead. The whole idea of travel was to discover new perspectives, including upon one's own choices and motivations, not dig yourself into another impossible situation.

"Are you still interested in seeing Ouro Preto?" she asked Pearl at the produce stand. "It was the one place I'd really hoped to visit, and I'd like to see it before I leave."

"Perhaps we could do that," Pearl said, softening. "I've wanted to go there, too."

"And in the spring you might meet me in Machu Picchu. I'll have made it to Peru by April, I'm sure. Do you think Victor could spare you?"

Pearl's gaze was passing over a bin of cashews, but Elizabeth suspected it was not the fruit that caused her expression to sour. "We'll see. He probably could."

Even if indecent, the cashews were beautiful to look at. That was Brazil in a nutshell. The skin of the fruit was the same saturated yellow-orange she'd painted her study in Key West. Mornings, when the sun came through the high window, the entire room had glowed. She chose two cashews from the bin, and after counting out her change to the pouting girl at the counter, Elizabeth waited for Pearl in the street.

First Ouro Preto, then Machu Picchu, Pearl or no Pearl. But probably Pearl. She'd write Lota and Mary clever postcards from along the route, and someday, when they visited her in New York or Amsterdam or San Francisco, the three of them would remember their days together in Samambaia. Lota would show her photographs of the house; Mary, of the children.

At her feet, the concrete sidewalk had been cracked by the roots of a tree. Sprouting from the tree trunk at eye level was a spindly stalk, on the tip of which bloomed an arresting flower. Scarlet petals, shading to rose at the center. In the place of pistil and stamens, there was the oddest appendage, a sort of pinkish-cream ladle lined with a feathery fringe, slightly aromatic. She'd never seen anything like it. Higher up, the long, twisted stalks grew into a huge snarl, sprouting more of the flowers, as well as spherical, wooden fruits nearly the size of soccer balls. "Look at that strange flower," she pointed out when Pearl joined her.

"How odd. I've never noticed those before."

"The language sounds absurd," Elizabeth said, "everyone goes around practically naked, with ludicrous, perfectly Greek bodies, the landscape is too absurdly beautiful to be believed, the flowers are like something from another world. What kind of country is this?"

"One we've both come to," Pearl said, "for some reason or another."

• • •

There is beginning, middle, and end, that is a fact. The end of things is not a moral act.

Thus spake the scrap.

In her notebook, Elizabeth attempted to describe the strange scarlet flower. Surprisingly, after days of lackluster writing, she found it pleasurable again to work with the words, to wrestle a bit and get the description just right. All that time in Samambaia she'd hardly put pen to paper; now she could feel the desire to work beginning to trickle back. Plainly, her craft was the only thing that had any real hooks in her. It had seen her through many different living quarters, many countries, many sad days and the occasional happy one, and if her nature could have been said to possess even one formidable ounce, then it was certainly anchored in the writing, in the act and discipline of writing.

During the night, a big storm had blown through, and the morning air possessed a clear, fresh quality. Elizabeth worked on the new poem until lunchtime, comfortable in her slip and bare feet, her mind sharp and lively in a fashion not to be rivaled by the false aliveness granted by constant doses of coffee. To piece together scraps into a thing of beauty and, one hoped, of at least limited use—that was her skill and purpose, to whatever end it might take her.

The coastline of Brazil, the impractical green mountains (*Green Mansions*, she heard in Miss Breen's voice), and Miss Breen herself, they had taken shape on the page. Rough shape, certainly, not much more than a prose outline. She'd talked her way through the poem and forged its bulk, with a few lines here and there that would probably remain. They were the backbone. That was the easy part. One had to continue shaping the lines as if with a minute chisel, shape and shape and keep shaping until eventually a distinct form began to emerge. A form nearly crystalline in its exactness and strength and grace. A form could be made visible, when previously it had existed only in the imagination.

And when she was really flying, the work was a kind of fever, a preemptive excitement that overrode all others. It became a physical force with the power to propel her person out of the chair and across the room to the window if she did not continually grip the tabletop to hold herself in place. After a while, she became so immersed in the poem that she no longer felt the anxiety of Lota. She did not miss the proximity of Lota.

·9·

*T*HE EARLIER INSTANCE had been merely a rehearsal for the second, the more fateful, arrival. The key scratching in the lock. The maid emerging from her room and advancing quickly to the front hall. The door flying open.

Elizabeth reached for a blanket folded over the back of the sofa, wrapping it around herself as Lota, arms laden with who knew what, kicked various bags of hardware into the apartment. Looking down, Elizabeth took in the wrinkled hem of her cream-colored slip, her stark white shins, bruised for some reason in two or three places, her broad flat feet on the wooden floor, indelicate, the little toe curling outward, with its split and yellowed nail.

"Good day, Elizabeechy."

"Why are you here?" She was displeased at the intrusion. She wanted Lota to know of her displeasure.

"I have some business in Rio. I won't be long, two days at most."

"It's your house. You can come and go as you like."

"No, it's *your* house while you're here." Lota waved a hand. "Please continue writing. I have no intention of interrupting." Then she carried her bags down the hallway, and Lucia shut the door.

Elizabeth continued to stand beside the table while Lucia busied herself in the kitchen and the aroma of coffee began to permeate the apartment. Lota did not return. Her own bedroom, Elizabeth recalled, was a disaster area. Lota would think her an ungrateful guest. At the very least, she ought to close the door so that Lota wouldn't see the mess.

Elizabeth crept down the hallway and peered into her room. Not quite so bad as she'd imagined. She left the door open a crack. In the adjacent bedroom, Lota was digging through an overnight bag. "It is good to see you working," she said without looking up. "You should go back to it. Don't let me disturb you."

Elizabeth leaned against the doorframe. She still held the blanket around her, though it was unbearably hot. "Did you fix the leaks in the roof?"

"Yes, now we are on to other complications. We've actually begun to sleep there but live by candlelight. It is a little like camping in the forest. Spiders and frogs join us in bed. Elizabeth, come here. There's something I want to show you."

"All right." Drawing near Lota, in those few steps, Elizabeth had time to observe that the sensations of excitement and dread were on occasion indistinguishable.

"I've been wanting you to see these." Lota held a number of slim books. "But they've been here in Rio all this time."

"Yes," Elizabeth said. "The famous monographs."

"Here's the one of Costa and Niemeyer's Brazilian Pavilion at the World's Fair in New York that I told you about. And here is the Ministry of Health and Education that really was the genesis of modernism in Brazil, the collaboration between Le Corbusier and our young architects. I'd like to take you to see it while I'm here. I also have these designs by a good friend who is planning a book about Brazilian modernism, the first book of its kind."

Lota picked up one of the books, then another, spreading them upon the dresser as proudly as if she'd made them herself. "Here is another house by Sergio. You can see how, without my ideas, his concepts verge on the conservative. He holds back, as though he's afraid of the possibilities that modernism presents. And you must look at these photographs Lina Bo Bardi recently sent me of her house. I told you of her, a dear friend. It is her first building, but I promise you that one day she will be an architect of great prominence. Look, it is cube made of glass. There is actually a tree growing up through the center! She's gone to live in São Paulo. I miss her. I would like very much for you to meet her. We'll go there to visit."

Lota flipped through the photographs of her friend's house, pointing out the details she found particularly admirable or iconoclastic, while Elizabeth sweltered beneath the blanket she continued to clutch at her throat. She was too hot, and she was standing too close to Lota, close enough that their forearms were brushing. Or else she imagined they were but would not look down to verify one way or the other. Lota continued to go back and forth through the books, putting one down and picking one up.

Why don't you just do it? Elizabeth thought. *Just grab me.*

"Lota," she said, "I won't be going to São Paulo with you. I'm leaving Brazil."

Lota closed all the books at once and set them on the dresser. She smiled pleasantly and then turned to leave the room. Elizabeth watched her own hand reach forth and lay itself upon Lota's neck, right where it sloped into the shoulder, where the skin was cool on her hot palm.

Lota turned back. She was smiling still.

They drank each other in. Much later, when she had any time to reflect, that was how Elizabeth thought of their prolonged embrace. For eons they stood nearly motionless, simply holding one another. Lota's arms were tight around her, her fingers pressing into Elizabeth's back, and Elizabeth rested her feverish forehead against Lota's cool neck. They clung to one another as if the spot on which they stood were the single tranquil domain in all the world. After some time, Elizabeth could not have said when, they moved to the bed. Lota had closed the door, and this was also curious, as Elizabeth did not recall a moment of physical separation. They might have kissed, but she thought not. They continued to grip one another as they lay upon the bedspread, arms and legs intertwining with the purest need. Though Lota remained fully dressed and the blanket, fallen from Elizabeth's shoulders, had become entangled between them, the contact was beyond intoxication. Without a single word, they answered one another perfectly, with an equivalent hunger to be held and touched. An hour passed, perhaps more. The trees and birds of Samambaia passed through Elizabeth's mind, the waterfall, the clouds and light, standing with Miss Breen at the ship's railing, her mother holding her while she stared down into the whorl of a fern. Her hands began to rove. They touched Lota's neck, her face, her breasts, her backside. Elizabeth's thirst grew overwhelming; her arms turned to tentacles.

At last Lota pulled back. "Do you find the merchandise to your liking?"

Elizabeth withdrew her hands, deeply embarrassed. "I'm not sure this is happening."

"It is happening."

Lota rose from the bed. She kissed Elizabeth's forehead, then tucked in the tails of her work shirt and resumed unpacking her overnight bag. Elizabeth slipped out of the room and into her own, where she dressed quickly and brushed her hair before the mirror. She did not believe herself disastrously unattractive, but she wondered if her face might be criticized for the same faults as her poetry had been. Too precious, too cold. A precise miniature of a face. When she emerged, Lota was having coffee with Lucia in the kitchen. The maid was talking up a storm with the mistress of the house and making Lota cackle. Lucia's own laugh was deep, almost vulgar. Lota set her coffee upon the counter, took Elizabeth's arm, and led her directly out of the apartment.

The world had turned on its side, yet continued to behave as though it had not. The doorman leapt out of his midafternoon snooze to grant them exit from the building and onto the square. Beneath the trees, an elderly woman called out and Lota stopped briefly to speak with her.

From the terrace Elizabeth had watched this ancient little crab walking her Lhasa apso each morning. By now, she should hardly be surprised to discover that every neighborhood eccentric, artist, highflier, and busybody was an intimate of Dona Lota, or hoped to be. She couldn't understand a word of their exchange, yet as Elizabeth stood by, Lota's arm linked through hers, she felt keenly the privilege of her position.

"It's cooler by the water," Lota said, guiding them from the sidewalk onto the sand. They ducked beneath the arc of a soccer ball two men were lobbing off their heads. Elizabeth slipped off her sandals and let the surf wash over her feet. The water was bracing, the undercurrent strong. She took a step deeper. A wave wet her hem. From across the beach, an umbrella rushed toward them as if under its own power, two skinny brown legs sprinting beneath it. The umbrella came to a halt beside Lota, opened up, and stuck itself into the sand. A boy with dark hair bleached russet by the sun emerged from underneath and unfolded two chairs in the umbrella's shade. His bathing suit was a strip of carmine against his burnished skin. The boy was as skinny as the dogs Elizabeth had seen nuzzling trash in the street.

"Would you like something to drink?" Lota asked.

Elizabeth nodded.

Lota spoke a few words to the boy, who ran back across the beach to the nearest kiosk.

The sky was deep blue, pellucid; the mountains were more absurdly beautiful than ever. The emerald water was full of swimmers. A little girl was lifted up and pounded by a crashing wave, then came floundering out of the surf, nearly incapacitated by delight. Elizabeth remained silent, taking in the scene. What use were words here, really?

She turned to her companion, but Lota continued gazing directly ahead, as if deliberately posing herself for study, jutting her chin forward, her alert eyes focused on the horizon. *Look at me, know who I am. I am the world's conqueror. And yours.* There was something about this formidable woman that was at the same time comical. The nose was a bit too large for her face, the lips succulent to the point of savagery. That

72

striking streak of white in the black hair. At times Lota's face was plain, at others it shimmered into a beauty that caused Elizabeth's breath to catch. There was also a quality to it that was nearly cruel. Around the eyes, perhaps, and in the way she held her mouth.

Elizabeth hadn't come here looking for a love affair. Quite the opposite. As the *Bowplate* had departed New York harbor, leaving that awful year behind, she'd felt at peace, for once, with the prospect of being alone. Just to be, to think, to work. But she could not deny the power of her attraction to Lota, so elemental it seemed to originate in her molecules. Truly, she'd never felt anything approaching this. Not merely physical desire—it was the desire to launch herself *toward*, to leap with the entirety of her being into the space between them, not knowing what might catch her fall. Was that love? Or even the beginnings of love?

Her previous love affairs had all taken root in a sameness of mind and opinion that had, in Elizabeth's understanding, been essential to form any attachment. With Marjorie, and with Tom as well, she'd held the same ideas on books, on aesthetics and morals; they'd laughed at the same jokes, enjoyed the same people, found the same ones insufferable. It was as though she'd needed to align herself with another who was similar in every way in order to bolster a weakness in herself, had drawn close to others out of the need to make herself stronger, safer. She hadn't begun to understand until now that *need* might be distinct from *desire*.

Lota was a different species altogether. She was alien to Elizabeth in a way inexplicable even by their different cultures and backgrounds. Say Mary didn't exist, say Elizabeth abandoned all reason and threw in her lot with Lota. She had a clear premonition that she would never truly know Lota, that Lota would forever remain outside of her understanding. And yet this very gulf excited her. The question of safety was moot. She wanted to make the leap. The odd thing was that for the first time in her life, she felt capable of performing such acrobatics. Or at least capable of the attempt.

"Talk to me a little," Elizabeth said.

"What would you like to hear, my heart?"

"Something about you. Not about architecture or books. We've talked enough of those."

"A confession?"

"Or personal history. Or a wish of some sort. Anything to help me know you better."

Apparently, everything Elizabeth said amused Lota. "Very well. I will tell you a personal history. And a wish of some sort. About a girl who thought she could do anything. She wanted to work, to have her own business, to study to be an architect, but her father said that was no life for a woman. What kind of woman wanted to live in the world of men? Besides, she was too ugly, too graceless. If she was lucky, he said, she might hope to follow the example of her beautiful sister and marry."

Mary had told Elizabeth about Lota's estranged father, the editor of an important newspaper. Elizabeth thought it a luxury beyond imagining to have a parent, still living, with whom you'd chosen to have no ties. "He actually said such awful things to you?"

"Many things more awful than those. What can you do in that situation but fight, as you would against any dictator? So I decided to become a painter. I believed I would be a great painter."

"You never told me you painted. I would love to see what you've done."

"I studied for years. That's how I know many of the people who have risen to prominence in the arts. All this was twenty years ago. I had some talent. It is hard to say now how much talent, or how far I might have gone."

"You stopped? I can't picture you giving up on anything."

"My father disparaged me, as in every endeavor. He enjoyed saying how I would never be good enough. He implied as a painter, but he meant as a human being. He could be very cruel, and I wasn't strong enough to stand up to him. Not strong enough *inside*, though of course we screamed at each other constantly. So I dropped my painting. Still, it is ironic that I have always had much greater ambitions for myself than he ever had for me. I believe he was very angry that I was not a son, that he had no male heir. But I've always felt confident I would show my father that a daughter can accomplish as much as a son, or more."

"I don't doubt that you will. You're the most impressive woman I've ever known. And you can still paint," Elizabeth added hopefully, as though that were the point.

Lota was gazing at her intently. "You will stay here in Brazil, Elizabeechy. With me."

Beyond Lota, the boy approached, bearing a green coconut as large as his head. The top had been sheared off by a machete, and two straws stuck out, as from a malt at a soda shoppe. Elizabeth took a sip of the coconut milk, cold and sweet, then could not stop drinking until nearly half of it was gone. She hadn't realized she was so intensely thirsty.

"Something is happening between us, something rare," Lota said quietly. "I recognized it at once. Life is giving us an opportunity we have no choice but to take."

"But Lota, you know it's not that clean."

"We were both wandering lost, and now we've found one another."

"You weren't lost," Elizabeth insisted. "You have Mary."

"It started in New York. I knew it even then, five years ago. I knew it the first moment I saw you at the modern art museum, and I knew it two days later when you came to my house for dinner. If you tell me that you did not feel it too, then you are being untruthful, with me and with yourself."

"Of course I felt it. I did feel it. But Lota, there's something you must understand. I am a sickly person. I'm sick in my body and my heart. I drink. I drink so much that more than once I've had to put myself in the hospital. Often I can hardly breathe because of the asthma I've had ever since I was a child. I can't breathe and I feel as though I'm dying. I'm not *normal*. I'm allergic to everything, and I can't love anyone. A few people have tried to love me, but I couldn't return their feeling. Honestly, I wanted to. I tried extremely hard. Something in me is simply dried up."

Lota placed a hand on Elizabeth's leg. She looked out to sea and her lips drew into a smile, as if every word Elizabeth spoke were in concordance with her own feeling.

"I told you about my mother to warn you off," Elizabeth said.

"I think you told me in order to invite me in." She took Elizabeth's hand, petting her palm as if it held something of rare value. "I know that you are capable of love. I felt it in the apartment, a moment ago. But you are afraid. You are simply saying that you have no ties."

Elizabeth had to laugh. "That's true. I have absolutely no ties. Not a tie in the world." She squeezed Lota's hand and dropped it. "But you do."

"You're right," Lota said. "It would be false to say I have no ties. But Mary and I, we are . . ." She shrugged. "We have become friends more than we are lovers."

LOTA'S LIPS WERE upon her face, on her eyes and neck. Lota was kissing her hands, her arthritic, worried knuckles. Lota was unbuttoning her blouse, bringing her close. The afflictions of the body—the asthma, the dyspepsia, the hangovers, the inflammations and rashes without apparent cause—Elizabeth had always borne upon her two stocky legs like a mule with a pack. But the body was not solely a burden.

As they kissed, Elizabeth's hands began again to rove, unembarrassed. To run through Lota's hair, to take Lota's hair in her fist and tug until she cried out. Lota's skin was a marvel, soft and silken, like a rose petal, and the color of a rose, pale beige with a suffusion of pink. She wished her hands were those of a giantess, to touch all of Lota at once. In bed, there were those who liked to be knocked around and those who liked to do the knocking. She'd sensed that the two of them would make the right match, and she was not disappointed. She found herself voracious; she would leave nothing but Lota's bones. But Lota had her own ideas. Her body pinned Elizabeth's; one hand held her wrist, the other slid below. A sickly body and heart might still exclaim, *At last, to feel!* Yet the pleasure of sex meant to converge with sorrow; Elizabeth felt herself on the cusp of weeping. She wanted to weep, she wanted her heart to be punctured.

Later, as Lota held her and slept, Elizabeth realized that she had not wept. She was unable to slip into peaceful dreams, as Lota had; she felt as though she'd indulged in the appetite for drink. To prevent her mind from churning and turning on itself, she left Lota's arms and retrieved the famous blanket off the floor. She returned to her place at the window overlooking the ocean. The maid appeared to have vacated the premises; Elizabeth wondered if she'd been told to scram. Evening was falling. In the twilight, the number of men on the beach had multiplied tenfold; they were enjoying themselves immensely. Maybe she'd take up football herself. In spite of the complications, Elizabeth thought how immensely *sane* she felt. This was what she'd imagined without believing it might be possible, this connection with another person, man or woman, this excitement and ease, this strength, this sex.

When Lota joined her and asked why she was smiling, she said, "I didn't believe I would ever feel this. I'd given up hoping. If I ever hoped for it in the first place."

Lota said nothing. She turned Elizabeth back to face the window and put her arms around her waist. On tiptoe, she rested her chin upon Elizabeth's shoulder. They looked oceanward together until darkness fell and the stars appeared.

WHATEVER BUSINESS HAD summoned Lota from the mountains, actual or fabricated, was forgotten.

"You'll come back with me to Samambaia," Lota said in the morning.

"Are you mad?"

"You'll come."

Elizabeth went to her bedroom and took down her travel bag from the shelf in the closet. She hardly knew what she was doing, but Lota did, and that would have to be enough.

In an alabaster bowl on the kitchen counter lay the two cashews

Elizabeth had bought with Pearl several days earlier. It felt closer to centuries, another lifetime ago—another Elizabeth. Pearl would be so disappointed in her. She picked up one of the suggestive fruits and considered it, then took a bite, immediately spitting it into her hand. Pearl was right. The cashew was much too sour to abide.

Only once during the drive did Elizabeth break the silence. Passing a park in Botafogo on their way out of the city, she saw one of the trees with the strange red flowers and asked if Lota was familiar with it, though they'd sped past too quickly for Lota to see.

"That must be an *abrico de macaco*," she said. "It comes from the Amazon. The landscape architect Burle Marx uses it in his gardens. He loves it, but many people don't like the tree at all. The fruits fall to the ground and break open, and the stink is terrible. Nuts of monkey? I don't know how to say the name in English. The monkey nuts tree?"

Elizabeth caught the edge of hysteria in her own laugh. *That's me, monkey nuts!*

On the winding road to Petropolis, they did not speak, not about modernism or the construction of houses or antique bird jails or fine how-do-you-dos. They did not speak about what they were doing or about what would happen when they arrived. The strangeness of their actions settled into Elizabeth's body as a physical unease. With every mile closer to Petropolis, the greater was her understanding that her life was about to change course, but at the expense of someone else. Of another heart.

They left the city behind, and then, ascending, they left the world behind.

In Samambaia, Elizabeth shut herself in the kitchen and prepared dinner with Maria the cook. Maria engaged her in a conversation about painting with local soils; she herself did so, drying the soils on the stove and making portraits of saints in beautiful, natural colors. When the meal was served, Elizabeth left Maria's company with reluctance and took her place at the table. Polite chat with Mary and Lota was torture. She had no hunger for the food. Exhaustion penetrated to her soul; it was a mistake to have come here. She should have had the strength to refuse, to take time to think. Lota was discussing plumbing fixtures with Mary. Elizabeth excused herself from the table and went to her room, where she attempted to read. Her mind couldn't attend to the book; her eyes kept falling shut. Her face, as well as her hands, began to itch, then to burn. The skin around her eyes began to swell, it was hard to the touch. At last she understood that something was wrong with her, something physical. She was ill. Controlling her panic, she returned to the dining room, where Lota and Mary broke from their conversation and looked up at her. Mary put a hand to her mouth. Lota stood and came rushing around the table. Elizabeth turned to the mirror and saw that she had become monstrous.

· I O ·

ON NEW YEAR'S, Elizabeth heard the fireworks on the beach and the roars of celebrants, but it seemed to happen in a feverish dream. She was inflamed from head to toe. Her eyes were swollen shut, and she was completely blind.

Lota shepherded out of the room the visitors whom she'd invited, to Elizabeth's horror, to view the patient's peeling, scabby face and hands. Then she sat by the bed and offered her own diagnosis:

"What is it when a toenail goes inside? Turns on itself and causes pain? Oh, yes, ingrown. *Encravado* means ingrown. And *tesao* is a word that means life, passion for life. Some give it dirty meanings, but that's not what it is. It is an excitement for life. It is yes instead of no. I know what has made you so sick. It is *tesão encravado*, ingrown *tesão*. And I also know the cure."

Lota held a hand so tender, it felt as though it had passed through fire, but Elizabeth did not pull away.

LOTA AND MARY unpacked some of the boxes they'd brought from Rio. The kitchen was nearly dark, lighted by the candles and oil lamps they'd placed among the rooms. The house was so clean and pure, Lota had recently considered keeping it completely free of objects so as not to break the lines. She'd come close to suggesting this to Mary but then laughed at herself to even think of doing so. Of course, it was an entirely impractical idea, and Mary would never sacrifice practicality for beauty. And the house was beautiful, beyond beautiful; it fulfilled her best imaginings, even when her eye snagged on the fault covered over with a patch of cement or on an imperfect joint in the roof.

They were back in the house now after the interruption caused by Elizabeth's illness. She'd really given them a scare, especially at first, when they'd rushed her back to the city not knowing what was wrong with her, if she was truly as close to perishing as she constantly claimed. And to think: the cashew! Dona Elizabeechy's extreme allergy was certainly unusual, the doctor said, but this sort of reaction to *caju* was not unheard of. Even some Brazilians responded in such a way. But she was much improved, and the doctor had agreed that moving her back to Samambaia would help her recovery rather than hinder it.

Elizabeth seems much better, Lota said.

Mary laughed. Sorry, I don't mean to be heartless, but this would only happen to her.

The doctor said it is uncommon but can be quite severe. Even dangerous.

I know, Lota, I was standing there when he said it. I'm just saying, next thing, she'll have a reaction to black beans, or to rain. Mary unwrapped a drinking glass from its paper, set it into the sink to wash.

It was time to tell Mary.

I've asked Elizabeth to stay in Brazil, Lota said.

Mary took another glass from the packing crate.

Did you hear what I said?

You mean you've asked her to stay here with you.

Yes, that is what I mean.

Has she accepted?

She will.

How convenient that you have two houses. One for the wife and one for the mistress.

Do not be bitter, Morsie.

Mary unwrapped the glass and held it in both hands. And have you made love to her?

I have.

I suppose I shouldn't be surprised. I saw it coming from the instant she arrived. When you have something in your sights, you don't stop until you get what you want.

Yes, Morsie, you're right. I don't.

Mary threw the glass into the sink with all her might, where it shattered among half a dozen other glasses. Then leave this house and go to her, she shouted. Leave me. Get away from me.

When Mary was angry, she was very fine. No one approached her.

Please don't get upset, my flower. Lota drew close to reassure her, but she did not try to hold Mary. She knew Mary would not allow herself to be touched. Our life together continues. It changes, but it continues. This is not the end.

She's a drunk and a hypochondriac! Everyone knows that.

She's a genius.

Mary began to sob openly. She did not attempt to hide her grief or to cover her face with her hands.

You know that it has been a long time since there was passion between us. I did not seek to find it with someone else, but it has come to me and I can't turn away from it.

But we've just finished our house. We've worked on it for so long.

It was wrenching to be so near a loved one with a broken heart and not be able to soothe her with a caress. Worse still that she was the cause of Mary's suffering. She stayed with Mary as she wept, her own heart aching.

Yet she could not deny her excitement.

She picked her way down the slope in the dark. She brushed away her own tears before she entered the house where Elizabeth was sleeping. Lota stroked her swollen face until Elizabeth opened her eyes, which gleamed in the blackness.

Now I have no ties, Lota said.

Song for the Rainy Season

. . .

[JULY 1952–JANUARY 1958]

Hidden, oh hidden
in the high fog
the house we live in,
beneath the magnetic rock,
rain-, rainbow-ridden,
where blood-black
bromelias, lichens,
owls, and the lint
of the waterfalls cling,
familiar, unbidden.

In a dim age
of water
the brook sings loud
from a rib cage
of giant fern; vapor
climbs up the thick growth
effortlessly, turns back,
holding them both,
house and rock,
in a private cloud.

· I I ·

ELIZABETH WROTE THROUGH the night. It was extremely cold. As the dark hours lengthened, she added sweaters one by one, finally pulling a heavy blanket over her shoulders. She'd cut the fingers off a pair of woolen gloves, like some waif out of *Oliver Twist*, and typed with bare, numb fingertips. From the darkness outdoors there came an intermittent *clang*, as if signaling the hour, a resonant, metallic note that sounded like a hammer upon an anvil. It was the mating call, Lota had said, of an enormous frog that lived in the stream. The frog was called the blacksmith.

Elizabeth continued to write even as the sky lightened and the household woke around her and Lota tiptoed past and the construction started up. An hour later, Lota passed by once more; without stopping she resettled the blanket that had slipped from Elizabeth's shoulder. It amused her that Lota would not dream of interrupting, not even to say good morning or to ask how the work was progressing. In Lota's view, artistic creation occurred through a mystical channeling of the gods and was not to be interfered with. This mad rush of typing was exactly what she would expect of a writer in the grip of inspiration. Lota would reject any suggestion by Elizabeth that the manner in which this piece had consumed her energies was so anomalous in her career that she hesitated to call it by the name of writing.

PRIVATELY, ELIZABETH DID not absolutely settle for some time the question of whether or not she was in Brazil to stay. It had taken nearly two months to recuperate from her clash with the cashew. Even though she was spoiled on her sickbed by Lota's attention and by that of Lota's kind friends, and even though by the time she left the bed Mary had moved to the apartment in Copacabana and Lota had begun building a writing studio for Elizabeth beside the waterfall, she still made a series of reservations on ships bound for Argentina, the next stop in her original itinerary, canceling each one as the departure date approached. Some perverse part of her desired to flee from a happiness that seemed to have sprung out of the ether.

The compulsion to continue south had finally abated. Elizabeth had instead conceived of a plan to return to New York in the company of her Brazilian friend. For Lota, the answer to any proposition of substance was an enthusiastic *Yes!*, and so they'd gone back to the States to spend the spring. A couple of months to show off Lota to her friends and to collect her things—that was how Elizabeth had thought of the trip. The city had never seemed so dazzling as when she and Lota revisited the shops, street corners, and galleries where they'd first encountered one another five years earlier, but it was in New York that she'd first begun to sense her own shift of reference, to feel that she was now a resident of *there* rather than of *here*. During the steamship passage back to Rio, the magic of crossing the equator had transported them from early summer directly into winter. Happily, as if throwing streamers from the ship's deck, Elizabeth had renounced all attachment to the sequence of seasons she had previously considered inviolable, to languages, fruits, and geography. To her own resistance to *Yes*.

Arriving back in Samambaia, she'd been surprised by how frigid the nights in their mountain enclave had become. The chill clutched at one's soul. She walked through the house stooped over from the weight of wool blankets, yet they did nothing to prevent her constant shivering. Lota's house was still only a handful of rooms more or less open to the elements, welcome to all varieties of neighbor, human and animal. The floor of the house remained an unfinished cement slab punctuated with the footprints of cats, dogs, and the gardener's children. No doubt there were monkeyprints as well. Around midnight, the floor was particularly refrigerating to the toes, socks or no.

Not long after their return, Elizabeth remarked to Lota that in Great Village a simple sheet-iron stove had heated the entirety of her grandmother's modest house, even in the dead of winter. It had simply *penetrated* all the rooms with warmth, and hadn't they such a thing here? Any intriguing architectural possibility Lota appropriated with fervor. She'd never seen a stove such as Elizabeth described in any of the old houses in Petropolis, nor for that matter in any house in Brazil, and so to the idea Lota formed of this old-fashioned, no-frills iron stove she attributed the allure of the modern.

They drove the next morning along the winding river road into Petropolis, to the workshop of a blacksmith called Rodrigo. The name was impossible for Elizabeth to pronounce; she could not get her tongue underneath the aspirated *r*'s. *Hodhigo.* Inside the ironworks, twenty or so men hammered away at hot, glowing metal. They threw open the doors of blast furnaces and were bathed in orange light. The heat and leaping flames, the tangy, molten smells, the screams of the buzz saws and the banging of the hammers, and the laboring, sweating, half-naked bodies—it was a vision of Hades. Yet it was an inviting Hades. In spite of the noise and the heat, it was a place where one might feel at peace. Lota shouted over the din to describe to *Hodhigo* the stove they wanted him to make.

A boy in partial shadow was hammering intently upon a piece of metal. *Bang. Bang, bang. Clang.* Elizabeth wondered what he might be forging: a horseshoe, an iron gate, a milking pail? The sound transported her to another time and place, one that was in memory's shadow. The sound was also deeply familiar, anticipating by many years this visit and the song of the frog that lived in the stream; however, she could not pinpoint the how or why. A door in her mind cracked open, but she was unable to see into the room.

From the covered porch of the ironworks, Elizabeth turned to gaze upon the street. She left Samambaia infrequently to come into Petropolis, but she always found it enjoyable when she did. For instance, the names of the stores on this block alone: Ladyman, Very Person, Mister Rats. What on earth did they all sell? Her mind, often too lively for its own good and rarely at ease with itself, now looked upon the world and found nothing that did not gratify.

Voices began to rise at her back, and when she turned to look, Rodrigo was shaking his head. Lota's voice grew louder. He might have been explaining that the design Lota wanted was impossible. Or perhaps not. Elizabeth had learned that what often sounded like the tones and mounting passions of an argument could as easily be a forceful account of one's liver problems. By now, though, she had certainly learned to identify annoyance on Lota's face. It was time to intervene.

"He swears the stove won't work," Lota said when Elizabeth took her arm.

"I know that it will. The principle of the thing is extremely simple. Tell him that."

Lota made a sharp-tongued comment to Rodrigo that Elizabeth suspected was not an exact translation of her words. Lota's hand upon her back guided her out of the ironworks.

THE NIGHTS WERE cold, but the days were hot and bright. By late morning, the sweaters were shed. After lunch, as she liked to do, Elizabeth took a brisk walk up the mountain. In no time she was very much in the wilds. The sky was a vertiginous blue, the forest a thousand brilliant greens, the vertical mountain black, like a great ship's hull cleaving the earth. Showy birds darted here and there, or rose up in a flock. No one she had asked seemed to know any of their names, not even Lota. They simply lived happily among them. As she ascended the hillside, the sounds of Rodrigo's workshop came back to her and Elizabeth's memory began to loosen and uncoil.

The blacksmith in Great Village had been named Nate. His smithy had stood directly at the back of her grandmother's garden, and you could hear him at work all day long. If you ran around the corner and stood in his open doorway, you'd hear the sizzle and hiss of hot metal dropped into a bucket of water, you'd see the glowing crescent of a horseshoe seesaw to the bottom. Nate was a bear in a leather apron, with jolly eyes and thick forearms covered with black hair. He picked Elizabeth up with one hand and set her upon a worktable while he shaped horseshoes or, better still, nailed the shoes to a horse's hooves.

"Make me a ring!" she cried, and he bent a red-hot nail into a circle.

The memory of Nate came to Elizabeth so piercingly that she felt she could close her eyes and observe his workshop as clearly as if she were sitting on that table now. A deep-russet horse with green crust around his mouth stood patiently while Nate shoed him. He shifted his weight and exhaled in a burst. He was so much larger than she was, but not at all frightening. He didn't make sudden noises or erratic movements. Nate was like that, too—predictable.

When Elizabeth looked back down the mountainside, the view of the Brazilian landscape seemed to have a screen laid upon it of a different, remembered view. From the Chisholms' pasture, you looked beyond the elms of Great Village to the long, green marshes and the sea. As the tide receded, the wet mud reflected the sky. The colors were more muted than here in Brazil but they were beautiful nonetheless: the soft, gauzy blue of the atmosphere, the lavender mud at dusk, the pale-ochre moths that fluttered everywhere over the grass.

It had been years since she'd recalled Great Village with such feeling. In the days after the visit to Rodrigo's workshop, these visitations of memory began to intrude with more and more frequency upon the current moment, as if the bank separating the past and present had begun to erode. A street on the outskirts of Petropolis shimmered into the lane leading out of Great Village on which Elizabeth had driven

Nelly to pasture. One of the men who worked for Lota, named Manuelzinho, rode past on his bicycle wearing a painted straw hat, and
instead she saw Dr. Gillespie, the minister who'd always worn a straw
sailor hat he'd painted black, pedaling along. Dr. Gillespie had been
kind to her, though for some reason her grandmother had found him
lacking as an interpreter of God's word.

One day, Elizabeth encountered Dona Fernandes down the road
from Lota's house. The elderly lady's mind had recently begun to fade,
and Elizabeth found her trembling with confusion, unable to remember
where she'd come from or what her destination had been. As Elizabeth
escorted Dona Fernandes home, the image of Miss McNeil returned
vividly to mind. Nearly forty years earlier, she'd come upon a stricken
Miss McNeil in the lane, turning this way and that. *I can't find my way
home*, she called out to Elizabeth. *Where am I?* Thinking it was a game,
Elizabeth shouted, *You're in Timbuktu!* and, laughing, ran on. When she
told her grandmother later how funny Miss McNeil had been, Gammie
became furious with her.

Elizabeth was not certain why all roads suddenly led back to Great
Village or why she was being assailed by these memories, but she did
not resist them. The sound of the ironworks was a key to a lock, opening a door to reveal something else to her, something important. It was
leading her to another sound, she realized; when it came to her what
that second sound was, she thought, *Of course.* She remembered it too
well, though it had occurred on only one occasion. At the time, she had
run away from it, to the safety of Nate's.

There were two sounds, and they were linked.

RODRIGO SENT WORD that the stove was finished. He greeted
Elizabeth and Lota with an enormous smile and his arms held wide, as
though he might pull both women to his barrel chest. With a flourish
he proudly presented his product, and Elizabeth had to clap a hand
over her mouth to prevent herself from laughing. The stove was ludi-
crously unworkable. Too small by half, with a door the size of a mouse

hole. Inside, the grate was positioned nearly against the top, leaving room for little more than a handful of twigs.

"What is this piece of *merde*?" Lota shouted. "Any idiot can see it's useless."

Before Rodrigo could respond, Lota launched into a tirade volubly dissecting the ironworker's craftsmanship, with some pointed asides on his further failings as a man. She was truly indignant, and yet it appeared to Elizabeth that it was also something of a game to her, or, rather, that the stove was merely an excuse to exhale her rage, not the cause of it. Rodrigo's face reddened as he attempted to interrupt, but Lota did not allow him the opportunity. Elizabeth took a pencil from her purse and began to sketch on a scrap of paper. She could picture her grandmother's stove as clearly as if she were sitting on the floor before it, warming her toes and drinking a cup of cider.

"In my opinion," Rodrigo finally shouted over Lota, "what you want can't work."

"I don't give a monkey's crap about your opinion. You should have done what I told you."

Rodrigo's men laughed, and Rodrigo turned to them. "Leave it to a woman to come up with this idea. I've never seen anything like it."

"Of course you haven't!" Lota screamed. "You are a peasant who pisses on his own feet."

The huge man and the diminutive woman continued to shout at one another while Elizabeth drew. The front view had the door open to reveal the interior and placement of the grate; the back view showed the connection to the exhaust pipe. The men in the workshop had stopped their work to watch the shouting match, obviously amused by the spectacle of Rodrigo's public demeaning by a woman half his size.

When Elizabeth was done with the sketch, she raised her own voice. "Stop yelling and translate."

Rodrigo was huffing like a bull, his eyes wild and fierce as he turned them to Elizabeth's drawing. "I grew up in Canada," she said, and when he showed no recognition of the place, she added, "It is very cold there, with ice and snow. This is the stove in my grandparents' house. It kept us warm all winter long. This is what we'd like you to make. I've marked the dimensions."

He studied the paper as Lota translated. "This kept you warm?" Rodrigo asked incredulously. "You are sure?"

"Yes, absolutely. I swear upon my mother's grave."

This call upon the sanctity of her dead mother's resting place at last conquered the blacksmith's resistance. Rodrigo shot a dark glance at Lota before he turned to the nearest assistant and, shaking the sketch in his hand, thundered at him to get it right this time.

"Maybe the second try will be charmed," Lota said.

"A gentle touch can work wonders."

"You must have your stove. I have to keep my poet warm." Lota kicked the misbegotten stove with her boot. "You'd think they'd never felt cold in their lives. Brazilians have absolutely no sense of their own comfort."

"Does that include you?"

"Of course not," Lota said, smiling. "I have an exquisite sense of my own comfort."

THE NIGHTS GREW even colder. Elizabeth woke two or three times with the sensation that a great fist was squeezing her lungs in its grip. She sat up, for some minutes in suspense. If the tightness bloomed into a coughing fit, she left the bed so as not to disturb Lota and moved into the little den, where one day, she hoped, her grandmother's stove would be radiating lovely heat.

"You can't sleep?" Lota stood in the doorway in her red long underwear. She looked just like a stout fireplug.

Elizabeth shook her head, slipping air in through her mouth and struggling to suppress the inevitable cough.

Lota's hand lay upon her back. "I think you must have a little bird trapped in your rib cage. I can hear him whistling."

She took Elizabeth's hand and led her outside. In the bracing darkness, Lota lay on a chaise and pulled Elizabeth against her breast, wrapped her in red arms.

"Look at the stars, my heart. You could never see so many stars in New York. It is a different sky completely."

"Yes, it is," Elizabeth breathed. The stars made a creamy texture across the night above.

"Doesn't it look as though they are pressing down to earth? So many of them. Can you feel them brushing your hair?"

Yes, she felt the soft caresses on her hair, on her face. The streak of white in Lota's own hair was like a comet's tail. Elizabeth loved to wash it in a basin by the stream. They lay on the chaise until she fell asleep in Lota's arms.

BRAZIL WAS KIND to the soul but punishing to the body. It was hardly a mystery why the asthma had become relentless. The humidity and cold, the upwards of ten thousand flowering plants simultaneously releasing their pollen into the air, the jungle of molds and mildews in beautiful shades of gray-green, black, chartreuse, and magenta that seemed to sprout overnight on decaying fruit and the walls and even your own clothes you'd folded upon a chair the previous day—any of these alone would be enough to induce respiratory red alert. Bundled in blankets, Elizabeth guided herself through one wheezing breath and then another, fighting the sliver of panic that could often be worse than the physical constriction of her lungs.

She was quite fond of molds, however, even if they were a hazard. Such subtle, intricate forms.

The attacks eventually subsided, but the constant deprivation of sleep made of her days a dreamy stupefaction. It was perhaps for this reason she'd become susceptible to the rush of memories of Nova Scotia; they were more nearly like visions from the unconscious than recollections. Her old reliables, adrenaline and norisodrine sulphate, provided momentary relief at best. In fact, the inhalant only caused her lungs to feel on fire. At the advice of her doctor in New York, Elizabeth agreed to try an experimental drug called cortisone, though its effects, both salutary and ill, were not fully understood. The cortisone worked like a miracle. After just a few days, Elizabeth could breathe. Once again, she could freely indulge in her fondness for molds. But she still couldn't sleep. The new drug sent her flying.

It was during these sleepless yet blissfully oxygenated nights, soaring along on the magic carpet of cortisone, that she began to view her memories of Nova Scotia in a different light, to observe them with a writer's eye. Elizabeth realized that she was in fact revisiting old material she'd first worked on twenty-five years earlier, in boarding school. It had not been evident during these last weeks how the vivid images of Great Village and the intense, frightening thoughts of her mother might be used in the service of writing. Poetry had never been the appropriate form for dealing with that period in her life, for representing the experience of a child passed among relatives while her mother was in and out of mental institutions. That was not the sort of poet Elizabeth was. One should not abuse poetry in order to confess one's sorrows—nor one's crimes, for that matter.

But now Elizabeth did think back to the handful of times she'd attempted to explore the subject in stories, and to the extensive notes she'd made for a novel set in Nova Scotia during the early part of the century. Tucked in a drawer somewhere ever since. Though she was hardly a fiction writer, this small collection of stories was one of the first serious projects she'd attempted as a teenager, aware even at the time that she didn't yet possess the power or skill to get it right. She'd done what she could, and then she'd put the stories away.

Truthfully, she'd hated her mother's visits to Great Village. When Gertrude had come home from the sanatorium for a holiday, or had been in between different hospitals, or when the family had summoned her, hoping to discover their daughter and sister cured and ready to return to them for good, the visits had been without fail disruptive. Or much worse. The young woman was simply not well. Then, after her mother left, Elizabeth would long for her to return. As she'd told Lota,

Gertrude was lost in grief and failed to recover her balance in the years following her husband's death. Elizabeth knew this from fragments of overheard conversations and much more that she'd absorbed.

When Gertrude came home, the household held its collective breath. Elizabeth's grandmother and aunts treated the mute and nervous young woman like some ethereal, delicately beautiful moth that had alighted at the windowpane. Her mother's visits were strained, and in the end it seemed everyone was relieved when she left, though gloom settled on the house for weeks afterward. During the summers in Nova Scotia, thousands of big, horrible brown moths beat against the windows and fluttered around Elizabeth's reading lamp at night, and sometimes she still dreamed that the moths were engulfing her and she couldn't breathe. She woke from these dreams with a shout.

There were two sounds, and they were linked: the sound of Nate's hammer and, once, the sound of her mother's scream. Her mother had made this sound, Elizabeth now remembered, on her last visit to Great Village before she'd been sent away for good. Elizabeth had not seen her mother again. On that visit, Elizabeth's grandmother and aunts had urged Gertrude to finally leave her black mourning clothes. It's been five years, they'd said. It's time.

Elizabeth had no memory of her father, no real sense of his presence in her infancy or how much or little he'd loved Gertrude. His sole legacy was this husk of a woman who stood before a mirror, a woman so thin you could crack her in your fist, whose white claw of a hand gripped the sumptuous purple fabric in which she was newly swathed.

The dress was almost done. The dressmaker knelt on the floor working at the hem, her mouth full of pins; she looked like a big insect with dangerous spiny mandibles. Elizabeth sat in her aunt's lap as Gammie and her mother's other sisters fawned over the dress. Gertrude grew more and more agitated, and then she screamed. The scream frightened the child and she ran out of the room, out of the house, finding refuge at the blacksmith's. The hammering and beautiful ringing sounds blocked out the scream. Perhaps it had not been a real scream. Gertrude may have been crying out in surprise or confusion over the clothes, or even in pleasure at the rich fabric. Yet the cry gained force and volume in the child's ear until it became a scream so loud she wanted to press her head to the anvil and fill it with ringing.

Later, the scream was over, and Gertrude giggled among her sisters, eating ice cream on the front porch. Elizabeth did not stay with them but instead helped her grandmother in the kitchen. Tears fell from Gammie's face into the potato mash. When Elizabeth asked if she was crying, she said no.

In the white schoolhouse, Elizabeth learned that a sound makes a wave, and that waves of sound continue circling the globe for eternity, even after they are no longer audible. Forty years later, Elizabeth could hear in her mother's scream exactly what had terrified her as a child: the grief and loneliness, her mother's recognition of how distantly she'd drifted from those to whom she was most attached in the world, the understanding that she could not find her way back to them. Beyond the grief and loss, Elizabeth now heard a secondary note. It was a kind of assertion, more like a battle cry than one of despair. As if Gertrude were defending the last territory that remained her own.

THEY WERE STILL waiting for the completion of the second stove on the evening Elizabeth began to write the story. She began quite late, wide awake long after Lota had gone to bed, her whirring thoughts fueled by the cortisone. Shrouded in sweaters and blankets, she typed by the light of a kerosene lamp. She wrote for hours and did not tire. An injection of cortisone, two cc's of adrenaline, a whiff of norisodrine sulphate, and a blast of gin and tonic to ignite the fuse.

The single drink was enough. She did not crave more. She did not want to upset the chemical balance.

Elizabeth wrote on the typewriter with unusual confidence and speed. The piece came to her in a form that felt complete, instinctively right, though the form was not a conventional one for prose; it lay somewhere between story and poem. The writing of poetry was such an exacting labor that it could take years to bring one poem to an acceptable state; she might work for months on a single line. Yet with this piece she did not second-guess her choices.

She wrote all night, something she had not done probably since Vassar. Midmorning, Elizabeth finally stood and left the typewriter. Discarding sweaters as she went, she walked up the streambed to the pool. She heard Lota shouting in the distance, amid various sounds of construction. Elizabeth had not abandoned the work; she was immersing herself in it more deeply. Incognizant of her surroundings, she paced beside the pool, hitting the palm of one hand with the fingers of the other, as if keeping time with her racing thoughts. She worked through the story in her mind once more. The ideas rushed upon her so rapidly, the galaxy of associations and details and memories made so many spontaneous connections, that she felt they were pressing against the physical confines of her skull. All the details sprang clear: the houses and citizens of Great Village, Nate and his smithy, her mother's hand. The story began with the sound, one sound that opened up into another sound, the sound of her mother's cry in counterpoint to the sound of the blacksmith's hammer. It was the balance between those two that had eluded her before and that now provided the frame. Elizabeth laughed out loud. It could be that yes, just perhaps, she was a genius.

On her way down to the house, she tripped over a shovel that had been left on the ground. The shovel flung wet concrete onto her jeans. She bent to wipe it off and was nearly overcome by a wave of lightheadedness. The effects of the cortisone were beginning to flag. Elizabeth went to her room to rest and did not wake up for many hours.

LOTA WAS ENTERING the room with a tray. Sammy the toucan perched on its lip, chortling as he did when he was pleased. Elizabeth found that she lay fully dressed on top of the bedclothes, though a blanket had been tucked around her. The light in the room was dim;

she'd slept until evening. When she sat up, she smelled coffee and toast. Looking to the window once more, she realized she had slept long past evening and into the following day.

Lota put a hand to Elizabeth's forehead as if she were testing for fever. Her attention was so intent and encompassing, it was like being taken physically into her arms. You could not encounter Lota without acknowledging the physical force of her. Lota swept over you.

"Are you rested, my poet?"

"I'm famished," Elizabeth said, reaching for the toast.

Sammy cocked his head and fixed his electric blue eyes upon her breakfast. He was exceedingly handsome, with glossy black plumage and a sulfur bib and an enormous, waxy green and yellow bill he wielded as dexterously as Lota did a machete. For a creature with no real face, he had a remarkable range of expressions. The first time he'd plunged into a bath, Elizabeth had discovered that beneath the black feathers, his skin was the same deep blueberry blue as his feet. On the first birthday she'd spent in Brazil, still bedridden from that dreadful cashew poisoning, the Polish zoo couple down the hill had given her Sammy as a present. That day, she'd received two gifts: a toucan and a ring. The ring was tight on her swollen finger. It had remained for several days on the bedside table before she'd kept it on. The engraving was a simple date: 20/12/51. The day Lota had asked her to stay.

"Why doesn't Sammy fly away, do you think?" Elizabeth asked.

"Why would he do that?"

"Look at him. He's still wild, even though he's eyeing my bacon."

"He's smart," Lota said. "He knows that he wouldn't be taken care of nearly so well anywhere else."

Elizabeth tossed a piece of mango purposely short so that Sammy had to lunge to catch it. His tail shot straight up, brandishing his red rump like a flag. She had to write something about him one of these days. Sammy cried out for a poem.

"How's the construction business?" Elizabeth asked.

"Soon you'll have two new bedrooms and a superbathroom with a sunken bathtub," Lota said proudly. "I'll put a window there, and as you soak you can look out at the mountain."

"And who will be looking in?"

Lota slid her hand under the blanket and began to knead Elizabeth's calf.

"I had a Portuguese nanny when I was a child," Elizabeth said. "I remembered that yesterday. It was in Worcester, while I was living with my father's parents. It was only for a short time; then they replaced her with a very severe Swede. Probably the Portuguese one was too nice to me."

"That explains it," Lota said.

"Yes?"

"She planted a seed in you. *Uma semente.* The seed grew into a plant, the plant produced a flower, the flower made a fruit."

Elizabeth laughed. "Is the fruit a cashew?"

"No, *coraçao*, the fruit is Samambaia."

THE ELIXIR'S EFFECTS, Elizabeth discovered, were repeatable. The recipe had a nice ring to it: cortisone, adrenaline, norisodrine, gin. The chemicals swirled in her bloodstream; her fingers flew across the typewriter keys. She finished the piece around three in the morning. Short story, prose poem, or autobiographical sketch, she did not know exactly what to call it. Still, she knew she'd hit something dead-on.

She had never felt much kindness toward Gertrude—not as a character in a story, not as one in life. She had occasionally found herself voicing, in conversation as well as in the privacy of her own thoughts, *Poor thing.* But she hadn't felt the sentiment, not deeply. Most memories of her mother were overshadowed by impatience. Once or twice she'd imagined herself as Gertrude's own mother, at her wits' end, slapping the young woman and telling her to get on with living, not to be so self-indulgent. When someone's grief was completely entangled with your own, it was impossible to feel true sympathy for her.

The first attempts Elizabeth had made in adolescence to write about her mother, she understood now, had been her way of trying to silence the plaintive cries that used to break into her thoughts before she could push them back into the dark.

Why did you leave me alone? Why couldn't you love me enough to get well?

Those stories failed, both as fiction and as exorcism. To act as a scientist objectively testing hypotheses could lead nowhere. The father died. The mother wandered down a path and became lost. The child was given up. She'd posed this case believing that the missing pieces of the story might be revealed and organized if only they were subjected to clinical examination. Elizabeth finally understood that the missing pieces—the private world of her parents, its intimacies and interdependencies, the quality of their life together—were irrecoverable. She would never know precisely what her mother had lost or why that loss had driven her mad. But she could imagine it. She knew that if she herself were to be separated from Lota, even after such a short time together, forced from safe harbor out into the storm, she, too, might wander too far down a dark path ever to find her way back. It was only now, twenty years after Gertrude's death, that Elizabeth could reach out to her mother with compassion.

· I 2 ·

I USED TO be merely embarrassed at being American, Elizabeth exclaimed. Now I'm horrified.

At last you are in exactly the same position we Brazilians have been in for some time! Rosinha said.

So shy and nervous when she'd first come to Brazil, Lota thought proudly, and now look at her Cookie—at the head of the table, holding everyone's attention: the queen bee!

When I read my friends' letters, Elizabeth said, what's happening in the States sounds completely absurd. Is that what you feel here? Such absurdity you think it must be a joke? I can hardly believe this terrible business with William Carlos Williams, thrown out of his post at the Library of Congress because someone, no one even knows who, called him a communist. The country is obsessed with communism, just rabid. Remember, Rosinha, when we went to Robert Frost's reading at the American embassy, how the ambassador was so rude and stupid? He sat next to Frost's daughter with an unlit cigar clamped in his mouth. Frost may be a malicious old bore, but the ambassador could not have been more disrespectful. All he could talk about was who was or wasn't a Red.

Americans have less respect for poets than we Brazilians, I think, piped in Marietta. Lota was shocked. Without the husband around, her sister turned back into a human being. Once again, she actually had opinions.

Yes, didn't you know? Elizabeth said. We're quite dangerous elements. If it weren't so terrifying, I'd have to laugh. As if a poet had any real power in the first place.

At last, Lota had to interrupt. She raised her voice to call down to the other end of the table. You'll never be a great poet if you think like that.

Well, I do think like that, Elizabeth called back.

Lota laughed. Her Cookie did not think like that in the least.

Last week, Elizabeth had confessed that all her life, the approach of the American holiday Thanksgiving had made her miserable; she had no real family with whom to share it, no real home. And yet this year she had begun to hope she might host a Thanksgiving dinner at Samambaia. She would invite all the members of her Brazilian family. Did Lota approve?

Lota gave her a squeeze and a kiss. Anything my Cookie wants, my Cookie gets.

Elizabeth hand-painted beautiful invitations and sent them to Mary, to Carlos and his wife Leticia, to Lota's adopted son Kylso and his family, and to Rosinha, Elizabeth's favorite among Lota's friends. She pressed Lota to deliver one of the invitations personally to Marietta. This is an occasion when we put our differences aside, she said, and Lota could not refuse. Even though she had instead handed the invitation to Marietta's maid and told her not to disturb the mistress, she was extremely touched by Elizabeth's gesture and was pleased, now, that Marietta had come. Fortunately, without her loudmouth husband.

The evenings had grown warm enough that they were able to set up a long table outdoors. Early in the day, the two of them had walked through the woods, stealing a private moment to hold hands outside and collect orchids and fallen branches ornamented with lichen, which they had fashioned into the table's centerpiece. Lota had thrown a rope over a branch and hoisted a chandelier overhead; hanging from the tree above the table, it was now alight with flickering candles. Lota beamed at her dear Elizabeth at the far end. The dinner had been a lovely idea. The courses themselves were impeccable, simply superb; Cookie was as much a genius in the kitchen as she was on the page. She'd improvised some Brazilian variations on the meal's traditions: *jabuticaba* jam in place of cranberry sauce; cassava meal in the stuffing.

Only when they began talking politics did the evening threaten to become disagreeable. Lota could see that Carlos was growing offended by some of Elizabeth's remarks about America. He frowned at his plate as he repeatedly aligned his knife and fork across its top. Besides, politics was not a subject to discuss in English. You couldn't trust English. It did not fully declare itself, unlike Portuguese. It pretended dispassion while hiding its true intent.

Finally, Carlos broke in. You speak so lightly about these things that I suspect you do not grasp their larger significance.

Carlos, Elizabeth said with a laugh, I have the right to criticize my own country.

And a blindness, perhaps, to what gives you that right? he said with some force. Communism would hardly allow you that right. Not all of us at this table share the rights you take for granted.

I'm hardly blind to that. But you can't be an apologist for every American stupidity. If the same thing happened here, you'd be the first to attack it. You're as critical of extreme nationalism as I am.

Yet nationalism forms only in opposition to a threat. Such as communism.

Or to an imagined threat. Or even to a *manufactured* threat.

Lota couldn't stand it when Elizabeth picked a fight with Carlos. Carlos is very brave, she said. You should not attack him. For instance, the list he published in his newspaper last week of the policemen in Rio receiving payoffs could put him in real danger. But he believes it is right.

I'm hardly attacking him, Elizabeth said. You know I respect Carlos highly.

There was the problem. The words did not match the feeling with which they were spoken.

Corruption is a cancer corroding the federal district, Carlos said, rapping his index finger against the tabletop. Lota was relieved that he was steering the conversation to more familiar ground. She was gearing up to join in when Elizabeth loudly exclaimed, Is that a little frog on the table?

She was pointing at one of the branches they'd gathered from the woods. A trick, Lota assumed, to retain the table's attention. Then she shouted, Oh! and leapt to her feet. She reached one hand into her dress, shrieking and wiggling her torso as if suddenly compelled to dance a samba. Not half bad, for an American.

Cookie, what is it!

A frog has just leapt into my bosom!

Everyone roared with laughter, even Carlos. She was perfect. Lota's *saborosa* Cookie was perfect.

Lota was arguing with Sergio over the angle of the concrete ramp leading to the new wing when Leticia rang. Carlos has been arrested, she said. He was taken from the offices of *Tribuna* and is being held at the police headquarters. We're gathering there to protest his arrest, and can you come?

But why . . . ? Lota was unable to form the rest of the question.

The list of corrupt policemen, Leticia said.

On the drive down the mountain, Lota battled unusual emotions: fear for Carlos and fear for herself if any injury came to Carlos. He was the only man who had ever truly *seen* her. He recognized the value of her ideas, he encouraged her passions, he requested her ear when refining his own thoughts and positions. Women were so easy to charm and bully that their good opinion didn't register. Lota took it for granted. Men were different. Generally, she had to kick them in the balls before they might turn their heads to acknowledge her presence. But not Carlos. He had always given her respect.

Intent on these thoughts, she didn't take in Elizabeth's words. There was an odd shimmering in her gut that only after some moments did she recognize as panic. She carefully took her Cookie's hand and asked her to repeat what she'd said.

I only remarked that Carlos is a clever man. First he provokes the authorities to arrest him, then he gains even more admirers for sticking to his principles and therefore gains greater notoriety and power, and at the same time he'll sell a heck of a lot more newspapers. Elizabeth chuckled. Very clever.

Lota was speechless at Elizabeth's ability to give offense. She withdrew her hand and returned to her thoughts for the remainder of the drive.

It was raining in Rio. When they arrived at the police headquarters on Rua da Relação, they were informed that Carlos's presence had caused too great a disruption and that he'd been moved. She had to raise her voice quite loudly and prepare for the kick in the balls before they told her where they'd taken him: to the barracks of the military police, several blocks away. Lota had no patience to move the car; she ran to the second location without an umbrella, Elizabeth trailing, and arrived soaked to the skin. A gate barred their entrance. Lota shouted to be let in. She did not like gates blocking her way. As a child, before her family had been forced into exile, she had stood at the gates of the Belgian embassy holding a box of cigars for her father, who'd taken refuge there from Vargas's thugs.

She banished these thoughts as a policeman now opened the gate and she rushed into the barracks. She was relieved by what she saw there. The magnitude of the response to Carlos's arrest was far beyond what she might have hoped. Throngs filled the reception area and the halls of the barracks. Lota saw immediately that it would be impossible to reach Carlos. A line snaked from the rear quarters of the building into the reception area; she assumed these people were waiting to visit Carlos in his cell. Leading politicians from the União Democrática Nacional and other friendly parties were present in great number, but Lota also noticed at least as many *getulistas* and congressmen from parties opposed to Carlos. So cynical of them to appear here. Surprise! His cause had become fashionable. Look over there, at the ultimate proof: society-page ladies in Chanel suits who didn't even know Carlos or have any idea what he stood for. Their primary interest was to hover in a group near the newspaper photographer like pale butterflies. In every doorway stood men in uniform, soldiers or policemen, who knew which? Lota could never distinguish between the two. This country was so rife with uniforms you couldn't tell a garbageman from a general.

A man knocked against her, smelling strongly of cologne. No, not cologne, it was cachaça! On the other side of the room, he offered a glass to a woman. Someone turned up the volume of a radio playing sambas.

Are we to start dancing? Lota cried out in frustration. Do they think this is Carnaval?

Elizabeth's bewildered expression only irritated Lota more.

Carlos will be freed by the end of the day, Elizabeth said softly. This is all for show, Lota. A power play. That's my guess.

Yes, but you know nothing, Lota snapped.

Who was in charge here? She would demand an explanation of the charges on which Carlos was being held. She would insist upon his release. When she spotted Odilon Braga, leader of the UDN, Lota felt a great burden lift from her. Odilon was Carlos's greatest friend in Congress and he was no fool; she was not, after all, alone among do-nothings. Lota moved quickly toward him, pushing through the crowd.

The sight of the man beside Odilon brought her to an abrupt stop.

Lota looked to every corner. She looked where she might hide. All her anger had abandoned her; now she was weak, afraid. Why had Elizabeth left her alone! Jose Eduardo must not see her. Yet she felt it was inevitable, as if she were standing in the center of a room that had suddenly cleared. Everyone else seemed to have moved to the perimeter. The helpless feeling made her furious, yet the fury did not make her strong. Only later, when she thought of the things she might have done or said, could she tap into that strength. Right now, she was a child again.

He'd seen her. He'd nodded and was sliding across the floor in her direction. He moved as though he believed himself a waltzer. On his arm, of course, was the usual woman at least forty years his junior, so beautiful it was a joke. This one wore a blue dress that cupped her breasts like two hands and left her slender brown shoulders bare. The kind of dress they called a *tomara que caia*—let's hope it falls.

Where had Elizabeth gone?

A phenomenon occurred during earthquakes, she'd read somewhere: liquefaction. Under excessive force, rock melted.

She couldn't move. There was no escape.

Over there, she saw now, Elizabeth was laughing with Manuel Bandeira. How like her! When Lota had first introduced them, she'd had to make plain that Manuel was *the* poet in Brazil before Elizabeth had taken any real interest. It wasn't enough that Manuel was a gentleman, elegant and mannered in the old style.

As Lota approached, Elizabeth's tone of address to Manuel struck her as overly familiar, verging on disrespectful. Manuel, she was saying, if you asked a poet in New York what you just asked me, you would be completely *shunned*. No one wants you to know how their work is going. They're too afraid you'll jinx it. But I'm happy to report that I've been working very hard. Or at least I was. I wrote some new pieces and actually *sold* them. I feel close to finishing a book of poems that's been lying fallow for four or five years. I've even begun a translation. Lately, though, I just want to lie in a hammock and watch the birds fly by.

You must indulge that impulse, Manuel said. My best ideas often come to me in a hammock.

Elizabeth ceased laughing when Lota gripped her arm.

You shouldn't have left me alone, Lota said in a low voice. He's following me.

What on earth? Elizabeth said. Then her gaze shifted past Lota, and Lota knew that Jose Eduardo was upon them.

If I could show him my house, Lota thought, *I would not feel this way. I would not be* reduced. *He would know what I am capable of.*

But he will never step inside my house as long as I live.

Good day, Manuel. Good day, Carlota.

Lota held herself erect. She would stand eight feet tall not five. Good day, Jose Eduardo, she said. She smiled, or rather, her face felt numb; she could not tell what it was doing. If only Carlos were not in danger. That was why she'd become incapacitated. Lota nodded to the girl on his arm, who, she noticed, had a big dark mole behind her ear, like a button.

Manuel pardoned himself.

Jose Eduardo took Elizabeth's hand and kissed it. It is an honor to meet you, Miss Bishop. His English, so crisp and fake. How irresistible he believed himself to be. Elizabeth fell for it, of course. Look at her pleasure. She thought she was being recognized by an admirer of her work. There were further inconsequential words before Jose Eduardo took his leave of them.

Who is that charming little man? Elizabeth asked, and then she fully took in Lota's face. Lota, dear, what is it?

Lota shrugged. He is no one.

No one?

He is my father.

That little man there?

Lota nodded.

Each weekend, when she'd come home to Petropolis from the convent school in Rio, he was at the train station to meet her. The most distinguished of papas in his dark suit and hat. How she'd scandalized the nuns—even as a child! She saved up the stories to tell him; he threw back his head and laughed as he held her hand. He was so tall, he cast his shadow over her. She skipped ahead through the streets, always running back to him.

Elizabeth clasped Lota's hand, draping her rain jacket over the indiscretion as she held on. For some moments, she said nothing. The room full of people rotated around them; they looked only at one another. Lota had grown used to their life in Samambaia, just the two of them. Perhaps she had already begun to take it for granted.

She told Elizabeth she wanted to leave. She wanted to go home.

That was when Carlos's voice spoke beside her. *The accusers have become the victims*, he said, *while the victims are becoming the accomplices of criminals.*

Everyone fell quiet. The words came from the radio nearby. An interviewer from the radio station must have been with him, broadcasting Carlos live from his cell. The sound of his voice was enough. She knew he was safe. The fight had not gone out of him.

I have been jailed for the crime of defending the interests of the people of the Federal District, Carlos continued defiantly. *However, I feel honored to be held under the fascist laws of the Estado Novo.*

·13·

THE ROAD TO Ouro Preto was a joke. Before they'd gone fifty kilometers, they already had a flat. With a cigarette dangling from her lip, Lota crouched at the roadside spinning the tire iron, while trucks came sputtering up the mountain pass and playfully tooted their horns. Investigating, Elizabeth found that Lota's wraparound skirt had fallen open, treating the truck drivers to a view of her glorious white Victorian bloomers. She shielded Lota with her coat until the new tire was in place, then on they went through the mountains.

They'd planned to drive the jeep, but two days before their trip Lota had run into the wife of the director of the Patrimonio Artistico, who claimed she had *just* been to Ouro Preto and had traveled over the most marvelous new road, simply skimmed along for miles, so they'd loaded up the Jaguar instead. The old cow had obviously lied through her false teeth. Three hours out of Petropolis the new road had still failed to materialize and Lota erupted in colorful language every time they hit a pothole, though the horrendous condition of the pavement by no means slowed her speed. Descending out of the mountains, she flew past warnings of *curvas perigosas* and grazing livestock and signs that indicated they were in peril of having boulders fall on their heads, until one of the donkeys munching grass along the shoulder ambled nonchalantly onto the asphalt and stood directly in their path. Lota hit the brakes and the car began to slide, a cliff face to their right, a precipice to their left, the donkey fore. That a vehicle was approaching at high velocity did not appear to enter the animal's consciousness until the last moment, when Elizabeth could see, at extremely close range, its eyeballs rolling back in terror. The car came to rest within inches of the donkey's rump. Only then did it lunge back to the safety of the grass.

"Why do you have to drive like a maniac?" Elizabeth cried. "We could have been killed."

"Look, my dove, what a beautiful valley."

Elizabeth's heart was still galloping as Lota took her hand and kissed it passionately. Sideways in the road, the car faced a vista of low hills. The light on the patchwork of cornfields below, she had to agree, was especially gorgeous. But she looked at the hand Lota held as though it were not a part of her.

THE ROAD DID not improve. Elizabeth began to imagine a new highway that was not entirely a figment of the imagination of the wife of the director of the PA. Perhaps she and Lota had simply missed the turn, and right now all sorts of people were flying along a beautiful, oil-black ribbon that had no potholes nor donkeys nor, as they encountered next, soldiers holding automatic weapons.

Children playing dress-up—they were simply too *young* to have machine guns slung over their shoulders—stood in the center of the road, checking vehicles. One of them motioned Lota to pull to the side of the highway. The fact that Lota did precisely as he said and got out of the car without backtalking or muttering any of her standard oaths alarmed Elizabeth even more than the guns.

On the roadside near the checkpoint, a line of stalls sold goods to travelers fortunate enough not to be terrorized by the armed forces. Weary-looking women cooked over open fires, and a man sat patiently

beside a pile of blackening papayas with a bugle in his lap. At one untended stall, a line of cloth dolls hung from strings, as though swinging
from the gallows. In theory, these images should be used in the service of poetry, or so Elizabeth had heard herself say in any number of
non-life-threatening settings. Poetry should be so present and constant
to the poet that it intrudes upon all other thoughts and experiences.
One's art should act as the prism through which all of life might be
thoughtfully observed.

Lota's conversation with the soldier on the side of the highway did
not, fortunately, appear to be turning into an argument. On the contrary, Lota suddenly pulled the soldier into an embrace. She was shaking her head with amusement as she returned to the driver's seat.

"He wanted money, of course," she said once they were on their
way. "He told me the car was in violation because the muffler had come
loose and was making an unpermitted noise."

"It's only loose because of this absurd road!"

"I told him I was taking a famous American poet to meet the United
States ambassador in Ouro Preto, and that we should not be delayed."

"He believed that?"

"He lied, so why should I not? Then I asked him what his mother
would think if she knew he was harassing ladies on the road who'd
done nothing wrong. He backed down. They all do."

"Well, he's hardly more than a child."

"He said that it gets so hot standing in the sun all day that if we
don't want to be stopped again, we should hold out a cold drink as we
approach the soldiers in the road. That's all it takes. A cold drink. I gave
him a little money anyway. They make nothing, these poor boys."

IT WAS CLOSE to sunset when they reached Congonhas, where they
were to stop for the night. The muffler's rattle resounded through the
town's narrow streets as Lota began shouting out like a madwoman to
the people on the sidewalk. "The Prophets! The Prophets!" she yelled,
while without surprise the locals waved them onward. One old woman

sweeping her front porch warned that the way ahead was *perigoso*, and directly, the road slanted nearly vertical, as if to launch them toward the planets.

At the crest of the hill stood a church.

In the dying light, the hilltop was utterly still. A samba on the radio drifted up from the town below. Dogs barked distantly, back and forth. "I wanted to surprise you," Lota said, and gazed at Elizabeth adoringly. Her love was offered so freely, and with such ease, that at times it pained Elizabeth as much as it pleased her.

She and Lota left the car and drew near the church. Upon the steps and parapets stood ten or twelve figures made of stone. The sculptures towered above them, their silhouettes against the deepening blue of the night. A bit spooky, really, if magnificent.

"So these are the Prophets," Elizabeth said.

"Your friend Manuel Bandeira describes them as a poem in stone. They were made over two hundred years ago by a sculptor called Aleijadinho, the little cripple. He was a leper and a mulatto. His mother was a slave. If he had not been a genius, he would have been an outcast. By the time he sculpted these Prophets, his hands had become useless from the leprosy. He worked with chisels strapped to his forearms."

"Is there anything you don't know about?" Elizabeth asked.

"I know a little about everything," Lota replied, uncharacteristically rueful, "but not much about anything." She moved up the steps.

Hacking away at stone with chisels strapped to one's useless hands—it was not an entirely unfamiliar feeling. Even so, Aleijadinho had rendered the Prophets with an exquisite touch. Some of the figures pointed toward heaven or outward to an imminent danger, while others cast their eyes upon the ground. And though the men's robes were of Old Testament times, their expressions were so precise, and so feeling, that no modern person could fail to recognize them. A prophet would necessarily stand alone, friendless. No one would have wanted to hear the messages these fanatics delivered: that the human race was a disappointment to its creator, that the earth, so freshly wrought, was already close to exhaustion.

It was not wrath or moral outrage or the certainty of God's judgment that clouded these men's faces; it was profound loneliness.

As night fell, the Prophets turned to dense black outlines against a sweep of stars. Brazil often made Elizabeth feel that she'd traveled backward in time; it was no great stretch to transport herself back to her Nova Scotia childhood, or even to a colonial era, when all the daily social formalities, the little rattling coffee cups that made their appearance at every call upon a neighbor or business, and the pageantry of religious and secular festivities appeared hardly to recognize the modern world. The Prophets catapulted Elizabeth even further back. In the beginnings of human history, all tribes regardless of continent had felt themselves dwarfed by powerful forces they could never counter or understand, by extremes of weather, phenomena of earth and sea. You saw it in the literature, from Homer on. Life in Great Village had not been so different, really. You endured, and you found fellowship in the endurance; you did not hope or wish to gratify personal pleasure. Lota, of course, refused to submit to forces greater than her own, or even to acknowledge them. Perhaps, Elizabeth thought, she herself was in a way more Brazilian than Lota would ever be.

Lota gazed up at the Prophet Isaiah. "Look at his face," she said. "As if he thinks he's the last Coca-Cola in the desert. Men haven't changed in a thousand years! The sculpture is genius, but still I want to knee him between the legs."

"Lota, you don't ever change."

White teeth flashed in the darkness. Hands took hold of Elizabeth's waist. "Thank you, dear Cookie. I take it you mean I am true to myself."

"That's certainly undeniable," Elizabeth said with a laugh. But that had not been her precise meaning.

In the valley below, amid green, a sea of red-tiled roofs. Churches stood like high fortresses upon outcroppings of stone. On the outskirts of town, they were stopped by a length of rope held across the road by ragged girls in ragged dresses. Their pretty faces were nut-brown, and each offered two or three bags of cassava bread and cakes.

Lota honked the horn. Elizabeth put out a hand to stop her, but the girls had already let the barricade drop and run off on the tips of their toes like dainty, timid deer. The cord, Elizabeth saw, was not a rope at all, but long lengths of grass they'd entwined and laced with flowers. The girls huddled under a tree and stared at the American woman in the sports car.

"Oh, please, let's buy a cake."

Elizabeth waved to them to come close and laid coins in one delicate open hand. "*Obrigado*," she said, taking the bread, and all the girls giggled.

"*Obrigada*," corrected Lota with a smile. "*O* is for men."

Light eyes bore upon dark. Elizabeth could not turn away from the children. She felt a sharp, essential lack; it was like hunger or lust, a physical need to possess one of these girls, to keep her and hold her, bring one into her lap and enfold her there, rest her chin upon the perfect child's head, breathe in the aroma of her tangled hair. To protect her and love her.

"They're so beautiful."

"And you, too, are the most beautiful woman they've ever seen."

Lota moved on slowly, as if not to frighten the girls. Elizabeth bit into the cassava cake, tough as shoe leather but perfectly sweet.

A pothole on the edge of town finally dislodged the muffler completely. It dragged along the last bit of cobblestone road, scraping and shooting sparks, the loud rumble of the engine drawing the attention of the townspeople they passed. A group of men followed them into the hotel's parking lot, where they surrounded the car.

"This is a Jaguar?" one of them asked.

"Yes, of course," Lota replied, leaping out as though preparing to defend the automobile with fisticuffs if necessary.

"Congratulations. You are the second of this type ever to come to Ouro Preto."

"You don't mean the first?"

"The first arrived last year. Unfortunately, it ruptured its gasoline tank on the road coming in."

THEY STAYED AT the new Niemeyer building, the Hotel Grande. Everyone agreed that building modernist architecture in a three-hundred-year-old colonial city was pure hubris; at the same time, it was delightful. Their two-level suite had a sitting room below with a private terrace, and they climbed a chic wooden spiral staircase to the bedroom above. "It's so elegant," Elizabeth said as they prepared for bed, after spending the evening with the car mechanic. "I feel as though I should descend in an evening gown, with long white gloves up to my elbows."

"No," Lota cried, "you should be descending nude!"

Then Lota herself slid down the banister in her nightgown.

THE RAGGED NYMPHS had opened the gates to a dream of Brazil. The terrace of their hotel room had a panoramic view of the town amid tropical greenery, with a backdrop of high, rugged sierra. Three centuries earlier, they had mined gold and built this opulent city, though, according to Lota, the buildings had now decayed virtually beyond repair. She had gone to see her friend Lilli, a preservationist, while Elizabeth had begged to remain at the hotel and work. She could not pass up the opportunity to write down her impressions of Ouro Preto under the guise of a young girl named Helena.

For over a year, she'd turned her back on poetry to work on a translation project. One of the Brazilian books that Lota had insisted Elizabeth read was the diary of Helena Morley, who'd grown up in this area of Minas Gerais half a century earlier. Elizabeth had been instantly charmed by the writing and by Helena herself, whose girlhood in the mountain town of Diamantina bore countless similarities to Elizabeth's own in Great Village. Again and again, Helena proved herself resourceful, pragmatic, unsentimental. She did not take it too greatly to heart when she was misunderstood or neglected, yet she felt things deeply.

Reading the diary, Elizabeth had developed a protectiveness for the girl so passionate it verged on love, though the real Helena was no longer a girl at all but a rich matron living in Rio. She'd left her humble origins and married a wealthy banker. In spite of Elizabeth's recalcitrant Portuguese, her working life was now devoted entirely to translating the diary into English. Each morning, with her dictionary in hand, she labored over the passages, discussing with Lota at lunch how she might infuse the woodenly translated phrases with life. Over the last year, her wish to visit Ouro Preto had sharpened into a desire to draw closer to Helena, to look at Brazil through Helena's eyes.

She worked past lunch. Then she began to wonder what was keeping Lota. It was the mystery of the new road that finally drew her out of the room. The hotel lobby was a long glass box bathed in diffuse light, with no more than a few pieces of spare furniture set here and there, apparently more for visual effect than for the traveler's comfort. Far down at the other end of the vacant space stood the reception desk, a bank of white stone.

"*Bom dia*," Elizabeth said as she approached.

Two officious, good-looking young people regarded her, one young man and one young woman. Aside from sex, they were nearly identical in most other respects: black, glossy hair, black-framed glasses, dark jackets, crisp white shirts. The young man busied himself with some papers. The young woman replied, "*Boa tarde*."

"*A estrada nova* . . ." Elizabeth began, before abandoning the language altogether. "I heard there is a new road to Ouro Preto, coming in from the south, and I wonder if you know anything about it."

The young woman nodded. "Yes, of course. There is a new road. We are preparing to celebrate the official opening. That is why the entire hotel is booked."

Elizabeth took in the vast, silent lobby, untread by a single soul. "Booked?"

"For the delegation. The governor of Minas Gerais and thirty others who have come for the ceremony."

"But the hotel is entirely empty!"

"They have yet to arrive, obviously."

"When do you expect them?"

The young woman conferred with her colleague in murmured Portuguese. Elizabeth noticed that she wore a shiny name tag of apparently recent vintage, on which there appeared no name. She turned back to Elizabeth and pronounced, "Soon."

"Well, if there is a new road, would you happen to know where it enters town?"

A pleasant, receptive blankness spread over the young woman's face, as though Elizabeth were still speaking or had yet to pose her question. The only obvious thing was that the girl was completely deluded and didn't have any idea at all if there was a new road or a ceremony or a delegation arriving or not.

"The wife of the director of the Patrimonio Artistico said she'd traveled on the road herself just last week," Elizabeth suggested helpfully.

"No, that lady came by train."

"She did? How can you be sure?"

"She requested a car from the hotel to meet her at the station." The nameless girl turned again to the young man for another private conference. "Paolo was at the Office of the Prefecture this morning. He says they are preparing the invitations to the road's inauguration. Perhaps you might check there for more information?"

Emerging from the hotel, Elizabeth nearly collided with a mule clomping by with enormous bunches of greenery on his back, led by a boy with a stick. Still wet from the morning's rain shower, the cobblestone streets of Ouro Preto glistened in the sunlight. Grand white colonial buildings with portals and windows painted all sorts of bright colors lined the roads, which curved and ascended so that she was continually pulled along to discover what was just out of sight ahead. Elizabeth attempted to follow the directions she'd been provided to the prefect's office, but one hill was too steep and treacherously slick, and she had to make a detour—and then, no matter, she'd find the office eventually. The pleasure of Lota's guiding hand upon her back was absent, but she had forgotten the luxury of wandering lost.

Topaz and amber jewelry lay upon tables set outside shop doorways so low even she would have to duck to enter. Elizabeth passed by, lingered at one or two, while dark heads emerged in a line up the block to gawk at her. A shopgirl rushed into the street, not to hawk the merchandise but to stare, as though Elizabeth had sprung to life from the pages of *National Geographic*, and then disappeared inside. Helena Morley's reaction to an American woman passing through her town with an umbrella and a purse would no doubt have been considerably more polite. Elizabeth was confident that Helena would have approached the foreigner and offered assistance. She imagined the two of them, arms linked, chatting warmly on their way, discovering all sorts of shared interests.

At the center of town, Elizabeth came upon a large square, where a statue commemorated a national hero named Tirandentes, the tooth puller. A dentist who'd become a revolutionary, Lota had told her, and who'd been executed here in Ouro Preto after attempting to liberate Brazil from Portuguese dominion. Helena would have learned about him in school, in a one-room schoolhouse like the one Elizabeth had attended in Nova Scotia. At the edge of the square, she found a seat, tucked her skirt beneath her, held her purse in her lap.

A tree above cast its shade upon her; from within its low, protective branches she observed the world as if through the bars of a wooden cage. She felt unperturbed, happy. The colonial buildings in beautiful shades, the light upon the wet cobblestones, all the people moving past—she might simply sit on this bench watching them forever and never grow bored.

Her gaze was drawn to a group of children huddled near the base of Tirandentes' statue. She realized they had followed her from the street of topaz shops and now were staring at her, growing bolder in their laughter and taunts to one another to approach, as though Elizabeth might bewitch them. She wished she could draw them near, give them sweets or pat their heads, but when she waved for them to come close, the urchins scattered instantly.

Ouro Preto had been Elizabeth's first idea of Brazil—long before her ship had docked in South America, before it had even crossed the equator, this was the place she had imagined most vividly. Many years from now, it will be the last place in Brazil she leaves. She will buy a house here, she will repeatedly seek refuge in Ouro Preto, and this is where, after Lota's death, she will make her last stand. She will try to remain a citizen of the country where she will have lived for seventeen years. But Brazil will not have been hers—it will have been merely on loan—and in the end she will leave for good and return to the States.

After Lota, and after Brazil, she will love other people and other places, but it will be a different species of love, so different she will wonder if the feeling can be called by the same word. The greatest surprise will be to discover that her lover's abrupt end does not also bring about the death of *love*, that after two years of numbness, then grief and anger in equal measure, again there is love. Love, simply. As naturally as if Lota were still alive to receive it. But that is precisely what Lota will have taught her—that to give love is its own reward, that to give love is in itself perhaps the most profound variety of liberation, that the more she gives, the more she inhabits herself and is alive to the world around her. To discover that capability after so much pinched, mean subsistence will be the gift of Elizabeth's lifetime.

Her last apartment will overlook Boston Harbor, and it will hold many beloved possessions from her years in Brazil: a mirror with a seashell frame, a paddle carved with the Brazilian flag, a wasps' nest made of mud, an antique birdcage, an *oratorio* of Saint Barbara. In those last years, she will reach a kind of peace, not completely free of drinking or painful shyness, but those she will allow to wash over her, and then she will reemerge. It will be to her Boston apartment that all her books and papers will finally be shipped, after packing up her Ouro Preto house. She will unpack them, lingering over the termite-eaten Oxford dictionary, the few notes and letters from Lota that survived Mary's purge of fire, even a handful of papers Elizabeth saved from high school and college. On one, she will read the professor's comments and laugh, accidentally calling Lota's name to come look at what he said.

Your argument suffers, Miss Bishop, from your insistence, against the evidence, that there is no opposition between passion and virtue.

AT THE DOOR to the Office of the Prefecture, Elizabeth heard gales of laughter. Three women were writing out by hand the invitations to the opening ceremony for the new road. So much attention devoted to the beautiful ivory cards, to the elegant script; however, the ceremony's time and place had been left blank.

"There is no date on these invitations," Elizabeth attempted to say in Portuguese. The words tumbled too quickly out of her mouth to be certain of their precise meaning. "How will anyone know when to come?"

The women nodded their heads, smiling. "You speak Portuguese very well," one said. The other two kissed her cheek and insisted Elizabeth take a seat and share their lunch.

LOTA'S FRIEND LILLI had short dark hair and a square sturdy face, and she spoke perfect English with a slight trace of her native Denmark. She'd been married to a Brazilian painter, and, though she was the town's only foreigner, she'd taken it upon herself after her husband's death to mobilize interest in preserving the decaying colonial buildings. Elizabeth had felt certain she would like Lilli immensely, yet as the Scandinavian woman gave them a tour of her ramshackle old house, the rooms full of paintings and beautiful, old, odd things on shelves and in cabinets, her tight unsmiling mouth and hard blue eyes made conversation impossible. The house reminded Elizabeth of a provincial museum where she might find Indian bones unearthed from someone's backyard or her own uncle's artwork or a two-headed chicken. From a front room, Elizabeth spied on a group of women who'd gathered in the street below, gossiping and laughing at a fountain. A child emerged from the skirts of one, and his mother cupped water in her hands and held them to his mouth. Across the road lay a derelict house, the tile roof sagging and full of holes. From its window, Elizabeth saw, one would have a daily view of the activity around the fountain. The house was in ruins, truly unsalvageable, and instantly she wanted to possess it.

She gathered courage and broke the silence. "Do you know who owns that house?"

"Why do you ask?" Lilli's eyes looked as though they could scratch glass.

"It's beautiful."

Lilli made no answer then, nor later in the day, as she walked beside Elizabeth on a mountain trail, did she offer a single word. It had been Lilli's idea to come to the cloud forest above Ouro Preto, yet she seemed to take no joy in it.

Lota strode ahead with their guide, a boy who couldn't have been more than fifteen years old. His name was Apollonio and he spoke in a grave, high register. Lota walked with a hand upon the boy's back, as if he were her ward rather than a hired guide. It was Lota's easy tendency, her instinct and her gift, to pull anyone she perceived as vulnerable or needing protection into her orbit—the gentleness always a surprise in someone so quick to ignite. But also so necessary. The country was full of children like this one: the shoeshine boys and five-year-old jugglers and fire-breathers at street intersections, and those beautiful ragged nymphs with their cassava cakes. It was just a crime.

Lilli spoke at last. "The house that captivated you, it takes a special eye to see its beauty. I do know something about its history. It was built during the early eighteenth century. I might arrange for you to see it, if you'd like."

"I would love that." Elizabeth smiled at Lilli, but the woman did not return the warmth; she kept her gaze forward. There was something about the stolidness of her neck and chin, the erectness of her spine, that caused Elizabeth to recall the women of Great Village.

Ahead, Apollonio lifted a branch revealing a trail that led down the steep hillside. Elizabeth passed beneath his arm and entered a forest more mysterious than any she had ever seen.

Remain in a single line, the boy said behind her, so we do not disturb the nature.

Mist drifted through the trees and turned the light yellow-green. The ground was a thick, soft mat of green covered with tiny red flowers. Tree trunks were furred with dense, vibrant moss and leafy lichens, while curtains of more moss hung from the branches, brushing Elizabeth's head like witches' hands. The landscape was primeval, too otherworldly to fully apprehend. The four of them walked in a hush.

From a waterfall above, a stream cut through the green mountainside. The forest protects a rare and unusual creature, Apollonio said in his high voice. It has a soft body, with legs like a caterpillar's. This creature is called a velvet worm.

"What a beautiful name," Elizabeth murmured, not sure if she'd even spoken aloud.

Lota pinched her lightly on the bottom.

With care, Apollonio said, we can overturn rocks at the edge of the stream to find one of these living fossils.

Lota and Lilli bent to search for velvet worms in the stream, but Elizabeth stepped away from them and sat upon a fallen, rotting trunk. She watched Lota's small, quick hands lift the rocks and debris at the water's edge, then carefully set them back in place. Hands unafraid of labor, calloused and rough, yet capable, Elizabeth knew, of the most delicate caresses. Hands that had traveled over her body, giving pleasure. Hands Elizabeth had taken in her own and kissed, but only in private. To act with discretion meant that she and Lota could never publicly reveal any sort of intimacy. Lota was always trying to defy the rule—the stolen public kiss, the sneaked tenderness—but Elizabeth pulled back from these gestures; even when the charade became unbearable, she could not let herself *want*. Their public performance as dispassionate spinster companions sought to erase the private world of touching, explaining, loving, perhaps with too much success. Elizabeth could parse out love in dribs and drabs, no more. She had warned Lota, from the beginning. Even when the two of them returned to their room and were once again together, with no one else near, Elizabeth could not cross the great distance from her feelings.

The light in the forest appeared aqueous, filtered by the green mist, as if Elizabeth were submerged beneath the sea. Sounds were muffled. The others at the streambed grew blurry. Elizabeth noticed a cloud of black particles descending into her vision, jumping and jiggling like atoms. She nearly called to Lota before she realized it was a phenomenon visible only to her. The particles hissed and crackled. It really was the most unreal sensation. Then she heard shouting.

A poeta está desmaiando! The boy's voice came from far away. The poetess is fainting!

Three faces floated above her.

The succulent green mat pressed softly against her back. Long shreds of moss hung from the tree branches, a tangled lace against the yellow sky. Elizabeth had no recollection of falling from the log, nor of being caught and laid upon the ground. She perceived Lota at her side, kneading her hand vigorously. Her lover did not care that the others witnessed her bending so close to Elizabeth that their lips nearly touched.

Elizabeth sat up. Her mind was clearing, but the vertigo lingered. Lota helped her to sit again by the stream, where she offered Elizabeth a handful of bread on which she might nibble.

"You gave me a scare, Cookie."

Staring into the flow of water, Elizabeth discovered the most marvelous optical illusion. If she kept her eyes for some moments on the rush of a waterfall, then turned to look upon the adjacent rock, the appearance of motion was transferred from liquid to solid. The stone itself flowed, it bloomed like a mineral flower, as if the rock had come alive.

"Cookie, can you speak to me?"

Elizabeth reached out to place her palm against Lota's soft cheek. "Did you find any velvet worms?"

"Oh, Cookie."

Lota leaned into the touch of Elizabeth's hand. She could never decide if her lover's constitution was truly as fragile as Elizabeth claimed. Sometimes she suspected Cookie would outlive them all, yet the possible loss of her was never far from Lota's mind. She felt she'd tossed her heart into the middle of the highway. Craziness to leave it there, it was certain to be mashed at any moment, yet nothing in the world had made her feel more thrillingly alive. Not her house, not art, not even, she thought sadly, Mary. When Elizabeth had fainted, sliding from the log to the ground and then, almost gently, laying her head upon the green cover, Lota had felt herself approach the verge of extinction.

Now Elizabeth cried out, Look at the waterfall, Lota! Then look at the rock. The rock actually moves!

Lota was overcome with a strange feeling of pride. Cookie, she said, you are learning to love.

Elizabeth's eyes filled with tears. Lota reached for her hand.

I don't know what's wrong with me today, Elizabeth said. Maybe it's the altitude. It's made my head go soft.

Her eyes shifted to look past Lota, and her expression changed in that lovely way she had. In Elizabeth's face, Lota could see her as a little girl discovering a mystery of nature for the first time, a chrysalis, a bird's blue egg in a nest. Lota turned to follow her gaze.

Through a break in the trees, she could see far below into the valley that led back to Ouro Preto. A soft black band undulated through the hills, like a velvet worm.

Elizabeth nearly whispered, Could that be the new road?

BEFORE THEY LEFT Ouro Preto, Lilli presented Elizabeth with a gift. It was an object from her own home, a wooden altar eight inches high, painted red, with doors that opened like those of a miniature armoire. It was called an *oratorio*. Inside was a wonderful carving of a saint. "It's from the eighteenth century," Lilli said, "like the house you have fallen in love with. Travelers and pilgrims carried these on the road so they would always have a protector nearby. This one is from Diamantina, where Helena Morley lived."

"And who is the saint?"

"Saint Barbara. She offers protection from sudden death, from thunderstorms and lightning, fires and explosives."

"Explosives! In that case, she can protect Lota, too."

THEY TOOK THE new highway out of town, the fresh asphalt sheathed in red mud rinsed from the mountains by the rain. Within the hour, the new road collided with the old, potholed one and disappeared. You really had to laugh.

They stopped at a hotel en route, a modernist monstrosity outside Juiz de Fora that Lota had been curious to see. Sitting at the poolside bar, they struck up a conversation with a salesman in a bathing suit on his way to Belo Horizonte. Elizabeth sipped a caipirinha made with passion fruit, really the most delicious drink that seemed to have absolutely no alcoholic effect, and watched the salesman's young daughter paddle around the pool inside a circular inflatable float. Before she was halfway through the first drink, she already wanted another; she could have had twenty in a row. Even with her eye on the girl, she remained attentive to the conversation, so familiar with the sounds and rhythms of the language that she didn't quite register when she lost comprehension of the Portuguese. Like a dog, she kept her ears perked up, wagged her tail at tones that seemed to be aimed in her direction.

The girl splashed about, talking and singing to herself, apparently happy to play alone. You didn't know the difference, Elizabeth remembered; you didn't register your own friendlessness or the fact that you'd never felt the touch of your mother's hand, because your mind and imagination, the stories you'd read and the ones you made up, filled in the space that human contact might have occupied.

She didn't see exactly how the girl flipped over. Elizabeth had turned to sip her drink and to smile at the salesman, who she sensed was telling a joke, and when she turned back, two skinny brown legs were frantically scissoring upside down in the air, trapped by the float. The little legs were mesmerizing. She wanted to say something— truly, she tried to—but dogs could not easily form words.

Flying from her seat, Lota knocked past the surprised salesman and dove into the pool fully clothed. She pulled the sobbing girl upright and held her close, calming her tears, repeating over and over, "It's all right, my dove, you're safe now, you're safe."

Elizabeth traded looks with the salesman, who didn't seem to have fully taken in the rapid sequence of events. She finished off her drink.

At dinner in the hotel restaurant, Elizabeth thought to comment on the hotel's architecture, how it was truly one of the most dreadful places ever conceived and executed, and that when they'd been shown to their room through dark cement passageways smelling of mold, she had felt like an ant following trails dug out of the dirt or like a miner in tunnels about to collapse. But Lota's silence and the hushed, deserted restaurant were oppressive, so Elizabeth said nothing. She felt sure Lota would interpret her criticism of the hotel, even if she agreed with it, as an attack on the country, and, to be honest, maybe it *was* an attack on the country, which just never ceased to confound her. Brazil had squandered such enormous wealth, with its pretensions to a grandeur that would never materialize or that could not be sustained longer than a historical instant. Just look at the imperial palaces of Petropolis or the grand opera house of Manaus in the middle of the Amazon jungle or Ouro Preto decaying beyond help. All of it fated to fall into decrepitude, just as all these monuments to modernism would no doubt also fall.

Not a soul crossed their path as they strolled back through the hotel grounds. As if her silence had harbored no ill feelings, Lota took Elizabeth's hand and drew her beneath an arbor, kissing her neck. Then she said pleasantly, "What do you think of the outdoor lighting here? Should we do something like this at Samambaia?"

"Yes," Elizabeth answered, "if we want our house to look like a concentration camp."

"Well, I like it."

The path took them past the poolside bar, now closed. Lota stopped and said, "I'll stay and have a smoke."

"All right."

"Would you like to keep me company?"

"I think I'll go on up to the room." A look of confusion passed over Lota's face. Elizabeth herself did not understand why she had to flee, why the moment had become painful.

"Please stay," Lota said softly. "I want you to stay with me."

"All right, then."

In the shadows of the untended bar, Lota smoked while Elizabeth wished for the trip to end. She wanted to be home again in Samambaia. Lota stubbed out her cigarette and, instead of suggesting they head back to their room, began to undress, leaving her clothes where they fell. She entered the pool with hardly a splash and swam its entire length beneath the surface, her stout, strong figure gracefully moving through the dark water.

Before Lota surfaced, Elizabeth hurried to the pool. She sat upon the steps and slipped her bare feet into the cool water. Lota came up for air beside her, unsurprised to find Elizabeth there, and folded her arms upon the pool's edge. Her shoulders were plump, ripe for a bite. She smiled up at Elizabeth. With her hair slicked back from her proud forehead, she looked like a boy extremely pleased with himself.

"This hotel makes me feel like a canary asphyxiating in a mine," Elizabeth said.

"Yes, bad modernism is terrible. It hurts the soul."

"It is the precise opposite of everything wonderful about your house, the lightness and glass, the luminousness."

"*Our* house, Elizabeth."

"Yes, our house. Our house is like a translucent balloon that could float above the earth. I love that house."

Lota regarded her seriously, then kissed Elizabeth's foot. "I am very happy you love it."

Lota was so natural in the water; she was so natural in air. But Elizabeth thought it could as easily have been her instead of Lota who'd jumped in earlier that day to save the girl, righted the skinny scissoring legs, held the girl to her breast. There was so much need for protection in the world, and so little supply. Was it unthinkable that she might provide some small bit of it? Then a horrible thought returned to her. *All you give is scraps.*

"I want a child," Elizabeth said.

Lota hooked her arm around Elizabeth's leg. "I have raised a child already. But if that is what you want, then you will have it. I have no doubt you will be a wonderful mother."

LOTA DROVE WITH one hand nestled in Elizabeth's lap, like a cat curled up for a nap. As dusk approached, the landscape was a blue-green blur, punctuated every now and then by a bright spot of color, pink house or yellow bird. On a curve, Lota went shooting past a truck with the words Materiais Perigosas painted in fanciful script on the back. "It's certainly"—the word that came to Elizabeth's mind was neither English nor Portuguese—"a *perigous* existence in Brazil."

"*Sim*," Lota agreed. "*Há muito perigo aqui.*"

Elizabeth propped the *oratorio* on the dash. "Good thing we have Saint Barbara to keep us safe."

She will be looking at Saint Barbara when she dies, in Boston, twelve years after Lota's death, following a period of ill health. In spite of Saint Barbara's alleged protection against lightning and other varieties of sudden death, it will happen suddenly. It is the sort of irony both she and Lota would have relished, to die beneath the gaze of Saint Barbara of an aneurism, a lightning bolt to the brain.

IN THE LAST kilometers before home, they hurtled through a dark void. A storm had passed through earlier in the day, so in addition to dodging mud-filled potholes Lota had to contend with branches and other debris littering the roadway, illuminated at the last moment by the car's headlights. At last, they turned onto their own road. In a fit of impatience, Lota went speeding up the hill in the pitch black.

"How on earth can you see anything?" Elizabeth asked.

"I don't need to see. I've done this a thousand times."

An enormous *thump* brought them to a stop. Lota put the car in reverse, then forward.

"We're stuck in the mud," she finally said.

Elizabeth laughed in a burst, delirious with fatigue and the joke of being unable to travel the last quarter mile. "The mighty Lota is stuck."

"We'll walk the rest of the way," Lota said, unamused.

They left their luggage and Saint Barbara and began trudging blindly up the steep hill. Elizabeth was so exhausted that even with her eyes on the ground she repeatedly stumbled and slipped in the puddles. Half a dozen times she nearly toppled over. Lota held her arm to steady her, but Elizabeth kept slipping from her grip. Her foot sunk into the mud, and her shoe was vacuumed off. Before she could regain her balance, Elizabeth took a dive toward the earth. She landed flat on her back in the slop and began to laugh uncontrollably, wave upon wave of feeling.

Lota stood against the stars, a dark outline with an arm outstretched.

"You look just like one of the Prophets."

"Can I help you get up, Cookie?"

Elizabeth grasped Lota's offered hand and pulled with all her strength. Shrieking like a girl, Lota tumbled upon her. "You are in big trouble now," she cried, laughing. "I am going to kick your behind."

Love crossed a new latitude. There was a notable change.

Lota lay quietly with her head on Elizabeth's breast.

"You've helped me feel happier than I've ever been in my life, Lota. It is very hard for me to believe in happiness. I resist it. I've spent so much time just trying to survive."

"And now you thrive."

Elizabeth held her close and kissed Lota's throat, and for a time they both looked up at the stars, as humankind had for millennia. In that moment, Elizabeth was unable to see through the eyes of the Prophets; she could not perceive portents, or warnings, or any promise of the end. For two thousand years, every age of man had believed itself to be the last, the most corrupt and exhausted, the final creaking era before the whole dangerous, precarious enterprise of human existence must collapse under its own imperfect design. And yet it hadn't proven to be so. Here they were, still trudging through the mud. But hardly alone. Perhaps friendlessness affected one's powers of divination.

Elizabeth helped Lota to her feet. They walked hand in hand up the hill toward their house, which lit up the dark like a glass lamp held in a giant's fist.

·14·

This place is wonderful, she wrote to Pearl, who'd returned to New York. *I only hope you don't have to get to be forty-two before you feel so at home.*

She did not know what she'd done to deserve this happiness.

Since sunrise, Elizabeth had remained in bed with several of her favorite Englishmen: Dickens, Darwin, and Sir Richard Burton. Morning fog filled the valley below the house, like a big bowl of cream. Another sky of absolute blue and the entire sweep of mountainside gone rose-red from the flowering *matto*. One little black bird hopped up and down on a twig, a bouncing ball of a bird. Among the bedclothes lay a number of literary quarterlies that had finally found their way from the States, tied with twine into a batch, most arriving months after their publication date. Something of her own appeared in one of them. The poem had been written so long ago that Elizabeth felt as if she were reading a message in a bottle. Thrown into the sea by a castaway who'd been marooned for a very long time.

And then Friday came.

A cloud flowed over the great rock peak, and mist floated in through her open window. As it cleared, Elizabeth spotted Lota near the new wing. Dressed in her bathrobe and slippers, she was shoving dynamite into a fissure in the mountainside.

The new addition to the house flew from the main body like a gesticulating arm and was cantilevered off an enormous boulder. Lota had begun to supervise the dynamiting after the first fellow miscalculated a blast and showered them all with granite, rocks small and large raining down on their lunch, like a tea party in Pompeii.

Lota retreated at a sprint, with her fingers to her ears. The explosion caused Elizabeth's bed to tremble.

Two years now, living in a construction zone. The racket from dawn until dusk, the ceaseless banging and pounding and scraping and blasting and shouting—early on, it had nearly driven Elizabeth off the deep end. One day, they'd tested a new doorbell. *Ding dong ding dong ding dong ding dong ding dong* until the noise was inside her head. Why have a doorbell when there was no door! Another time, when Elizabeth's exasperation had gotten the best of her, Lota had led her outdoors and described the new wing, how it would become their private enclave, apart from the rest. "I'm not building this house just for myself, Elizabeth. I don't think you always understand that, but you will."

Elizabeth learned a new phrase: *tapons do oveido*. Earplugs.

THE COOK WAS not in the kitchen. In fact, ever since Maria had confessed to her love affair with the gardener, the two of them had rarely been in evidence. At the blasting site, a temporary armistice appeared to have been declared, but Elizabeth did not hear Lota sneak up behind her. Arms encircled her waist, and a nibble on her neck sent an electric tingle down her spine. "Good morning, Cookie," Lota breathed into her ear.

"Someone might see!" Yet she drew Lota's arms around her and leaned into the embrace.

"I hope they do. We will show them what love can be."

"Did I keep you awake last night? I was up five times at least."

"Sweet Cookie. The cortisone isn't working?"

"It works, but you know it makes me terribly anxious." Beyond the patio, the yard looked like a quarry, rocks and tools strewn everywhere. "Are you finished with the dynamite?"

"For now. I need the engineer's opinion, but he can't be here until the afternoon. That is very frustrating! It is a powerful feeling to shape the mountain."

"I wish you'd wear a hardhat with that bathrobe."

"Cookie."

"If you need me, I'll be in the studio."

"Yes, go. Write your masterpieces."

JUNE AGAIN, AND breathing was impossible. In the middle of the night, Elizabeth became a mad scientist conducting experiments by lamplight, mixing quantities of inhalant, injections, and pills, introducing them into her own body like Dr. Jekyll to register their effects. Only the cortisone gave her any real relief. But cortisone was a fickle friend; it hadn't taken long to show its sinister side. Not simply the insomnia and jitters—worse, it gave her a sense of imminent doom. The medicine made her fat, to boot. So she tried not to lean too hard on the cortisone, until a week of nights like this made it the only option. Struggling through another wheezing fit at 3:00 am, she could stand it no longer. She employed the full battery.

Ah, blessed breath!

The miracle was short-lived. Elizabeth could breathe, but her heart raced as though from a sudden fright. She thrashed about in bed, eliciting groans of protest from Lota. On previous restless nights, Elizabeth had moved to the other bedroom, but Lota abhorred waking up to discover herself alone. Elizabeth forced herself to lie still, her arms at her sides, calling to mind any number of serene images: the clouds coming in the window, washing Lota's hair in the stream, her hands rubbing Lota's scalp.

It was no use. She left the bed. There was one thing she could do.

The jumpiness and nerves weren't caused by any *real* reason; they

were merely a physical reaction to the medicine. Yet the feeling mimicked another state of mind that Elizabeth didn't care for in the least.
She had no interest in revisiting the anxious panic that had once been
her constant.

So she didn't need the alcohol for any *real* reason, simply for a
physical reason: to counter the effects of the cortisone. She needed to
bring herself down, away from that old, treacherous feeling. So she was
doing it for her own safety, surely not only a wise, but also a necessary,
course of action. It was no more than one or two drinks, in the middle
of the night, to take off the edge.

It was enough for Lota, who had a sixth sense of people's failings, to
notice. The next morning she asked in an offhand manner, "So you are
back to your old ways?" while her mouth made a twisted little smile.
Then she passed out of the room, not waiting for a rebuttal, and it was
her dismissiveness even more than the remark itself that cut Elizabeth
so deeply.

She caught up with Lota in the passageway of the partially constructed new wing. "That was unfair," Elizabeth said.

"You should not drink. You told me so yourself. You can't control it.
Do you want me to say nothing?"

The hurt whipped into heat, and the words were spoken. "You have
your own ugly habits, and I don't go hounding you about them."

It was liberating to be a little cruel.

Lota stormed into the yard where the men were working and blew
up at the first unfortunates she encountered there. Then she returned
to her room looking very pale and tired.

Halfway up the path to her studio, Elizabeth stopped. She had to go
back and apologize, to explain that she'd had the drinks out of desperation, to plead with Lota not to lose faith in her.

But wasn't it Lota who ought to apologize? Since Elizabeth had
come to Brazil, her drinking had dwindled to nearly nothing. A glass
of wine over dinner, every so often a bourbon. Maybe a handful of
times she'd slipped further, hidden away with a bottle for a few hours,

but Lota had always found her before any real damage had been done. And in a larger sense, she no longer craved drink as she had, nor did she experience, when she did pour herself one, the wave of absolute relief or even revelation that had once come over her with the first sip. Not just the need for it, but the pleasure as well, was virtually absent. Couldn't Lota see this, instead of leaping to the worst assumptions? Personal transformation did not happen overnight simply because you willed it. Cal would understand, even if Lota didn't.

A brilliant little thing on the ground caught Elizabeth's eye. Shiny, a beautiful shade of purple-red, it scuttled along like a miniature patent-leather shoe. Whenever she saw one of these tiny crabs that lived in the stream, she wondered how it had ended up here in the mountains, so far from its marine origins. As she admired him, the crab tilted back to brandish one large, lopsided claw. If Lota had been nearby, Elizabeth would have tugged on her sleeve and said, *Look at this tough little customer*.

Instead she called to Julinho, who was working in the garden alongside the house. They stood side by side watching the crab, Julinho nodding his head and murmuring words too softly in Portuguese for Elizabeth to make them out. Once, she'd lived among the brightest minds of New York; now, these amiable, hardworking men—these Julinhos, Manu-elzinhos, Paulos, and their families—made up the bulk of her human society. For days at a time, when Lota left for Rio on her various errands and forms of business, Elizabeth might see and speak to no one else. They worked for Lota, though were not officially her employees. Nor were they squatters, exactly. They'd lived on this land for generations, longer than Lota's own family had, planting on the steep hillsides their haphazard gardens that yielded scant harvests. Lota made certain they had clothes and the attention of doctors, but they remained entrenched in poverty. Elizabeth had always been taken slightly aback by their smiles and readiness to help with whatever task lay at hand, yet there was still something wretched about the whole lot, especially all those children, brought into a world that did not want them.

Crawling over the landscape, hard-shelled, tough customers from some faraway place—the men were like the tiny crabs. And not unlike her, either. In fact, all of them—she, the men, the shiny purple crabs—were bound in a loose confederacy under Lota's protection.

Julinho lifted up his shovel. Elizabeth quickly reached to stop him from smashing the crab. Instead he slid the blade beneath the hard, bright, scrabbling little legs and set the crab down beside the pool. He smiled shyly at Elizabeth and moved back to his work.

In her studio, she set some water to boil and peeled a handful of bananas while Sammy made a noise like two gourds knocking together. He would eat as many bananas as she gave him, she was sure, right until he popped. He had no sense of pacing himself. As Sammy gorged himself, she looked over some recent letters from friends. The people who understood her well lived so far away that at times she wondered if they were products of her imagination. Some days she might write six or seven letters describing in each precisely the same events, simply in order to convince herself these friends still shared her life.

She began to write about the incident with Julinho by the stream. *I pointed out to him one of the beautiful little wine color and yellow crabs that live in it*. In a burst of excitement, she continued, *and* wham *went his shovel and that was the end of that crab. Sometimes one gets awfully tired of primitive people, I must confess.*

She poured a second cup of tea; another banana disappeared down Sammy's gullet. Looking over the lines, she thought what an odd thing she'd written to her friend. But why not? It wasn't pure misrepresentation. Surely it, or something like it, had happened a thousand times since she'd taken up residence here. Brazilians were all primitives, incapable of judgment, and so wretchedly made, like the clothes and the furniture and the roads and just about everything else.

SHE COULDN'T BREATHE. She took the medicine, and then she couldn't sleep. It became Elizabeth's habit to take a single drink, or two or three drinks, every night. This did not prevent her from working long hours on the translation of Helena's diaries; in fact, it made it possible. Nor from rising early and bringing breakfast to Lota in bed, but Lota's eyes would not meet hers, even with the comical distraction of Sammy on the breakfast tray. Her silence was more ominous than the grim expression. There was no atoning. Elizabeth felt as though she might shout, *Yes! You've unmasked me! I'm not who you wished!*

TOO MANY KISSES. That was the problem with Brazilians; they always wanted to cover your face with their lips. At least with Mary she could count on a good old-fashioned handshake.

Their guests had come from São Paulo to see the house, Luiz and Roberto Cusi and Lota's nearly deified friend Lina Bo Bardi, with old Mary also tagging along. Such a strange creature, Mary, a wraith haunting the house that should have been hers. Elizabeth supposed she should feel guilty, but if Mary hadn't been so humorless, Lota never would have had to go searching for someone else. Elizabeth's predecessor in Lota's affections should count her lucky stars that Lota had set her up in the Rio apartment, where she might consider occupying more of her hours, instead of spooking about Samambaia.

They'd hardly put down their bags before Lota ushered them on the grand tour. Elizabeth begged off to finish preparations for dinner.

"What are you cooking for us, Cookie?" Lota offered her first smile in days.

"Chicken pot pie."

"An American delicacy," Roberto Cusi said. His eyes were kind and full of mischief.

From the kitchen, Elizabeth was able to track the group as they moved through the house and outside along its perimeter. Lina's exclamations meant that Lota would return in a brilliant humor. Though far from finished, the house had won an international prize in architecture last winter, and ever since they'd been subject to weekend busloads of architects and students arriving for unannounced tours. Of course,

Lota would always puff herself up like a fighting cock for these visitors, while Elizabeth scrambled to prepare an impromptu lunch for thirty, only too aware of herself as a most unpleasant sort of person, utterly mean in spirit. Now, she sipped a glass of wine as she worked in the kitchen, and by the time the guests had returned from their tour and the meal was ready, she gratefully felt herself slipping back into her normal, more generous skin.

Lina was broadcasting her pronouncements on the house as Elizabeth took a seat at the table. "The industrialization of the design is much more radical than you described, Lota, and yet framed by these elements and planes, the landscape is even more irresistible and seductive."

Lota hung on every word. Lina had recently received the commission to design the new museum of modern art in São Paulo. It was the kind of recognition Lota might have craved for herself; still, it was embarrassing to see her fawning over her friend.

"But how is the aluminum roof in the rain?" Lina asked.

"Fantastic!" Lota exclaimed. "The noise is tremendous."

"So you've come to Rio to teach a symposium?" Elizabeth asked politely.

"A three-day workshop at the university," Lina replied. "Lota set it up for me."

"Do you often teach?"

"*Lo adoro*. The minds of young people, they are very hungry. They have not yet been corrupted. And all of them are open to me. Have you taught? If you haven't, then you must."

"I'd rather eat glass."

Luiz, she noticed, smiled at his plate. She had adored both of the brothers ever since she'd met them the day she first arrived in Samambaia, at the lunch Lota had thrown in her honor.

"No, you mustn't be afraid," Lina said, placing a hand on Elizabeth's arm, "not of the students. Not of anything. Right, Lota?" The Italian woman was undoubtedly a fascinating creation, with that impressive self-confidence and long red hair and translucent skin and intelligence sharpened like an instrument of war. She'd been a member of the Italian resistance against fascism and was now on her way to being one of Brazil's most prominent intellectuals. All the same, she appeared to find herself even more fascinating than she deserved to. Lota, at least, was not a narcissist.

Roberto said, "Elizabeth, the potted pie is fabulous. But please tell me where do you get your clothes? You are so elegant, and we expect a poet to be a frump."

"But I am a frump." Kittenishly, she pulled up one leg of her slacks to reveal a magenta sock.

"Surprise!" said Roberto, throwing himself back in his chair.

"Lota got them for me at a store that sells clothes to the clergy."

"And your hair," he said, his eyes darting around her head, "it's genius. It's so . . . *alive*."

"*Isso*," Luiz, who until now had remained silent, said softly.

In physical appearance, the two brothers could have been mistaken for twins, yet in character they were inversions of one another, Roberto outgoing and big-gestured, while Luiz turned a fierce beam silently inward, as plainly uncomfortable in his skin as Elizabeth was in hers, which she always found an endearing trait. Recently, the furniture they designed out of scraps and discarded materials—a sofa made of cardboard, a stool of a coiled garden hose—had been collected by museums, and every so often she saw their work featured in the newspaper. All of it was quite imaginative and outlandish and playful. Slightly insane, as Lota had asserted Brazil to be.

The conversation circled and returned to the house.

"It is unlike anything I've seen, Lota. A triumph."

"She has thought of nothing else for years," said Mary.

"That's not entirely true," Elizabeth corrected.

"Well, yes, we cannot think of only one thing. We must strive for balance," Lina said. "But personally, I think balance is overly prized." Elizabeth found herself the object of Lina's scrutiny, as if there were a crumb on her shirtfront or gristle between her teeth. "I am just like you," Lina pronounced at last. "When I first came to Brazil, it was not in my mind to stay. Remember, Lota, we met at that exhibit at the ministry of health, well-meaning but terrible? My husband and I had come from Italy, after years of fascism and the war. Like you, Elizabeth, we found it so enticing we could not leave. That was ten years ago."

"Yes," Elizabeth laughed. "It entraps you."

"Everything is new here," said Lina. "You can do anything, create anything. Like this house. You can redefine your own possibilities. When I design, even more than beauty, I search for freedom. The only limits are those you impose upon yourself. Do you find that to be true?"

There it was, thank heavens, the internal shift back to being a human being, and just in time. "Yes, I do," Elizabeth agreed. "Truly, I've not ever been so productive as I have here in Brazil. For a while now, I've been working on a translation of the diary of a Brazilian girl named Helena Morley. It's called *Minha Vida de Menina*. An extremely charming book, but even more than that, I find it very moving."

"We read it in school," Luiz said. "A wonderful story."

"Yes, it is," Elizabeth said, with great warmth for the man—atypical for a Brazilian, so modest and quietly mannered.

"But it is taking too long," Lota said sharply. "Elizabeth does not work enough. She stays in bed very late."

"Brazil," Lina went on, "is very inspirational. In Rome, everything is in ruins. It is all dead. *Morto. Estinto!*"

"But sadly," Roberto said, "here we have no gladiators."

"We do not all work at the same speed," Luiz said to Elizabeth, but it was too late. She'd already shifted back.

"Yes, Lota," Mary said. "Not everyone works all day and all night, like you. Some of us need sleep." She smiled at Elizabeth, who felt she might begin to claw the flesh from her own arm.

"But what is the point if you are not completely absorbed by the work?" said Lina.

"Then you'd just be a big fake," Elizabeth nearly shouted, and sucked in a viscous mouthful of wine. "Not like the two of you, of course. You've each built a tremendous house."

"You have seen my glass house?" asked Lina, showing her glistening teeth.

"Only in photographs. Lota insisted I see them when I first arrived in Rio." A sensation came over her, oddly physical, even a little vulgar, but really rather wonderful. Why on earth had she been wound up so tightly? Smash that goddamn crab! "They had a very naughty effect, I have to confess. Lota showed me the photographs of your house, and the next thing we knew, we were—"

"Elizabeth!" Lota cried.

She refilled her wine glass. "Let's just say your house is as inspiring as Brazil. It makes you feel as though you could do anything."

Lota slammed her hand upon the tabletop. "Stop now!"

Elizabeth looked into air.

Roberto broke the silence. "Lina, perhaps I might have some copies of those photographs for my own use?"

Mary added, "I always say the power of good architecture is under-estimated."

"Bravo," Lina said, holding up her glass.

Lota reached toward Mary and squeezed her arm. It was too sickening.

Luiz looked as though his insides had begun devouring themselves. If only she could speak to him, human to human, she might rescue them both. "Tell me, Luiz, how does one start designing chairs? I love what I've seen of your work. It's like poetry."

"It started in Bahia," Luiz replied gravely. "I'd gone to live there dur-ing a time of change in my life. I'd been working as a lawyer, and I found that I had to stop. It was not a choice; it was a matter of survival. In Bahia, I hoped to clear a small space in my mind, in my living, to see what might grow. I arrived in summer. You must see Bahia in summer. The excitement, the music and dancing, it is consuming. Everyone was out, their asses full of heat. I was very restless myself. I couldn't sleep."

"You couldn't sleep?" she asked.

He shrugged. "It was impossible. Every day I walked on the beach for many hours and collected seashells. This became my ritual. At night I worked. I used the shells to make mirrors—"

"Mirrors out of seashells!" she howled. "How charming."

Why was she being so awful?

Luiz spoke no further. The remainder of the evening passed in a manner that Elizabeth did not commit to memory.

IN THE MORNING as their guests prepared to leave, Elizabeth remained in her room. She begged Lota, who was escorting them to Rio, to say goodbye on her behalf.

"That is very rude," Lota said.

"Yes, I know, but Lota, I can't do it."

Lota's irritation became something even less tolerable. She sat on the bed and put her arms around Elizabeth, squeezing tightly. Not anger or blame but love filled her eyes. How could Lota keep loving her, after such a disgusting performance? Elizabeth couldn't help but despise her just a bit.

"Are you sure you'll be all right?" Lota asked.

"Of course I will."

"Why don't you come with us?"

"No, Lota, it's better if I stay."

The thing about drinking was that it gave you a sense of humor about the absurdity of your own existence, your own *self*-ishness. Was that, she wondered, the origin of the word? To have a self and to be selfish, yes, they were inescapably one and the same thing. Drinking also provided a context, a frame, if you required one, for the disorganized desire to cause injury to yourself, operating somewhat like the formal structure of a poem.

But it was not immediately upon Lota's departure from Samambaia that Elizabeth committed herself fully to the art of drinking. She did not advance upon the liquor cabinet the instant the jeep disappeared down the hill. She savored the idea most of the day, and it was only in the evening that she went up to her studio with her watercolors and a bottle of gin. There, she began to drink in earnest, sipping the gin straight from a glass while sketching the objects and papers on her desk. It was a relief, really, after all this time pretending to be someone she had no business being, and no desire to be. She felt extremely purposeful. It was her mission to empty the bottle in a methodical fashion while maintaining enough composure not to fall down and break an arm. That would be hard to explain, and it would make her feel stupid. Her drawings devolved into nonsensical shapes and colors. When it became difficult to remain seated upright in the chair, Elizabeth moved to the daybed. There, she must have nodded off.

Someone was shaking her awake. A light was sharp in her eyes, it hurt. Maria and another face behind. She slapped their hands away. They held her up, carried her down to the house.

In the morning, a breakfast tray stood beside the bed when she woke. The coffee was ice cold.

Elizabeth heard the jeep come up the road late in the afternoon and then Lota's voice calling out for her. It was a while before Lota entered the studio. She sat on the daybed and looked at Elizabeth very hard.

"How was Lina's class?" Elizabeth asked brightly.

"Maria says you were drinking last night."

Lota would give her a stern lecture, Elizabeth would apologize and swear never to do it again, and that would be enough to get her back on track. It wasn't as if it had never happened before.

"Maria doesn't know what she's talking about."

Lota stood over her. "No more."

"No more what?"

"You are going cold shoulder."

Lota's apocalyptic face uttering the malapropism caused Elizabeth to burst out laughing.

"What is funny?" Lota said angrily, and yet she too began to laugh.

"The expression is cold *turkey*."

Lota rushed upon Elizabeth and embraced her. "I love you, Elizabeth. I love you. I love you."

ELIZABETH DREAMT SHE could breathe water. She left the bed where Lota lay sleeping and removed her clothes like a false skin and without fear she went into the river and took water into her lungs. She swam from the mouth of a tributary into a great river, past a sunken canoe and enormous fish with eyes the size of silver dollars, but she was not afraid. Above, sleeping villages were unaware of her moving swiftly in the strong currents. In the dream she knew she must leave the water, but she did not wish to return to the world of air. She woke with a sharp, indrawn breath. The dream remained so real that even as Elizabeth became aware of her body and surroundings, she was surprised to find herself in bed, with Lota's arms tightly around her.

GOING COLD SHOULDER lasted several days. Lota didn't hover, though there were awful moments when her great brown eyes turned liquid with helplessness and Elizabeth felt she stood at the shore of a sea of rage with waves lashing at her feet. Still, she slept soundly through four glorious nights. During the fifth, she woke with a parched throat. She produced a series of pathetic opera coughs that would not stop; the sensation was like that of steel wool abrading the lining of her lungs.

There was no deliberation regarding the rightness or wrongness of the act she was preparing to commit. No remorse. It was very clean.

Elizabeth left the bed roughly. Lota did not stir.

The fire in the stove still produced a warm glow by which Elizabeth made her way across the room to the liquor cabinet. Oddly, the shelves were empty, as if she'd misremembered the alcohol's location, and she opened several adjacent cabinets before she understood. Very clever. She could picture Lota standing over Maria as she ordered her to clean out all the bottles and hide them where Dona Elizabeechy's greedy little hands could not reach.

No matter. She had a trick or two up her own sleeve, though it was extremely irritating to have to brave the freezing night in her stocking feet. She slid open the glass door and tiptoed up the steps. Once she was inside her studio, it was unnecessary to light the lamp; she could navigate the dark room, having prepared for such times of scarcity, though she'd had to pony up a hefty sum to the American cultural attaché in Rio for a decent bottle of bourbon.

She removed the bottle from its hiding place. The taste of the liquor was harsh at first, but she loved how the suffusion of alcohol in her blood greeted the buzz of the cortisone, like the froth of a wave advancing up the beach. She had rarely known the forest outside to be so silent: no bugs humming, no birds calling, no monkeys whistling.

Her mind began to grab at fragments.

The world is asleep, and here am I.

I am an eye.

She hadn't bothered to light a fire, and soon the chill banished thought altogether.

When the shivering became intense, Elizabeth put the bottle and the glass away and returned to the house, stepping carefully upon each step, her hand on the wall to steady herself. What a communicative surface the wall was against one's fingertips, rough and smooth at the same time.

At the foot of the stairs, she turned from the terrace to enter the house. A great reverberation sang out, causing Elizabeth to stagger back and topple over, as if she'd been felled by Zeus's thunderbolt. Flat on her back, she did not feel any pain, though her head was ringing. Then she remembered: *Oh, yes.* Some of the plate-glass windows had been installed, right where she had long been used to walking directly through the wall. They'd even taped big *X*'s over the glass to prevent birds from snapping their necks. How silly of her. She'd walked smack into a window.

The cold was extreme, yet Elizabeth lay for some time marveling at the vastness above. Unbelievable how clear the night sky could be here in the mountains, the stars so close and sharp they seemed to prick her scalp.

. Time slid along. She may have, mercifully, slept. Then there was Lota standing over her, hands on hips, her expression so severe Elizabeth laughed out loud. She looked just like a disappointed mother. That was, if a person actually had a mother.

"Elizabeth, you're drunk!"

"You've a keen eye."

"You must stop this!"

Elizabeth rolled onto her side. "And you have to stop trying to stop me."

Lota gripped her arm and yanked Elizabeth to her feet. There was such violence in her eyes, Elizabeth was certain Lota would actually strike her.

"Lota, you look extremely pitiful at the moment."

"Elizabeth, please." Lota's face collapsed in that helpless, defeated look. A weak animal lays itself open to attack, and Elizabeth seized her opportunity.

"You're even sicker than I am, to want someone like me. Something is *wrong* with you."

It was odd how one aspect of Elizabeth stood apart, observing these words as though they'd been written on a page, finding them wanting, even laughable, while another aspect of her filled to bursting with the most hateful, vile feeling. "You're quite a little despot. I suppose you have to have someone weak close by for you to bully."

"Please do not say any more."

"The bully can't take being bullied!"

The charges were cruel, yet at the same time they were not cruel enough. Elizabeth's voice rose until she found herself shrieking. "It's really pitiful, pitiful, pitiful. It's just pitiful, building this stupid house out here in the middle of nowhere."

At last, Lota left her.

But Elizabeth would not let her off so easily. Lota slipped behind

screens and halls ahead, eluding her like a bird in the trees, as Elizabeth
followed through every half-finished room of that stupid house, spewing the most odious charges. At the door to the bedroom, she finally
caught up. Lota's face was wet. For an instant, Elizabeth was startled
by the tears. Then she pressed her advantage.

"It's almost perverse, Lota, don't you think? You really should see
someone about this. You need to take a good, long look at yourself. Or
are you afraid what you'd see would be too *ugly*?"

Lota put a hand upon Elizabeth's breast and gently pushed. Shuffling
back, Elizabeth felt Lota's touch begin to lance the abscess; if only she
never removed her hand, this horrible soul-sickness might be drained.
There would be no need for drink, there would be no thirst.

"I'm sorry, but I must do this for your own good," Lota said
softly. The hand was withdrawn and Lota retreated, closing the door
behind her.

Elizabeth went after her, but the door would not open. Lota had
locked her in. She kicked at the door and shouted until she exhausted
herself.

When morning broke, her head was clear; her stomach, however,
was reminiscent of the insufferable Miss Lytton's aboard the SS *Bowplate*. Poisoned from the alcohol, of course, but beyond that, the poison was of her own manufacture. A little packet of it had burst inside
her like a rotten appendix. Putrid yellow bruises ran along her hip and
arms, and both elbows were scraped. It was some minutes before she
remembered walking into the plate glass. Lucky to have escaped with
mere bruises.

Elizabeth lay for quite some time gazing out the window as the sun
appeared and soft yellow light filtered into the valley. The window also
framed the main structure of the house, where through the glass she
could see Maria sweeping. That was the thing about Lota's house, there
was nothing hidden, there was no pretense; what you saw was what
you got. It wasn't *corrupt*. She loved this view with the entirety of her
being. Perhaps that was why she was being punished so severely. She

should have known never to love anything so much she couldn't bear to lose it. That was life's lesson.

But impressive really, to have lasted this long. She had to give herself that much. Now it was time to pack her bags, to turn her mind to the next part of her journey. Maybe she really would get to Machu Picchu. Brazil had been only a stop to refuel, after all, not the final destination.

Lota knocked lightly on the door before she unlocked it, a final politeness offered to the criminal. She entered with a breakfast tray, sans toucan. The smell of coffee appealed to Elizabeth and was at the same time revolting. "How are you, Cookie?"

"Just peachy, officer."

Lota set the tray aside. "I'm sorry that I shut you in here. I did not know what else to do."

"Well, you should have known. You should have had a plan."

"Please do not become angry."

"I'm not angry, Lota. I'm ill. Why do you think all your friends advised you to steer clear of me? I'm a drinker. I told you so when we met. I've tried to stop before, but I'm too weak. I'm not going to stop drinking, and I don't want to."

Lota gazed at her hands in her lap. "I love you, Elizabeth."

"I think you *are* the sick one," Elizabeth cried. "Why would you want to put up with this? All this time, it's been a trick."

Lota drew Elizabeth close, wrapped both arms around her, then a leg, she seemed to have as many limbs as an octopus. Rocking her, she shushed Elizabeth's protests. "Here is what I propose," she said. "First, I will take you to a hospital to get the asthma and the drinking under control. I realize now that I can't do it myself. I thought I could. After that, you will tell me when you feel the desire to drink. You will come to me. You will not hide from me. I am not your enemy. I will be with you in the day and in the night. It is not your destiny to hurt yourself in this way."

"It's no use." Elizabeth felt extremely tired.

"There is a medicine you can take."

"Antabuse. It makes you violently ill."

"Only if you drink."

"Yes," Elizabeth laughed bitterly. "Only if."

She was growing uncomfortable in Lota's tight embrace, but Lota held on.

"You do not believe you can change. I believe you can."

·15·

*S*LUMBER, INTERRUPTED BY brief periods of semiwakefulness. Her body did not want to leave sleep for long. Whenever Elizabeth opened her eyes, there was always a lively young nurse plumping her pillows, rubbing her calves or hands, smiling and cooing over her as if she were a baby in an incubator. They roused her for the injections and the tests, drawing blood out, putting something else in. The blurred, smiling white shapes hovered over her like angels, then a pinprick on her arm or wrist.

It was called the Hospital dos Estrangeiros: Foreigners' Hospital. Yet she did not feel a foreigner here. She did not feel unwelcome. Some of her happiest times had been spent in hospitals. Everything was soft, white, heavenly.

"WAKE UP!"

Against a white plane, a wall or a sheet, shadows glimmered and played. There was a draft on her skin, cool. It was not clear if the words had come from the real or the dreaming world.

"Wake up, Brazilians!"

The amplified voice was followed by cheers and whistles. Another political rally in the plaza outside.

Elizabeth's hand lay outstretched upon the white covers, tucked between the pages of a book. It was the study of the poet George Herbert, written by a friend, that she'd carried with her to the hospital. Her mind was too slack from the chemicals they fed her, or simply from exhaustion, to take in much of the book's substance, yet she wanted it near her, wanted to be touching it like a talisman. She owed Herbert so much; he'd guided her so well in art. When she'd come across her own name in the acknowledgments, her heart had contracted and she'd been unable to control her sobs.

Elizabeth looked to the window, and there was Lota. She stood with her back to Elizabeth, her head bobbing to and fro, intent on what she watched outside. The streak of white in her dark hair made her look just like a chickadee trying to fly out of the room.

> Love bade me welcome: yet my soul drew back
> Guilty of dust and sin.

The line was Herbert's. She did not think she would ever write one half so piercing.

"What are you looking at?"

"Sweet Cookie," Lota said, turning. "Sweetest of them."

"Anything new happening in the world?"

"The city has become very agitated. You can't walk down the street, it is so full of uncollected garbage. The bay is full of ships that the dockworkers will not unload. Carlos is very pleased. The strikes at last are eroding that dictator Vargas's support. The cruzeiro has lost half its value."

"Again? Lota, that's terrible."

Lota nodded, yet she was smiling. "That is simply life. We will make do. But I'm afraid we will have to postpone our trip to Italy."

"I don't want to go to Italy. I just want to go home, with you."

Lota again faced the window. "While you were asleep, I was taking a walk down memories lane. There used to be a big hill just over there, the Morro do Santo Antonio. They knocked it down and used the rubble to extend the waterfront all along Flamengo and Gloria. I was living in the Hotel Gloria then. The noise was terrible, constant. I'd had a fight with my mother, and for some reason my father put me up at the Hotel Gloria. Very luxurious! Me and the movie starlets. Perhaps he wanted a reason to be nearer the movie starlets. The *aterro* is so ugly now, a pile of rocks along the water. What is wrong with these people? They have no sense of possibility. They can't see what's right in front of their eyes. It could be made into beaches or a park, a place for people to gather and meet, not just a gravel pit. I was thinking that if I could only get my hands on it, I would make something truly beautiful."

"I don't doubt that you would. Like everything you touch."

LOTA WAS CHATTY in the car.

"We will have the house to ourselves. The other day I opened the pantry door and found Maria and Paulo while the act was blazing, so I had to give the lovebirds some time off. Lovers must have the opportunity to consummate their passion. Carlos is coming to lunch tomorrow. I'm worried about him. His campaign against Vargas has left him exhausted."

Elizabeth would have preferred for the two of them to be alone, but she knew it was important for Lota to feel they were resuming a normal life. You could forgive anything in the person who'd saved you from drowning.

The forest was lush and wild yet soothing to the eyes, a forest rendered by Rousseau. She found her studio precisely as she'd left it, her books open to the pages she'd marked, the daily list of Portuguese words and phrases from Helena's diary she'd had difficulty translating still with a pencil upon it. Each evening she brought the list down to dinner and Lota went over her work, explaining the subtleties of the language. Really, the book was not her own—it was a collaboration.

Elizabeth sat at her desk, took up the pencil. She felt a strong desire to work. Perhaps it was the room itself. In Elizabeth's first months at Samambaia, Lota had halted work on the house to build her a studio. Elizabeth loved the blue-gray rock with flecks of mica Lota had found on the mountain and used for the floor and fireplace; she loved her kerosene stove, the view of rustling bamboo from her window, the sound of the waterfall nearby. She loved them too much—she could not live without them. That was the lesson underneath the lesson.

Perhaps, too, it was Helena. Looking over the diary entries she had translated most recently, Elizabeth was struck again by the quality of the girl's writing that had first enchanted her: a seemingly effortless honesty she not only admired but also felt she might learn from. Family squabbles, the care of livestock, descriptions of civic and domestic life—Helena invested them all with her modest struggle to balance the hopes and wishes she secretly held for herself with the desire to do what was right and dutiful to others. Helena had not turned to alcohol.

Elizabeth had spent so many years wandering in the fog, right along the edge of a precipice, at war with herself and with anyone who'd tried to come close. All that time, this was what she'd lacked: bamboo outside her studio window, a toucan on a breakfast tray, the occasional blast of dynamite, language lessons. How simple it could be to accept the ministrations of one person. The drinking, that was old—it was the ruins of Rome. Everything that had come before was old. Here, everything was new. She could make anything.

Elizabeth worked through the morning on a passage in which Helena and her cousin attended a midnight mass in the countryside. The cousin wrapped a rosary around her arm, only to discover some time later that what she'd believed to be her rosary was in fact a live garden snake.

"I HOPE YOU are feeling better, Elizabeth. We have all been concerned for your health."

Carlos and Lota sat at the table on the terrace while Elizabeth lay in a chaise nearby, wrapped up in a shawl though the day was warm. "Yes, I'm greatly improved," she said. "The asthma at last seems under control." She wondered how much he knew or guessed, privacy being a porous border in this country. Elizabeth did not understand why, after all the time she'd spent in the man's company, and in light of Lota's nearly fanatical devotion to him, she still found Carlos so deeply annoying.

While he and Lota talked politics, she listened at a remove. The soporifics of the hospital still had her under their thrall. A hawk soared over the valley, with a small dark bird diving and fluttering around it. She loved it when the little bird chased the big bird.

Her companions' words also darted about each other.

". . . promiscuity with bandits . . . he is surrounded by thugs and criminals . . ."

". . . but he is weakening . . . look at the demonstrations . . ."

Apparently, the newspaperman planned to run for congress in October, intent on making the leap from private to public office that he had been calculating for some time. In recent months, his daily attacks on Vargas, in print and on the radio, had increased his already considerable notoriety.

There was no doubt as to his intelligence or passionate conviction. Carlos was anything but corrupt, and had such an altogether different way—hopeful, almost naive—of imagining political change in a system that in so many aspects was cynical and rotten to the core. She had written enthusiastically to Cal that he was far and away the best man in Brazilian politics. Yet she could not forget his first words when they had finally seen him in his jail cell after his arrest last December. "Some see a setback," Carlos had said. "I see an opportunity." His belief in his own destiny came off him in waves. Elizabeth often found herself charmed, lured in, and then again she saw the opportunism and experienced an aversion as visceral as an allergy to cashew.

"If it weren't for my place here," Carlos said, "just to come here to Samambaia and tend my roses, I think I'd go mad. Did you know that if you keep cutting roses back they will bloom continually almost all year? I notice you have none, Lota. You should have roses."

"I prefer native plants. We've just planted the hillside with three hundred Brazilian trees—*jabuticaba*, *pau brasil*, and *ipê*."

"Don't forget monkey nuts," Elizabeth said.

"Yes, and *abriço de macaco*."

"Then you are a disciple of the landscape master Burle Marx?" said Carlos.

"Are you trying to insult me? Who do you think he learned it from?"

Carlos grew serious. "Your father paid me a visit last week. He said to send his regards."

"His regards to whom?"

"To you, Lota."

"How is he? I heard he's looking terrible, very yellow in the face. He is in deep financial trouble, they say."

"He's been a good friend. He hates Vargas's cronies as much as we do."

"Yes, he always had enough hatred to go around for everyone."

"Lota," Elizabeth interrupted, "I received a note from Lilli today. Do you think we might go back to Ouro Preto soon? She's opening an inn and has invited us to stay. I was reading Burton again in the hospital. He went there nearly a hundred years ago, and his observations still hold true. Funny how I knew it would captivate me even before I ever saw it."

"Yes, it is stunning," Carlos agreed.

"It has that effect on you, too?"

"In fact, I've never been."

Then why did you say that? But Elizabeth held her tongue.

"You know what really could be made into something stunning?" Lota said. "The *aterro*. I could see it from Elizabeth's room in the hospital. You know, Affonso Reidy has already begun his design of the art museum to be built there. When you become president, I want you to give the *aterro* to me. Let me make it into something we could all be proud of."

"Lota, when I am president, I will name you as one of my ministers. Then you can take on any project you like."

"I will be vice president, you mean."

They both laughed, but they were not joking, neither one.

· 16 ·

*L*OTA CRIED OUT during the night. Her body leapt and jerked in Elizabeth's arms and then went slack. Elizabeth held on, urging her lover's troubled soul toward calm. Lota began to wail, a low, terrified sound, and at last Elizabeth spoke her name. Then again, more forcefully. Lota came awake with a shout. A moment of disoriented terror, then she pressed her face into Elizabeth's neck.

"I was having a terrible dream," she said, in a voice eerily vacant of emotion.

"I know you were."

"The same one, the one you don't like to hear."

"The swimming dream?"

"Yes."

"It's an awful dream, but that's all it is. It's not real."

"It *is* real. I've had exactly the same dream ever since I was a child. It is telling me something. It's telling me how I will die. And *when* I will die."

Give me straight talk, Elizabeth wanted to plead, *not more of your Brazilian mysticism*. She could not explain, as she might to any reasonable person, that a dream drew its power from metaphor and symbol rather than from concrete fact, that a nightmare was not a premonition of the future but an all-too-vivid expression of one's fears. For instance: fears regarding the disappearance of one's dear friend Carlos.

"I've had nightmares of dying, too, Lota, in a fire. Repeated ones. But I don't believe that's the way it's really going to happen. We've been through a lot these last weeks. We're all worried about Carlos."

"But Carlos isn't in the dream," Lota protested. "It's about swimming in the sea."

"Yes, I know——"

"The water is beautiful, very blue and clear. Maybe it is at Cabo Frio."

Elizabeth could not bear to hear the nightmare recounted one more time; it always upset her terribly. Yet from the very first words, she was mesmerized.

"We are swimming together," Lota continued. "That too has always been part of the dream, that I'm swimming with someone I love, the person I've loved most deeply. There's so much to see, so many beautiful things. We're below the surface, holding hands, looking at them together. We have no trouble breathing. It's as though we can breathe the water. I dive deeper to see more, and when I finally try to come back up, something is holding me down. A tide or current or a hand. At first I am frightened. I struggle to swim back to you. I see you above, floating on the surface. I want to get back to you, to be with you. I begin to feel terrified of being alone and drowning. And then I stop struggling."

It was the flatness of Lota's voice, even more than what she described, that caused tears to slip from Elizabeth's eyes. "But why do you stop?"

"Because it's finally all right. I don't have to struggle anymore. I can see you there, and I know you love me, and the pain is finally gone."

"Carlos is extremely resourceful," Elizabeth said. "He's already survived more than one assassination attempt. He has many friends who will protect him. He'll let us know he's safe as soon as he can."

Lota did not take in a single word. Her incessant fingers continued to knead Elizabeth's back. Lota, who had carried her through so many desperate times—she, too, could lose her way, plummet to terrified depths. So Elizabeth held her lover and stroked the back of her head and said nothing more.

On the first few occasions she'd seen Lota brought low, when the powerful Lota she knew and loved and depended upon turned weak, Elizabeth had recoiled. It was not merely surprise at Lota's sudden helplessness. Elizabeth's instinctive reaction was one of repulsion. The lost Lota became a mirror in which Elizabeth saw her own reflection, her own darkest, most twisted need. She could not tolerate what she saw when Lota became a mirror: a bereft, shivering girl in the wilderness, half-savage, half-starved. In her weakened state, Lota lost the power to soothe the desperation of that girl, so fearful and alone. And so at first Elizabeth had turned her back on Lota, as a matter of her own survival.

But after a time, Elizabeth had discovered that she did not have to turn away. She did not want to. The parched little heart inside her rib cage had grown large and compassionate enough to answer both Lota's need and her own. She'd stumbled across a steadiness in herself, rather than a lack. When Lota could not be strong, and even when Elizabeth felt she might literally die without the protection Lota offered, compassion was the door. Compassion for Lota, and compassion for the girl.

Now she put her hand to Lota's lovely, despairing face. Tenderness gave way to a pull of desire. "You are very beautiful," she said, and bent to put her lips to Lota's.

Lota pushed violently away. "Don't lie to me!"

"I would never lie to you, my love."

"I don't like it when you say I'm beautiful. Don't say that. I'm not beautiful."

Elizabeth did not answer, and Lota again drew close. "I'm scared," she whispered.

"I know, but it's going to be all right."

"You're never scared."

"That's hardly true. But I'm not scared right now."

Minutes passed. Elizabeth could feel Lota growing more agitated.

"You should go," Lota said. "Please go."

"I'm not going to leave you by yourself."

"I'm not so nervous if I'm alone. I can't stand it if you're here right now."

"Then only for a little while. I'll be right outside." She kissed Lota's forehead. "Please try to sleep."

THE LIVING ROOM was awash in silver moonlight. Beneath the bright moon lay a shimmering sea, its luminous waves brushing the shore. All of it so beautiful, so enchanting, yet Elizabeth had absorbed the horror of Lota's dream and the ocean appeared to her sinister, threatening, *perigoso*. Maybe she wouldn't miss this apartment as much as she'd thought. They'd come to Rio to rent it out, after many months of hoping to avoid doing so, but they desperately needed the money. The strikes and devaluations had brought the country to the verge of financial ruin, and Lota was completely broke.

Near the waterline, Elizabeth noticed a lone, wavering light, a pulsing phosphorescence on the sand. A beached jellyfish, perhaps, or else a candle left in offering to the ocean goddess Yemanja, no doubt complete with chicken entrails and bloody feathers. She should probably go down and say a prayer of thanks to Yemanja herself; without the Antabuse, she'd be heading this instant to the liquor cabinet to make an offering to a different god.

Lota would pull through. Whenever she became submerged in these dark waters, from whatever cause, she always came back up quickly. But the events of recent weeks had them all half-deranged. It was because they'd come down to Rio to fix up the apartment and find a tenant that they'd found themselves with front-row seats to the absurd political circus at summer's end. Seesawing from fright to jubilation to greater fright—it was no wonder Lota was having nightmares.

Three weeks earlier, Carlos had been shot outside his apartment building after speaking at a rally in Tijuca. His wounds were not mortal; in fact, they verged on ludicrous—he'd been shot in the foot. But the air force officer serving as his bodyguard had been killed. Visiting Carlos in the hospital, Elizabeth and Lota had discovered him in a state of near ecstasy, though unfortunately not from any morphine; he believed he'd finally been handed the golden opportunity to topple Vargas. After the shooting he'd become absolutely rabid; you could hardly talk to him anymore. He began pursuing Vargas's impeachment through the highest channels of government, and denounced him more viciously than ever. Each night, Elizabeth, Lota, and Mary took their dinners beside the radio, listening to Carlos's venomous broadcast. It was there that Elizabeth found an unlikely ally in Mary, who privately agreed with her on the subject of Carlos.

Listen to him, Lota remarked. He's so passionate, vehement, and still so charming, so humorous. He is a great journalist, but an even greater orator.

To Elizabeth, Mary raised one eyebrow.

The official inquiry into the plot to kill Carlos brought him a larger audience than he'd ever had. Even as the hearings began to implicate a ring of Vargas's closest associates, including his own son and the head of the presidential guard, Elizabeth felt increasing distaste for the inflammatory rhetoric Carlos used as a means to realize his ambitions. The country's terrible economic straits had already drained Vargas of so much power that he'd become paralyzed; in his own words, with the new allegations swirling around him, he was drowning in a sea of mud. But Carlos did not desist. He excited a mob outside Catete Palace, where Vargas had barricaded himself with the war minister and several generals. That night, Carlos called Lota very late, shouting over the line, We've won, we've won! Vargas has resigned! The thirty-year dictatorship has ended!

It was close to four in the morning, but the news spread quickly. The phone kept ringing, and neighbors and friends appeared at the door, some in their nightclothes and stocking caps, with bottles of champagne in hand. There must have been fifteen or twenty people in

THE MORE I OWE YOU

the apartment drinking and dancing when a call came with the second announcement, which stunned them into silence.

The president had submitted his resignation, then locked himself in his office and put a revolver to his heart.

The friends hurried home through the false calm of dawn. Lota made repeated calls to Carlos and Leticia's apartment but was unable to get through. From the terrace, Elizabeth watched the streets below begin to fill. At noon, a mob went marching up Avenida Atlântica, past the old lady walking her Lhasa apso and the men playing soccer in the sand and the beachgoers drinking beer at the kiosks in their bathing trunks. The same people who had gathered twenty-four hours earlier to demand Vargas's resignation now attacked the offices of Carlos's newspaper, shouting, Death to Lacerda!

Carlos went underground. They had received no word from him in days.

"Is Lota all right? I heard her calling out."

Mary stood in the corridor, an apparition in a white nightgown. Elizabeth was grateful to have the company.

"She was having another nightmare."

"Should I check on her?"

"She insists on being alone."

"Was it the one about the automobile accident?"

"No, the drowning dream."

Mary took a seat. "That's a bad one."

Elizabeth could not help but notice that the two of them occupied the same chairs as they had on the morning she'd first walked into this room three years earlier, her life held in cupped hands like the shards of a shattered teacup. Same chairs, while all else had changed. Once the apartment was rented, Mary would return with them to Samambaia, where Lota had recently given her some land just down the hill. They would all live in Lota's house while Mary built her own. It was hard not to be amused by the turns and ironies life presented: the three of them playing musical houses, musical hearts. More than once when she'd thought back to the early day she and Mary had gone to Correia, it had crossed Elizabeth's mind that Mary had been attempting, in her indirect way, to warn her or even prepare her for the difficulties of life with Lota. It might have been Elizabeth, and not only herself, Mary had been trying to protect. She'd been uncharitable to Mary in the past, in her mind.

"Well, it's no surprise why she's gone half-mad," Elizabeth said. "After Vargas's suicide, we all are. And who knows where Carlos has gone. I don't doubt for a minute he disappeared purely for theatrical effect. Honestly, does anyone in this country ever balk at the grand gesture?"

"I heard a radio broadcast today claiming it's a trick," Mary said. "They say there's no proof Vargas is actually dead. No one's seen his body. They say the *getulistas* will do anything to regain power."

"No, he's dead," Elizabeth said with certainty. She'd heard the suicide note read over the radio too many times not to recognize the cold fury of someone bent on his own end.

I fought against the looting of Brazil. I fought against the looting of the people . . . I gave you my life. Now I offer you my death. Nothing remains. Serenely, I take my first step on the road to eternity and I leave life to enter history.

It reminded her of another example of the genre: *Go to hell, Elizabeth.* Both of them catchy in their own way.

"Suicide is a terrible thing," she said. "So full of vindictiveness. But I suppose we might have expected it. This entire country is in a continual state of nervous collapse."

"Yes, it's become almost normal, the insanity."

"Not to me, it's not. It will never be normal."

THE BEEHIVES HAD to be moved. That was obvious now. She should have seen it at the beginning. If you were in bed looking out the window, they blocked your line of sight entirely. She was very stupid to have placed them so close to the vegetable garden.

Lota rubbed her arms. She was so cold, she could not get warm. Her arms were numb. She had no feeling.

The architectural tours of Samambaia must stop at once. She was ashamed to have anyone see the house as it was now, even if they were only students.

Where had Elizabeth gone?

Privately, Lota had always known the house to have failed. On the day of the party celebrating the roof's completion, they attempted to light the wood in the fireplace and the entire house immediately filled with smoke. The workers had bricked over the chimney to prevent rain from coming in. They were so ignorant, they'd never seen a chimney before! Half the doors and windows were still missing, the floor was unfinished, no better than bare rock. For months the fireplace had remained useless, but she didn't have the energy to attempt a cosmetic correction for a problem that ran, she suspected, to the very core. One night, she and Elizabeth had built a fire on the concrete floor and roasted their dinner over it, like Neanderthals in a cave.

She'd dreamed of a house that showed its seams, turned inside out to reveal that the mode of its construction—the very thing most architecture sought to hide—could in itself be a thing of beauty. No secrets tucked behind walls, no conjuring of tricks, everything transparent. A house that showed you exactly how it was put together and at the same time took your breath away.

Instead, it had turned into a cave.

Women don't own businesses! That's what her mother had said, the only instance in which Lota could remember the woman raising her voice. Lota had wanted to own a dress shop, to *participate* in the modern world for the love of God instead of chitchatting with all the other women and embroidering handkerchiefs behind the scenes while the men smoked cigars in the drawing room and decided all their fates. So they'd fought, she and her mother, and Lota had moved out. Her father had lodged her at the Hotel Gloria, had also put up the money for the dress shop in Copacabana. He'd had money then, as well as the desire to pique his ex-wife whenever the opportunity arose. But once in a while, even at that time, he'd shown affection for Lota, had still wanted to please her now and again. At the Hotel Gloria, you were treated like royalty. At Samambaia, like a Neanderthal! Welcome!

She was not blind to her qualities. Single-handedly she'd brought an exhibition from the Museum of Modern Art in New York to Brazil, to this backyard country. But no one valued that here. In Brazil, material-istic, beautiful people sailed through life. Look at her sister. They had no original ideas. She had too many ideas, they took her in every direc-tion. She had an eye, but everything she did was half-cocked. Nothing was finished just so. She ruined her own ideas. Her father had let her know he understood that about her from the first.

Now everyone would see that he'd been right all along, that she had no ability, that she was stupid as well as ugly.

Everyone would see she was a failure.

Except Elizabeth.

Where was her Elizabeth?

Elizabeth believed.

When at last the door opened and Elizabeth crept back into the room, Lota lifted the bedcovers to receive her. Elizabeth's body radi-ated heat. Lota drew close to the warmth. She felt so cold.

I have to move the beehives, she whispered urgently.

Elizabeth was searching her face. There was no light in the room, but Elizabeth's eyes gleamed like the sea beneath the moon. You don't have to do anything right now but let me hold you, she said.

Lota nestled close into Elizabeth's warmth. Elizabeth was a warm wave rushing over her. She revived her. She made her human again.

You bring me back, Elizabeth.

Back from where, my love?

From death.

·17·

ONCE THE PARTY had died down and most of the guests had gone, Elizabeth found herself surrounded by the young poets from New York. She was seated with her feet on a cushion while they stood before her like three valiants out of a fable come to seek her favor. One was tall and cool and barely registered emotion, the second was scared of his own shadow, and the last, skinny and exuberant, had come bounding up the stairs early in the evening and knelt before her, taking her hand to press his lips upon it and proceeding to kiss his way up her arm until, with a stricken laugh, she attempted to free herself. As undernourished as he appeared, he had a strong grip and wouldn't let go. His name was Frank.

She amused herself thinking what Cal would have to say about all this. He would have the right take on this sort of thing.

"Is it really true," Frank asked for perhaps the third time, "that you didn't know you'd won?"

Such a curious thing, these not quite men, not quite poets, hanging on her words, unbelievably fresh and slightly desperate. "Somehow time moves differently in Brazil than it does here," she said.

"I'd got it in my head that the prize had already been awarded. Then one morning the phone rang, and a reporter was screaming over the static that I'd won the Pulitzer. I thought it was one of Lota's friends playing a joke."

The cool one tensed his jaw and winced, as if he'd bitten upon aluminum foil. "Even there they care about a poetry prize."

"Yes, they care about it, and that's not a bad thing. In Brazil, poets actually have *value*. That night, we had reporters and film crews for the newsreels coming to the house in the pouring rain. They had us all pose on the couch like bumps on a log, Lota and me, our friend Mary, and the cook's baby girl—my little goddaughter. Then Lota entertained the journalists by flipping the lights off and on, because we had just gotten electricity after years of living by oil lamps."

"You lived without electricity?"

"Right in the middle of the jungle, with the monkeys and the snakes."

If they required a myth, she'd give them a myth. She'd hold that boulder over her head and put on a show. She'd done it before. The shy one didn't make a peep. She wanted to take him onto her lap and feed him a bottle of milk.

Elizabeth began to worry the poets would want to talk about poetry, so she made her excuses. At the other end of the swimming pool, the water's unsettled surface cast undulating light and shadow across Lota, who sat with their hosts Bobby and Arthur. She was still wearing a bib that covered her front with the stars and stripes. Joining them, Elizabeth let her head rest on Lota's shoulder. She felt depleted but happy. The day had been one long parade of interesting people, heaps of lobsters and clams and corn on the cob, then a little Fourth of July concert by Bobby and Arthur, culminating in an explosion of fireworks over the water, false stars of red, white, and blue.

Here it all was: America.

"It is good for Elizabeth to be appreciated," Lota said. "It is good for her to be the spectacle."

"Please don't say it will encourage me to write more."

"It's like watching three butterflies hovering over a lily," Bobby said.

"I feel more like a mushroom than I do a lily."

"Maybe it will help her to write more," Lota said. "She doesn't produce as much as she should."

Elizabeth appealed to Bobby. "Lota doesn't understand me in the least."

"That's what love is, didn't you know?" he said. "A whole world of not understanding."

Originally friends of Lota and Mary's, the two men had embraced Elizabeth without reservation; their generosity of spirit touched her immensely. A virtuoso piano duo, Bobby and Arthur performed all over the world and were equally brilliant in the domestic arts. Their dinner parties were infamous. Bobby was soft, pliable and eager, really a very tender man. Arthur was more refined, yet his perfect manners disguised a wit sharp enough to draw blood. Beneath his silky voice lay a rasp, like butter spread upon toast. They were as different in temperament, yet as complementary, as were she and Lota.

"Tell me," Elizabeth asked, "are only homosexual men writing poetry in America these days?"

"No, dear, only homosexual men are invited to our parties."

"Brazilians are so different. As crazy as they are, they have a modesty of sorts. They don't go parading their predilections about."

"Not like us."

"But they don't hide them, either. That's the interesting thing. They're just . . . exactly who they are." Elizabeth took Lota's hand and caressed her own cheek with it. "When will you come visit? I could ask the cultural attaché to invite you to Rio for a concert. Lota, don't you think they'd like to meet Luiz and Roberto?"

"Is that the pair who's replaced us in your affections?"

"They're not a pair. Though I suppose you tend to think of them as a pair, when in fact they're brothers."

"How extremely freethinking! In that case, Bobby and I will certainly arrange a visit to Brazil."

Across the pool, the New York poets were engaged in an animated conversation. It pleased Elizabeth that they appeared to be such good friends, touching, laughing, lighting one another's cigarettes. Every so often, all three turned at once to look at her. "The cool one makes me nervous," she said, staring back. "He just stands there and says nothing, and his eyes seem to judge you."

"He respects you enormously," Bobby said. "He told me so."

"I like the shy one best. He acts the way I feel most of the time—just paralyzed with indecision."

"Arthur likes the shy one best, too."

"Shush," Arthur said.

"I like the enthusiastic one," Lota said. "He is only thirty, but they say he has already written a thousand poems. He works at the Museum of Modern Art."

"He reminds me of one of those starving dogs in Rio that follow you down the street, hoping for a piece of your sandwich," Elizabeth said. "The shy one really is painfully shy, isn't he?"

"Poor Jimmy had a nervous breakdown a few years ago," Bobby said. "He began having a long conversation with the Virgin Mary, who told him the world was coming to an end. He might still be having it. We're not sure. You poets are very delicate—I finally understand that. But Arthur helped him through those dark days, didn't you?"

"Not the time, my sweet."

SINCE SHE'D ARRIVED in the States, Elizabeth's clock had been completely off. They'd stepped onto American soil the last day of March; here it was July, and she still bolted awake before five. Lota lay comatose with the white sheets twisted around her caramel legs. Elizabeth slipped out into the morning, where pale yellow light had begun to seep above the ocean. The beach at Southampton was as wide and white as Copacabana's, but not a single soul was kicking a soccer ball. All that good sand going to waste. After yesterday's party, with everyone treating her as though she'd gone to Hollywood and come back a star, she appreciated the stillness, just the soft light and the dawn waves and the shorebirds with scissoring legs.

Five years away; it had passed so quickly. She'd been excited to return to the States, only to find herself taken aback by the whole bloated enterprise. As much pleasure as Elizabeth took in seeing all her old friends, in their uniquely open American spirit, and in speaking her native tongue to an audience that caught her references and tones, the banter and the martinis and the glamorous crowds had all begun to feel like hardly more than a glittering surface. There was no real *texture* here.

She and Lota lived on an isolated mountaintop, yet nearly every morning some grizzled little man pushed his cart up the extremely steep, rutted hill to deliver water or canisters of gas, or to pick up the trash or sharpen the knives and hatchets. Each made a different sound to identify himself: The gasman rattled a chain, the trashman honked a horn that mimicked a cow, the knife sharpener blew an extremely shrill police whistle that could wake the dead. Then Elizabeth would go running out into the road to catch him. At first she'd wondered, *How on earth can a country even function like this?* And now—well, she couldn't imagine living without it. Cal had once told her that on rare occasions he entered a heightened state in which all experience felt as though it were being filtered through poetry, that it had actually *become* poetry. That was Brazil.

The day Elizabeth learned of the Pulitzer, Lota had gone to the market and she'd spent the morning in her studio, working on a poem that for months she'd been unable to break the back of. That was what she termed the moment when all the juggling and back-and-forth of words and form fell miraculously into place. Though the poem might still be rough, at last she understood how to push the work to the final stage.

Last night another big one fell, she'd written. *It splattered like an egg of fire / against the cliff behind the house.*

Every June on Saint John's Day, the villagers who lived near Samambaia released fire balloons into the evening sky, contraptions of sticks and colored paper and kerosene. From the terrace, she and Lota watched the softly glowing balloons ascend into the night. Some of them were caught by mountain drafts and whisked upward, and every so often, one was dashed against the rocks and burst into flame, terrifying the animals there, the owls and rabbits and, once, an armadillo she saw scurrying away from the conflagration. As beautiful as the balloons were, she didn't understand how the villagers managed to avoid burning down the whole mountainside. She'd been working with the fire balloons as the poem's central image, draft after draft, and though most of the important pieces were on the page, the whole contraption had yet to become airborne. This particular morning was not a bad workday, nor did she break the poem's back. Then it was time to put writing aside and attend to the needs of the household.

In a bright yellow flannel suit with matching socks, the cook's daughter Maria Elizabeth was crawling around on the kitchen floor unattended. Elizabeth picked up her namesake and lightly nipped her two fat cheeks. The child, called Bettchy, was more or less her goddaughter, except that Elizabeth was a non-Catholic heretic and therefore could not officially be named her godmother. Not quite two, Bettchy was so cheerful that her own father had asked if something was wrong with her, as if only an idiot child might find cause to smile so much. Elizabeth balanced the child on her hip as she began preparations for lunch, while the plump starfish hands grasped at everything. Elizabeth saw that Bettchy's mother Maria was out on the terrace, painting. Their cook had turned into quite an impressive primitivist—her paintings on tin sheets and cardboard and plywood scraps, of saints, mostly, and flowers and churches, and sometimes all three in one frame, leaned against walls throughout the house—but in the fever of artistic creation, the woman had basically abandoned her domestic duties, as well as her maternal ones. Elizabeth had taken over the cooking and most of the mothering. These days she hardly needed her own child when there were so many extras crawling around. Now that Helena was done, Elizabeth's next translation project would most definitely be Dr. Spock. Maria didn't have the faintest idea what to do with a child. All day long it was *no, no, no*, and a double slap on the hand or the behind.

When Elizabeth answered the telephone, the connection was so full of hisses and crackles she didn't register at first that the other party was speaking in English.

"Please, is this Miss Bishop?"

"Yes?" she shouted. "Hello?" Bettchy wriggled insistently until Elizabeth let her out of her arms.

"I'm calling from *O Globo*," bellowed the caller, a youth by his voice. "Can you tell me your reaction to the Pulitzer Prize?"

"My reaction? Bettchy, *vem cá*! Well, I think it's a fine prize."

There was a silence; perhaps the connection had been lost. "Dona Elizabeechy," the reporter shrieked, "do you know you've won the Pulitzer Prize?"

Outside, afternoon clouds were gathering over the mountains. The waterfall was gushing. They'd have another night of terrific storms. "Well, thank you for calling," she said.

"Don't you hear me?" he shouted. "O Premio Pulitzer! You've won!"

For some moments, she could not think of a proper or polite response. "Are you sure there's not some mistake?"

"It is no mistake. You have won the prize. Would you like to share your thoughts?"

"Well, then," she said, "thank you very much for calling."

"But don't you understand what I'm saying?"

"Yes, and I thank you again."

Elizabeth returned the phone to its cradle and reached down to remove a boning knife from Bettchy's hand. Fortunately, some weeks had passed since the knife sharpener had pushed his cart up the hill. She drifted out to the terrace, where Sammy clucked sharply at her from inside his cage. He'd not yet forgiven her for leaving him out in the rain the previous night. In the morning, he'd stood frozen stiff, his bill held vertically, until she'd coaxed him back to life with a banana.

"It seems I've just won a prize," she told Maria in a daze.

Maria clapped her hands in excitement. "How much did you win?"

"It's not the lottery. It's . . ." Elizabeth turned and passed quickly through the house, as if propelled. In the street, she came to a stop. A donkey tied to a fence post, with bundles of kindling strapped to his back, turned his dewy brown eyes on her. No other human being was in sight.

A drop of rain fell upon her cheek. Elizabeth put her hands to her face and looked into the cloudy sky, as if there lay the origin of her gathering euphoria. But what importance could the Pulitzer Prize possibly have when you lived at the end of the earth, with children, toucans, and donkeys as your primary company? Half in a dream, she went stumbling down the road, grinning like a deranged person. Wasn't there someone, somewhere, she could tell?

She missed Cal profoundly. He would know what to make of this news. He'd won the prize himself; he'd told her of his mixed emotions, the joy coupled with the skepticism. No one understood her better as a poet or had more sympathy for her struggle to produce. Yes, she did struggle, but she wasn't entirely an impostor. Since finishing the translation of Helena, she'd been writing poetry again, and regularly, not in her typical fits and starts. Even Lota was pleased.

At last, Lota's friends would have proof that she was not a fake, she was not a mere hanger-on.

Half a mile down the hill, she came to the house where Mary was living. She called out but received no answer. Most likely Mary had accompanied Lota to the market, then they'd gone on to other business. You'd have thought the woman might have shifted focus after Lota broke her heart, or tried to build something new. But no, here she was again at Samambaia, at Lota's beck and call. Funny how Lota had fixed that.

The rain began to pour, the daily deluge. Trapped for the time being,

Elizabeth entered the house. On the kitchen counter lay a package of American cookies, horrible chocolate things with white crème centers. She would have killed for a glass of wine. Didn't she deserve at least one celebratory toast? But of course the Antabuse would wrench her body inside out, so she'd have to make do. She poured a glass of milk instead. She made a silent toast to Cal and ate three of Mary's Oreos.

WHEN ELIZABETH RETURNED from her walk on the beach, she found Arthur, Bobby, and Lota at the breakfast table, all three in silk pajamas. The men wore pale rose and blue; Lota was queenly in maroon. Lota settled Elizabeth into a seat, placed a cup of coffee before her, and began to prepare toast and eggs while Arthur and Bobby looked on in amazement.

"It's a very, very beautiful thing to see, the way you tend to Elizabeth," Bobby said, then turned to Arthur. "Why don't you treat me like that?"

"Would you like some toast, light of my life?"

"I would love some."

Arthur crossed the kitchen. Moments later, a slice of toast came sailing across the room and bounced off Bobby's plate.

"You boys," Lota said, and drew them both into an embrace.

"Frank has already called twice this morning," Arthur informed Elizabeth. "He rudely woke me out of a very pleasant dream. He wants to know if he can come again today to worship at your feet."

Elizabeth sipped her coffee. "I think we've had enough of Frank O'Hara."

"Do you think Arthur and Bobby are all right?" she asked Lota. They were playing gin rummy on the train back to the city.

"They seem to be, now that they are back together."

"Yes, but just because Arthur has come back to Bobby doesn't mean they are all right. So Jimmy Schuyler is the one Arthur was in love with for so long?"

"The shy poet you like," Lota said. "They were having an affair for five years. Bobby told me last night the whole story. Arthur broke off with the shy one, Schuyler, and now has come home with Bobby. Fairfield Porter has a wife, but he is in love with Schuyler. But Schuyler is now in love with Button."

"Button!"

"He is a painter."

"And is no one fond of Zipper?"

"We must see Fairfield Porter's portrait of Schuyler. Even Bobby says it is exceptional."

"How on earth do they all manage it?"

"Boys will be boys."

"And I thought little old Mary made our lives complicated."

Lota hooked her stocking foot around Elizabeth's calf. "*That*, my heart, would be taking the mountain to the molehill."

THERE WAS SO much Brazilians could learn here, Lota thought as she watched the stream of pedestrians going past the café. Her countrymen were like a bunch of cocks in a farmyard, all competing to crow the loudest while secretly believing themselves lowest in the pecking order. But look at these Americans. Look at how well put together their clothes were, the hats at flirtatious angles and the bright neckties, and how they walked, facing forward with confidence and purpose and smiling! They did not question whether or not they deserved a place at the banquet; they simply took a seat and ate their fill. Even the women. Especially the women.

Lota smoked and watched the American women go by while the conversation continued behind her.

I hope you don't mind my inviting myself along, Elizabeth was saying. But a boat trip down the Amazon! I can't help myself. I've wanted to go forever.

It is not important, Rosinha said. Though you know I will be responsible for my nephew Manuel. The trip is for his fifteenth birthday.

That will be half the pleasure, Elizabeth said. Adolescents always gravitate toward me. Maybe because I'm just as awkward and uncertain as they are.

Lota nearly turned and said, *Are you deaf to Rosinha's hesitation?* It was funny—in Brazil, all Elizabeth could do was complain about the country's barbarity, and now, at last in a civilized land, she spoke incessantly about Brazil.

Enough, Lota said, banging her hand on the table. Let's leave Brazil for Brazil. I've forgotten what it is like to be in a real city. Rosinha, I'm so glad you were able to meet us here. What should we do first? Shall we go to the UN and have Candido give us a preview of his murals? Or first to the museum, to visit Frank O'Hara?

Or, she thought, might they go on another foray altogether, one she did not want to mention quite yet while Elizabeth was listening, to Central Park? Lota wanted to study its plan and flow, all the park's details, the light fixtures, sidewalks, plantings, buildings, garden railings—how Olmsted, in a context of egalitarianism, had made all of them work together. Now that the house was nearing completion, Lota's mind had begun turning seriously to another project. What had begun as a daydream of transforming the *aterro* into one of the world's great city parks was taking on the momentum of a new obsession. She had already spoken to her architect friends Sergio and Affonso and mentioned the possibility in passing to Burle Marx, to gauge his interest in designing the gardens. Once she had explained her vision of a democratic park, with beaches and playgrounds and theatre and art available to all peoples and social classes of Rio, they too had caught her fire. Now it was only a matter of getting the official stamp, which was not such a leap from reality as Elizabeth would undoubtedly believe. Less than a year after Carlos had been forced to flee the country—even after Vargas's death, he had continued to fight the enemies of a democratic Brazil, at great danger to himself—he had returned in triumph. Thousands had greeted his plane when it touched down in Rio, welcoming him back to power. All depended on how he built upon that power—Lota had little doubt he would soon enough be in a position to hand the *aterro* over to her.

I'm afraid I can't join you, Elizabeth said. I have to get back to the publisher's. They showed me the cover design for Helena this morning, and I nearly had a stroke. It was completely black!

Black? cried Rosinha. Do they think it is a book about death?

They must be insane, Lota said, but she felt more pleasure than outrage. Five years ago, her little woman of *bom desenho* would not have understood the malevolence of a black book cover. She had acquired an even finer eye, and for that Lota felt she must take some credit.

We'll see if they put up a fight. Though I really think they'll respect my opinion. I never imagined I'd say this, but I've almost enjoyed working with my publisher.

They recognize what you are, Lota said proudly. It is long past time you are finally being appreciated. Those monkeys in Brazil have no idea what to make of you. They'd rather eat bananas than see the treasure under their noses.

Please, Lota, Elizabeth objected, but the expression on her face, Lota saw, glowed with the praise. She often worried that Elizabeth was wasting away in Samambaia, with no one but Lota to keep her mind sharp. You could not sequester a genius so far away from the rest of the world. Maybe they were both wasting away there. On this trip, Lota had begun to think that they might move back to New York. Just for a time, until work on the park could be launched for real.

Rosinha, Elizabeth said, tonight we're having dinner with some dear friends of mine. Can you join us?

Yes, you must meet Elizabeth's poet friends, very nice. Not Robert Lowell, though. He was a great disappointment.

Rosinha demurred, then agreed to dine with them after the invitation had been repeated three times. Her manners were faultless.

Well, I'm off, Elizabeth said. Keep Lota out of trouble, would you please, Rosinha?

And then she entered the passing flow of humanity. Watching her

slender back recede down the block and finally disappear, Lota felt a
sweetness as exquisite as heartbreak. There were moments with Elizabeth such as this, more and more frequent, when Lota was possessed
not only by love's joy but by its rawness, its *dor*. Elizabeth's gait was not
like that of the other New Yorkers. She walked away like a child doing
her best to be brave.

Lota turned to Rosinha with excitement and a desire for mischief.
Let's go to Central Park, she said. I must talk with you about an idea
I have.

THEY SPOKE, at first, of the prize.

"I still think Randall Jarrell should have won," Elizabeth said. "His
book is certainly more fully realized than mine. The Pulitzer has probably never been awarded for such a paltry amount of work."

"It was awarded to you," Cal said, "and it was well deserved."

He sat at the head of the canoe, his back fine and straight, speaking to her over his shoulder while he pulled them along with strong,
even strokes of his paddle. She hardly dipped her own into the water at
all. Rather untidy and in need of a haircut, Cal was still exceptionally
handsome in that turn-of-the-century way she was drawn to. Women of
her mother's generation, Elizabeth felt certain, would have found him
irresistible. She and Lota had arrived from the train station not an hour
ago to find their hosts in the midst of a domestic crisis. "We're at war
with the nanny," Lizzie had said wearily as she greeted their taxi in the
drive, the screams of baby Harriet carrying from an open window, "but
we're lost without her." Inside, Cal had deposited the inconsolable child
in Lizzie's arms and turned his attention upon Elizabeth. That face again,
alive with the pleasure of your company yet insistent upon your absolute
attention—nothing less than total surrender would suffice. Before they'd
even gotten properly indoors, he had pulled her out the back toward the
shore, where a canoe lay in the grass. "Go on," Lota had said in Portuguese. "I'll help here." It was obvious she preferred to avoid Cal.

The slanted afternoon sun on the water's mercury, the forested landscape, ripples of surfacing fish, birdcalls here and there—it was a recipe for heaven. Cal propelled them toward the northeast, in the direction of Nova Scotia. The place of Elizabeth's childhood was so near it exerted a happy magnetism upon her. To sit in a canoe with Cal, surrounded by this northern, waning peacefulness, so different from Samambaia's, was precisely what she'd journeyed back to find, not the glitter of New York.

"The prize feels deserved and undeserved at the same time. I write so very little." She had to laugh at herself. "I must have said that to you a hundred thousand times. How many poems are you writing these days, in a good year? Ten, twenty?"

"Typically more. You just have to learn how to harness your mania."

"My mania, if I have any, sends me straight to the kitchen to bake. Which is better than straight to a bottle of gin, as it used to. As you know, a good year for me means that I finish one poem, maybe two. Of course, I've always got a dozen in the works."

"Waiting for the right word, no doubt. You of the twenty-year poem."

"That's right. I've got so many that simply require finishing, but I can't *finish*."

"What you do finish is perfection, and that exactitude is one reason you won. Everyone else sees it, even if you can't."

With anyone other than Cal, she might have dismissed the compliment outright. She'd never been able to speak about these things so openly, partially for want of trust and partially because she found discussing the subject as embarrassing as jointly examining a pile of one's undergarments. Yet it had always been easy with Cal, from the first instant. He had won the Pulitzer years earlier, and he was far more productive and acclaimed than she, but Elizabeth had never felt she had to defer to him or hide an opinion, even if it was in opposition to his. They could talk for hours on subjects that Lota would never have the patience for in a million years. Only with this man could Elizabeth appraise her work and her peculiarities related to the solitary craft of writing—even appraise, she might go so far as to say, *herself*—with a clarity and an honesty that never ceased to gratify her. This was the primary thing, in Brazil, she still hungered for.

"You have no idea how much I've missed plain talk with you," she said. "There's the work, and then there's all the fuss about the work. Most everyone is so deeply invested in the fuss. You should have seen Frank O'Hara kissing my arm."

"The boy admires you, that's all. As *I* do. The draft you showed me last month, I've been carrying it around in my pocket ever since. I can't get those fire balloons out of my head. The short lines make me want to change everything about how I write. And the final image is arresting. Those animals!"

"All my poems end with an animal," she cried, and splashed him with her paddle.

A great blue heron lifted off and glided along the shoreline. She kept her eyes upon the graceful bird until it alighted in a tree ahead and folded its wings.

"Lota thinks it's a sign of moral weakness that I produce so little. She thinks all I have to do is sit at my desk and poems will flower from my fingertips."

"Yes, she is a bit domineering," Cal said, then caught himself. "But it's obvious your welfare is her main concern. She is completely devoted, anyone can see. It's a great solace to me that you have her. You are lucky, Elizabeth, to have finally found a place in Brazil where you can be at peace."

"I am at peace, you're right. But I'm still not sure where I belong."

Right before they'd left for New York, a dinner party on the terrace at Samambaia had concluded with the most maddening conversation. In the moonlight, Elizabeth had argued with two of Brazil's supposed foremost intellectuals; she'd had to insist repeatedly that Edmund Wilson and *not* Henry Miller was the better representative of U.S. letters, and that Dreiser was not completely ignored but Henry James was far superior. Defending Henry James, for God's sake! The two men had looked just like Sammy the toucan when he became fixated on a shiny button—they had not really seen or listened. After she'd heatedly made her case, they had merely reiterated their unaltered opinions. They had no interest in ideas other than their own. Stifled into silence by these bombastic people, she'd looked forward to New York, imagining the many vibrant conversations she would have there with investigative minds.

But once she and Lota had settled into their East Side apartment, it was really no different. Mary McCarthy had rung to invite them to a party. Flattered by the invitation, Elizabeth had arrived to find a group of America's supposed foremost intellectuals seated on Hannah Arendt's living-room floor, discussing, of all things, how to read a line of verse. She'd soon suspected that her reception into this inner circle had almost everything to do with the Pulitzer Prize and very little to do with her. As the group had strayed further and further into abstractions about poetry and truth, Elizabeth realized that she'd traveled thousands of miles to sit with another bunch of bombastic people enthralled by their own words. From another continent beckoned the room where she and Lota might curl up among the bedclothes and talk of Trollope and compost late into the night.

More unfortunate was that Lota, at the party, had shown herself at her worst. Insecure among all the big names, she'd started marching about, giving orders to people and name-dropping. Mary McCarthy had watched her as if she were studying the lines of an anatomical dissection.

Elizabeth dipped her oar into the water. "When do you think you'll come see Brazil for yourself?" she asked Cal.

"Lizzie and I would both love to."

"Please say you will, and *soon*. Then I can tell Mary McCarthy we're all booked up."

"Is she threatening to visit?"

"Imminently. I think she fell in love with Carlos Lacerda while he was exiled here. Every time I see her, I can't help thinking of the day Lota and I were having lunch on the terrace and the gardener came racing up to tell us a snake was eating baby birds out of a nest in a tree. We all went running to look, and there it was, with its long, green reptilian tail hanging out of the bird's nest, swallowing the baby birds with no pity whatsoever."

Cal had swiveled around on his seat, the paddle held across his lap, watching her with a smile and those brilliant, penetrating eyes. The canoe rocked softly in the breeze. Elizabeth had seen this expression on countless occasions, but now, for no good reason, it made her shy, and she nattered on.

"Anyway, you have to come. Brazil overwhelms you with sights and smells and sounds. You become a voluptuary by necessity. The density of experience has to be embraced. Everything in the States is so *sanitized* in comparison. I don't think there's ever been a country so filthy rich and so hideously uncomfortable at the same time. Though of course in Brazil there's the total anarchy and political instability. Every time we have a little revolution, Lota has a nervous breakdown and some of our friends have to flee the country."

"You have a special opportunity to use what you are living through," Cal said reverently.

"If you mean the politics, I'm not that kind of poet. Brazilian politics are like a school playground. One boy's a bully, one's a bookworm, one's a miner's son, one's an aristocrat's, all fighting over a game of marbles and thinking they're deciding the fate of the world. I'm not like you—I can't turn everything into poetry."

She spoke with bitterness, thinking of the politicians responsible for so much of the country's, and Lota's, anguish. Yet when Cal turned abruptly and resumed paddling, she worried she might have offended him.

"I am trying to write about Brazil," she went on, "but I also don't want to become the American poet who writes about Brazil, about exotica. They always try to pigeonhole you. I can't stand it when they say I'm one of the best living *women* poets." The words were hardly out of her mouth before she remembered that it was in fact Cal who'd written precisely that about her first book, before they'd really known each other.

"If you want to talk pigeonholing, you're in a canoe with one of the best living crazy poets."

"Who cares what labels they give us? Lota says it's not others who categorize us. We categorize ourselves."

"Yes, I imagine she would." He laughed in a way that was not terribly kind. "I've missed our conversations, too, Elizabeth. I always feel they transform my work. Lately, I've wanted to change everything, to push my poetry to a much more personal place."

"Please don't. You know I detest that sort of thing. It's unhealthy."

"You think so?"

"Absolutely. Best saved for your journal."

He turned again to face her directly and spoke with great gentleness. "Yet every time you hint at the personal, as rare as it is, I feel almost unbearably moved. Reticence is your virtue, but it's also your limitation. You might risk more yourself, go out on a limb."

"That limb will snap," she said.

"I don't think so. But even if it did, would that be so terrible?"

For some minutes, the canoe drifted. Elizabeth broke from his look to gaze across the water, remembering the August day years earlier when the two of them had spent a magical afternoon on the Maine shore not far from here. She'd gone there for the summer, like an ascetic in retreat from worldly attachment. Cal and his girlfriend had come to visit; then Elizabeth had heard the two of them fighting in their room, and the girlfriend had left early. To Elizabeth's great pleasure, Cal had stayed. They'd waded into the cold water, skipped stones, talked and talked and talked. They were twin souls, she had thought that day, perfectly aligned. Cal had stood against a tree and posed as Saint Sebastian, a stick tucked beneath his arm like an arrow piercing his breast. He'd hoped to make her laugh and to charm her, and she'd drunk up every moment.

Now she turned her gaze to his. "Since I've been so far away, Cal, I've come to rely on you more than ever. There have been so many times I've wished you were there. You've no idea how much I count on you and admire you, how lucky I feel to know you. I think of you every day of my life."

AND YET HE'D been unspeakably rude to Lota. At the beginning of the summer, Cal and Lizzie were in New York and invited Elizabeth and Lota to dinner. Elizabeth was in a high mood. She'd spent the previous weeks at the publisher's making final revisions to Helena. Under most circumstances, she'd rather have walked on live coals than deal with a single soul in the publishing world, but her editor was so conscientious and respectful that she had truly begun looking forward to their exchanges. The moment they entered the supper club, however, Lota's hackles were raised. One look at the Cuban band's bongo drums and the colorful ruffles on their arms, and she said, "Do we expect Carmen Miranda to perform next with bananas on her head?" To Elizabeth, she added disparagingly, "You people," lumping her in with all the rest who would put exotic foreigners on display along with the parrots and the big cats.

Part of it was show meant for Cal, Elizabeth knew, by whom Lota had been immediately starstruck. Coquettishly, she attempted to engage him a number of times across their table, but he kept pointing to his ear and shaking his head to indicate that the music was too loud to allow conversation. Then he returned his attention to Elizabeth beside him, an arm across the back of her chair lightly touching the skin at the nape of her neck. She would have been embarrassed by his behavior if she hadn't been so concerned about his drinking. He repeatedly ordered a new highball before he'd finished half of the one in his hand, and he spoke so rapidly, on such a variety of topics, that she caught only a smattering of words. It was like trying to keep up with a conversation in Portuguese.

After the meal, Lota came around the table and invited him to dance, at her most charming and playful, and he surprised them both by brushing her hand roughly off his shoulder. Then he pulled Elizabeth from her seat and onto the dance floor, where he gripped her shoulders and drew her against his chest, shockingly planting a gin-flavored kiss on her mouth. He had drunk far too much, of course, and didn't have any idea what he was doing. Fortunately, Lizzie was on the phone with the babysitter and saw none of this. Lota became understandably furious, and the final half hour of the evening was exceedingly disagreeable.

IN THE EVENING, after they'd brought in the canoe, Cal suggested a driving tour along the coast. In the car, Lota appeared bent on making him pay.

"All the trees look as though they are planted in rows," she said.

"It's not tropical here," Elizabeth said. "Maine has a different type of forest."

"An artificial forest?"

"That's the turn to Stonington," Cal remarked. Stonington was where they'd passed that long-ago day together.

"And you call this a beach? It's only rocks. Where's the sand?"

"It's not really a beach, Lota. This is a rugged coastline."

"In Brazil, a beach has miles of white sand."

"Parts of Nova Scotia are like this," Elizabeth said wistfully. "Even the air feels the same. We're very close, you know."

Lota at last relinquished a smile. "I would like to go there, *minha pombinha*. Can we drive there now?"

"We're not quite *that* close. But one day I would like to take you there."

Night had fallen by the time they returned to the house. Not the swift, deep, black curtain of Samambaia, but a pale, soft firmament in which only the brightest stars were suspended. As Lota went ahead, Elizabeth reached for Cal's arm to have a private word with him on the porch. He turned back upon her with that startling intensity.

"Cal, can you please apologize to Lota? She's still very upset by what happened in New York."

"Anything you want, dearest. I was awful, I know." Such a large man, he continued staring down at her, standing too near, crowding her so that Elizabeth thought she would be forced back down the steps. Then a noise at the side of the house drew Cal's attention, and he moved to the railing to investigate. He remained there, very still, until at last Elizabeth went to his side. In the darkness, she began to make out an animal rooting around in the trash bin. A bushy tail, held straight upward. A raccoon or, no, a skunk!

At her laugh, the animal raised its striped head and stared back at them, unafraid. "A skunk in the trash," Elizabeth said. "Who cares about politics or confessions when all you need is right there? Why don't you do something with that skunk?"

"Yes, you're right." Cal was amused, but she could see she'd piqued his interest. "Why don't I?"

"He is a pain in the ass," Lota said, when Elizabeth joined her in their bed. She was filing her nails, peering through black eyeglasses on the tip of her nose.

"Please, Lota, they can hear you." She nestled against her lover's solid warmth, laying her head in Lota's lap. "Something is different about him."

"Yes, he is brilliant, there's no doubt, and he's handsome, and that's why all you women put up with his *merde*."

"That's exactly what I think about Carlos!" Lota gave her a slap on the rump. "But that's not what I mean. A few things he's said today, and a way he's looked at me, they worry me. Or maybe I'm imagining it. I used to have this same feeling with my mother, this *instinct*, when she was growing unwell, and I always wanted to run in the other direction."

"Then perhaps you should run."

"But I love him, Lota."

Lota caressed Elizabeth's face. "I know you do. You are not heartless like me. You are kind, and that is why I will not give him a kick in the tail."

As Lota slept, Elizabeth's concern for Cal kept her awake. She had not mentioned her true suspicion, that somehow she was to blame. It was beyond coincidence; on a number of occasions, seeing her had seemed to trigger the onset of Cal's illness. Yet she would not stay away from him. That summer in Stonington, she'd been bereft. The day with Cal had sustained her for months afterward.

A soft fluttering noise came from the shadows of the room, and two dark shapes emerged, moving back and forth across the wall. She thought she must be imagining them, or dreaming, they were almost too rapid to be real. Yet there they were again, two little bats or two strange nocturnal lizards, pursuing one another from one side of the room to the other. She reached to turn on the light. Electricity at her fingertips—what wonderful science.

Lota groaned and covered her eyes. "Elizabeth, what is the emergency?"

Standing on the mattress, Elizabeth gazed at the ceiling. Motionless, each dark shape was larger than her hand, flat and nearly invisible against the wooden planks. Two giant, sooty moths, with a delicate mottled pattern.

Lota saw them and cried, "Get those out of here!"

"It's only moths. They're beautiful."

"A black moth in the house is not good," Lota said fearfully. "It means someone will die."

"Please, Lota, save that for Brazil. We're in the good old US of A now."

"Yes, I forgot, where even the wild trees are planted in rows."

"MARY MCCARTHY WAS telling me that you are simply transformed," Lizzie said. "And she's right! Look at you. You're so thin and radiant."

"I'm down to 115 pounds," Elizabeth admitted. "It's paradise there. I don't know what I've done to deserve it."

"You have to stop saying that," Cal said, passing through the room with Harriet in his arms. "You deserve everything you have."

During dinner, they'd been unable to pursue any line of conversation for long. Lizzie and Cal had taken turns with the crying child while the other sat at the table. Cal was drinking prodigious amounts, though possibly, when you yourself were off the sauce, any amount appeared prodigious. Now he'd taken little Harriet and was making laps around the house. It was the first moment Elizabeth had seen Lizzie, an intelligent woman frazzled by motherhood, relax and speak her mind.

"On the subject of Mary McCarthy," Elizabeth said, "do you find her as much a puzzle as I do? She is of such penetrating intellect, every time I see her I find myself drawn in and opening up. But even as I'm doing it, I have the feeling she's looking for ways to exploit me. Still, I can't help but admire her accomplishments. Do you think that's what women with any brains have to do to succeed?"

"Maybe that's our only recourse," Lizzie said, "to eat our own."

"In my opinion," Lota said, "you must refuse to be eaten. By men or women, it doesn't matter. They will all try. Put up your spines so they choke on you. Every time I have wanted to do anything, others have tried to stop me. The resistance I encountered while building my house was unbelievable."

"Lizzie, you have to see Lota's house. I was telling Cal today that you both must come visit. It's really quite fantastic."

"We are almost finished," Lota said proudly. "We are finally building the front entrance, and we are putting glass in all the holes. The master architect Neutra himself is coming to visit. Even he has heard of my house."

"Right before we left, Lota sat like a queen in a big armchair, directing an army of workers to build a stone fireplace," Elizabeth said. How lucky she was to be witness to such creativity and passion; what a privilege to live alongside a force of nature. Of the two of them, Lota was the true creator—why wasn't there a prize for that? "Every weekend, at least thirty people come up the hill in a bus, most of them unannounced. There are dogs and cats everywhere, and the number of children seems to multiply by the month. Several families all dump their children on us for the summer. I feel like a mother to twenty orphans. And I've never been so happy."

"I don't know how to thank you for visiting us," Lizzie said. "You have no idea what a pleasure it is to have a conversation with adults."

Cal continued his revolutions through the room, looking increasingly unhappy and excluded. The next time he passed through, Elizabeth held out her arms for the child. Cal complied, and within moments, Harriet stopped wailing. Elizabeth put her nose to the baby's forehead and inhaled; she felt she could hold the warm weight of her until dawn.

"You're a natural," Lizzie said.

"As I said, I get a lot of practice at Samambaia. The cook even named her little girl after me, though I have to say the child looks more like the handyman than like her husband. She had a terrible crush on the handyman for a while."

All three of Elizabeth's companions watched her with the child, each with a different variety of admiration. After a time, Harriet fell asleep.

"It's a miracle," Cal said. "Let's get her to bed, Lizzie."

"Please let me keep her for a while. It's no trouble."

"If we wake her later, we'll all pay the price," Lizzie said.

Once Lizzie had taken Harriet upstairs, Elizabeth's arms remained cradling the absent child. Cal came out of the kitchen with a pot of coffee and made a show of serving Lota.

"How do you drink this pool of coffee?" Lota complained, looking deeply into her coffee cup as though she were reading the future there. "It has no flavor, no charge."

"Lota," said Elizabeth, "I beg of you."

"In Brazil, we get more in a thimble of coffee than you get in this pool of coffee. I'll show you real coffee." She stood and passed into the kitchen, as if through the gates of Rome.

Cal instantly leapt up and took Elizabeth's hand to draw her out of the house. He whispered, "There's something I want to show you." She did not resist. They went down the grassy slope and to the end of a pier, where the water lay twinkling romantically in the moonlight. Before them, Elizabeth could hear gentle laps and splashes, while behind, Lizzie was again singing to Harriet. Cal breathed audibly through his nose.

But he did not speak. He looked away, across the lake, and Elizabeth followed his gaze, attempting to guess what he'd intended to show her. Her eye could find nothing extraordinary.

At last she said, "Cal, shall we go back in?"

Abruptly he turned, and Elizabeth made a little cry of surprise. "I'm going to come to Brazil, just as you said. Not with Lizzie and Harriet. I'll come alone. What you told me today, the sounds and textures, I have to see it for myself. It sounds fantastic."

"Cal, you know I want you to come visit, but Brazil is not the sort of place to be alone. I feel very strongly about that. People like you and I, we need someone to help us keep our feet on the ground. You must bring Lizzie and Harriet. There's room for all of you at Samambaia."

His gaze was deeply admiring; at the same time, he didn't see or hear her at all. That was the curse alongside the gift of his intimacy. At times, she felt like no more than a character moved here and there in the brilliant diorama of his making. Yet when he spoke again, it was with extreme tenderness.

"You remember our day in Stonington?"

"Yes, of course I remember it. I remember every minute."

"You told me then you were the loneliest person ever to have lived. You told me that should be written as your epitaph."

"I suppose it felt true at the time. It's fortunate that things can change so greatly. I don't feel at all lonely now. But it took a very long time. It isn't easy to allow yourself to feel loved. We both *are*, Cal. We are both very fortunate."

"And that winter, there was the poetry reading at Bard," he went on. "We were riding together in a taxi afterwards, and I was so drunk my hands turned cold, like ice. I couldn't get them warm. You took my hands in yours. *You* were my anchor, *you* kept my feet on the ground, you—" He broke off.

"Cal, I think you may have had very much to drink tonight. Why don't we go inside?" She attempted lightheartedness. "I have to tell you sometime about the wonders of sobriety."

"I've been carrying your armadillo around in my pocket."

"Yes, so you said."

"Those fire balloons are fantastic! *O falling fire and piercing cry / and panic—*"

"Cal, stop," she cried. "Please don't quote me."

This feeling! A wild heap of fury was building inside her; it wanted to smash everything to bits. If she allowed him to, this man would absorb her, yet she remained staring into his eyes, unwilling to break away.

"There's something I have to confess to you, Elizabeth."

"You and your confessions!"

"Elizabeth, dearest of Elizabeths."

"Cal," she forced herself to say, "I'm not sure what you're trying to tell me, but I'm going to go inside the house now."

His face fell. He turned his back.

"Won't you come with me?"

That he would not respond pained her. She could not help a feeling of failure; she had failed to live up to his expectations of her. She was not the poet he thought. In a sense, it was against all her desire, yet Elizabeth left Cal and made her way through the dark to the house, where a light illuminated every window. Reaching the door, she turned to see him still looking away across the black water, his hands in his pockets. The temptation to return was nearly irresistible. She had not asked what it was he wanted to show her. He still had not told her what he could see that she was unable to see on her own.

ON THE SHIP, they brought twenty-six pieces of luggage, including, thanks to the glory of electricity, a new hi-fi—or *eee-fee*, as Lota called it—to play the records Elizabeth had not heard in five years, and two portraits in big gold frames that Aunt Grace had sent down from Nova Scotia, of her mother and Uncle Neddy as children. Even with its cast of characters constantly testing one's patience, shipboard life was as much to Elizabeth's liking as ever, though the boredom and monotony of the voyage nearly drove Lota mad. When she finished the last detective novel from the pile she'd stocked up on, Lota threw the book over the railing and into the sea with a howl of frustration.

In Rio, Cal's manuscript was waiting when they arrived.

For New Year's, they went to Rosinha's house in Cabo Frio, where they gorged themselves nearly beyond the limits of human endurance on platters of freshly caught shrimp and fish. Each morning Elizabeth took a long walk on the beach, collecting shells, and thought fondly of Luiz Cusi and his mirrors. All afternoon she swung in a hammock, the sounds of the surf lulling her, an unopened book in her hand, and thought of Manuel Bandeira and his preferred method of composing a poem. In the evenings she turned to Cal's manuscript. She hadn't been imagining it at all. Once they'd left Maine, he'd had another breakdown. Thankfully, he'd soon recovered his balance of mind. She read and reread his poems and formulated her response, not only to the work but also to his rather spectacular letter in which he apologized for his behavior in Maine and also confessed a long-unspoken desire, once upon a time, to have married her. The confession was not a complete surprise, but still shocking to see on the page. Also lovely, in its way.

And the poems! How did he do it? In spite of her appeals, he'd forged ahead and mined all varieties of personal experience—his own as well as his family's—to create something astonishing. That he could take such intimate information and derive so much larger meaning, elevate the material undeniably into the realm of art, was far beyond anything she could imagine herself capable of. His assurance never ceased to amaze her, even if, at times, her sympathies remained with those who'd become the unwitting subjects of the work.

Lota declared the poems masterful. It wasn't the *poetry* she had a problem with, she said, nibbling the nape of Elizabeth's neck.

Cal had written about the skunk after all. It was Elizabeth's favorite poem of the bunch, yet still she had to smile. He was so insistent on himself, on forcing the symbolism upon you, rather than letting the material breathe and live on its own. He'd dedicated the poem to her; the transformation in his work had been inspired, he claimed, by her armadillo fleeing from the fire of a Saint John's Day balloon. How beautiful the fire balloons were, he wrote, and how quickly they turned dangerous.

At night, Elizabeth put the poems aside and switched off the light. She left a candle burning at the bedside.

Since they'd returned to Brazil, their lovemaking had taken on a renewed urgency. Lota's hands reached for her and slowly began to stroke Elizabeth's skin, as acutely sensitive from the sun and the sea as if it were freshly made. Lota drew widening ellipses upon her back; her touch made Elizabeth feel lighter, weightless. The lightness turned to warmth, the warmth to fire. A gust of desire abruptly swept her up, took them both in a fierce ascent. She took hold of Lota in both fists, her cries smothered by Lota's kisses, until at last, descending, they returned softly to the earth.

*N*o Coffee Can Wake You

. . .

No coffee can wake you no coffee can wake you no coffee
No revolution can catch your attention
You are bored with us all. It is true we are boring.

No coffee can wwake you no coffee can wakeyou no coffee
    can wake you

                                        No coffee

·18·

THE DAY BEGAN with an argument, once again about the goddamn roads. The two men were waiting outside the Shack when Lota arrived, Enaldo Crava Peixoto, the new director of SURSAN, and his chief engineer. Enaldo wore a white linen suit and was cooling himself with a black fan. The engineer, whose name was Gilberto, paced back and forth and mopped the sweat from his dark, angry face.

Thank you for being so prompt, Lota said before he could open his mouth.

In fact, said the engineer, we have been waiting here boiling in this heat for nearly one hour.

Dear Gilberto, may I offer you some water? She pressed Enaldo's hand and kissed his talcumed cheek. Good morning, Enaldo.

Hello, Lota.

Please come inside and have a seat. She unlocked the Shack and opened windows to air out her workplace, already an oven even at this early hour.

Gilberto stood petulantly in the doorway with his arms crossed.

Please, Gilberto, do not remain angry with me. I work every night until one in the morning, you cannot expect me to arrive precisely at

7:00 am every day. I also might remind you that I carry out my duties as director of the *aterro*'s development without compensation of any kind, out of dedication to the governor and to the betterment of this marvelous city.

My commitment is no less—

Let's get to the reason I asked you here. For months, we have discussed this issue of the roads, and it was my understanding we had agreed that only two roads were to be constructed through the *aterro*. Yet Tuesday in *O Globo*, Gilberto was quoted as saying we knew very little about how the *aterro*'s space would be used, except that there would be *four* roads! Please help me understand.

Enaldo, leaning against a bookcase, said nothing. Gilberto at last took a seat and said, The plan for the *aterro*'s development was approved three years before your appointment. It clearly specifies four roads.

That plan, as far as I'm concerned, has as much significance to our work as a speck of shit left by a fly. Enaldo, perhaps in the few weeks since you've taken over the directorship of SURSAN and its myriad urbanization projects you have not had the opportunity to look at this plan? The agency you've inherited is full of myopic engineers and architects who are only looking for a way through a traffic problem. They do not see the larger picture and they want to turn Rio into cloverleafs and concrete highways. Isn't that how you hope to be described by history, Gilberto, as the men who turned Rio's waterfront into a stretch of concrete, from downtown all the way to Rio Sul?

The engineer glared but said nothing.

Still fanning himself, Enaldo offered his opinion. We must also consider the practicalities of modern urban life, Dona Lota. The city is growing rapidly, and the citizens of Rio do not want to sit in traffic all day. They require growth and progress.

So you plan to fill the city with underpasses smelling of urine? That raises another question for me. Why is it that men feel compelled to relieve themselves in public? Just this morning, I passed three men showing off their unpeeled bananas to the world. I suppose you are right. We are a nation of primitives and would do well to enter a modern century.

Both men laughed. Lota could always make them laugh with a little vulgarity. It was the sign she used to begin to outmaneuver them. Yet precisely then the conversation took a turn for the worse.

But is progress really the uncivilized notion that human beings are less important than machines? she asked lightly.

If a snake could smile, it would have looked like Gilberto as he spoke. I understand that in your advisory capacity you feel bound to express colorful opinions.

Advisory! Lota cried.

However—

I am not an advisor. I'm the director.

Instead of matching her emotion, Gilberto's voice grew softer, velvety, seductive. Why was it that when men smelled blood, they acted as if they wanted to make love to it? I've seen many political appointments come and go in my time at SURSAN, he said. I'm not sure why they are so interchangeable, I suppose it is a matter of expediency for the governor. I do not have a clear understanding of your own professional training, Dona Lota, though I understand you have tried your hand at painting. I am trained as an engineer. In my opinion, the problems presented by the *aterro* require an engineering solution.

Are you insinuating that I lack qualifications, you unimaginative little dwarf? As far as I'm concerned, you are merely a handyman. Your job is to turn the screwdriver.

Enaldo fanned himself more rapidly. Fury overcame Gilberto and made him impotent. He could not speak.

Is it because I am merely an expedient appointment by the governor, Lota went on, that I have assembled a team of the most talented and visionary men in Rio? Affonso Reidy and Sergio Bernardes are two of Brazil's foremost architects. Roberto Burle Marx is a master of landscape design, he is known throughout the world. I am here for the duration of this project, and you may as well get used to taking your orders from a woman. Your previous supervisor could not do so, and I ask you, where is he today?

The engineer stood, clenching his fists as if to restrain himself from striking them against an object. I bid you good day, Dona Lota, he said in a strangled voice, and departed.

It is very hot this morning, Enaldo said after a moment. It has affected all our tempers.

It is always hot here. I have grown used to it.

Ah, Lota. Tell me what you would propose.

I will not allow four roads.

Can you not compromise a little? You are making the men feel humiliated. They will keep opposing you.

Lota laughed. Humiliation builds character. Ask any woman.

Well, then. Enaldo kissed her cheek. Until later.

The members of her team had begun to arrive. Lota loved the morning best, the Shack turning into an industrious hive as everyone took up their work. She had hand-picked all her staff. Most, like her, worked until nearly midnight, for little or no money, because they believed passionately in the project.

Out the tiny window of her office, she could see a sweep of broken rock and rubble meeting the bay. For her, it was a simple leap of the imagination to envision trees, a beach, children white, brown, and black together in the playgrounds—a park not only beautiful but also serving and bringing joy to all the people of Rio. Every encounter with the small minds whose province it was to develop this park offered her another glimpse of how revolutionary such a vision might be. Every imaginative suggestion, every idea that did not have as its aim the sacrifice of humanity and beauty to practicality, was attacked; or worse, first the idea itself was attacked, and then the attack became personal. That was one reason Lota always scheduled her most difficult meeting of the day first. She often arrived late to keep them off balance and so maintain the upper hand. She was certain to emerge victorious and for the rest of the day feel invigorated and alive. Just as she did now.

Lota wasted no time putting in a call to Carlos. Or, rather, to the first in a series of assistants who formed the barricade between her and the governor. To how many underlings did she have to explain herself before she was allowed access to Carlos directly? His secretary had her own secretary, and the undersecretary had an assistant, and the under-undersecretary had a receptionist who was actually the sharpest of the bunch. Behind that line of defense, Carlos was working at his massive desk in Guanabara Palace. One had to enjoy the irony, and the occasional justice, history could deliver—to think of Carlos overseeing the state's business in what had once been the private home of the dictator Getulio Vargas. At last, someone passionate and honest to make things right.

Waiting on the line, Lota thought back to the day Carlos had sent for her immediately after his inauguration. She had been driven through the streets in a black sedan with the flag of Brazil fluttering at its hood. What would her father have thought of his unmarried, ugly daughter if he could have seen her at that moment, or later, when she and the newly elected governor had gone up in the palace helicopter and flown over the *aterro*, and Carlos had told her that *now* was the time, that *she* was the one who could create a park as memorable as Sugarloaf and Corcovado, and would she do it for him?

Back at the palace, they had celebrated and talked until four in the morning. Rio does not have enough water, Carlos told her, not enough schools, not enough sewage capacity, not enough roads, not even enough telephones! And certainly not enough money to meet one-tenth of the need. Sordid political practices and swindling have denied this poor city the proper infrastructure. It defies belief that it is still functioning. And everyone works to further his own interests instead of for the general good. Can you believe that last year our schools were so overcrowded we had to refuse admittance to over one hundred thousand children?

As always, Lota said, you are in a canoe, attacking a cruiser.

Carlos cried, Yes! Yes! Absolutely! and laughed heartily. And you are right beside me.

Sometimes she thought she might have married him.

Finally she was informed that Carlos would speak with her. Yesterday you wouldn't even take my calls! Lota cried before he could say hello. Today your secretary made me wait ten minutes. How many times are you going to piss me off before I really get pissed off?

And good morning to you, Carlos said, chuckling. He loved the game of their friendship as much as she. You must realize, dear Lota, that there are aspects of governing Rio state beyond the directorship of Flamengo Park. That is your job, not mine. Have you not read the newspapers? I thought perhaps you had called to congratulate me on my negotiation of the prison riot on Frei Caneca street. Or to offer advice on how I might answer the current proposal by my enemies in the legislature. Less than one year in office, and they are already trying to have me impeached.

No, I have not read the papers. I don't have time. Listen, Carlos, the engineers at SURSAN do everything to obstruct me. Enaldo was just here with his chief engineer, Gilberto Paixão, who was so obstreperous I was forced to suggest I might have him fired, just as I did Landim.

First, Landim resigned, I didn't fire him. And second, Enaldo has just had a heart attack, so please don't give him another one. He is a good administrator, and I need him to continue as secretary of works, in addition to directing SURSAN.

Every day we revisit the same issues. Three or four incompetent imbeciles are wasting all my time. I'm sending you the list of those I'd like you to replace as soon as possible.

Lota, I want you to work *with* SURSAN, not remake it. We're not going to fire everyone who doesn't agree with you. That is the strategy of despots like Vargas. Use your skills to draw people to your way of thinking. Now I must go. Today, I am proud to say, we are inaugurating two new primary schools. Then I will tour the Rebouças tunnel construction and the new water mains in the Rosinha favela.

All right, Carlos, you stick with that rubbish of sewage, water, and whatever. You think you will be remembered for that? When they find that toilets work, they are not going to remember you. Water and schooling are things every government has the duty to provide, especially yours. The one thing they will remember is that *you* made Flamengo Park.

Carlos laughed again, extremely pleased. And I have no doubt you will create something that will make people remember me kindly. You and I both detest mediocrity, Lota.

Yes, but if you continue being so difficult to reach, I'm going to have to start communicating with you by letter, and I promise you won't like the letters I write. Goodbye for now, dear friend.

IN THE AFTERNOON, Ethel Medeiros arrived to discuss the designs for the children's recreation spaces. Thank God there was a woman on the project to provide at least one moment's peace before Lota had to prepare herself for another battle. Today, Ethel was accompanied by the head of the mothers' association of Catete and Gloria. When they showed her the plans of the pond for model boats, the train and playgrounds, the puppet theatre, Lota wished she had a photograph of the mother's ecstatic face to show Enaldo. One look would banish any doubt.

SURSAN would have you run across four lanes of traffic of insane Rio drivers just to take your children to the playground, Lota said. But I promise I will not make you risk your lives.

Who is Sir San? the mother asked.

A wonderful aroma filled the Shack. Lota looked up to see Elizabeth! Among the hustle and bustle, she clutched a shopping bag before her with both hands, looking completely lost.

Cookie, what are you doing here?

You said you'd be home for lunch, but when you didn't come I decided to bring it to you.

I'm sorry, Cookie, I forgot the time! I am just meeting with a mother from Gloria who is very excited about our plans.

Elizabeth's face had that tight look, and she did not answer. Lota begged Ethel to continue the meeting and took Cookie by the arm. In her office, she swept the papers from the desk. Let's have a picnic right here.

I made you something special, Elizabeth said as she unwrapped the meal. You can hardly find meat anymore—or rice or sugar either, for that matter—but my butcher friend saved me some. Then of course you never know if the taxi or bus drivers are going to be on strike, so I wasn't sure I'd even be able to get here. Honestly, this country!

She watched while Lota ate. It is absolutely delicious, like everything you make.

Kylso called. We talked for a long time.

In the doorway, Lota's assistant was trying to catch her attention. Lota waved her away. The mention of her adopted son instantly soured her mood. I suppose he tried to bring you over to his cause.

No, not exactly.

Did he tell you he has now hired a lawyer? He is making very extravagant demands. I took him from nothing! I gave him education, surgeries so he could walk, every opportunity. Is it my fault he is ruining his life with too many children he cannot afford? Now he is suing me because he wants my money? I see no choice but to cut ties.

A series of expressions fluttered across Elizabeth's face: so many shades of sad! She spoke so softly Lota could hardly hear the words. Maybe he just wants a little of your attention.

Everyone wants my attention. I must answer to engineers who want four roads and students who want a restaurant on the waterfront and mothers who don't want to imperil their children's lives and admirers of Carmen Miranda who clamor for a memorial to that fruithead. It is enough to send me to the luna bin. But listen, Burle Marx showed me some preliminary plans of the gardens. How would you like to go to the Amazon with us to help collect some plants?

Nothing gave her as much pleasure as turning Cookie's sadness to joy. You know I would love that, she said. You know I dream of going there again, and with you this time. Then she asked, Do you think we'll be able to get away to Samambaia this weekend?

Of course. The weekends are sacred, just the two of us. I leave all this behind. I told you that.

Lota finished the meat pie. It was extraordinary. If only Elizabeth cared as much about her poetry as she did about her cooking. Still, since Lota had taken over the park's development, she was not the only one who had been productive. Elizabeth had written at least six or seven poems in the last year, three times her normal output. It was probably a good thing that Lota had been so busy; maybe all along she'd simply been getting in Elizabeth's way.

Though she wasn't crazy about that poem with the man who turned into a fish. It didn't make any sense.

Tell me of your morning, Cookie. Did you write?

Elizabeth did not answer immediately. This was a habit Lota still had not grown accustomed to. So much time might elapse between her question and Elizabeth's reply that Lota could not help but jump in to offer one herself. Today she remained patient, however, gripping her knees and waiting for Elizabeth's words.

I've been asked to write a book, Elizabeth said at last. One of those awful coffee-table books about exotic countries. They want to pay me ten thousand dollars.

Lota leapt to her feet, clasping Elizabeth to her and crying, Ten thousand dollars!

It's more money than I've ever made writing anything in my whole life.

And it's less than you deserve. But what is the book about?

Brazil, of course. The hilarious thing is that before they made the actual offer, they asked me if I'd ever been a communist. She laughed in a bitter way.

But what do you know about Brazil? You don't even know Portuguese.

That's not the point, Lota. I've certainly lived here long enough to know it's a hysterical country constantly on the verge of collapse.

She stared at Lota, who could not help but smile. She liked it when Elizabeth was roused to emotion.

I thought I might buy a house in Ouro Preto with the money.

Buy a house in Ouro Preto? Ten years together, and Elizabeth was still a complete mystery. Why buy a house hundreds of miles away in a town she'd visited only once or twice? For now, she gave Cookie a squeeze and said, I must run. I have a meeting with Brigadier General Gomes, who promises he will finally get a contract so Affonso can be paid. He has worked without a salary for nearly a year. I will see you tonight by seven thirty. That's wonderful news about the book. I'm very proud of you.

Lota's last appointment of the day was with a journalist, whom she took to task for describing her in a previous article as a chain-smoking friend of poets and artists, a woman who wore men's clothing to work. Gossip about the director was hardly constructive journalism and was a waste of space that might otherwise showcase the park itself. Instead of alienating the young reporter, however, she knew she could convert him. She took him on a tour of the *aterro*, and discovered that the construction of a pedestrian bridge had stalled because the supplier had failed to deliver the proper building materials. At that moment, Enaldo also appeared, and she ordered both the journalist of her father's newspaper and the director of SURSAN to climb into a dump truck parked at the Shack. Lota had never before navigated a dump truck through Rio's downtown at rush hour, but it was no great trick—the other cars knew to get out of her way. She drove directly to the supplier and demanded that it be filled with the correct materials at once.

When they returned from the adventure, Enaldo was in a very good humor. He stayed late into the evening, and they went over all the plans again in detail, how it would work with two roads instead of four. This area is a gift, Lota said, it is a beautiful poem written to the citizens of Rio. We are entrusted with it for only a short time, and then others will take our places. It is a great responsibility and we must do · our best to live up to it.

In the end, she prevailed. Men always believed their ideas superior, until she made them bend, even when they didn't realize they were bending.

LOTA DID NOT arrive home until after eleven. There was a light beneath Elizabeth's closed door. Lota put her ear to the wood; she could hear the rustle of pages. She wouldn't disturb Cookie's work. There were still at least three calls she had to make that would keep her up again until long past midnight. And tomorrow, at sunrise, another difficult appointment would be waiting for her at the Shack.

· I 9 ·

Today Rio is no longer the capital of the country. The actual drive to move the seat of government to the interior began in 1956, but the idea of establishing a utopian capital had existed for more than a century. As a site for this dream city, the government decided on a bleak, almost barren plain eight hundred miles to the north of Rio de Janeiro.

The ultramodern city of Brasilia is a testament to progress and the future, yet the ironies are endless. It's simpler to launch a rocket to the moon than to drive an automobile over the hundreds of miles of muddy roads to the new capital. In a city of monumental concrete and glass architecture, the only real human life exists in the workers' town built of wooden shacks. The city conceived and designed by its makers to eliminate social inequality has so bankrupted the country that there is no money for the basic services of schools, medical care, and electrical power in any of the cities where people actually live. ~~So why not bring in the best architects, fly in tons of Carrara marble, and build an Oz while many go without the basic needs to survive?~~

At the time of the author's visit, the presidential residence, called the Palace of the Dawn, and the Brasilia Palace Hotel were the only two buildings completed, while the skeletons of five blocks of apartment buildings, or super quadras, rose into the distance like pyramids on Mars, with its miles of blowing red dust. The dust covers everything in Brasilia, one's clothes, the cars, and the few scrubby trees. ~~In the lobby of the Brasilia Palace Hotel, red grit is ground into the new white carpets.~~

The first building to be completed in the master plan of this modernist city was the Brasilia Palace Hotel, which appears to float magically in the air. Entering the lobby, one's attention is drawn to a wall made entirely of drinking glasses laid on their sides, with the sunlight passing through the glass bottoms. The effect is beautiful and ~~fiendishly hot. In my room, I could hear the person next door taking a bath because there are holes in the wall for ventilation, and at my dressing table, I could only see my chin in the mirror. That's the thing about modernism, it goes for the grand effect that disregards personal need or practical use, that's what will doom the whole enterprise because people will do what they need to do, you can't shoehorn them into way of life through architecture~~

The Palace of the Dawn is a masterpiece of lightness and grace, a great glass box with swooping white columns, looking as if it has just touched down on earth. Even the best of Niemeyer, however, is alive with contradiction. Inside the palace, the sun streams through the glass, a lovely effect, though one feels likely to perish from the heat. And outside, one views the empty plain of red dust, kept at bay on the other side of a barbed wire fence and guarded by two soldiers in tin helmets with tommy guns under their arms.

Modernism: a new façade for the same old barbarism!

· 20 ·

FEATHERS, MOSS, SHEAVES of bark, an opossum's skull. The forest's detritus that Elizabeth scavenged on her walks through Samambaia she left in a loose collection on her desk. The new housekeeper, Beatriz, might store the charcoal in the refrigerator and leave a dozen cobwebs hanging in the corners of a room, but she had a poet's eye. She and Elizabeth had stumbled into a daily conversation, using, in place of words, the vocabulary of nature. Each afternoon, Elizabeth would pose a question with the objects she had collected, and the next morning she would receive Beatriz's reply. A handful of leaves, eaten away to lace skeletons, were arranged into a nest, in which lay the fragments of a speckled eggshell. Concentric circles of stones radiated outward from the four legs of a worktable. Twigs and seedpods with undulating edges were configured upon a flat stone like hieroglyphics on a tablet.

The editors of *Time* had turned their backs on the natural poetry of this country; they'd wanted a book about Brazil with nary a bird, beast, or flower. It was beyond them to understand all the manners in which Brasilia was a complete disaster, but the modern city had been exactly what they wanted to emphasize—an exhibit of the new, the shiny, the engineered. All these months later, it still made her temperature rise. Writing that idiotic book had been the most scathing experience of her professional life. She'd hoped to make something beautiful, or at least with heart; then her relationship with the editors had deteriorated into an exchange of irate letters, and hardly a word of what she'd written remained in the final text. The published book was simply propaganda. What they knew about Brazil would have fit on the head of a pin, yet the gall, the arrogance, the condescension!

Ever since, the entire task of writing had soured. In six months, Elizabeth hadn't managed a single decent thing of her own. She was stuck writing bad poetry about her pet toucan.

> *Uncle Sam, I killed you.*
> *Poor Sammy, I didn't mean to. I cried and cried.*
> *It was all my fault.*
> *You were so funny, Sam. Most comical of all in death.*

Twenty drafts at least, and she'd never got beyond *You're dead. I killed you. The End*.

Elizabeth abandoned her work and descended the hill to the house. Certainly she knew better than to disturb Lota, but some things couldn't be helped. Lota was at her desk, peering through eyeglasses on the tip of her nose and surrounded by countless papers—sketches, accounting sheets, memoranda. The report she was studying so furiously was marked red with the ink of her notations. Elizabeth remained in the doorway and did not speak.

"Is there something you want from me?" Lota said, without looking up.

One of her own unfortunate habits, Elizabeth had noted, was that the fouler Lota's mood, the more she pressed for Lota's attention. "Why don't we do something fun today?" she chirped. "Let's have a picnic by the waterfall."

"Elizabeth, I beg of you. I can't leave the house on any whimsical outings. I must go over these hydraulic studies by Monday. I've brought an expert all the way from Lisbon to advise us on creating the beach."

"I know, I know. And the dredge has come all the way from the Panama Canal. You certainly can't disappoint the dredge."

"I cannot go on a picnic."

She should have gone, of course, gone anywhere—to collect some sticks and snakeskins, or take her watercolors to the pool, or work on her dreadful poem about Sammy—but instead Elizabeth entered the lion's den and took a seat. "Sammy's empty cage looks so forlorn behind the house. I miss that guy."

"Then you should not have poisoned him."

"I was thinking maybe we could—"

"No. We are taking a vacation from toucans for the time being."

"Why are you being so horrid to me? It's not my fault you're over-worked."

"I should not be here, Elizabeth!" Lota erupted. "I am very uneasy in Samambaia when there are a thousand things in Rio that demand my attention. You have no idea what pressures I'm under. I let you convince me to come here because I know you want to, but I have a lot on my mind, a lot that I am responsible for."

Yes, here she was in Samambaia, they'd come for the weekend at her insistence, but she was no more than a visitor, a tourist in her own home. The house that Lota had built was so gorgeous Elizabeth could wander through its rooms and stare and sigh as though she were in love. Every architectural detail was in dialogue with nature—the windows that invited light from every angle, the stone walls covered in lichen, the wild animals that passed through these rooms with as much freedom as its human inhabitants. How could she have understood they were to leave this home, which had taken her half a lifetime to find, so soon? Ten years had passed too quickly. Maybe Elizabeth's happiness had drugged her into a sort of trance; she hadn't received the news flash that everything necessarily changes, even enchantment. Enchantment most of all. Happiness was a state with no tension; that must be why it floated past like the clouds spilling over the mountaintop. The mystery was that Lota, too, had been happy, but for those days she had no nostalgia whatsoever. Once the house had been completed, she hardly seemed to acknowledge it. Nowadays, it was the park, the park, and nothing but the park.

She and Lota stared tensely at one another until a bright flash of crimson outside the window caught Elizabeth's eye; it was that little drab bird with the brilliant red breast. She hardly ever saw him, and here he was, perched sideways on a stalk of bamboo, showing off his one impressive color. Lota had told her that on the rare occasion this shy bird offered a glimpse of his red breast, that day you would receive a pleasant surprise.

"Lota, look!"

Lota turned to the window, and then, glory to God, she broke into a laugh. When her eyes again rested upon Elizabeth, they had grown kind again. Lota rose from her work and knelt before Elizabeth, laying her head in Elizabeth's lap. Her jet-black hair had silvered over the years—it was so elegant, so handsome. "Please forgive me," Lota said. "I need you now very much. Please don't leave me, don't go away from me."

Elizabeth put a hand to Lota's cheek. "I don't know anymore whether you're heroic or completely out to lunch."

CAL, AT LAST, in Brazil.

They sat together on a cliff face, watching seabirds wheel and dive into the sea. From their perch, the jagged rocks fell at least a hundred feet into the surf, which boiled and seethed below. He'd arrived a week earlier, bringing Elizabeth a wonderful present—a pair of binoculars—and now she kept them pressed to her face, studying how the birds folded their wings and plummeted into the rough water. They hit so near the rocks they risked being dashed against them, then took flight as they were still gulping down the silvery beakful of their catch. Then they dove again.

"I never should have accepted the assignment," Elizabeth said, passing Cal the binoculars. "I knew from the beginning I couldn't write the kind of propaganda Life World Library wanted to publish about Brazil, but I just kept beating my head against the wall. Promise you'll never let me write again for motives of profit."

"I promise you," Cal said.

"But how else are we to survive? My last royalty check for Helena was $4.90."

"I've considered taking a job at the local five-and-dime. It's about all I'm qualified for."

Sameness of mind was restorative. Elizabeth had forgotten. She did not spend hours wondering what Cal's thoughts might be or trying to second-guess what he needed from her or upon what system of logic he operated; she already understood. Yet ever since she'd met his plane and helped Cal and his family settle into their suite at the Copacabana Palace, Elizabeth had been studying him, examining his face as though that might tell her the truth of his state of mind. In the five years since she'd seen him last, on the disastrous visit to Maine, he'd had another handful of breakdowns. Each time he'd managed to pull himself back together, but who knew how; it seemed a superhuman effort. His wife Lizzie was a saint, that was sure, but Cal's sufferings broke Elizabeth's heart.

Still, he seemed well. What had first struck her as jet lag from the long flight appeared to be his steady state: rather calm and subdued, though not at all melancholy. She'd seen none of the swings or effusions of his sickness.

"It's nice to be alone with you finally, Cal."

He set down the binoculars and reached across her shoulders, drawing Elizabeth close. She looked at his big warm hand upon her bare arm. "I'm doing wonderfully, just to let you know. You don't have to worry about me. I'm thriving. And I'm writing up a storm."

"You just got here!"

"You never told me how inspiring Rio was."

"I suppose it can be." Elizabeth still focused on her arm, where the skin, spotted and slack, wrinkled up in the crook of her elbow. The length of the limb looked like the skinny, jointed leg of a crab. Cal was so hale and vigorous. How had she become a scrawny crab?

"Would you like to see Rio by helicopter?" she asked. "You swoop up and down over all the mountains, and it's absolutely terrifying. Lota can arrange it."

"I would love that!"

"I'm sure she'll want to take you to her park, too. Though there's hardly anything to show. She's been working on it for two years, and all she does is have fruitless meetings with lazy bureaucrats, then come home with mysterious aches and dizzy spells."

From the beach below came a chorus of shrieks. Lota was chasing sandpipers with Cal's wife and daughter. Mary stood apart, holding her recently adopted baby at the water's edge and dipping the child's toes into the waves. Elizabeth took the binoculars; it was wonderful to see Lota's face like this, her joy so clear and sharp, magnified through the lens, such an infrequent sight since she'd started working in the government. You'd have thought Lota's manner might be too gruff for children, too overwhelming, or that she would be disinterested in them, but on the contrary she was brilliant, full of stories and games, open to wonder; she became childlike herself. As Elizabeth watched, Lota began to run in ever tightening circles around Cal's daughter Harriet, faster and faster and at an increasingly precarious angle, until she fell over onto her side in the sand. Harriet pounced upon her, while all the women laughed.

All three in the scope of her binoculars, Elizabeth noted, were mothers. And she, upon the cliff, watching them from behind glass.

"Did you see last night how Harriet stood on a stool to help me cook?" she said. "She's a little marvel, Cal."

"I'm totally sold on her. I can die knowing that I made at least one beautiful thing. It's as if before I'd been lacking some prime faculty, like eyesight or reason. I'm sold on my Lizzie, too. Those two are my anchor."

"And look at Mary. You didn't know her earlier, but she was just the driest thing before she adopted Monica. I always wanted a child myself. I wanted one very much."

"That would be a very lucky child."

Elizabeth shook her head. "No, Cal, I'll *always* lack some prime faculty. It's not in me to be a mother. I'm not dependable. Before Lota began on the park, we used to have so many children running around, Kylso's babies and all those nieces and nephews. It was relentless, and it was paradise, too. But I'm the eccentric aunt, the fairy godmother. I bake cakes and tell stories. I'm not good for much else."

"Elizabeth, that's nonsense. If *I* can rise to the occasion, then you would soar."

She paused, and then admitted to Cal something she had never breathed aloud to Lota.

"Remember Uncle Sam, my toucan that I adored? A couple of years ago, he had an infestation of some kind, that drove him mad with scratching. He completely lost his beautiful sheen. The man at the pet store gave me a spray. Safe for people, he said, yes, of course, and inoffensive to animals. I didn't trust him, though. He drank too much, and had a young beautiful wife that he mistreated. Still, I sprayed Sammy with the poison. It killed him in half an hour. He was like a cartoon dead bird, on his back with his blue feet curled in the air. I cried so hard that Lota grew impatient and told me that was enough. The worst, though, is that I did it even when I knew I shouldn't have. I did it anyway."

The binoculars rested between them. His attention was fully upon her. "Dear Elizabeth."

"It may sound silly, but that's when I gave up the idea of ever having a child of my own."

THE MORNINGS WERE blue, pure, cool. Rio in winter. On the terrace, Elizabeth swept the view with the binoculars—she couldn't get enough of them—from the rocky point on the north end of the beach to a Brazilian navy cruiser heading out to sea, full of sailors in blue hats with red pompoms and stubble on their chins, then past the islands tarnished like silverware, and down to the beach below, where a soccer ball made impact with a bare chest, golden hair glistened on an arm, and a swarthy foot caressed the smooth shapely leg beside it. Skin, such a lovely invention.

A year from now, Elizabeth will turn the binoculars Cal gave her away from the ocean to the Morro da Babilonia, the hill's steep slope dense with the pitiful hovels of the poor, where she will witness the life of the favela close-up. On the first day, she will see a woman slapped by her husband; on the next, three young toughs smoking marijuana cigarettes, and a child slipping down the hill to a precipice, wailing there while his father attempts rescue. Later, Elizabeth will watch a bandit being pursued by the police. He will climb into a tree, and the police will shoot him out of it. Days after, she will draft a poem about the bandit's demise in one sitting, and it will be the first good thing she's written since the book on Brazil.

This morning, as she trained the binoculars on the sidewalk in front of the Copacabana Palace, Elizabeth did not have to wait long. Taller than most yet slightly stooped, wearing powder-blue swimming trunks and a white towel slung over his shoulder, Cal emerged into the sunlight and stood in noble profile. Elizabeth ran down to the beach to meet him for their daily swim, ready to plunge into the bracing current at his side.

I tried to persuade him to give up the rest of his trip and go back to New York, she wrote Lizzie. *Please remember that I did try to get him to go back.* But in fact Elizabeth had felt a sort of sick relief when Cal had left Rio for Buenos Aires.

He'd waited until the end of his visit to go completely mad before her eyes. By then, Lizzie and Harriet had already boarded a ship home; Cal was to continue to Argentina for a series of readings before following them a week or so later. This time it was particularly bad. The reports that filtered back to Elizabeth from Buenos Aires—the drunkenness, the political ravings, the scuffles, the hospitalization, the awful flight back to the States under sedation with his arms and legs bound— served to confirm her suspicion that in some way she was at fault for his collapse.

But what more could she have done? It was only looking back that she recognized the warning signs. Cal had become terribly overwrought after the departure of his wife and daughter. In her own defense, trying to understand the hows and whys of insanity had really lost its allure of late, and what she didn't have the resources or gumption to see, Elizabeth pushed from her mind.

It was during the last dinner, on Brocoió Island, that Cal's disintegrating state became impossible to ignore. The entire meal was deranged, but Cal was more deranged than the rest. Even so, everything turned on its head so quickly.

On the speedboat out to the governor's residence, her friend appeared in fine spirits. Elizabeth remarked on how distinguished he looked in evening dress, standing at the vessel's bow like an elegant sea captain. All around them, Guanabara Bay was unbelievably beautiful in the setting sun, the folds of mountains and city limned in gold. She'd loved Cal's visit, and told him so. Even Rio hadn't seemed so terrible in his company. As they looked at it now from the water, the city was spectacular. A marvelous city, or at least a marvelous setting for a city.

She amused him with gossip about Carlos.

"Did you know he actually chooses his wife's clothes for public appearances? Not only does Leticia have to put up with a controlling, paranoid gasbag for a husband, but the poor thing also has hearing problems. Constant noise in one ear, a buzzing or a humming, I can't remember. Maybe that's how that marriage has survived. She simply can't hear him!"

"I'm sensitive to sound myself," Cal said, smiling.

"Who knows what state we'll find Lota in," Elizabeth went on.

"She's been out here all day with Carlos, plotting the overthrow of the president. If I didn't know their main intrigue was political, I'd worry it might be amorous."

"You needn't worry. It's obvious she's hooked on you. Deeply, deeply hooked."

Perhaps, but it was as Elizabeth had suspected. By the time the boat docked on the island, Lota and Carlos had worked themselves into quite a state, like two alcoholics who'd spent the whole day drinking together. Leticia drew Elizabeth and Cal into the foyer, where she helped remove their coats and offered them drinks and a tray of canapés, while the two conspirators found it impossible to desist from their conversation. They remained apart, speaking in angry bursts.

Looking especially beautiful, Leticia took Cal's arm to provide a tour of the governor's residence. Elizabeth drifted along in their wake, thinking that Carlos had to be commended: He'd done an excellent job on his wife's presentation. She also noticed that Cal was answering their hostess's questions in a near murmur, leaning down to speak directly to her bad ear. There was something strangely purposeful to it—as if he were flirting with Leticia, or worse, taunting her—that made Elizabeth suddenly desire to hold a glass in her hand.

By the time they reconvened with Carlos and Lota, Elizabeth was in fact holding one. She sipped daintily from a glass of claret. She wasn't going to hide it. Lota gave her a hard stare but otherwise said nothing. She had already made the only comment she was going to make, for the time being. So, you are off the Antabuse? she had asked the first time she'd seen Elizabeth drinking, with resignation rather than anger. When Elizabeth had tried to explain, Lota interrupted. I don't want to hear your reasons. If you so desire to kill yourself, I cannot stop you.

"President Goulart's style of communism," Carlos pronounced, "calls itself pacifist and only promotes war, speaks to the humble and only robs them, even of their right to think, speaks of self-determination and instead creates a new totalitarian imperialism."

"Please, Carlos," Elizabeth said. "You're not being interviewed on the radio. You're among friends." To Cal, she explained, "The last president was a big triumph over the Vargas dictatorship, but he resigned after a few months, thanks to Carlos's attacks. We're not sure why Carlos disliked him so; they had once been great allies. Now we have Goulart, an old crook from the dictator gang, but he calls himself a reformer."

"Which is only a disguise," Carlos said. "We won't tolerate his concept of reform either in the shape of terrorism or false populism."

"When everyone around you is disguised," Cal said, "it is difficult to know who to trust."

"I trust my friends," Carlos responded.

"Your *true* friends, you mean."

"Of course. They are the ones—"

"Yes," Cal interrupted, "but do you always know your true friends?"

Impatiently, Lota broke in. "Your true friends are those who agree inflation of 40 percent is not acceptable, who believe that people rioting because of food shortages and sacking stores so that the army has to come in and the result is forty-two people dead is not acceptable, and who think that a president encouraging constant strikes of railroad, port, and maritime workers is not acceptable."

"And when every rant is disguised as civilized conversation," Elizabeth said to no one in particular, "it is difficult to know when to listen."

Leticia ushered them into the dining room. Mercifully, at least for the beginning of the meal, they spoke of Cal's reading and lecture schedule in Buenos Aires, his impressions of Rio, parenthood. Leticia became animated describing her eldest son's wedding preparations. It was all quite pleasant. However, Elizabeth could set her watch by the instant at which Carlos steered the conversation back to the only subject he had any real passion for. Twenty-two minutes, no longer. He ignored dinner-party etiquette altogether, directing his comments to Lota alone. Ever since Elizabeth had washed onto Brazilian shores, and probably for long before, in social settings Carlos and Lota had alternated opinions at an increasing level of volume that excluded everyone else and made talking around them impossible. Either you joined in the fray, at your own peril, or you absented yourself completely. When those two really got going, Leticia's placid expression was an advertisement for the blessings of deafness.

Did it matter who said what? Lota and Carlos simply parroted each other.

"The nation is struggling against two powerful forces that want to destroy it: inflation and the fifth column."

"It is difficult to see any option but for the military to reestablish order."

"Yes, Goulart has begun openly preaching revolutionary war. Expropriation of private property. Nationalization of petroleum refineries."

"He must be suppressed."

"You want a military government?" Elizabeth said, unable to prevent herself. "Surely you can't mean that."

"Historically, the military has always intervened when the country becomes ungovernable."

"It will return Brazil to democracy, as it has done in the past."

"Goulart has unleashed the tide of communism, and we are all drowning in it."

"The communists are like children. They have no discipline."

"But they are very dangerous children."

"Yes, bring in the army," Cal said in a near shout. "Round up those commie bastards!"

The wonder of Cal's outburst was that Lota and Carlos actually fell silent. Both eyed him with suspicion. You could not honestly tell if he was ridiculing their fervor or if he was actually caught up in it. What was apparent, at least to Elizabeth, was that Cal had grown much more agitated than he'd been on the boat. He jiggled one knee and gripped his fork so tightly that the knuckles had turned white. He was amping up for more when she spoke in his stead.

"I think what Cal is trying to say . . ." Elizabeth began, and then had little idea how to conclude that particular opinion. "Well, the debate has become so incredibly polarized, hasn't it, that no one listens to anyone anymore. On one side, communism is pure evil, and on the other, *lacerdismo* is totally fascist. There's nothing in between. How are we to achieve any sort of balance when no one seems to value it? Every channel on television has a different politician giving a hysterical speech."

Her comments fell on a general lack of reception. Lota did not even bother to look in her direction. Could it be that they were *all* deaf?

"Yesterday there was an interesting item on the news," Carlos said thoughtfully. "It now appears that I am being held responsible for the prime minister's brain hemorrhage. According to reports, his death was due to the hatred and inhuman malice of the cold-blooded and vile Carlos Lacerda."

"Yes," Lota said with a laugh. "I read in the paper that Lacerda is uncivilized and deserving of condemnation."

"He is a killer of beggars."

"He is Paleolithic!"

The two of them chuckled. Cal muttered into Leticia's ear.

"Lacerda is intemperate," added Elizabeth, an observation of her own.

"Carlos is not corrupt, Elizabeth," Lota said seriously. "He is the only one. That is why they will try to drag him down."

Cal raised his glass. "Governor, you are a brave man. You also have an extremely beautiful wife." He turned to Leticia, studying the side of her face. "With the most delicate, lovely earlobe."

Leticia's eyes did not seem to know where to rest.

"All I can say about the current situation," Elizabeth said with desperate cheer, "is that the food shortages make it very difficult to bake cakes. Now that Lota's on the city council, maybe she can do something about that."

"I intend to." But she did not match Elizabeth's attempt at humor.

"Lota got on the Rio city council last May," Elizabeth told Cal, "along with a rhinoceros."

He began to laugh.

"It's true. People were so fed up with politics, they actually elected a rhinoceros from the zoo as a write-in candidate."

Cal's laughter did not stop but escalated in pitch until it became a high, hysterical scream. Then it passed out of the register of human hearing. His body continued to quake while his face became crimson and wet with tears.

Elizabeth put a hand upon his back. "Cal?"

He stood abruptly and left the room.

Carlos and Lota turned to her in alarm, at last understanding that something was not right with him.

Elizabeth went after her friend. She found Cal in the front hall, rubbing his face with his hands.

"I'm fine," he said. "Don't worry. I'm just very tired. I miss my family."

"Of course you do." She stood beside him and placed a hand on his arm. For several moments he made no response, then abruptly he turned and caught her in an embrace. Cal pressed his lips to hers and then released her so quickly, pushing her away from him, that Elizabeth hardly had time to register surprise.

They stood looking at one another, both breathing heavily, as if from a tide of passion. It was beginning again, the whole nightmare. There was only one way the story between them ever ended.

"Tomorrow we'll go see a doctor," Elizabeth said. "I know someone good. I can take you to see him."

"All right, Elizabeth." Inexplicably, he appeared calm again. "If you want me to, I'll go."

"It's best to get help now, don't you think? Before it gets worse."

"It comes in waves. It's like a big, vulgar blast of enthusiasm. It's not a bad feeling at all, not while it's happening. Everything is very clear and focused. There's so much I want to make happen."

"You have to take care of yourself, Cal. You must think of those who love you and depend on you."

"I will, Elizabeth. I want to."

They returned to the dining room, where he did not speak through the rest of the meal. Even the political diatribe had lost its conviction. Elizabeth brought the evening to a conclusion as rapidly as politeness made possible. They stood in a group at the front entrance, where Leticia bade them goodnight and retired upstairs. Lota stepped into the vacant place at Carlos's side.

"Lota, dear, where's your jacket? It's chilly on the boat."

"I will stay here tonight," Lota said.

"What on earth do you mean? You've been here all day."

"Carlos and I still have much to discuss."

"Really, Lota, I have to insist you come home."

"I will be there first thing in the morning."

Surely Lota understood exactly what was happening with Cal. Why would she not relent? "Please come now."

It must have been the desperation in her voice that caused Lota to harden further. "I'm sure the two of you will be fine without me."

By night, Guanabara Bay was even more beautiful than it had been at sunset. Elizabeth shivered from the chill until Cal put his arm around her, and she leaned into his warmth. Perhaps she had overreacted after all. He appeared fine now, though quiet, chastened. Lota was so maddening—she disguised her work as some kind of noble sacrifice, when really she was addicted to the insanity. If she was not engaged in mortal combat with a behemoth, then she did not know if she was truly alive. All of it was her own creation—not of course the absurd politics, but the hysteria in which the two of them had come to live and breathe.

"What does Carlos actually stand for?" Elizabeth cried out. "He attacks everyone, but is he really trying to build anything constructive? There's so much wonderful humanism and imagination in this country, and it's just squandered, over and over. When I first got here, Kubitschek was running for president and you saw his campaign posters everywhere with the slogan in big red letters: Fifty Years in Five. He promised to single-handedly forge Brazil into a modern nation. So he built Brasilia and bankrupted the country, and now it's even more ruined than when he started."

"It's a beautiful line, though. I can see it in a poem. 'Fifty years in five.'"

"Yes, it's beautiful and totally disastrous. As if you can maneuver change just because you've passed a resolution, that you can forgo the *process* of change, the slow, painful work of it. Change comes at its own pace, and almost always from a surprising quarter."

"If it comes at all," Cal said, and squeezed her close to him.

From the dock, they returned to Copacabana by taxi. Their driver kept one hand out the window, holding a cigarette, while he raced along the length of the *aterro* as if hell-bent on breaking the sound barrier. To one side lay Lota's park, to the other Christ on his mountaintop. How could you look at either without feeling the lie of monuments? All the way, her fist lay balled up in Cal's ice-cold grip. When they arrived at her apartment building, they stood together in the little square bathed in bright moonlight. From the beach came the thunder of waves. Someone had suspended a tarp among the trees in the square, and beneath it lay two or three sleeping bodies.

"I'll call you first thing in the morning." Elizabeth didn't yet want to leave him, and she sensed he felt the same. "We can skip our swim and go directly to the doctor."

"You have always been my girl." Cal's gaze was intent upon her face. But he wasn't seeing. Again, the disregard. It wasn't him, really; it was the madness's disregard. She'd been the object of this look too many times to count. It was a look that preceded the most extraordinary statements spoken in the most rational tone, the look that drew you in until you no longer knew what was normal and what was mad.

"You're so beautiful," Cal said. "Like an actress."

"No, Cal. I'm not."

"Yes, you are. Too beautiful to touch."

She did not answer.

"I threw away my crazy pills," he said.

"Oh, Cal, please tell me you didn't!"

"Right after Lizzie left."

"Then I don't know what to say. I just give up."

"I wanted to feel free, and I do. Not at all like a monster, did I say that I did? It's like a wonderful bright fever."

She no longer tried to keep the annoyance from her voice. "Then you're in no shape to go to Buenos Aires. You must postpone your trip. I insist. At least until you see a doctor."

"There's no need." He smiled lovingly as he backed away. Elizabeth had only to step forward and she might still have caught hold of his jacket.

"Wait, Cal. Where are you going?"

"Goodbye, darling poppet."

Out of reflex, her arm went up, then fell slack at her side. Cal had already turned and was walking briskly along Avenida Atlântica. Elizabeth determined to go upstairs immediately and call his hotel—perhaps they could restrain him somehow until a doctor arrived. But she didn't move. She watched Cal's back disappear into the dark.

Five years will pass before Elizabeth sees him again, in New York. By then, all of this will have been forgotten. She will be utterly alone. She will depend on him more than ever, and Cal will not fail her.

ELIZABETH REMAINED on the terrace at Samambaia with a glass of wine, having read and reread Cal's letter from the hospital in Connecticut. He was spending a lengthy recuperation there, and reported that he was doing as well as could be hoped. At least he was recovering, a little more each day. The letter contained his usual postbreakdown apology, but this one moved her even more than most. She'd come alone to the house for the weekend; Lota could not get away. It was evening. This was always the most difficult part of the day for Elizabeth; as the light drained completely from the sky, her spirit was at its weakest. Yet she was not terribly worried that her glass of wine would turn into something more destructive. Her motivation for taking a break from the Antabuse was quite the opposite. Elizabeth had taken in so much poison with Lota's involvement in politics that she had no desire to take in more—that included both pills and gin.

From the forest emanated the calls of birds and monkeys. Here was paradise directly before her. She must remember this, not allow it to slip through her sights.

Later, having retired to bed and deep in the letters of Coleridge, something drew Elizabeth from the house and into the frigid dark, up to her studio. Earlier in the day she had gathered jacaranda seeds in her skirt and placed them on her desk, the dark wooden pods beginning to open like a dozen gaping mouths. Before she slept, she wanted to see what the housekeeper Beatriz had done with them. She found the jacaranda seeds scattered throughout the studio—one held the drafts of a poem in its jaw, another stood upright on the lip of her teacup. Several had been set along the edge of a paddle Elizabeth had brought home from her trip with Rosinha down the Amazon. The paddle was shaped like a lollipop, and carved into its flat plane was the Brazilian flag. A man in one of the dugouts that had constantly approached their riverboat had noticed her admiration for the paddle and had offered to sell it. She'd hesitated, but Rosinha had urged her on. But how will he get back to shore? Elizabeth had asked.

For months after the trip, she dreamed of the river constantly. Sometimes she was on the boat, and sometimes the dreams were more surreal, she swam beneath the water like the riverman in her poem, she spoke to the river's denizens, the birds and snakes. She wanted desperately to go back and begged Lota to accompany her, but she could have predicted the response. *I'd sooner drown than be trapped onboard a boat for that long.*

From Rio, they'd flown over the River of Souls, the River of the Dead, the Xingu. In Manaus, she, Rosinha, and Rosinha's nephew had boarded a riverboat packed with over five hundred passengers. The *caboclos* hung their hammocks on the lower deck or else slept on mats among their livestock and sacks of goods. Elizabeth shocked a fellow passenger in first class, who'd mistaken her for the wife of a rich plantation owner, by descending the stairs to visit them. A handful of pure Indians, handsome and plump, waved her over like gentle children. One wore beads and red and black paint on his body, and before her visit ended he made Elizabeth an offer of marriage.

Below Manaus, the Rio Negro was joined by another tributary, the Solimões. The two waters did not mix but flowed side by side for many miles, crystalline black on one side, *café com leite* on the other. For the next two weeks, they floated down the great river, making eighteen stops along the route to Belem: Itaquatiara, Urucurituba, Oriximiná—names out of prehistory. Some were towns and others were settlements discernible in the night only by candles or lanterns on a pier. The boat took on even more passengers and cargo, including game from the forest—a gutted deer, a muzzled live alligator, a fish eight feet long—and a number of sick people on their way to the hospital at the river's mouth. There was a girl bitten by a snake, a feverish pregnant woman, and a dying man wrapped in a sheet with a nightcap on. The ill, like the cargo, were loaded into the hold.

With every breath, she wanted to speak Lota's name.

At night they traveled side channels so narrow the forest swept at her cabin door, like hands scratching to get in and claim her. During daylight, her eyes were constantly upon the river. A hundred herons ornamented the branches of a dead tree, luminous white against a stormy blue-black sky. Elizabeth loved the river traffic, boats of all sizes scuttling back and forth, crowded with people and their daily commerce. The dugouts were propelled by the lollipop paddles, and their rears popped out of the water as though the front ends were overloaded. At every stop, the boats came out to meet them, laden with fruit, rocking chairs, chickens and turkeys with their legs bound, anything and everything on offer. One sold ironing boards, another shirts and trousers. She acquired a tin basin in which to wash Lota's silver hair and the paddle from a father and son who'd sold out of their woven baskets and rubber balls. Without the paddle, they lay in the dugout upon their stomachs and pulled themselves back to the dock by hand.

Lota hates boats so much, she would have lost her mind on this trip, Elizabeth told her companions as she dealt another game of Hearts. But I think she would have loved it, too.

The town of Santarem had no pavement, just deep orange sand among the beautiful houses, and absolute silence. On the ground lay blossoms from Brazil nut trees, smelling divine. That town in particular Elizabeth hated to leave. It was ideal for a rest cure, and she discussed with Rosinha how they might return at the earliest possibility. But Elizabeth will not return to Santarem. She will dream of the Amazon for the rest of her life, she will write about it, but she will never go back, not with Rosihna, not with Lota, and not alone. When the boat's bell rang, she left Santarem and boarded with the other passengers. In her hand she held tight to a souvenir, the hard mud nest of a wasp given her by a friendly pharmacist.

Even she had to admit the food onboard was inedible. After fifteen days on a diet of hard-boiled eggs and ready for a little variety, they reached Belem, near the river's mouth. Along the riverbank, the houses balanced precariously over the water on stilts. The wharves were full of miserable houseboats, their names written on the hulls, *Flotuante* this and *Flotuante* that, though most of them were waterlogged, listing, barely afloat. *Flotuante Maria*, *Flotuante Flor*, and one that made her cry out to Rosinha, Look at that one! That one's mine! *Flotuante si Deus Quer*. Still floating, as long as God wills it.

· 2 1 ·

CURIOUS HOW ONE grew accustomed to living in a state of siege. The first time Elizabeth took notice of a shift was on the night she last saw Cal, when several men lay asleep on the ground beneath a tarp they'd unfurled in the little plaza beside the apartment building, but really it must have begun a while before that, in countless smaller ways, or even those sleeping men would have struck her as more remarkable. No one really seemed to notice or asked them to move in the following days. It crossed Elizabeth's mind that perhaps they were owners of one of the kiosks across Avenida Atlântica or drunkards who'd rolled down the hill from the favela and were too soused to climb their way back up.

They were striking workers, it turned out, and they began to arrive in profusion. For some time, there were maybe twenty-five or thirty, men and women both, who sat all day under the tarps and slept there as well. They spliced into the electrical lines and watched television or made fruit juice in blenders. You had to be careful not to trip on the cords running over the pavement, but otherwise there was nothing overtly menacing about their presence. You got used to them. They didn't bother anybody. Many simply lay on cots and read books. At night, during the blackouts, they talked softly by candlelight. Some strummed guitars while others sang. Elizabeth did not understand why they'd settled here; they did not display any signs protesting a specific injustice. Lota dismissed the entire issue with a wave of her hand. Meaningful conversation was reserved for one topic only. And that was the park.

After the workers took over a radio station up the block and began their pirate broadcasts, the encampment grew rapidly. From the terrace, Elizabeth looked down upon the multicolored surface of the tarps, which overflowed from the small square and into the nearby streets like an outdoor market, blocking traffic. Pedestrians were forced to duck beneath the lines that fastened the tarps to street lamps and buildings. Manholes were pulled aside, and latrines fashioned out of wooden scraps and tin were positioned directly over the sewers. In order to protect their fellow unionists living in the street, the strikers erected barricades at the intersections, first using stones and branches, and later shiny corrugated-tin sheets and barbed wire. After sundown, an acrid smell carried into the apartment when they began to burn tires in front of the barricades, where two or three men with machetes kept watch through the night. A scorched mark remained on the pavement in the morning along with the tires' radial wire rings.

Elizabeth began to use the freight elevator at the building's back entrance, around the corner from the encampment, in order to avoid the men at the barricade who asked for her identification. Refuse to provide it, Lota told her. Barge right past them, like I do. They are afraid of me.

A bus was burned and remained blocking Gustavo Sampaio Street.

Beyond the tarps, the city functioned normally, and there Elizabeth found a taxi so that she might take lunch to Lota at her workplace; otherwise, she found that she did not leave the apartment for days at a time. On the way to the *aterro*, she often passed soldiers or tanks guarding positions near the government palaces and public squares. It was unclear who commanded them, since it might have been either the governor or the president, who distrusted and hated each other and so maintained their own loyal armed forces, and unclear also what, precisely, they protected, whether the liberty of the strikers to protest or the right of Rio's citizens, amid the chaos, to conduct their daily lives without fear.

A worker in the port who did not support the strikes was ambushed and murdered in the middle of the day.

Elizabeth realized she had not seen a single policeman in more weeks than she could remember. Soldiers, yes, but no municipal police force. Of course there are no police, Lota said. Carlos has pulled them off duty. He cannot afford to provoke a confrontation with the striking workers, who have the sympathy of the president. And can you believe, she continued, only now growing heated, that those peabrains at SUR-SAN resist my ideas for the lighting of the park, even when the world's greatest lighting expert has agreed to design the plan?

You could no longer travel out of Rio with any certainty, as the bus lines, train station, and airport might be shut down when you arrived. You could not reliably purchase beans, coffee, rice, or sugar. You could not buy meat unless you took your place in line at the butcher's by 4:00 am. You could not withdraw your money from the bank. You could not walk along the beach after dark, or anywhere in the city where the streetlights no longer functioned, without risking your safety.

As the city fell further into anarchy, Carlos announced his candidacy for president, though there were still two years before the elections. If he wins, Lota said, and of course he will win, he wants me to be his minister of education. Elizabeth could not find words to respond, and she immediately left the Shack before Lota finished eating her lunch. In Cinelândia, there was an encampment ten times the size of that in Copacabana, with banners draped across the façades of the buildings and speeches being made continuously through a megaphone. She ducked into a movie theatre, expecting it to be empty at midday, but instead it was nearly full and she had difficulty finding a seat. Minutes after settling herself, Elizabeth began to cry uncontrollably. She understood now that the park was only the beginning of Lota's public career; they would never return to Samambaia. The woman two seats over put a hand on Elizabeth's arm and offered her a handkerchief.

On one occasion, the protest erupted. Elizabeth opened the door to the terrace early one morning, and there was an odd pungency in the air, not the smell of smoldering tires that she had grown used to but something else, acrid like burning plastic. Then her eyes began to sting and stream tears. A helicopter was circling low over the beach, and a great roar rose up from that direction, as from a soccer stadium after a goal. Hundreds or even thousands of people were blocking the tunnel that led from Copacabana to downtown. A figure in black was braced in the helicopter's open door. He wore a hood and aimed a gun with a wide barrel at the multitude. A canister of billowing gas shot into the mass of protestors, who began to run in every direction like terrified chickens in a farmyard. One man holding his shirt to his face retrieved the tear-gas canister and pitched it ineffectually back into the sky.

Elizabeth realized that for some time she had felt a flickering desire for violence to break, for the growing tension to explode and spill over, that she had been waiting and wanting it and dreading it, knowing the explosion would come, though not when or in what form.

· 2 2 ·

*Y*ES, SHE WAS drinking again. They were living through difficult times, so her detractors would just have to cut her some slack. Generally she kept it under control. However, there did occur with some regularity the chain of causes and effects, including, but not limited to, sleepless nights, a lack of poetical production, and a harsh word or breakdown, or both simultaneously, on the part of Lota, that necessitated Elizabeth's holing up in her room for a few hours, or days, drinking until there wasn't a drop left in the vicinity, tearing out her hair in private anguish over what a horrible person she was, then pulling herself back together and carrying on.

The less fuss made over it, the better, and that was the only fortunate consequence of Lota's being away so much. Often she missed the entire spectacle. She was usually in meetings until midnight, and once or twice a week she stayed the night with Carlos at Guanabara Palace or Brocoió Island. Park business, of course. Yet more and more, the discussions centered on how to counter the communist rise to power. Since the announcement of Carlos's presidential candidacy, Lota had become more than a mere park director. She'd assumed her place in the inner circle.

Lota had also mentioned in passing that at the palace they watched movies of an inspiring nature.

"You watch movies?" Elizabeth asked, with the hint of a shriek.

"Yes."

"Inspiring like *It's a Wonderful Life* or like *The Guns of Navarone?*"

Lota stared blankly. She'd completely lost her sense of humor.

Perhaps she was watching a movie at this very minute about extraordinary people accomplishing extraordinary feats, such as the one Elizabeth was accomplishing now in her own home: cooking dinner for her predecessor in Lota's affections while Lota herself was absent. Mary had come down from Samambaia with Monica and to show off her second daughter, Martinha. Having to play hostess to Mary and her children, well, that was when Elizabeth needed the inspiration only a glass of wine could provide. Instant relief! One unfortunate effect, however, was that she began chattering like a parakeet.

"First the sewing girl arrived, feeling very blue," she said, "so I set her up with a soap opera on the radio. Then big tears began rolling down the maid's cheeks for a reason that was not entirely clear to me. It was either for love or for liver, with Brazilians it's almost always one or the other, as you know. Her second cousin is staying with us until his hand heals—he cut it badly working for Lota at the park—and he wants to help out so much around the house that he began washing the terrace, very vigorously, until water flooded into my study from underneath the door. An absolute tidal wave. Then his wife, who caught him with another woman not long ago, arrived and went into hysterics as soon as she saw him. Finally, once everyone had calmed down, I made them all sit in a circle like schoolchildren while I read aloud from the newspaper about how we're living in an atmosphere of irrational delirium unleashed by extremists on both the right and the left. They nodded their heads and said, 'We're all going to the workers' rally on Friday, Dona Elizabeechy, aren't you?' And people wonder why we refer to them as the lower orders!"

Mary gazed down at her new daughter asleep in the bassinet.

She tucked a blanket around Martinha and told a story of her own. Some friends lived in an apartment that backed up on Widow's Hill, one of the steepest inclines in Rio. Returning home one night, they'd heard terrible noises inside and had opened the door fearing thieves, only to discover that a horse had fallen from an outcropping on the hill directly onto their terrace and was crashing around in the living room!

The world had certainly turned upside down of late. On this they could agree.

The meal was not one of Elizabeth's best efforts. The pork was over-cooked, the greens soggy. Mary didn't touch her wine. They picked over their dinner by candlelight while all across Copacabana each window glowed with the same soft, flickering warmth. The nightly fires were going in the streets around the encampment. There was beauty to a blackout, Elizabeth thought. At least there was that silver lining.

Silence between them had never been comfortable. They resorted to the one topic on which neither ceased to hold opinions: the dazzling, the maddening Dona Lota.

"She's killing herself with work," Elizabeth said. "Her teeth have started to fall out, if you can believe it, and she never stops complaining about some new ache or pain."

"But she's recovered from the typhoid?"

"I suppose so."

"Did she tell you that Affonso Reidy has been diagnosed with lung cancer?"

"Yes, isn't it awful? He's so kind, and he's the only real ally she has left on the working group. She's alienated practically everyone else."

"It's true. Even many of her friends who have nothing to do with the *aterro*."

"She doesn't have any sense of proportion anymore."

Mary smiled and at last reached for her wine glass. "When did she ever?"

Elizabeth almost warmed to the woman in moments like this. "Not long ago," she confessed, as if it were something for which she should feel guilty, "I received an invitation from the University of Washington in Seattle. They've asked me to come teach there for six months. The letter came out of the blue, and at first I nearly threw it in the trash. I'm frightened even to mention it to Lota. Do you think she would consider it?"

Mary laughed. "Surely that's a joke."

"It could get us out of this insanity, if only for a little while. Maybe that's all we need, just a break."

"You can't even get her to Samambaia for the weekend. She wouldn't leave Rio in a million years. And she'll forbid you to go alone."

"I wouldn't go without her, of course. But last year she took two months off, and it wasn't the end of the world."

"That's only because she was hospitalized in the intensive care unit!"

"At least there's a precedent."

Last winter, Lota had come home one night complaining of a stomachache, and by morning she was undergoing emergency surgery for an intestinal occlusion. She had insisted on returning to the Shack within two weeks, refusing to take time off, then was back in the hospital immediately with typhoid fever. Elizabeth had taken the opportunity to check into a clinic herself, for ten days or so, to indulge in a rest cure and reclaim a modicum of balance.

"It doesn't really matter what either of us thinks, does it?" Mary said. "She's going to do exactly what she pleases, no matter what. We just have to stand by, and if she falls ill again we'll be here to take care of her." Mary gave one of her thin smiles and gathered the plates from the table. Elizabeth suspected that in some peculiar way she actually enjoyed Lota's illnesses. When Lota was rushed to the hospital, it was little Miss Mary who came to pack her bags and who parked herself day and night at Lota's bedside, sleeping on a pallet on the hospital floor. Lota lapped up the attention, of course. But really, hadn't the woman a life of her own?

"This country is enough to send all of us to the hospital," Elizabeth remarked, pouring another glass of wine.

"Yes, but Lota was ill with something she could not control."

FOR DAYS, WORKERS poured into the city on trucks and ferries. They came from São Paulo, Sergipe, Pernambuco, and Minas Gerais to attend the rally of Goulart loyalists. Over a hundred thousand people were expected. Most congregated in Cristiano Otoni square, across from the central railroad station, but bands of workers roamed through all the neighborhoods of the city, wearing packs on their backs and carrying water bottles or banners with revolutionary slogans. For the first time, Elizabeth was afraid of the strikers in the Copacabana encampment, who had grown restive and excitable with the arrival of their comrades. She feared the communists' rally might finally ignite them into a flare of violence. It was under circumstances such as these that one became familiar with one's inner fascist. She finally agreed with Carlos and Lota. She, too, wanted the army to come clear out the protestors and restore order by whatever means necessary.

"CARLOS IS AN imbecile!" Lota yelled as she slammed down the phone. "He won't take my calls."

"I thought you were one of his closest advisors," Elizabeth said.

"He is no longer available to me."

"These days he's probably spending all his time trying not to get kidnapped or killed. That last time was a near miss."

"Maybe I will go on strike myself. Then he will see all I do for him. He will not take me for granted." Lota came to the corner of the Shack where Elizabeth had spread out her papers. She rested her hands on Elizabeth's shoulders and surprised her with gentleness. "I like it when you are here, Cookie. You look after me."

Uncomfortable alone in the Copacabana apartment, Elizabeth had begun to accompany Lota to her workplace. She fiddled with a poem while Lota rushed between meetings and inspections and planning sessions. Oddly, her concentration did not suffer from the constant high pitch inside the Shack, nor by the escalating political unrest outside of it. The poetry was neither inspired by, nor a respite from, the craziness in which she lived and breathed. It simply was what it was, and by whatever lucky alignment of the stars, it seemed to be going well. Her next book of poems was scheduled for publication in a little over a year, and though it might end up a slim collection, for once she believed she would actually make her deadline.

Mostly, Elizabeth liked coming to the Shack because she liked having Lota in her sights. She'd forgotten how remarkable it was to witness the woman in action—how she bullied, cajoled, and flirted to get her way, whatever the matter under discussion. This was the Lota of old, rather than the depleted shell who made occasional appearances at home between the hours of midnight and 6:00 am. Here in the Shack, while Brazil cannibalized itself, the park director trounced one spoiled, temperamental man after another, and Elizabeth took note from her corner, speechless with admiration.

Her admiration was in full bloom later in the day as she walked with Lota through the park grounds to check on preparations for that evening's ceremony. While President Goulart was preaching revolution across town, they were to inaugurate one of the first park projects to reach completion, a model airplane field. Three years earlier, this landscape had been nothing more than an expanse of gravel and dust. After so many meetings, so much bureaucracy, so much nervous energy, Lota's beautiful vision had begun to take shape. She had created a mile-long beach, now covered with bathers and colorful umbrellas. Palm trees towered overhead; the warehouse near the Shack was full of hundreds more trees Burle Marx had collected from the Amazon, ready to go into the ground. To think of the headaches it had taken just to get the dirt! And now everything around them was turning green.

She turned to Lota to congratulate her, but the exclamation died in her throat. Lota stared down at the path as she walked. Elizabeth knew the look, she knew that Lota's mind was churning and growing more befouled with her own thoughts and suspicions. Elizabeth could also guess what was disturbing her. In recent days, the park grounds had acquired some low contours, hills and dales that not all members of the working group had been in favor of. In best Rio fashion, the argument had spilled into the daily papers. One colleague was quoted as saying that Dona Lota had railroaded the entire process against the wishes of the majority. There really was no event too small for these people to get hysterical over.

Lota had done so much, but at such cost to herself.

"Look around you," Elizabeth pleaded.

"What?" Lota said, with great irritation.

"Look at that beach, and those trees. At those children over there, playing soccer. You made all this, and it's beautiful. Why are you blind to it?"

"Carlos has one more year as governor. After that, how do I know what will happen? *You* look. Look out there in the world, at the thousands of people eager to pull this country apart. This park, too, will become politicized. I have worked too hard to have a government full of small minds come and destroy it. There has got to be a way to protect it from the whims of all those stupid sheep."

To Elizabeth's surprise, at least a thousand people showed up that evening for the ceremony. For a model airplane field! That's how desperate they all were for something nice. Along with the *aterro* team, she and Lota took their places on a wobbly stage, sitting in wobbly chairs. Carlos sat to Lota's left, but she treated him coldly throughout the interminable remarks. First came the director of SURSAN; next, the president of the city's model airplane club. For a humorous touch, the head of the Rio airport. Affonso, pale and thin from his illness, turned to Elizabeth with a kind look and shrugged.

Beyond Christ the Redeemer rose the mountaintop where Elizabeth had gone to the clinic last year after Lota's surgery. She could see it now from her seat. Up there, the blue and green undulations of Rio had looked so beautiful; its crookedness and waste were invisible, as were the millions of poor whom everyone but Goulart preferred to ignore, and the workers' encampments, and even Lota's park. Each evening, the Seventh Day Adventists who ran the clinic sang hymns—it was really very sweet; she had even sung herself—but as the days had progressed, Elizabeth had begun to long for home, for Lota. By the end she'd been desperate to escape the shrieking children and cockroaches. Still, the visit had accomplished its purpose: to break her nasty habit of filling up the empty hours beside the liquor cabinet. After Lota got so sick with typhoid, Elizabeth had determined she would not add to her troubles.

The two months of Lota's convalescence they'd spent in a Samambaia dream. Lota had slept ten hours at a stretch, and they'd drifted through languorous hours of reading and playing cards and enjoying one another's company. Why, Elizabeth wondered, did they both have to draw so near the precipice before they could find this peaceful accord?

Concluding his remarks, the airport director called Lota into the limelight. To enthusiastic applause she untied the ceremonial ribbon on the airplane field, and her arms were weighed down with so many white roses, all you could see were her big round eyes peeking over the flowers. She said nothing into the microphone, just gazed at the people clapping and cheering wildly. Dona Lota was famous now, she was beloved. Yet she looked as traumatized as a prisoner of war.

When she returned to her seat, Elizabeth squeezed her hand. Carlos stood at the podium to give the final address, and she prepared herself for the certain hour or more of grandstanding against his political enemies massing on the other side of the city. Yet all of his words were reserved for Lota. He praised her energy, her devotion, her vision, her humanity, her wicked humor, her unselfishness, her relentlessness, her moral courage, and, most of all, her long-standing, loyal friendship. None of this around them, Carlos said—this great, enduring gift to all the citizens of Rio, young, old, rich, poor, black, and white—would have been possible without Dona Lota.

Carlos was never more charming than to a crowd of a thousand. The people in the audience were enthralled. Throughout, Lota sat perfectly still in her chair beneath the mound of roses, which were beginning to wilt in the heat, and watched him with the most hideous scowl.

"Try to look nice," Elizabeth whispered. "Everyone has their eyes on you."

At the edge of the stage, two little mulattoes were trying to climb onto the shaky platform.

"She is a lover of children," Carlos continued, "a champion of the less fortunate."

Lota hissed at the boys to get off the stage, then began kicking out at them wildly with one foot. The white roses cascaded from her arms to the ground.

Jan-go! Jan-go! Jan-go! A hundred thousand workers roared the president's name as he took the stage.

Elizabeth was not by nature a rubbernecker. On the mountain road to Petropolis, she turned away from the not infrequent automobile casualties, the sheet pulled over the prone body on the asphalt. But that night she sat before the television until very late, watching the live newscast of the Goulart rally. It was debatable whether the man outdid Carlos in the monomania department. But how could you tell who was more deluded—Goulart, with his dreams of a workers' state, or those who denied the lure of his promises and the desperation of the country's poor? The president was surrounded onstage by men of power— labor leaders, governors, admirals, and congressmen—and his speech showed no faintness of heart. He vowed to expropriate private lands, nationalize petroleum plants, and rewrite the Constitution, granting himself greater powers to challenge the entrenched cronyism in the government. I hope you are listening up there in the White House, he cried. We are no longer here to do your bidding.

As Goulart went on, Elizabeth felt a perverse pleasure in picturing the American ambassador frantically dialing the number to Washington.

But our worst enemies are on our own soil, he said. Governor Lacerda is a traitor to the nation, a pawn of the elites and the Yankees.

And so on in that vein.

The crowd was frenzied; one notch higher, and they'd become a mob. But in Brazil you could usually count on any sense of peril to be tempered by the comedic touch. From below the podium, a farmer handed up a mandioca root of enormous proportions, easily twenty-five pounds. The president accepted the offering and finished his speech holding the huge phallus under his arm.

The following day, the streets were deceptively quiet. "Those delinquents should be massacred," Lota said.

"Don't say that! Even in jest."

Unrepentant, Lota continued. "Well, they must be answered. The governor of São Paulo is organizing an anticommunism rally for this weekend, to show Goulart what the people of Brazil really want. He has invited Carlos to speak. Carlos has invited me."

"So you have his ear again?"

"I never lost it. Would you like to come?"

"I'd rather drink kerosene, to be honest."

"As I suspected."

"I think I'll go to Samambaia instead."

"If so, you will not be alone. Luiz Cusi is staying there."

"I don't need a babysitter, Lota."

"He did not want to stay in São Paulo for the rally either, so I invited him to Samambaia. Besides, I am not going to babysit you anymore. You may poison yourself drinking whatever liquid you wish."

SOLDIERS WERE STOPPING cars on the road to Petropolis. Elizabeth had never seen that before. With the delay, the trip took three hours instead of one. Even so, once she reached Samambaia, Elizabeth felt no desire to poison herself drinking any of the variety of liquids at her disposal. Amidst the tranquility of birds, beasts, and flowers, she could forget that the rest of the world was going up in flames. Luiz had already arrived and was at work on the prototype of a new chair, a strange and uncomfortable-looking contraption made of steel rods onto which he wove and knotted rope. Lota's twenty-year-old nephew, Flavio, had also come to stay at Samambaia, needing a break, he explained, from his mother. A fellow asthmatic and bookish from an early age, Flavio had been Elizabeth's favorite of Lota's relations ever since he was a child. For three days straight, Elizabeth cooked, listened to jazz recordings, and happily tuned out Brazilian politics in the company of her misfit confederates—then came Sunday afternoon, when the three found themselves seated around the radio to listen to the São Paulo rally.

Was it the misuse of *language* that lent the entire enterprise an aspect of farce? The hyperbole of the accusations and counteraccusations made Elizabeth want to laugh—the words were all so extreme and ill considered, you couldn't believe any of it. It was too *facile*. The mere sound of Carlos's voice was an irritant; his nasal whine compelled her to speak over him.

"It is impossible to know the difference between people who really want to change this country for the better," she said, "and the opportunists who want to destroy everything that's not of their own creation. I have to tell you both the most amusing story." Last year, she went on, Carlos had fled to Samambaia and sought refuge not in his own house but in Lota's, when Goulart, tired of Carlos's daily attacks, had sent his thugs to kidnap and most likely kill him. Poor Mary had seen the car racing up the hill in the middle of the night with the headlights off and roused Manuelzinho from sleep; wearing nothing more than boxer shorts, he'd tiptoed into the house holding a stick, with Mary creeping in behind him. A bodyguard with a machine gun had come round a corner, and all three had nearly gone into cardiac arrest.

"Carlos is like Tobias the cat," Elizabeth said. "He's been bitten by a snake, fallen off a cliff, come home full of cactus spines, and still he seems to have a million lives left. In Brazil, comedy and terror are never far apart. I'm still not sure if that's what dooms this country or what will save it."

Luiz and Flavio smiled politely but turned their attention back to the radio. Elizabeth knew perfectly well that Carlos was not the source of her restlessness—it was imagining Lota on the stage beside him, imagining Lota's sense of triumph as she stood before a crowd of two hundred thousand people. No, not triumph, more like a certainty that at last she was fulfilling her destiny. But *why* did she require that? It was a sickness. Over a decade ago, Lota had enticed Elizabeth with the most tantalizing dream—this mountainside, this house, this peace. And then she'd pulled the dream away.

In the evening when Elizabeth went up to her study, her mind resisted work. From the drawer of her desk, she removed a small bundle. The pistol Lota had recently pressed into her hands was small, delicate, almost feminine. A true lady's firearm, lacking only a pearl handle to complete the aesthetic. She could slip it out of her sequined handbag with a velvet-gloved hand whenever she found herself in a jam.

Steps came up the path, hesitating near the door, then Luiz appeared. "I am sorry to interrupt . . ." His eyes fell upon the gun.

"Please come in. I promise I won't shoot."

Elizabeth shut the gun back inside the drawer as Luiz entered the studio, his gaze absorbing the sum of her material possessions: a wall of books, an antique bird cage, photographs of Marianne and Cal, the mirror Luiz himself had sent only days after she'd drunkenly insulted him during his visit with Lina Bo Bardi. The gift had surprised her not simply for its generosity, but even more for the striking nature of the object. When he'd described making mirrors out of seashells, she'd imagined mere kitsch, but the mirror frame was fantastically gorgeous. Thousands of tiny maroon shells were arranged in spirals and waves, the work obsessive, exact. What had touched her most deeply was the note that came with the gift. *Elizabeth, from the beginning I felt as though you are like a sister.*

"Is the rally over?" she asked.

"It will go on all night. I think even they are surprised how many people came." Luiz sat on the edge of the daybed, his back very straight.

His eyes gleamed as they continued to roam over the room. "This is a wonderful space to work."

"Lota built it for me. Though it wasn't in her original plan. *I* wasn't in her original plan. I think that was when I knew I would stay in Brazil, long before I really admitted it. In my whole life, no one had ever done me such a kindness."

"Lota changed after you came. She became more soft. It was shocking to see, in someone so strong."

"Now I'm afraid she's become hard again."

"We all have. We are forced to."

"She gave me the gun. She says Samambaia may not be safe for me any longer. I can't even imagine what she means."

"In times of unrest, many find themselves persecuted, especially those who question beyond black and white. There could be that danger now. We must know when to go underground and hide so no one can find us."

"Like grubs," Elizabeth said.

"It might be necessary."

"I've had an invitation to teach in the U.S. next year. I want Lota to come with me. She hasn't said no, but she hasn't said yes, either. It all depends on the park, of course. But it's getting so desperate here, I feel we have to leave."

He noted the pages spread before her. "No matter what she decides, you must think of the work."

"It's hardly that! Strangely, I've been working more steadily than ever. I have a book of poems coming out next year, which I think may be the best work I've produced. Yet I can't help wondering what good is any of it! I'm just sitting here in my little room in the clouds, making marks on a page. Sometimes I look at the favela near our apartment in Rio, and I have the oddest thought that not a single person living there will ever read one of my poems. I know that sounds self-absorbed, but what I mean is, they don't truly *benefit* anyone."

"I make chairs," Luiz said simply. "The world is full of chairs, so why make more? I can't say why. I'm not an intellectual. Maybe when I think of a new way to use the material or a new form, it is still a good thing to do."

"All of us need to sit down, Luiz. At least you help us take a load off."

"We also need poetry. Maybe even more than we need chairs."

THE ARMY MADE its move.

A week after the rally in São Paulo, a thousand sailors rebelled in Rio with the support of Goulart, demanding better working conditions. The mutiny proved too much of an affront to many in the military who had previously opposed action against the president. In the hours following the naval rebellion, high-ranking officers in all branches of the armed forces began to shift their loyalties and seek new alliances. Half had lost confidence in Goulart and wanted to remove him, while others remained faithful and vowed to prevent a coup. On the last day of March, General Mourão, who had long been vocal about his hatred of the president, mobilized a battalion in Minas Gerais to advance upon Rio. It was impulsive, endorsed by none of his allies, yet it forced them all to choose sides. Civil war became a near certainty.

In Copacabana, the day was at odds with the grim occasion. It was hot and glaringly bright, with blasts of wind that shook the trees and rattled the windows. Flavio had come back to the city from Samambaia with Elizabeth; listening to the radio, he shouted out to her across the apartment every update on the situation. She was grateful for the company, as Lota had not been home since their return. In an ecstasy after General Mourão's announcement, Carlos began making preparations for Guanabara Palace to be defended by sandbags and volunteer gunmen against the soldiers Goulart was sure to send. Defying the counsel of his friends in the military, he barricaded himself inside the palace with his family and close associates. Lota, of course, had been first in line. When Elizabeth finally got through to the palace phone after hearing of General Mourão's plan, Lota told her she could speak for only a moment; they had just gathered in the screening room to watch an inspirational movie.

Elizabeth could not at first respond.

"About John F. Kennedy's wartime heroism," Lota added.

"Are you insane? Come home!"

"Do not worry, my dove," Lota said, "the palace is protected. Armed police surround us. I even have a pistol of my own. And they've closed all the streets with garbage trucks."

"You're surrounded by garbage?" Elizabeth said acidly.

"It is true they will not be much help if Admiral Aragão makes good on his threat to attack Carlos with tanks."

"This is not a joke, Lota. They're saying there could be war. And that palace is the primary target."

"I am hardly joking." Lota's voice had gone hard. "Now is the time to fight. We will only leave this palace dead."

Elizabeth hung up and turned to Flavio. "Your aunt's completely lost her senses."

Throughout the day of March 31, Flavio sat on the floor beside the radio, turning the dial in search of the latest news bulletins. "The unions have called a general strike in Rio," he called to Elizabeth, who was distracting herself with a new recipe in the kitchen.

An hour later: "There is no longer transportation in or out of the city. A grocery store in Ipanema is being ransacked because it sold out of bread."

Later: "A crowd has broken the windows at the Banco do Brasil in Gloria, demanding to withdraw their money."

"Please turn it off. I don't want to hear any more," Elizabeth told him. "I'm going to get you out of this country if it's the last thing I do." As a child, Flavio, so vulnerable and lost, had endeared himself to her. Sometimes Marietta had dropped him off, not saying when she'd return, and the boy had stayed with them for weeks. He'd sit with Elizabeth in her study, quietly reading while she worked. He was very

bright and sensitive, but now he was being wasted in Brazilian university, where the classes had stopped meeting and the only allowable
conversation was about the coming communist revolution. Elizabeth
wanted to get him a scholarship to Harvard so he wouldn't be ruined,
and Cal was pulling what strings he could. Flavio was looking especially handsome with his new haircut; it wasn't quite as avant-garde
as before, though he was so self-conscious she couldn't utter a peep
about it.

Every half hour Elizabeth dialed the palace line, but the calls would
not go through. When their own phone rang, it was not Lota but Manuel Bandeira warning them not to go outside, the streets were turning
dangerous. Luiz also called from São Paulo to ask if they were safe and
if they had stocked up on water and other rations. As the afternoon
waned, they put on some jazz records, Flavio's latest passion, and he
read to her from a music magazine.

The next call was from Flavio's mother in Petropolis; she said that
Mary was trying to reach Elizabeth on the short-wave radio. Elizabeth
opened the cabinet where they kept the radio they used to communicate with Mary in the mountains. She turned it on and attempted to
call, but there was no response.

Flavio was listening again to the news. Troops of the First Army
were now heading out of Rio to confront General Mourão's regiment
marching from Belo Horizonte. They were expected to clash sometime during the night.

So there would be war.

Elizabeth went out to the veranda. On the beach, the usual throngs
soaked up the glare, played soccer, and splashed about in the waves as
though it were any other normal day in paradise. Flavio called to her
from inside the apartment. Mary was on the short-wave radio. Elizabeth
rushed in and took up the microphone. Mary had been putting Martinha down for her nap, she said, when Elizabeth had tried to reach her
earlier. The phone lines had all been cut at the palace, and that was why
they'd heard nothing from Lota all day. But Mary had other friends there

who'd been able to smuggle out messages. Carlos still refused to evacuate, against the army's advice that they didn't need any more martyrs.

As darkness fell, it began to rain. Elizabeth prepared dinner. Fish, which you were still able to get. She and Flavio lit candles all over the apartment. As they ate, they ran out of words. At least the boy had a voracious appetite, so the meal was not a total waste. Outside, the streets of Copacabana were empty; even those in the workers' encampment had decided to pack up and scram. After dinner, Flavio returned to the radio and Elizabeth tried to read, but her attention failed her and she made little progress. A bit before midnight, General Kruel in São Paulo announced that the Second Army under his command would side against Goulart and the communists. Flavio turned the dial from station to station, back and forth, but there were no further details, simply the same announcement over and over on different stations. It wasn't for another hour or more that another proclamation was released: The First Army, marching to defeat Mourão in Minas Gerais, had instead been ordered to join his forces.

Flavio and Elizabeth looked at one another. They leapt up and grabbed the other's arms, dancing in a circle while the rain beat at the windows.

There would be no war.

After 2:00 am, it was Carlos's voice they heard on Radio Roquete Pinto, live. She wasn't surprised; it was a voice that could defy any opposition, including severed electrical lines. One of the telephone lines had not been cut, Carlos reported, and that was why he was able to deliver this update from inside the besieged Guanabara Palace. So far, it had been a terrifying night. The palace was encircled by enemies. On the orders of the president, two Marine battalions were preparing to attack. At any moment, they might be overwhelmed by the superior force of the Marines' tanks. Yet many valiant defenders lay on the palace floor with weapons in hand.

Bleary from lack of sleep, Elizabeth said, "Do you think we can believe even a word of what he says?"

"Maybe half, but which half?"

"You know what today is, don't you? It's April Fools'."

Flavio grinned. "Here we call it the Day of the Lie."

Shortly before daybreak, Carlos raised a second alarm. Though every minute brought new defectors from Goulart's camp, the president was growing desperate. An attack on Guanabara Palace was imminent, and Carlos appealed to all citizens of Rio to close ranks around him, to take to the streets and help combat those who would take away their freedom.

"What do you think?" Elizabeth said. "Shall we go?"

Flavio leapt to his feet. "We shall!"

"Let's straighten your eyeglasses first."

Even in the pouring rain, thousands of people were heeding Carlos's call, filling the streets. Elizabeth had to grip Flavio's hand not to lose him as they were carried by a human tide through the Copacabana tunnel. Everyone was sopping wet from the rain, their clothes clinging to their perfect bodies, and they were all jubilant, shouting and calling to one another, just like Carnaval, when people were soaked to the skin with sweat and joy and cachaça. After two hours they neared the palace, pushing past the blockades of cars and trucks and a few vendors grabbing the chance to sell fruit juice and fish croquettes to the converging hordes. At the end of the avenue, Elizabeth could see a knot of figures in front of the palace, surrounded by police. That one was Carlos, certainly, and there, beside him, that had to be Lota! Elizabeth frantically waved her arms and shouted, but they were at such a great distance that she was merely one more shouting, waving lunatic in the crowd.

Carlos's voice suddenly reverberated in the air, like God's. She could see him speaking into a microphone set up on the palace steps. She took Flavio's hand and pushed forward, all the way to a formation of policemen in riot gear who prevented her from advancing further. Carlos was making a joke about the garbage trucks, and then he stepped away from the podium. Lota was nowhere in sight.

For a long time, she and Flavio waited. The rain came and went. Elizabeth was so exhausted and chilled she had to sit down, right there on the curb. She rested her chin on her knees and smiled weakly at Flavio.

"That reminds me of when we were children," he said. "Your sitting like that, like a little girl. Do you know what we used to call you? *Cara eterna.* You had the face of a young girl, always smiling and shy and kind."

"I'm sorry," he said when he saw that she'd begun crying. "I did not mean to make you sad."

Carlos reappeared, and Flavio helped her to her feet. The governor was brandishing a gun over his head, shouting that Guanabara Palace was being attacked at that moment by a band of desperadoes. The crowd cried out and ducked to avoid the exchange of gunfire. Carlos challenged his invisible foes to settle their dispute in man-to-man combat. Elizabeth wondered why his leather jacket looked so familiar.

There was no gunfire. After a while, they realized there were no desperadoes either. Elizabeth's thighs ached, and she stopped crouching down.

She was terribly hungry. By now it must have been long past lunchtime, and they'd eaten nothing since dinner the previous night. Flavio went in search of the vendors they'd seen earlier. As he left her, Elizabeth reached for his arm, momentarily uncertain if she should voice her thought.

"What a nice haircut," she said adoringly. Flavio ran his hand through his bangs and disappeared into the mass.

She won't be able to save him. She won't be successful in finding him the scholarship to America. In two years, Flavio will score well on his test for the Brazilian foreign service and begin a career as a diplomat, though for a government growing increasingly repressive under military rule. So repressive, in fact, that Flavio will start to fear for his own safety. However, he will always remain fiercely loyal to Elizabeth.

In the fight over Lota's estate, Flavio will side with Elizabeth against his own mother, testifying in court that Elizabeth had not exploited Lota's derangement in order to alter the terms of her will, as his mother charged. Elizabeth will not be the only one stunned by the news, three years after Lota's death, of Flavio's suicide. Even if it were true he'd died by his own hand, nothing will convince her that Flavio was not a victim of Brazil's insanity, just as Lota was.

From the crowd behind her, a murmur rose, moving swiftly and volubly up the avenue. The asphalt trembled. She heard shouts. *Tanks! Run!* A rumbling and clanking, then the human sea parted before three tanks advancing toward the palace. Down the slope behind the tanks was a perfect vista of Lota's park, of the bay and the mountains beyond Niteroi. People began to push and shove in panic. As they were about to be attacked, Elizabeth thought with dry humor how it all looked like an elaborate float at Carnaval, one with a military theme.

She was so far from Lota. It wasn't fair or right. And Flavio had disappeared. She was alone. Elizabeth thought she should run, as everyone else was, try to flee out of the tanks' range, but she stood still and watched them move toward her, more curious than frightened.

The tanks halted. A soldier emerged from the first and waved the Brazilian flag. The crowd grew hushed, confused. Then utter pandemonium engulfed them all as it became apparent the army had deserted the president to side with Lacerda.

In the revelry, Elizabeth was pushed up against the palace barricade. A policeman in riot gear took her face in his hands and pressed his lips to hers, then threw his helmet into the air and caught it. Elizabeth, too, yelled and waved—she had never screamed so hard or for so long in her life—until at last Lota emerged and came rushing down the steps, hitting the surprised military guards with her fists and pulling Elizabeth through.

She kissed Elizabeth's face over and over, right there in front of the world.

They ascended the steps and stood near Carlos at the dais. The leather jacket, Elizabeth saw now, was the same one he'd modeled for them after he'd returned from his last trip to Italy.

There would be no war. There would be no war. There would be no war.

"There is no need to cry," Lota said. "We are victorious."

Carlos was trying to address the crowd, which stretched so far Elizabeth could not see its end, but the noise of a million people in celebration drowned out his words. Beside the palace was a children's park. Two soldiers, hardly more than children themselves, had laid their guns upon the grass and were swinging on the swing set. They swooped back, then forward, competing with one another in earnest to attain the greatest height. They swung out their legs, reaching so high their backs went horizontal to the ground. At the top of the arc, their momentum failed. They went into free-fall, were caught short by the yank of the chains.

· 2 3 ·

VERYONE HAD left her.

Everything involving the park had become so toxic, each day Lota felt more poisoned.

Sergio had left her. He'd grown much too big for his britches, as Elizabeth said, and he'd been fired after that fiasco with the student restaurant. Affonso had left her. Her one true friend in the working group, the only man not so full of himself that he was blind to everything but how he appeared to others. His death had been a great loss and, to be honest, very inconvenient. Carlos, too, had left her. He was never in Rio anymore, he was running around the country, already fighting with the military government so he could become president, Elizabeth was right, he only created division, he had not even attended the official opening of Flamengo Park in April. After all her work, Lota had not expected that slap in the face. And all those idiots at SUR-SAN! She wished they would leave her, but no, they preferred to attach themselves to her ankles forever and suck her dry, like leeches.

Even Elizabeth had left her. She had said she was going to Ouro Preto for two weeks, and already it had been two months. She was probably spending all her time with the bottles, not writing. Lota could not take care of her the way she used to, but Elizabeth was an adult, she had to learn to take care of herself.

But *this*, this open letter in the newspaper, was the worst affront of all. So public, so calculated to harm her reputation. And from someone she had counted among her closest associates for over thirty years. When she opened *O Globo* that morning and saw the name of Roberto Burle Marx on the front-page editorial, she began to read with pleasure—until she realized that the article was a venomous personal attack upon her! Why in God's name did he feel compelled to broadcast his discontent to all the citizens of Rio? As she read his charges, her disbelief turned to cold fury. Lota de Macedo Soares ruled despotically, imposing her decisions without the slightest regard for discussion or consensus. Lota de Macedo Soares did not digest ideas deeply. Lota de Macedo Soares was vastly unqualified for the position of park director, even more so for the directorship of the proposed Flamengo Park Foundation, though it was undeniable she had an eye for choosing fine objects for the home. She was contemptuous of others' ideas; she was untrained, unskilled, and incompetent. She did not understand lighting or any other concept of design, and her own plans for the park's public spaces and playgrounds were unimaginative and vulgar.

The editorial continued to the bottom of the page.

Roberto's betrayal stung like acid thrown in her eyes, but once her rage subsided, Lota decided to calculate, not merely react. The bullfighter did not attack the charging bull; she stood her ground, danced lightly to the side as she thrust her sword. With Carlos's enemy recently elected to succeed him as governor, the park was terribly vulnerable. For political reasons, the new administration would use any excuse to remove the park from her control. They didn't care if it was destroyed; every measure was taken simply out of spite for someone else or to further their own fame, but mostly out of spite, to prevent others from appearing as if they'd accomplished anything

important. That was why she had worked so hard to get the park des-
ignated as an independent foundation, free of government meddling,
with herself as director. Not to stoke her own ego, but so the park
would not be ruined.

Besides, didn't Roberto know that shopkeepers recognized her and
shouted from their doorways, "Bravo for the Flamengo Park, Dona
Lota"? Didn't he know that people leaned from their automobile windows to blow her kisses?

Lota pulled out a sheet of paper and laid it across her desk. She
would answer his accusations one by one, in her own letter to the
editor, reasonably and damningly. She would detail all that Roberto
had conveniently excluded from his diatribe. For one, the playground
design he attributed to her vulgar sensibility had in fact been designed
by his esteemed colleague Affonso Reidy. How dare he slight the dead
architect? And he had no say over the lighting! He had not studied
modern concepts of lighting for six months with the world's greatest lighting designer, as she had; he knew nothing whatsoever about
the subject. His expertise was limited to flowers and trees. That was
why she had hired him. The real reason Roberto was so vindictive, she
knew, was that he had attempted to extort millions of cruzeiros from
the city treasury by providing the grass for the park's open spaces at
highly inflated prices. Lota had thwarted him by finding a different
supplier. She had thought it a game of strategy, that Roberto might
even admire her ability to outwit him, but obviously he was furious.
More likely, his manhood had been bruised and so now he had to let it
be known he was no underling to a woman. He wanted people to think
it was he who should have been making the decisions all along.

Lota finished her letter in under an hour and had it delivered by
messenger to the offices of O Globo. Afterwards, she was euphoric. This
must have been how Achilles felt when he faced down Hector on the
battlefield, this elation, this fulfillment of one's own power.

But the apartment was so quiet. Where was her Cookie?

SHE'D LEFT IN August, after a fight.

She'd left in August, after a fight.

It was a very difficult day, Lota had said when she arrived home that evening. She'd come straight home after a terrible, contentious meeting with the sewage engineer, and though it wasn't too late, she saw that the glass beside Elizabeth's chair, where she sat reading a book, was already empty.

Yes, Elizabeth said in that awful screeching voice she got from the alcohol, every day is difficult for you.

That's because everyone tries to make me fail. It is their sport.

It's a beautiful park, Lota. People love it. And it's almost finished.

There is still time to destroy it.

It's never enough for you, is it? All you see is disaster, everywhere you look.

Why was Elizabeth attacking her? Couldn't she see that if you gave up fighting, you stood to lose everything you had gained? But perhaps, Lota thought later, she might have resisted turning nasty herself. You have no reason to complain, she said. You wanted to go to Italy, I took you to Italy.

Yes, Italy was nice. We had fun on those bikes in Florence. That was the only fun we've had in the last five years.

Lota picked up the empty glass and smashed it on the floor. And what do you do all day—nothing! Drink drink drink. You don't write. You have no ambition. You play at being a poet. You are not serious about truly being one.

Lota, stop, Elizabeth said wearily. This has nothing to do with my poetry.

You haven't learned Portuguese in ten years! You could speak it if you wanted, but you're lazy. You Americans expect everything to be handed to you on a platter. My friends warned me—Americans, their hearts are very cold—and still I am always surprised.

Elizabeth left the room. Later, Lota found her packing an overnight bag.

So you are leaving me now?

I think I'll get out of your hair for a while. Lilli has invited me to Ouro Preto.

Lota was overcome with remorse. Please don't leave me, Elizabeth.

I'm not *leaving* you. Elizabeth smiled and shook her head. If only you could see your face. But, to be honest, Lota, you are making yourself sick, and I am trying very hard to stay well. Everything with you is the end of the world. I can't live like that and I don't want to be around it. It's just a park. You're killing yourself over a park.

It's just a park? What if I were to say, It's just a poem?

That would make sense to me. I have no illusions that poetry is going to change the world. Most poems are trifles, baubles. Mine certainly are.

You're right, Lota finally said, maybe you should go.

Two weeks after Roberto's letter, another notice appeared in the paper, this one a hundred times more troubling. The military government had passed Institutional Act No. 2, banning all political parties and declaring that there would be no direct election of the president. There was hardly even a public outcry. Carlos would not take her calls. Lota read in an interview his intention to retire from public service as soon as the new governor took office. So she was dumbfounded to learn in the following days that one of his last acts as governor was to create, by decree, the Flamengo Park Foundation, naming Lota de Macedo Soares as director. In this way he circumvented those in the new administration who opposed him.

Lota immediately called Lilli's house in Ouro Preto. The housekeeper told her that Lilli and Elizabeth had gone across the street to look at a property. Lota requested that she retrieve her mistress at once, it was urgent.

Yes, ma'am.

There is so much to tell you, Cookie, she said as soon as Elizabeth came on the line. Roberto's letter in *O Globo*, the victory of Carlos's opponent Negrão for the governorship, Carlos's last defiant act of creating the Fundaçao Parque Flamengo after Institutional Act No. 2 destroyed his chances of ever becoming president. It all came out in a rush.

When are you coming home, Cookie? I miss you. I need you so much.

Soon. After a silence, Elizabeth said, I'm buying a house, Lota.

In Ouro Preto?

Remember the one right across the road from Lilli's? The beautiful house practically falling apart?

No, I don't remember.

A wealthy mine owner wanted it, and Lilli couldn't bear the thought of him as a neighbor. Of course, it's completely uninhabitable. There's scarcely an even floor in the whole house, but the walls are three feet thick, and they're made of mud and sticks tied together with *hide*, if you can believe it! They say that method hasn't been used since 1730 at the latest. There's even a legend that gold was buried under the house, and the owner has dug holes all through the foundation looking for it. The garden is huge, with all kinds of fruit trees and a stream running through it. But it needs a new roof, new paint, and a septic system, because there are no real bathrooms.

Have you already given them money?

The owner is Senhor Olimpio. He's a little gnome of eighty, with ten children. He keeps climbing the avocado trees, and they think any day now he will fall out of one. He lives in one room in complete squalor, with ducks and hens and cats sitting on his bed with him.

Lota had not heard such excitement in Elizabeth's voice in a very long time. I think you are crazy, she said, but I can't say I'm not intrigued.

Lota, you'll love it. You always said you wanted an old house to go with your modern one.

Tell me one thing. Do you mean to move there?

Lilli says she'll take charge of the restoration while I'm in Seattle. There was a long pause. But no, Lota, I wouldn't live here without you.

LOTA LEFT THE next morning before dawn, nine hours straight on roads that had grown only more perilous over the last decade. She didn't stop to eat, and when she arrived in Ouro Preto she was trembling from lack of food and the vibrations coursing directly from the potholes and through the steering wheel. Lilli raised an eyebrow on finding Lota at her doorstep and nodded toward the second floor to indicate that Elizabeth was in her room. Lota ran up the stairs. There was Cookie coming out onto the landing. They stood looking at one another, then Lota went up the last stairs to Elizabeth and took her hand and they entered the bedroom, closing the door behind them.

They embraced shyly. They sat side by side on the bed without speaking, as if they hardly knew each other.

You came all this way, Elizabeth finally said. I'm touched.

I couldn't be without you any longer.

You work eighteen hours every day. I'm surprised you notice if I'm there or not.

You are right, Cookie. Carlos is a dreadful politician. It is probably a good thing that he cannot now become president.

Elizabeth said nothing. Lota went on. Brazilian politics are absurd. The new governor would be glad to be free of me if I were in Seattle for six months.

Don't joke, Lota. Don't say that unless you really mean it.

Lota picked up the book that lay on the bedside table. What is this you're reading? What a pretty book.

The cover was blue, with a drawing of a sixteenth-century map of the New World. *Questions of Travel*, by Elizabeth Bishop. There was a quote by Lowell on the back. Say what you would of him, he did love her, that was plain. Instead of a photograph on the inside jacket, there was a portrait of Elizabeth in pencil. Very sophisticated, Lota said.

I just received it.

It's beautiful. She flipped through the pages. Had Elizabeth really written so many poems? All this time, had she been quietly building her own monument to history?

Then she read the dedication.

For Lota de Macedo Soares

. . . To give you as much as I have and as much as I can,
The more I pay you, the more I owe you.

Camões, Elizabeth said.

Lota tried to speak. She couldn't make any sound. She felt unbearably, painfully moved. She tried to speak again, and a sob burst from her. She wept, holding the book away so that her tears would not damage it.

Cookie, she said at last. How do you put up with me?

I love you.

Do you? Are you sure you still do?

I've been very lonely for a long time, but Lota, I love you. I am in it until the end, whatever that might mean, to the end of you or me.

She could not meet Elizabeth's eyes, but stared at the beautiful book in her hands. I do not feel strong anymore, Cookie. I do not think I have ever felt so absolutely depleted. All the time, I see in people's eyes that I am failing, that I am a failure. And there's nothing to help me, there's nothing left inside of me.

Oh, my love, Elizabeth said. How you torture yourself. She pulled Lota's head to her lap and stroked her hair. After a long time, she asked, Would you like to meet Senhor Olimpio?

Yes.

And his ducks and chickens?

Yes, Elizabeth. Show me your discovery.

·24·

ELIZABETH WOKE AROUND eight thirty. Lota lay snoring lightly at her side. In the dark bedroom, the sound of waves was thunderous, as if there'd been a storm out at sea in the night. She felt a vague anxiety that it was already too late, she had overslept and should have started the day earlier. She gathered her books and went upstairs. The upper floor of Rosinha's house was open on three sides, with a panoramic view of Cabo Frio and the coast. The morning sea was rough and iron gray, the sky overcast, though as Elizabeth read she kept thinking she saw breaks in the clouds. She was looking through poetry collections, trying to create a lesson plan for the class in Seattle, but it all felt rather a joke. After two hours, she returned to the bedroom and tried to rouse Lota, who moaned and drew a pillow over her head. Elizabeth left her again and began to prepare breakfast. Lota emerged, groggy and with her eyes half-closed as if she were drugged. She ate in silence from the plate Elizabeth served. Her expression was not promising. Elizabeth attempted to engage her every few moments, under the delusion that it might lift her spirits. Don't you think the vegetation is beautiful this time of year, with all those flowering cacti?

Hmm. Do you think they'll ruin Cabo Frio just like they've ruined everything else? Yes. What's on your mind? Nothing. Then, finally, I guess I'm depressed. Do you think it's beautiful here, at least? Yes, Lota said. I do.

Lota finished her breakfast. She began examining the details of the house's construction: the masonry, the woodwork, the patterns of white and black stones in the floor, the vines used to lash the beams together. "I want to take photographs of all this," she said. "The vernacular architecture is so real and direct, straight from the earth. Look, it's just rocks and sticks and palm leaves. It's not trying to trick you."

She seemed to be perking up, but only moments later Elizabeth turned to find her lying supine on the couch and staring at the ceiling with that forlorn look she knew only too well. "What is it now?" she asked.

"I am sad I will never have a house this beautiful."

"You do have a house this beautiful. Even *more* beautiful."

"It means nothing. It's false."

Elizabeth thought, *If I don't walk away now, I will throttle her*.

She walked away. In the kitchen she washed the dishes from breakfast, trying not to bang them around too much. A good houseguest would not break Rosinha's plates out of ill humor. The gray sky seemed to be opening up; she noticed one or two blue streaks. Lota came close and stood nearby without speaking. Elizabeth felt the physicality of her so keenly, she ached for Lota to put her arms around her.

"Would you like to walk with me to town, my dove?" Lota asked.

"Yes, I would. I would love that."

At the market, right where the fishing boats came in, Lota finally came around. They filled their woven sisal shopping bag with fruit and vegetables and beer and an octopus from a fisherman with enormous beautiful dark eyes and whose eyelashes were, Lota agreed, to kill for. The sky was clear blue by the time they returned to the house. They packed their beach gear and went down to the dunes. How Cabo Frio managed to escape the mad crush of humanity that had engulfed the rest of the world continued to be a wonderful mystery. On the beach there was never another soul in sight. All the cacti were covered with magenta and yellow flowers, with butterflies in frantic ecstasies around them. A turtle was swimming in the water and raised his head to watch them spread their towels on the sand, as if he did not know enough of humankind to be afraid.

Without a word, Elizabeth took Lota's hand and drew her into the warm water. The surf had calmed since the morning, and now it undulated in rolling blue swells. Lota resisted at first, but Elizabeth coaxed her in. In these moments, when she was so terribly tender, you had to treat her almost like a newborn child, she had absolutely no defenses. They slipped on their masks and submerged beneath the crystalline surface. Elizabeth loved the stark contrast, the motionless desert landscape above and then, below water, the wild effusions and vibrancies of life. Thousands of living creatures, swimming, darting, swaying every which way. Immediately Lota dove deep, pulling Elizabeth down. She was so graceful in the water, like a marine animal. She could hold her breath for the longest time to look at everything that caught her attention: fish, corals, fanworms. Elizabeth bobbed right back to the surface like a cork. She saw, drifting close by, a nearly invisible mass suspended in the water, quivering with subtle hues and light. It was a school of squid, twenty or so, each about six inches long. The entire group was continuously shifting color, first completely clear, hardly distinguishable from the water, then in an instant turning dark, then blue, then mottled like rocks, all in unison, as if trying out anything to please her. She wanted to show Lota, but Lota had drifted away in the current. She was head down in the water, kicking her legs to remain in place while she gazed beneath a boulder.

The squid jetted off. Elizabeth continued to float while Lota explored. She noticed that a man had appeared on the beach and was sitting on some driftwood near their towels. Another human being on the shore was momentarily so surprising she did not at first become suspicious. He was already moving on as Elizabeth swam in and discovered that

Lota's sandals had disappeared. A wave had washed over their things. She wanted to believe that the surf had stolen Lota's shoes, but that was too great a stretch.

Elizabeth lay on the towel, drying beneath the hot sun. Lota surfaced so rarely for breath that she began to worry. She stood and searched the water until she saw Lota again. Was loving another human being with all you possessed to live in a state of grace or a state of masochism? Truly, it was hard sometimes to know the difference.

A school of fish was moving swiftly along the shore, breaking the surface with silver flashes and a hundred little sprays and splashes. A school of something much larger was in pursuit. Dolphins! Their curved backs bowed out of the water, agile and powerful. Infant dolphins swam among the adults, leaping entirely clear of the water. She saw that Lota lay directly in their path, treading water and watching the dolphins approach, her dark head above the water's surface as they engulfed her.

When they'd passed on, Lota returned to the beach. "Did you see that?" she said, exhilarated. "One actually let me touch him!"

"It was marvelous. Were you frightened?"

Lota shook her head. "I'm starving. Let's go in for lunch. Where are my sandals?"

Elizabeth feared spoiling her mood. "I think a wave absconded with them."

"No matter." Lota grinned. "They were a piece of *merde* anyway."

After lunch, they showered to rinse off the day's salt and sun. It was after four o'clock, and the afternoon was still very hot. As Elizabeth combed her hair before the mirror, Lota shut the door to the room and approached in the dim light and embraced her, pressing her lips to Elizabeth's neck. She couldn't remember the last time Lota had done anything like that, it had been so long. She turned to receive Lota's kiss. Lota led her to the bed, and they began to make love. The intensity of her own excitement took her by surprise. Elizabeth kept trying to rush, but Lota slowed her down. Near the end, the excitement faded, somehow she couldn't maintain it. But it did not matter. It was so lovely to be intimate like this, touching one another, cherishing one another, she could have wept with relief. After, Lota stroked her face as they lay in silence.

In the evening, they emerged to a sky and sea that were nearly purple, right before all the light went out of the world. Things were now easy and playful between them. Elizabeth sharpened a knife and Lota cut up the octopus and made a vegetable sauce while it boiled. They battled an invasion of wasps that flew out of the stove's exhaust pipe, and then Elizabeth spoke with great feeling of trips she'd made as a child to cold seas, off the coasts of Canada and New England, the landscapes and seascapes so different from this. There were parts of her, she told Lota, that had never stopped longing for the north. Her inner compass still pointed there. She was scared to teach, of course, but she thought Seattle was going to be a wonderful adventure.

The octopus finished cooking, and Lota tossed it into the sauce and said it wasn't half bad.

Then she put her hand to Elizabeth's face.

"It was a dream," Lota said, "to think I could go with you to Seattle. I can't go, Elizabeth. Governor Negrão has already made concessions to me. I have to see if I can work with him. Otherwise, there are so many who hate Carlos they would go to any lengths to undo all we have accomplished."

Elizabeth felt such little reaction, she actually smiled. "I suppose I never really believed you'd come."

"I meant to."

"Yes, I think you did."

"Would you like some octopus?"

"No, thank you. I don't have much appetite."

They continued to talk with ease and even laughter while Lota ate. It was around eleven by the time they cleaned up the kitchen. They went downstairs to read for an hour or so before they turned off the light.

· 2 5 ·

$\mathscr{T}$HE HOTEL MEANY could not have been more appropri-
ately named. Mean in dimension, mean in comfort, without a bit of
light to brighten things up. All the overhead lamps were of such low
wattage Elizabeth could not navigate her single room—so cramped it
had no proper desk, so she'd begun typing her letters to Lota on the
ironing board—without bumping her shins on the bed frame. Hardly
any sunlight passed through the windows, as it had rained constantly
since the moment she'd arrived, except for the few hours the rain had
turned to snow. The view was of a city half-glimpsed through dark
swirling clouds.

That she could still cancel her contract and head home on the next
flight remained a tantalizing option. What prevented her from doing so
was the thought of Lota's gloating expression when Elizabeth walked
in the door. *So you finally realized what I knew all along*, she would most
certainly say. *You are not cut out to be a teacher, poor Cookie.*

Well, poor Cookie would prove her wrong.

Elizabeth prepared herself for the plunge into dismal weather, with
her new yellow slicker, galoshes, gloves, and umbrella. More than once
in her life she'd arrived in an unfamiliar city, never doubting her capa-

bility to handle whatever challenging circumstance arose; for far too long, the idea of herself as a competent world citizen had atrophied. Besides, how hard could it be to find a goddamn reading lamp to cheer up this dark hole of a hotel room? All those charming streets around the university were full of little shops selling lace and teapots. She needn't go far.

Outside, the rain was so fierce it appeared to be falling *up*. It got inside the sanctuary of her umbrella, and this was quite annoying. Just a block over, however, a window display of a desk with a stack of books and a standing lamp warmly illuminating the scene enticed her inside. Upwards of a hundred lamps hung from the ceiling, in every conceivable style: Tiffany glass, arts and crafts, stainless steel. However, not a single desk lamp was in evidence. The shop turned out to be a daunting labyrinth of extremely tall shelves full of boxes of doorknobs and hinges. Elizabeth went up and down the crowded aisles until she was thoroughly disoriented. Nothing was clearly explained. There was no one to assist her. She sat heavily in an armchair marked Half Price.

Perhaps Lota was right. If the most simple errand so easily defeated her, then she'd be hopeless in the classroom. In the weeks leading up to Elizabeth's departure, Lota had been so sweet and funny; then right at the end she'd turned awful. She'd offered, free of charge, a number of brutal imitations of Elizabeth attempting to teach—arriving at class drunk, stumbling and dropping her valise so that papers and books went flying, slurring her words, unable to finish any idea or sentence. Really, just hilarious. The memory was so horrible it continued to have a glaze of unreality. Any feeling person might simply have said, I'm going to miss you too terribly, that's how much I love you and need you. Instead, Lota had decided to be cruel.

Then, the night before her flight, the desperate pleading. *Don't leave me, I can't bear it if you leave me. Who will take care of me?*

"Can I help you in some way?"

Elizabeth found a young woman standing over her. How she managed to look so pleasant and at ease while her customers were wandering lost around the store like Jews in the desert made Elizabeth extremely cross. "Yes, you can help me, thank you for asking. All I want is a simple reading lamp. I don't understand why that's so difficult."

"A bedside lamp, something to read by?"

"Isn't that what I just now said?"

"Give me a moment. Wait right here, and I'll see what I can find."

"Don't trouble yourself," Elizabeth grumbled as the young woman disappeared down a passageway. She returned in moments with three lamps in her arms, as if she'd plundered a secret stash not available to the public, and set them on the floor at Elizabeth's feet. "Do you like any of these?" she asked. "This one's practical. Look, it clamps to your desk."

"I don't have a desk. I have an ironing board."

"All right, then, moving on. Number two has a bendable neck. Though it might become a breakable neck in the state of mind you're in, so let's put that aside. And here's number three, my personal favorite."

"You can't be serious. That color is hideous."

"Oh, but this color is one of my favorites."

"That shade of green is almost putrescent."

"You're right, it is," she said, lighting up. "I love putrescent green!"

What a curious young woman! She knelt before Elizabeth with a brilliant smile, beams of vitality and youth shooting off her like solar flares. The young woman could hardly have been older than the students Elizabeth was presently to face. She was very pretty, with a high, intelligent forehead and a perfect small nose, and her long auburn hair spilled from a funny round rain cap sitting snug on her head and down past her shoulders. She wore a short dress that left her long legs bare. *Rather informal for a salesgirl*, Elizabeth thought, and besides, wasn't she chilly in this climate?

Yet Elizabeth's spirits could not resist the girl's buoyancy. "Why don't you leave them all for a minute," she said with a reluctant smile, "and I'll decide which suits me best?"

"Very well. Good luck. Oh, look, your galosh has slipped off." The young woman pushed on the heel of Elizabeth's overshoe, and then she stood. "What a funny word, *galosh*. One never seems to hear it in the singular. Bye now."

And then she was gone. Elizabeth had been away such a long time that American youth had become a complete mystery. If her students were half as charming as this young woman, however, teaching might be bearable. The entire lamp episode had cheered her up immensely. What the heck, she'd buy the putrescent one. It proved to be a wonderful choice. Back at the Meany, the lamp made her room almost inviting. That night she read without a bit of strain to the eyes.

After Elizabeth switched off the light, she lay awake, continuing to be amused by the young woman. In Brazil, such behavior toward one's elders would be insolent; here, it was something else altogether, a sort of vibrant expectation of nothing less than the happiest possible outcome. It was the first time since leaving Brazil, alone in a strange and uncomfortable Seattle bed, that Elizabeth did not feel absolutely sick at heart. Smiling to herself in the dark, she became aware of a low, sighing noise emanating from a corner of the room. It was regular, rhythmic, like breath. But it was louder than breath, rougher around the edges. It was snoring! Someone was snoring in the corner of her hotel room.

Elizabeth had long ago ceased resisting the idea of spirits, portents, or premonitions; she'd been in Brazil too many years. But a snoring ghost!

THE OPERATOR PUT the call through even after Elizabeth told her to cancel it. She'd wanted to wish Lota a happy new year, then realized in Rio it was already long past midnight. Lota was groggy from a sleeping pill she'd taken, and the connection was terrible. Still, there was no disguising the happiness in her voice.

"I miss you so much, Cookie."

"I miss you too."

Within moments, though, she was complaining about the park. The new governor was already trying to erode her authority. Could Elizabeth believe that? He said that Carlos had created the park foundation illegally.

Elizabeth noticed that she did not react in her customary way, with the usual flash of frustration followed by mild, pervasive despair. Perhaps it was good, this separation. Maybe when she returned to Brazil, she wouldn't so easily be sucked back into the morass.

"Then quit and come here," she said. "It's as simple as that."

"No, Elizabeth, I can't."

"The park is nearly finished, no one appreciates you, and they all make your life a constant hell. Don't you wonder why you stay?"

"If I leave, they will say it's because I am a woman. That I am too weak to stand up to men. That's how I will be remembered, as a weak woman who failed."

A noise like a rushing wave filled the line.

"Are you still there?" Elizabeth said.

"Yes."

"Maybe you *don't* have to stand up to the men any longer, not because you're too weak but because they're all crooks and liars."

"How much are you drinking in Seattle?" Lota asked, after a pause. "It's easier to drink, isn't it, when you are away from me?"

"I'm not drinking at all," she said, by which she meant she was not drinking to excess. "Even though I'm living in terror of my first class."

"What did you say? I couldn't hear."

"I'm not drinking," Elizabeth shouted.

Lota chuckled. "Oh, Cookie, you expect me to believe that?"

IT WAS EITHER spend New Year's Eve alone in the Hotel Meany, wearing a housecoat and slippers and coaching herself not to down an entire bottle of gin, or else attend the dinner party to which she was invited as the guest of honor. So here she was, not inelegant, if she did say so herself, if a little damp from the constant deluge, in her nicest black dress, hair freshly done at the beauty parlor, and a smile plastered to her mouth, while a number of extremely nice and terribly young Seattle-ites waited in line to offer their compliments on her poetry. It was very tedious, but probably less tedious than lonesome inebriation.

A tall and rather lovely young woman kept smiling at her from across the room. Her hair was piled on top of her head in an assemblage of loops, and she was wearing a dress encrusted with plastic gems and with an odd sheen—the fabric was turned inside out, Elizabeth realized; the girl must have sewn it herself. The dress was so exceedingly short it nearly revealed her altogether, though there was no denying the long bare legs were perfection. As the hostess called them to table, the young woman found her way to Elizabeth's side. "Did you find the light?" she asked with a penetrating look.

Elizabeth stared back into her eyes, glittering green and gold like the fake jewels on her dress. Hard to say which color was predominant. She'd heard that religious fanatics often prowled public spaces in search of lost souls to ensnare, but Elizabeth had hardly expected to encounter one at a dinner party.

"No," she said. "But it looks as though the light is trying to find me."

The young woman laughed and laid her fingers on Elizabeth's arm. "I'm sorry, you don't recognize me. I helped you with the lamps the other day."

"That was you? I thought you were an evangelist." Elizabeth felt a rush of relief and bright spirits, just as she had felt when the young woman presented the three lamps at her feet. "Yes, I did find the light. I chose the putrescent one, and I adore it. You should recommend it to all your customers."

The eyes grew amused. "But I don't work at that store," she said.

"You don't?"

"I saw you sitting there, looking so frustrated, and I'm something of a busybody, so I had to interfere."

"Oh, dear." Elizabeth suddenly felt more moved than the situation merited; in fact, she found herself close to tears. "That was extremely kind of you." She left the girl and took her place at the table.

During the meal, Elizabeth sat next to a young painter whose vociferous passion for abstract expressionism allowed her to forgo her own performance as the prizewinning poet from the tropics. She was grateful, even if his soliloquy was a bit hard on the nerves. He required no more than the occasional *hmm* or *oh yes*, though she suspected even those interjections were unnecessary to keep the conversation rolling. For an hour, her greatest challenge was how she might most politely swallow her yawns. Several times Elizabeth glanced down the long table to find the young woman watching her with a worried, apologetic look.

Long before the meal was done, she began to feel it was high time to return to the Meany and kick off her shoes and curl up with the poems of Gerard Manley Hopkins. She and Lota had always had such wonderful New Year's celebrations, either quiet ones at Cabo Frio looking at the stars or else big, raucous dinners in Rio or Samambaia. She remembered one year in particular, when they'd had to move all the furniture out of the living room in the Rio apartment to make one enormous table seating thirty people. She and Lota had sat at either end, while between them had been all the people who mattered in that maddening, lovable country—Carlos, Rosinha, Luiz, Roberto, Mary, Flavio, and so many others. Somehow Lota had even lassoed a famous soap opera star into joining them, and she'd brought the French heartthrob Jean Paul Belmondo, who was in Brazil making a movie. Who at this table tonight would have pictured Elizabeth comparing impressions of Brasilia with an international movie star right there in her own home? Just another day in her glamorous South American life. After the meal, they'd crowded onto the veranda as fireworks exploded over Copacabana. The beach had glowed with the many thousands of revelers in white gowns wading into the water with their offerings to the sea goddess Yemanja.

"You and Lota are perfectly matched," she remembered Luiz saying beside her. "You are the north to Lota's south." Even Luiz was prone to poetics after a few glasses of champagne.

"But look down there," she said. "The south sure knows how to have more fun."

"But without the north, it does not know what it is."

"WAS THAT COMPLETE torture?" The young woman had slipped into the seat recently vacated by the painter.

"You mean the sermon on Jackson Pollock?"

"That was my husband sitting here, boring you to tears. I felt terrible I couldn't save you."

"There you go again, seeking my salvation."

"Yes, I have faith we can help you find the light, Elizabeth." The moment stretched out as they continued smiling at one another. Then the girl spoke again. "Actually, it's my husband who's the religious nut. Pollock is his God. He thinks putting random lines on a canvas makes him an abstract painter and a genius, but between you and me, he couldn't paint a still life to save his ass."

The vulgarity on those lips was oddly titillating. "At least he is passionate about the work," Elizabeth said carefully.

"I much prefer *his* subject matter." The young woman indicated a lean, bearded man wearing a plaid jacket. "He paints ducks. That's all. He just loves ducks."

"Well, who doesn't?"

"The cretin who doesn't love ducks probably hates kittens!"

Her eyes were really the most extraordinary color. Elizabeth held them until the young woman's cheeks reddened. "You must think I'm silly," she said, looking away.

"Not at all. I think you're refreshing."

The party began counting down from ten. Midnight was upon them. There was shouting and cheering and blowing horns all around. "Happy New Year," Elizabeth said softly.

"Happy New Year to you," her new friend said. The long graceful neck curved like a giraffe's or a gazelle's, Elizabeth observed, as she bent close. Then she closed her eyes to receive the young woman's kiss.

Elizabeth pulled back and glanced about at the immediate company. The husband was thumping the painter of ducks on the back. She moved to tap her champagne glass to the young woman's and noticed that the young woman was drinking water. "Aren't you celebrating?"

"In a private way. I'll tell you a secret. I just found out I'm going to have a baby." She spoke with the barely contained effusiveness with which she seemed to say everything.

"Well, congratulations," Elizabeth said. She was surprised at first, and then was overcome by a profound weariness. Yes, it was certainly time to be heading home.

The young woman continued to look at her. She bent close and spoke in Elizabeth's ear. "Have you accepted Jesus Christ as your personal savior?"

My word! Could a married, pregnant girl thirty years her junior actually be flirting with her?

EVERY DAY THERE was a letter, sometimes two or three. How Lota found the time to write them, Elizabeth could not fathom; she'd rarely been free for so much as a conversation before Elizabeth left Brazil. Most were funny, sharp descriptions of daily life—meetings with their friends, the animals at Samambaia, and of course the latest tribulations regarding the park. She didn't complain or scold Elizabeth too much—it was obvious she was trying hard to win her back. *You haven't lost me*, Elizabeth thought as she read, *I still adore you*.

AND THEN Miss Bishop was a teacher.

For the first few meetings, she stood before her students in such a paroxysm of anxiety she was almost unable to speak. They slouched there, staring at her, so much more informal in their beards and their beads than she ever would have dreamed of being when she herself was a college student.

And to them, she must have appeared like one of their grandmothers, hopelessly old fashioned, practically from the Middle Ages.

Yet almost immediately she began to dread her classes less. In all her worries about teaching, it had never occurred to Elizabeth that what would become quickly apparent was the fact that she actually knew a great deal more than her students did. Her students knew nothing! There were one or two bright lights, fortunately, but on the whole she had really expected them to be more advanced. When handing back their early assignments, it was only through a supreme effort of will that Elizabeth prevailed upon herself not to explain to one student and then the next why he or she was her most hopeless pupil.

You never learned how to spell.

You have a vocabulary limited to eight monosyllables. And that is a generous assessment.

You are addicted to comma splices.

You are as sloppy in language as you are in personal hygiene.

You couldn't punctuate a road sign.

There was learning of her own to be done, of course. She greatly appreciated her students' attempts to cross the generational gap and help her along into the modern era. One girl complimented Elizabeth's eye shadow and within minutes was discussing the use of birth control among her contemporaries. Not infrequently, in the middle of speaking to the class, Elizabeth found herself struggling to articulate her thoughts about writing in a way that might teach these young people something they could actually use.

"Some of your lines are just atrocious," she said. "I could spend the entire semester giving you grammar lessons, but that's not why we're here. You can do that on your own, and truly I urge you to. What I keep seeing in your poems is that you're all trying very hard to tackle weighty subject matter—war and social inequality and God and the question of whether or not we're all living in a dream. Ambition is good, and praiseworthy. But it doesn't generally serve you, and frankly, it's a little taxing to the reader, to use material that is too far beyond your experience. From what I've read of your poems, it looks as though half of you have spent your adolescence in the madhouse. If you really had, you'd probably be writing about something else altogether, flowers or skunks. Madness isn't romantic, and in itself it's no more meaningful than this pen in my hand. Writing should be about observing your own experience, taking a magnifying glass to your immediate world. You can make anything into a poem, but it's your observations of the subject that invest the poem with meaning, with depth and layers, just as they give life meaning. Do you understand the difference?"

They looked at her in silence, their eyes big and glistening with a hint of angry desire, like cats waiting to be fed.

"Today we'll do an exercise to illustrate my point. I've brought several different objects, and I want you to choose one and write a poem about it during class. In fact, I'll write one too. What I want you to keep in mind is that the more closely you observe, the more distinct and interesting, the more meaningful, your words are going to be."

From a paper grocery sack she drew a fork, a packet of seeds, a potato, and one of the scuffed black shoes she'd worn on New Year's. That morning she'd swept into the bag whatever lay in immediate sight, as she'd been running extremely late.

THERE WAS ANOTHER poetry teacher Elizabeth took to, a handsome, acerbic Englishman who called on the phone frequently to report on his exercise regimen. He read from his students' work the most blundering offenses to the tradition of poetry, until they both nearly died of hysterical laughter. At social gatherings, he always aimed directly for the bar and put a drink in her hand, then spoke in snide terms about nearly everyone else present. He might bring out the worst in her, but he certainly helped to pass the time. He encouraged Elizabeth to think of students as kin to parasites that had to be periodically purged or poisoned, like tapeworm. To her own surprise, she did not agree. She'd come to feel quite fond of the young people in her classes. For the most part, she found them touchingly sweet if a bit rambunctious, more like goats. They called out *Miss Bishop* from across the campus lawn, and on her birthday they brought her flowers

THE MORE I OWE YOU

and cupcakes. The show-off in class turned shy when he asked her to sign his copy of *Questions of Travel*. On some days, Elizabeth noticed she looked forward to meeting them in the classroom.

On other days, nothing could convince her to go. Different city, but the same old story. Some undermatter in her being seemed to be in a state of decay, the kind of precarious feeling that most often led to a binge; she could not leave the hotel room until it passed. That was why, one February afternoon of furious rain, she found that class time was approaching and she had not yet gotten out of bed. By then, Antabuse was a thing of the past. She'd used it erratically for some time, then run out completely months ago and had no intention of getting more. It was scientifically proven to cause despondency—she'd seen this in a magazine article and cut it out to send to Lota. But neither did Elizabeth wish to get roaring drunk; the close observation of that personal experience she preferred to leave behind as well. It would help to have some company, she decided, some talk, and so she called one of her students and asked him to come by. He was an older boy who had once invited her to tea, named Wesley. She'd been impressed by his impeccable manners. He was a painter.

Surprised by her invitation, he nevertheless said he'd dash over in the rain. He also brought what she'd asked for: a six-pack of beer. Beer in conversation was much healthier than gin by oneself. Elizabeth met him at the door in her housecoat.

"Please pull up that chair," she said as she settled back under the bedclothes. He was plainly uncomfortable with the arrangement, but there was really no other choice. There was the one armchair, with the bed affording the only other seating option. "I know this is unconventional," Elizabeth said, "but accommodations at the Hotel Meany are far from luxurious." Then she almost laughed to think Wesley might suspect he'd been invited to the scene of a seduction. She opened a beer and drank from the can. "Now tell me, how do you think the class is going?"

Wesley's eyes roamed all over the room. "It seems to be going all right," he finally said.

"From what I can tell, the real problem is that none of you seems ever to have heard of iambic pentameter. I'm going to begin assigning sonnets and sestinas, I think. You need to learn these forms, it's very important. You young people think of traditional forms as a *constraint*. You all want to write free verse, whatever you think that means, but what you don't understand is that form, and working within those structures, that's what can truly free you. And what is all this about Buddhism? Everyone is turning in haikus."

Wesley laughed, beginning to relax. "You have to remember we're on the Pacific coast. The Far East is our point of reference."

"How fascinating. Sometimes I haven't a clue how to talk to you all."

"Well, some of the students might not really get where you're coming from, but I think there are four or five in the class who would listen to just about anything you have to say."

"That's very sweet of you, but I know I'm hardly the most talented teacher. Teaching takes a lot of time, effort, and character, things I don't have any of. Here's my advice: You should be reading all day long, from the moment you wake up until you go to bed, everything good you can get your hands on. That's the best teacher. It was mine."

They sipped their beers. The rain beat at the window.

"Thank you for coming by on such short notice," she said. "I wasn't feeling well at all, and now I'm much better."

"I brought some of my paintings," Wesley said. "Would you like to see them?"

He opened his briefcase and removed a handful of pictures hardly bigger than playing cards, leaning forward to lay them out upon the bedspread like a game of solitaire. All were landscapes, scenes of the Pacific coastline in various seasons, viewed from a great distance. Elizabeth felt as though she were on a faraway hilltop, watching the line of surf through binoculars, and the effect was extraordinarily private and peaceful. Looking at these closely observed miniatures was the strongest antidote to that decaying thing inside her. She almost asked if she might keep one. "These are truly lovely," she said, setting down her beer. "Wesley, they're so good. What a pleasure to see really *small* paintings."

Blushing, he gathered them up and whisked them back into his brief-case. "Someday I'd like to carry a whole exhibition in my pockets."

WHENEVER THEY MET for tea, the young woman promised to take Elizabeth to the botanical garden as soon as there was a break in the weather. The first afternoon the rains let up, there she was, waiting in the lobby of the Hotel Meany when Elizabeth returned from class.

"I enjoy men," the young woman said as they strolled beneath trees still dripping with moisture, brilliant green moss covering their trunks. "I've always enjoyed sex with men."

Elizabeth admired the dogwood in flower. Apparently, the fad of open confessionalism was hardly limited to the younger American poets; it had become a way of life for the entire country. For some reason, she wasn't offended by this quality in the girl. "I suppose it's the pregnancy," her young friend went on, "but lately I can't really bear for my husband to touch me. It's as though my body wants something else, another kind of touch or excitement. It's trying to tell me something new but doesn't know how. It doesn't recognize this hunger."

Elizabeth was happy to listen but had no intention of participating equally in this style of conversation. It would have been the height of disrespect to begin speaking of Lota. To tell this young woman how it felt to be separated from a companion of fifteen years, how at times she craved Lota's physical closeness, her touch, the feel and the smell of her, with every cell of her being. And how strange to discover that even so, at this moment she could imagine nothing more pleasant than being here on this forest trail, hand in hand with a fresh young woman, the air cool and moist on her skin. No, these were private thoughts not to be discussed.

"I read that it was the son of Olmsted, the man responsible for Central Park in New York, who designed these gardens," Elizabeth remarked.

The young woman laughed in surprise and squeezed Elizabeth's hand. "You know just how to put a girl in her place, don't you?" she said. "You're a sly one. No one suspects it, and that's why it's such a delight to discover. I hope you won't be offended if I say that your company these last few weeks has been the thing I most look forward to, Elizabeth."

"Thank you. Yours is dear to me, too."

And then the sweet moment was spoiled. Elizabeth was so susceptible to poison oak that she had merely to walk near the plant, and it was like passing through the mist of perfume sprayed by a girl in a department store. The effects were instantaneous. A mild burning and then a fiery itching spread across her nose and cheeks.

The young woman knew exactly what to do. In five minutes she found a pharmacy nearby, rushed inside, and returned with a vial. There on the street, she fanned her hands over Elizabeth's face and used her thumbs to rub in the calamine lotion. It cooled the itching instantly. The young woman's touch reminded Elizabeth of how her grandmother had rubbed her icy hands in the winter, so vigorously she'd shaken Elizabeth's small body like a rag doll's.

As they drew near the Hotel Meany, the young woman gave her an even more pleasurable surprise. Anticipating their parting, Elizabeth felt a familiar lonely ache. She did not want to go inside alone; in fact, she did not want to go inside the Meany ever again. Then the young woman asked, as if she had read Elizabeth's mind, "How would you like to leave this hotel for good? I think I may have found you a home."

ELIZABETH DIDN'T HAVE to lift a finger. The young woman sent her off to the beauty parlor while she, Wesley, and another of Elizabeth's favorite students checked her out of the Hotel Meany forever and installed her in the new apartment. It wasn't spacious, but it wasn't mean. Best of all, even on a rainy day, light streamed in through windows in every room. The young woman had found it near the university and had pulled together furniture and kitchenware.

Wesley donated one or two of his own paintings to make it not so
spare. That evening, the four of them had a little party to celebrate.
Elizabeth cooked dinner for the first time since she'd been back in
the States. As they cleared the table to make room for the meal, she
noticed a packet of Lota's letters among the odds and ends. She swept
them into a box, then put on a samba record she had brought from
Rio, just in case a situation like this arose.

Samba, she told them as they ate, that's *real* poetry. So inventive and
playful. Every year there's a new batch for Carnaval, songs of love and
politics all shot through with a crazy, funny hope.

They ate the meal, they tripped over their own feet as she tried to
give them samba lessons, and at last they said goodnight and disappeared into the rain. The young woman remained behind to help clean
up. Elizabeth kept talking. "It's Carnaval in Rio tonight. I always loved
watching the samba bands. Samba can take anything from life, stories
straight out of the newspaper, and make it into art. That's the wonderful thing about Brazil. The way they live, it's so poetic, not hygienic
like it is here."

"So you've said, a number of times."

Elizabeth began dancing a samba for the young woman. She wasn't
bad for a northerner, that was what they'd always told her in Rio. The
young woman watched intently, but she was no longer smiling.

The song ended. Elizabeth stopped dancing. "Well, that's what I'd be
doing in Rio tonight."

"But you're not in Rio, Elizabeth. You're right here."

Irritated, Elizabeth turned and put the needle back on the record.
She danced a little more with her back to the young woman and with
her eyes closed. How could you long for a place and at the same time
feel so relieved to be free of it? It didn't make any sense. Maybe she'd
had too much to drink, because she tripped on her heel and nearly fell,
but the young woman was right behind her, catching her arm so she
didn't.

"Oh my, I'm getting old," Elizabeth said. "I never used to stumble."

"You're not old. You just need someone to hold you when you lose your balance."

The young woman's arm remained around Elizabeth's waist. Elizabeth turned and stared straight into the girl's sternum. She did not resist when the young woman pulled her close and slipped her arms around her. She was hardly in love with the young woman, Elizabeth thought. In fact, she had never missed Lota so much. But she'd felt so tired for such a long time, she deserved to rest. Her body gave itself over to this touch, its strength and its youth.

The young woman pressed her lips to Elizabeth's forehead, and switched off the lights.

It was only the body. Skin touching skin. She allowed the younger woman to take hold of her physical person, to position it this way and that, and it was exciting. There was no indecision.

Her pleasure came quickly. It was intense and muscular, like a cramp.

"I will never leave Lota," she whispered, her hand entangled in the young woman's hair.

·26·

THE ART OF blaming oneself is so very easy to master. Countless nights alone pondering infinite *if onlys*. For a time Elizabeth will be unable and even unwilling to imagine an end to this variety of self-inflicted torture. But she will not blame herself forever.

Three more cities lie ahead: San Francisco briefly, Ouro Preto off and on, and finally Boston for the last years. In the end, the North will draw her back. From her study overlooking Boston's waterfront, she'll watch the sailboats and fishing boats and tugboats crisscrossing the harbor. She'd been a good sailor herself as a girl, and the boats will always be mesmerizing. *But what a shame*, she'll think, *that there's no one playing soccer*. For nearly seventy years she will have wandered across a multitude of continents, but she'll die not fifty miles from where she was born.

It will happen most often in the mornings, before the day sweeps her into its present demands—that's when she'll think of Lota. A wake-up kiss on her Cookie's forehead. Elizabeth will not forget the intolerable years; hardly—how can you forget the scars knifed indelibly into your flesh? It is simply that the nightmare pervasive at the end of their time together will no longer take precedence. The horror will ebb, like a wave pulling back from the beach. So that, yes, it will still be possible to remember the evening Lota intercepted a letter from the young woman and then climbed onto the balcony railing, shouting and sobbing, threatening to jump to the street below; to remember as well her own screaming, insane response: *Just do it and put us both out of our misery*. It will be possible not to elide those events from her memory, and yet still recall the exquisite tenderness of floating side by side in the pool at Samambaia on a hot summer afternoon, such peace between them that butterflies alit on their arms and faces to drink the moisture from their skin.

Sometimes, while she gazes at the harbor traffic, the sensation of Lota's presence will rush upon Elizabeth with such force she will suspect she has only to turn and discover Lota standing there, watching her with a mischievous smile.

Loving was not about saving yourself, nor saving your beloved. Mary had tried to tell Elizabeth something of the sort, but at the time she hadn't been able to listen. Love was simply about loving, as ardently and willfully, as consciously, as you were capable.

The *oratorio* of Saint Barbara that Lilli gave her will sit on a shelf above her desk. Fittingly, on the autumn afternoon Saint Barbara witnesses her death, Elizabeth will be at work, making revisions to a poem that isn't yet right. Throughout the day, she'll raise her head from the page to watch the boats gliding upon the water. Since the recent anniversary of the date on which Lota slipped from the world, Elizabeth's thoughts will have been traveling back in time, back to the trip they made to Italy before Lota became so ill.

After arriving in Florence, they'd been on their feet without a break, Lota was inexhaustible when it came to museums, and even more so when shopping for the exact black leather briefcase she'd imagined finding there. Elizabeth's feet throbbed, she begged to rest. Wait right here, Lota said, and disappeared around a corner. Within twenty minutes she returned, wheeling along two bicycles. Elizabeth resisted at first, though she could not say why; it was simply her way, to resist while at the same time longing to be convinced. And Lota always convinced her. As soon as she was on the bicycle and pedaling through the streets, Elizabeth could not stop grinning. She had never imagined herself as graceful, but this was glorious, it was truly like flying. They wove daringly among tourists, rode out into the countryside and back—she did not want to stop. Late in the evening, near midnight, they propped their bikes at a café. The church directly across the little square had palm trees painted on its face. They look like an oasis, Elizabeth observed. They make me homesick for Brazil.

Lota caught up her hand and kissed it. Elizabeechy, she said. My life was arid, and now you are my oasis.

You are the same for me.

Lota called over the waiter and ordered a grappa for herself and, to Elizabeth's surprise, a limoncello for the lady. We are on vacation, she said, I do not need to be so strict with you. Just like the first day Elizabeth had arrived in Samambaia, when Lota had poured her a limoncello, the drink was syrupy at first and then it was delicious. It is a real lady's drink, Lota said, and you are a real lady.

Then they were back on the bikes, racing tipsily through the deserted city, up and down the cobblestone streets, over bridges, through plazas, and Elizabeth singing. Limoncello, she sang. Lotacello. La mia bella, Lotacella. They rolled down a curving sidewalk that suddenly broke into a series of stairs—*bump, bump, bump* on the bicycles—and there before them was the Duomo! Lotacella, sang Elizabeth, la mia bella. And on through the streets of Florence.

A BUS DISGORGED a tour group that entered the botanical garden in a queue, two by two. From a distance, they appeared to stumble and stagger down the long avenue beneath the imperial palms. "There's something odd about those people," Elizabeth remarked to her companion. "Look how they walk, as if their feet are bound together."

"Are they adults or children?" he asked. "They seem to be holding hands."

"Maybe they're war veterans," she said. "Damaged, somehow."

"Or suffering from terminal illness?"

"Who've come here for the healing properties of nature."

They'd been sitting on a bench in the shade of a jackfruit tree and playing this game much of the afternoon, conjuring stories about whatever caught their notice, be it animal, vegetable, or mineral. Her friend was a bright young Fulbright scholar she'd met before leaving for Seattle, who thankfully hadn't come to his senses and fled Rio before her return. He was good, clever company, and ready for any outing she suggested at almost any time of day or night. She appreciated that about young people. Even Lota found him agreeable, a rarity in itself, and trustworthy enough that she didn't give Elizabeth too much grief when they went out to hear music at Copacabana nightclubs.

From the bench, one's eye was first impressed by a pond full of those vigorous, thrusting elephant ears she remembered lining the banks of the Amazon. Beyond, one or two ladies beneath parasols, then all faded into trees and vines. The colors were elemental: blues, greens, browns, with a dash of yellow, pink, or red here and there—you could lose yourself completely, as if you were staring into a painting. Earlier she'd seen that one of her favorite old trees had died. Beautiful even in death, with enormous buttresses running down the trunk and bare black branches covered with green bromeliads. For an hour or so, three men had been working energetically to fell it with a giant saw.

The scholar followed her gaze. "Backyard forestry," he said. "Part of a new government program initiated while you were away."

"Yes, it's called Fifty Years of Regression in Five. I've heard it's been highly successful already. The first step was restoring the dictatorship." Then Elizabeth dropped the game. "Honestly, I find the political situation impossible to understand. Maybe you can explain it, but it seems to me the country's in worse shape than when I arrived fifteen years ago."

The scholar merely shrugged, as if confused by her seriousness. To amuse him, she began translating the inscription on an old plaque beside their bench, though of course her friend's Portuguese was far superior to hers. "'Sitting in the shade beneath this jackfruit tree,'" she read, "'Friar Leandro do Sacramento, in 1825, directed the workers excavating this lake.'"

"Perhaps the friar is buried here, and that's his epitaph." At times Elizabeth noticed that he seemed to imitate her inflections of speech.

"Yes, a lovely tribute to what can be accomplished while sitting in the shade. It's never too early to have a good epitaph prepared. I know what mine will be: 'Awful, but cheerful.'" He laughed, but this was in fact her second choice. Her first was more apt: "Here lies one whose name was writ in hooch."

Over her friend's shoulder, she saw the tour group emerge from the forest, lurching hand in hand out of the foliage. Docents in white caps kept them in line. The mystery of their confusing appearance was now solved. All proved nearly identical: short stature, droopy, sad eyes, broad foreheads, downturned mouths. It was an outing of mongoloids.

"Look," Elizabeth said, "here come a bunch of Brazilian politicians."

She was not a kind person, but she could usually draw a laugh. At least she had some spark left, a little fire, even if when she looked in the mirror she saw a crooked old lady.

And yet when she and her friend returned to the apartment and stood on the veranda, the view of the ocean and the long graceful curve of Copacabana still made Elizabeth's heart leap up, as if it were not yet through with the world.

They had just settled into chairs, each with a gin and tonic in hand, when Lota arrived home. Elizabeth hadn't expected her so early, but she didn't worry overmuch. Lota wouldn't be too terrible in front of company.

"What are you doing here?" Lota asked in an accusatory fashion.

"We're discussing *Moby-Dick*," Elizabeth said.

"That's not what you're doing. You're drinking in the middle of the day!"

"Please, Lota. It's not the middle of the day, it's after five. That's a perfectly civilized time."

Lota left them in disgust and retreated to the back rooms of the apartment.

"It's too bad you didn't know her when she was fun," Elizabeth said. "She used to be hilarious. She could make you laugh more than you'd ever laughed in your life. Now I find her opening my letters."

"While you were away, I came to see Lota quite a lot. She missed you very much."

"Oh, don't try to give me a pep talk. She missed controlling me."

Lota banged on the wall.

Elizabeth raised an eyebrow. "I suppose that means we'll have to change venues. Shall we see if Vinicius is playing tonight?"

Lota reappeared, lunging at Elizabeth and snatching the drink out of her hand.

"Lota, that's enough!"

"She is sick," Lota told the scholar, "very very sick, and she can't control herself. She is a sick woman."

CONSTANT NOW, the dread.

IT HADN'T BEEN so when she was preparing to return. During Elizabeth's last days in Seattle, once she'd turned her thoughts southward, back to Brazil, she had begun to believe in the prospect of a happy reunion. The separation had done her good—Miss Bishop was cut out to be a teacher after all. And it was better to be leaving Seattle before things with the young woman became too complicated. She was excited to take up her life again with Lota. Yet she almost did not know the woman, so haggard and thin, altered virtually beyond recognition, who leaned on the faithful maid Lucia's shoulder at the airport. Had she really changed so much in such a short time, or had some amnesia about Lota's condition fallen over Elizabeth in Seattle like a veil?

On the way back to the apartment, Lota talked nonstop in a kind of angry mania. Elizabeth had had her six-month drinking binge in Seattle, but now she was home and there'd be no more of that. And now that she knew what a failure she was as a teacher, there'd be no more of that, either. She did not allow a single word of rebuttal. By the time they arrived home, Elizabeth was completely drained. Lota followed her into her room to continue the harangue. Elizabeth pulled a pillow over her head, and still she went on. It appeared there was not to be any joy between them.

Through July and August, Lota's moods grew only more extreme and unpredictable. Mornings were the worst. Elizabeth woke to discover the bed shaking with Lota's sobs. No gesture or word of compassion was allowable, because the moment the crying fit passed, it was replaced with a temper so befouled with rage and suspicion you would be cut down instantly if caught in its crosshairs. Better to remain hidden like a rabbit in a burrow until the danger passed. When at last Lota left the apartment for work, Elizabeth and Lucia stared at one another, at first too brutalized to speak.

"Has she been like this for long?"

Lucia nodded. "But it is worse now that you are back, Dona Elizabeechy."

The park consumed her; that circumstance remained consistent. The power struggles, the idiocy, the feuds—ongoing. Lota was seeing her analyst five times a week, and it was that, Elizabeth thought, that kept alive whatever rationality remained. Week after week, however, her physical condition deteriorated. Lota tossed and moaned at night, unable to sleep. She did not possess enough concentration to read, denied even that consolation. When Elizabeth remained at her side she was contemptuous, yet she refused to be left alone. She began to suffer dizzy spells of such severity she could hardly walk across a room without stumbling. Her doctor was useless, blaming the vertigo on a liver imbalance and prescribing the intake of macaroni and gelatin. But he narrowed his eyes accusingly at Elizabeth when he suggested that the true cause was emotional distress.

Thank heavens for the Fulbright scholar, for the botanical garden, for the samba clubs in Lapa, for escapes to Ouro Preto, and for cachaça, Brazil's national pastime.

One morning in September, Elizabeth found Lota at the dining table with her forehead pressed against her fists. She drew near but hesitated to come too near.

"Lota, dear, what's wrong?"

"I can't do it," Lota murmured.

"You can't do what?"

"I can't do it!" she shouted, slamming both hands upon the tabletop.

In the back room, Lucia was watching a soap opera; the overwrought voices could be heard through her door. Outside, the day was flawless. A bird floated on a draft, as if suspended motionless from above with his wings outstretched, and then alighted on the veranda railing. Elizabeth did not speak. She willed herself to enter the tiger's cage, offer her hand. Carefully she placed a palm on Lota's back and began to rub lightly between the shoulder blades.

Lota mumbled something, arching her back.

"I'm sorry, Lota, I couldn't hear you."

"I don't like to be touched," she said.

Elizabeth withdrew her hand. Until now, it had not occurred to her that love could be completely beside the point.

"*O Globo* has started reporting on the number of people killed in the park every day by speeding cars," Lota told her. "Children are dying as they cross the road to the playground. And they blame me! I told them not to put in so many roads."

"I know you did. They would have put in even more if you hadn't fought them so hard."

"Negrão has requested to meet with me this morning. He is looking for any excuse to terminate the park foundation and has already filed a lawsuit challenging its legitimacy. He plans to give jurisdiction to SURSAN, to those imbeciles. And I'm supposed to make a case for why he should not take it away from me. After everything I've done. I can't face him. I can't do it."

Lota now turned to Elizabeth with a terrible, desperate look.

Elizabeth had seen the expression before, but she could not at first remember where. The mule on the highway to Ouro Preto, watching their car fly toward it, thinking it was going to be hit—its eyes had rolled back in terror just as Lota's did now.

"Please try to calm down." It was all Elizabeth could think to say. Were there no other words more helpful, more loving? "It will work out for the best, I just bet you it will."

"'It will work out for the best?' That is a ridiculous thing to say. You have no idea, Elizabeth, of the stress I am under. Why are you standing over me like that? Everyone wants something from me, even you. What is it *you* want from me?"

Lota spoke with such spitefulness that it was a relief to snap as well. "I want you not to attack or mock me at every opportunity," Elizabeth cried. "I am not your enemy. And, Lota, it's just—" She stopped herself in time.

"Yes, say it, it's just a park! I know that's what you think. Just because you have no idea what it means to be committed to anything. You're not even a poet anymore, you're just a drunk. You had to leave me for six months so you could go drink without anyone telling you to stop. And now you drink here, right in front of my face."

"You make it impossible not to drink. It's the only way I can bear living with this insanity."

"When was the last time you took your pills?"

"I'm not going to take the Antabuse anymore. It makes me very despondent. It is not good for me."

"Well, that is too bad. So we are both despondent. You will take it."

"No, Lota, I won't. Don't ask me to."

"The time has passed for asking."

Lota stomped out of the room. For such a small person, her footfalls made an inordinate amount of noise. As did her opening and closing of cabinets, her slamming of doors. The peace of a room Lota had recently left was exquisite, almost musical—like the ringing deafness a soldier must experience on the battlefield after a nearby detonation. Elizabeth made a motion toward the veranda, but she saw the bird still perched on the railing and didn't want to disturb it. It was one of those compact little terns she loved, the ones that traveled hemispheres. Still, it took fright and lifted off, its wings outstretched in perfect strong arcs. Then, gracefully, it set itself back down in precisely the same place.

Lota returned, a clenched fist held before her. "Open your mouth."

"What are you talking about?"

"I said open your mouth!" Lota was shouting.

Elizabeth looked to the maid's room, willing Lucia to emerge. She was truly afraid now. She thought to call out, then decided it best to leave the room altogether. Lota grabbed her arm and held her back.

"You let go of me this instant," Elizabeth cried.

"You will not drink anymore."

"You're hurting my arm."

Elizabeth tried to pull away, but Lota yanked her toward the couch and forced her to sit down. With one hand she seized Elizabeth's jaw and dug her fingers into the sides of her face. Elizabeth tried to speak but could not. All the will drained out of her.

"Open your mouth!"

Elizabeth's body did as it was told.

Lota pushed her head back and dropped the pill at the back of her throat, as she would have done to a dog. "Now swallow it."

Elizabeth's mouth was completely dry. Water leaked from her eyes but she was not crying. She looked up at Lota's determined, heartless face.

"Swallow it!" Lota screamed.

"Give me some water," she said.

Lota filled a drinking glass and watched as Elizabeth drained it. Once she was satisfied Elizabeth had swallowed the pill, she left the house. Elizabeth remained on the couch for she did not know how long. Lucia's soap opera went on. The bird was still perched on the veranda.

FLIGHT BEGAN TO present itself as the only option. Elizabeth went back and forth in her mind: It must be either her own flight, away from Lota, to Seattle or somewhere new, to a new life, or even a very long trip—that might be enough, back down the Amazon, or any river for that matter. Or else, no, she would not leave Lota—she was in it to the end, they would go away together. Her mind snatched and grasped at anything like hope. To Europe! They'd had good luck there before. Yes, to Europe. To Holland, somewhere cold, with taciturn society. Some reliable Dutch stolidity could be precisely the thing to counter this plague of Latin hysteria.

·27·

THEY NEVER SHOULD have gone to Europe, in Mary's opinion. It was obvious Lota was in no shape to travel, and that Elizabeth was desperate, clutching at straws. Hardly a surprise when Mary heard they were cutting their trip short and rushing Lota home, to the hospital. Why Lota's psychiatrist had ever approved the trip in the first place was beyond her, as if a mere change of scenery could cure the gangrene infecting Lota's soul. But no one had asked for Mary's opinion.

Now she and Elizabeth stood on either side of Dr. de Souza in the doorway of Lota's hospital room, speaking in hushed voices, as if the numb lump of Lota might actually overhear them.

"We are keeping her sedated for the time being," the psychiatrist was saying. "She is extremely agitated."

"Her state is very grave, isn't it?" Mary pressed, rigid with anger.

"Decio, do you think it might simply be her inner ear?" Elizabeth asked, with her mouth twisted into a weird grimace. "We were at an exhibition in London, and Lota was so dizzy, she was teetering like a drunk. She fell down, and then she was furious and impossible. Her doctor says it's all psychological, as if it's *my* fault, but maybe it's an infection in her ear. I told him to check that, and he never did."

Lota and Elizabeth called the psychiatrist by his first name; they both thought he was so wonderful because he'd studied with the famous Melanie Klein. Mary judged him, but she couldn't afford to judge him too severely. When Dr. de Souza met her eye, she gave him a look as if to say, *See! This is what I've had to deal with for years. They're both crazy.*

He turned back to Elizabeth as she continued to ramble.

"I know it was probably a bad idea to take her to Europe, but I've always believed in the good old-fashioned notion of change. I thought a change might be good for her. We had good luck there before, when we went to Italy. We rode bicycles. But she hated London. Nothing was good enough for her. I finally realized she was in ghastly shape. Maybe it was my fault for taking her away."

"It's not your fault," the doctor said gently. "She's been under intense strain for five years, and it is finally taking its toll."

"Yes, you're right. She's been under such strain. She would never listen to me, never take a break. All she does is criticize me. Everything I do or say is wrong. She doesn't believe that I'm on her side. She's more violent and rude every day. She's been just intolerable." And then Elizabeth began to cry into her hands.

Dr. de Souza observed her, then turned to Mary. In a tone so soft it belied the severity of his prescription, he said, "My feeling is that the two of them should be separated."

"Separated?" Mary kept her voice even, surprised at her own sadness.

"For at least several months. Miss Bishop's presence is not beneficial. It triggers Lota's paranoia. Two women, living together in close quarters . . ." He shrugged, as if this result confirmed a common hypothesis. "It compounds the hysteria."

It wasn't that Mary blamed Elizabeth, not exactly; she'd known Lota too well and for too long. But nor did she hold Elizabeth faultless.

Mary could see that the woman was suffering, and she felt for her, truly. But it wasn't by mere chance that Elizabeth and Lota could no longer be in the same room for any length of time without acrimony, nor that in the immediate crisis it was Mary who could provide what Lota needed most.

Dr. de Souza took hold of Elizabeth's frail-looking shoulders, to offer comfort, it seemed, but also to communicate that she must pull herself together. "What are you doing for your own health?" he asked.

"What do you mean?"

"There is nothing you can do now for Dona Lota. You must take care of yourself however you can."

He said good day. Elizabeth did not move. Her eyes were wide, liquid. Mary had never seen anyone look so bereft, like a child informed she'd just been made an orphan.

MARY WAS RELIEVED when Elizabeth called Lilli and left on a bus for Ouro Preto. Knowing she had friends to go to, Mary didn't have to worry about taking care of her on top of everything else. Yet she also wished Elizabeth had not left her alone; in its sly fashion, fate had made Elizabeth the only person with whom Mary could now commiserate. And though it might not speak well of her, Mary couldn't help but resent the woman for leaving everything in her hands. Of course, there was no question that Mary would move down from Samambaia to attend to Lota, leaving her daughters in the care of their nanny, to perform whatever duty was required for as long as necessary. But in the following weeks she could not prevent the bitter thoughts that crossed her mind. In Ouro Preto, Elizabeth did not have to rush back and forth between the apartment in Copacabana and the clinic in Botafogo, bringing the meals Mary and Lucia had to cook, since Lota could not stomach hospital food. Nor did Elizabeth have to wash sheets every day, since Lota refused to sleep, even under sedation, on inferior hospital bedding. Elizabeth did not have to provide the company Lota required without respite, as she could not bear to be left alone for any longer than was necessary to fetch her food and linens. Nor did Elizabeth have to sleep on a pad on the floor, Lota's hand gripping hers throughout the night, holding the arm elevated with drug-induced strength until the blood drained out and left her right shoulder numb for much of the morning. Elizabeth had to do none of those things, and those were the easy things.

Unlike Mary, Elizabeth did not have to accompany Lota daily down into the hell she had come to inhabit.

The insulin treatments were the most gruesome torture Mary had ever seen inflicted upon another human being. Dr. de Souza warned that the therapy might subject Dona Lota to severe shock, that was a danger they must risk, but Mary felt it was she instead who was receiving the shock. In the States, they never would have allowed her to be at Lota's side during the procedure, but here everything was excessively casual; they did not take into account the danger to the witness.

The first time she watched Lota go into convulsions brought on by the injection of insulin, tears began streaming down Mary's face. She had to force herself to remain still, not to run out of the room. A nurse told her the seizures were normal, but they were anything but—they were criminal. Mary prayed for the fit to end, but when it finally did, what followed was hardly better. Lota fell into a coma. Her face was bloodless, deathly white, and her hands were laid over her chest; she remained utterly still, as if truly deceased. Dr. de Souza told Mary that none of this diverged from the expected sequence of events, that the treatment would help Lota get better, yet as she sat beside Lota in this state, Mary felt she was being introduced to the eventuality of losing Lota completely.

And then, when the doctors brought her out of the coma, for a too-brief, miraculous hour or so, it was as if the Lota of old had woken from a long hibernation. Not just coherent but playful, naughty, even vigorous. She joked with the doctors, bossed the nurses around in that charming way of hers that made you rush to do her bidding, talked of the future—there was life in her eyes. But always, after a while, the fire began to fade and Lota descended back into the blackness.

Elizabeth never saw any of this. Once a day, she checked in by phone from Ouro Preto and talked about the renovations to her new house, for God's sake! She wasn't there to see Lota's eagerness for these calls, her hunger. Lota was usually in that state of grace following the coma, when she could banter and laugh. "The park is lost," Mary heard her say one afternoon in an almost jovial tone. "Negrão has won. He's given it to SURSAN. It is time to look forward, Elizabeth." Elizabeth wasn't there when Lota set down the phone—the look on her face was enough to shatter you.

This went on for a month. Mary delivered the meals and the laundry, endured the seizures and comas. In her few private moments, she wrote notes to her daughters, promising she'd see them soon. Lota's periods of lucidity grew longer, and one day she decided it was time to attempt a normal life again. She was much better, certainly. Dr. de Souza agreed to release her from the hospital for a trial period. Elizabeth returned from Ouro Preto, and the three of them drove up to Samambaia just in time for Christmas. As if the last few months had not even happened, Lota and Elizabeth were easy and affectionate with each other. Mary asked to be let out at her own house at the base of the hill. She did not wait for the car to pull away before she rushed inside. Her daughters came running in from the garden and she gripped them both, pressing their bodies to hers, breathing in their green smell like salvation. "Oh, how I missed you," she said, again and again and again.

All remained stable for nearly a week. Until the morning Mary knocked on their door and could hear the shouts and sobs inside. The dread for which she had braced herself now returned. The door opened. Lota's face, rageful, grief-stricken. Elizabeth's, completely broken down. Her own, no doubt resolute.

RATHER THAN READMIT her to the hospital, Dr. de Souza kept Lota at the apartment under his daily supervision, with two nurses and Mary in constant attendance. Elizabeth could not stay there. That was imperative. Neither Lota's health nor her own permitted it, and this time the doctor was adamant about the separation. Mary now had full confidence in his judgment.

Elizabeth packed a battered suitcase while Mary stood in the doorway. Between her hands she held a hot cup of tea she'd made for Elizabeth. The heat felt good on her arthritic joints. None of them were young any longer, of course, but the years seemed to have treated Elizabeth particularly unkindly. She looked like a shrunken crone, white and hunched, like a character from a children's fable who would promise you a treat, then trap you and eat you.

Had Elizabeth really believed Lota would not find out about her dalliance in Seattle? Though Mary did not feel much outrage on Lota's behalf. She herself knew only too well the keen despair of losing Lota's gaze, what depths it could drive you to. It had been awful to watch the two of them grow more and more estranged, more disregarding and suspicious. And now this—no options left but rupture. So very sad, though of course much sadder for Lota.

Elizabeth filled her suitcase, inattentive to the items she placed there, then thread the leather tongues through the buckles and cinched it closed. She looked in the mirror as she put on a hat and gloves. She might have been preparing for a journey to another continent, rather than to the hotel down the street where she planned to stay a few days, only, she'd said, until a place opened up for her at the clinic. Elizabeth checked in for rest cures the way other people went to the beauty parlor; she had a standing appointment, going in haggard and emerging redone.

Elizabeth sat heavily on the bed and pulled the suitcase into her lap. "Here I am again," she said wryly, almost with a sense of humor. "Off to a hotel alone after fifteen years."

"It won't be forever," Mary said helpfully, though, to be honest, no one really knew.

"I feel completely at the end of my rope. I don't know what to do anymore."

"I'm truly sorry, Elizabeth. Let's just hope that Lota gets better."

"Yes, I have to believe she will. I suppose I should be off." She made no motion to leave. Her eyes had become pleading. "Help me, Mary, I feel so lost." Elizabeth began to cry, bitter jagged tears. You could not help but be moved, even if you disapproved of her choices.

Mary set down the tea and knelt before Elizabeth, clasping her hand. "The way out is to keep loving. I know it's not easy. We always want love to give us something back, something we need deeply, but I don't think that's the way it works. Love is like faith. We have to keep reaching into ourselves to find it, even when we think there is nothing left inside us and nothing returned. It can be terribly painful. But when you are lost, that's the way to find yourself again."

Elizabeth looked down at her. Mary smiled, thinking perhaps she'd gotten through her misery and helped in some small way. Elizabeth was not her rival after all, but her colleague; they both loved Lota.

"Well, I'm not a nun like you." Elizabeth's voice was low and hateful. "I have needs, too. I can't just serve."

Then she carried her suitcase out the door.

Mary remained crouched beside the bed, stung beyond comprehension. How unjust! As if she were some dried-up old maid who had no need for love. Did Elizabeth have any idea how excruciating and lonely it had been on occasions too numerous to count to spend the day or evening with the two of them, then return alone to her own house or room? To be evicted from the very house she had helped plan and build? Of course not. She thought of no one but herself. Elizabeth had no idea what love might truly be, other than the gratification of her own selfishness.

Lota was awake when Mary went to check on her. The afternoon light coming through the window washed across Lota's gaunt face, still

THE MORE I OWE YOU

so beautiful even in this wasted state. Finally she might have a chance to improve, with Elizabeth out of the picture.

"How are you, dear?"

Lota did not answer.

"Would you like something to eat?"

"Has Elizabeth gone?"

"It was Dr. de Souza's recommendation. She took some of her things."

"Where will she go? Did she tell you?"

Mary said nothing. Truthfully, she did not care where Elizabeth went. Let her go to hell.

Lota turned away from Mary, craning her neck to look out the window, as if she might spot Elizabeth on the street below. "My poor, sweet Cookie," she said.

·28·

*I*N MARCH, LOTA appeared at the door of Elizabeth's room in the Botafogo clinic. "What are you doing here?" she asked gently. "I thought *I* was the sick one."

Elizabeth did not want to believe what she saw, she did not dare allow herself to hope. "My asthma came back," she finally said.

"Well, let's get you out of this dump," Lota told her. "I'm taking you straight to Samambaia."

ELIZABETH WROTE throughout the day. The words came in a flood, in surprising forms she'd never before thought to attempt. She could not remember when she'd last felt such energy or inclination, as if the enormous tension she had been holding inside herself for months or even years had now burst forth and taken shape in writing.

Each morning, she rose early and took her coffee beside the waterfall. The dry season had begun, and the creatures who inhabited the pool, the snails and toads and crabs, squeezed into crevices among the rocks, seeking moisture. It was the time of year when large pale-blue butterflies drifted along the meadows and the edge of the forest, flopping slowly before one's eyes, and the Lent trees bloomed purple all over the mountains. Looking back down the hill, Elizabeth saw how the house had become nearly overgrown by jungle and vines after many months of neglect. It appeared abandoned, or else home to the sort of people who collected bales of newspapers and were overrun with cats. But when she returned inside, the sun was streaming through the leaves that grew over the windows, like green stained glass, and the light was perfectly beautiful.

Nearly two decades earlier, when Elizabeth had first come to Samambaia, the house had been a mere four rooms. She'd written in the little den, banging on an ancient typewriter whose letters had worn off the keys. This was where she returned to work now. She preferred to stay in the main house rather than disappear into her studio; she did not want to stray too far from Lota. On the sofa across the room, Lota lay sleeping with a blanket tucked around her, while the Calder mobile suspended above took a twist or turn every so often from a draft. It was warm for March, but Lota said she could not rid herself of a chill that went to her bones. She wore sweaters and blankets, and Elizabeth, in a slip, kept the fire roaring in the sheet-iron stove as she worked.

The day progressed. Elizabeth wrote about the toad. Lota whimpered in her sleep, and Elizabeth tiptoed to her side to pull the blanket back over her shoulders. The woolen blanket was moth-eaten, pinpricked with holes. Lota's recovery was a miracle—Elizabeth could not yet fathom it—but she wasn't completely out of the woods. For no apparent reason, she still experienced crying jags or sudden fits of bad temper. In most ways, however, in the ways that mattered, she was Lota again.

Lota woke as Elizabeth stood over her, and her eyes darted about, filling with panic. She was often afraid when she first gained consciousness, as if she did not recognize where she lay.

"It's all right," Elizabeth said, sitting beside her. "I'm here."

Lota's gaze finally rested upon Elizabeth, and she grew calmer. "Have I slept long?"

"It's nearly evening now. Here, take these."

Obediently, Lota swallowed the two white pills Elizabeth held in her palm.

"Shall I make you some dinner? I can bring it to you here, on a tray."

"With a toucan?" Lota said, smiling.

"No toucan, I'm afraid."

"You miss your Sammy the toucan, don't you? You loved him so much. Why don't I get you another Sammy?"

Elizabeth slid her hand beneath the blanket and stroked Lota's calf. "For now, I'd rather take care of you."

"I was terrible to you about Seattle, Cookie."

"Yes, you were. You were impossible."

"I was jealous. All those letters from your students. You must have been a very good teacher for them to miss you so much. I knew you were happy there, so far away from me."

"I wasn't happy being away from you. But it's true I wasn't as unhappy as I'd been here before I left."

"And you are over all your nonsenses, aren't you?"

Elizabeth nodded, though it was easier to speak about one of her nonsenses than about the other. "When I'm away, the drinking is not so much of a problem. It's only with the constant strain that I can't control myself."

"Then we must eliminate the strain. And we must trust each other more."

"I feel very hopeful, Lota, as strange as that sounds. After all we've been through together, I feel as if we finally have no illusions left. We just have each other, as imperfect as we are, but also as well-meaning."

Whoever could have told her that deep sorrow was inextricably bound to deep love? Was that what Mary had meant, that in the end you must submit, humbled, before love? In the clinic in Botafogo, her mind had filled with plans for escape. She'd catch the next flight to Seattle, or New York, or Key West, or Mexico. No, not Mexico—no more Latin countries ever again. Instead, she'd been given another chance to love, to love better, and she would not squander it. She would not leave Brazil—not this vine-enshrouded house, not the pool, not the snail, the toad, the crab. And not Lota, never Lota.

As Lota gained strength, she also regained the capacity for boredom. Elizabeth had never known another person who responded to boredom with such a personal and almost moral fury. In retrospect, she understood this had always been so. During the years they'd spent peacefully in Samambaia, before the park, Lota had lived in a state of ceaseless motion. All her waking hours had been devoted to working on the house, with hardly a moment for rest or contemplation, for a stillness of soul. Then, it had not occurred to Elizabeth that Lota's energy might contain an element of desperation; instead she'd thought it enviable, passionate and creative, qualities she deeply admired. Once the house was completed, however, Lota had pursued a project of an even greater scale to avoid drowning in her own impatience.

"*Merde!*" Lota exclaimed.

Elizabeth looked up from the typewriter. Lota had thrown the pages she was reading to the floor. It was another letter from Carlos. He wrote nearly every day, trying to woo her back.

"Carlos is so full of bullcrap it makes me sick," she cried. "He wants me to come work for him again. I think he honestly believes the two of us alone can overthrow the dictatorship. If I don't work soon, I will truly go mad, but if I work for *him*, I will go madder sooner." As she held Elizabeth's gaze across the room, Lota's anger softened. "Why did I not listen to you?" she said. "You were right all along. Carlos does not want to reach accord with anyone, he simply wants to fight. I miss him, but I do not miss all his *merde*. A cloud of *merde* follows him everywhere."

"That's true. But I have to believe that, like you, Lota, he is only fighting because he believes so deeply in his cause."

Lota replied, "I am tired of fighting. I don't have any fight left. Cookie, I've been thinking. Do you think you could make a very special lunch, if I asked you?"

"Of course. Anything you want."

"I would like to invite my father to come. And my sister Marietta. When I feel a little bit stronger. It is time to make peace."

LOTA WAS AGAIN able to drive, to read, to take walks with Elizabeth in the forest, to bully the gardener. She began to take charge of getting the house in order, and now there was much bustle and activity around Elizabeth as she wrote. Their idyll was broken only by one daily unpleasantness: Mary's visits. Mary no longer entered the house freely at any time of day but arrived each afternoon at three o'clock, knocking on the door like a formal visitor, and strode past Elizabeth without a greeting. Elizabeth hardly remembered what vile things she'd said the day of their quarrel, she'd been so distraught and poisoned by self-loathing. But obviously Mary remembered every word, and she had not forgiven her. Now she spoke to Elizabeth no more than was necessary to maintain the bare minimum of civility.

Of course, this did not escape Lota. "What happened between you?" she demanded.

"Nothing, Lota."

"It was more than nothing. Morsie does not easily take offense."

"Well, she took offense from me."

"Tell me why." Her expression was wonderfully stern and Lota-like.

"We fought over you, if you must know."

Lota took in the information, and a pleased look settled over her face. She let the matter drop.

FINALLY, THE BOREDOM was too great. Cleaning the house was not enough; it was work for a maid. One of the former members of Lota's staff at the park had moved to the federal office of inflation control. He offered her a job, and she accepted.

"That sounds absolutely deadly," Elizabeth said. Lota's announcement had taken her by surprise, but it also made plain another fact equally difficult to accommodate: Samambaia would never again be their permanent home. "I am only worried that going back to work for the government will make you . . ." She searched for the word.

"Unhinged?"

Elizabeth nodded. "Something like that."

"I promise you I won't allow myself to become swallowed as I was before," Lota said. "I will keep perspective. Besides, I will be a low-level bureaucrat, and who will care enough to fight me? But Elizabeth, you know I cannot be idle. That is the greater danger."

So they left the mountains and descended back into the deafening city. Lota had new clothes made and began to meet with her prospective employers. Three days a week, she had an appointment with Decio. It was now Elizabeth, alone in the Rio apartment, who was forced to confront idleness. The crisis appeared to have passed, and catastrophe narrowly escaped. If they were to take up their lives again, in which direction was she now to turn her own energies? The answer was close by. In fact, it had been percolating for years. At last it was time to tackle the project she'd wanted to devote herself to for as long as she could remember: the book of essays on Brazil. Not the airbrushed Time Life version full of naked happy savages and gleaming modernity, but her own version, one that encompassed the staggering loveliness *and* the terrible waste, the Brazilians' capacity for *saudade* as well as the consuming delight they could take in any moment—the whole wrenching, beautiful mess of which she'd become a citizen.

Once her mind quickened again to the work, Elizabeth knew exactly where to begin. Another river trip, this time to the Rio São Francisco, Brazil's second great waterway, which cut northward from Minas Gerais to Bahia. At the end of May, Lota accompanied her as far as Belo Horizonte, where Elizabeth boarded a bus with the other passengers who'd signed on for the river journey, fourteen intrepid souls who were all, curiously, rather obese.

After a long day's drive, they arrived in the town of Pirapora, where the river became navigable, and boarded the sternwheeler. Elizabeth began to take notes at once. In Portuguese, the boat was called a *gaviola*, or birdcage, for the iron framework built around the paddles, and indeed there were also birdcages all along the lower deck, filled with canaries, ferocious little green birds that were set upon each other to fight for sport.

As they set off down the river, the paddles splashed softly, a lulling, hypnotic *ppph . . . ppph . . . ppph*. The landscape was arid, desolate, a thousand times less lush and beautiful than the Amazon, yet this was exactly what the doctor had ordered: drifting with the current, gazing into the sky or water, losing all sense of time and place and distance. Her mind was cleansed. The hours passed.

All day long, the crew fished from the sides of the boat and grilled what they caught for lunch. The paddle wheel turned. *Ppph . . . ppph . . . ppph*.

The clay of the riverbank was a yellow-brown, and the color had worked its way into the water, the hides of livestock, the paint on the houses, the skin of the people. As they passed the yellow river towns, the yellow women washed their yellow clothes and yellow plates and yellow children in the yellow water. They stared at Elizabeth, and Elizabeth stared back. A breeze blew from the shore, carrying with it the perfume of jasmine and, underneath the sweetness, the scent of feces and carrion. Each evening, she made notes in her calendar book while the captain blasted a scratchy recording of *Lakmé*. On the last day before they arrived in Bahia, Elizabeth was gazing downriver when a thought lightly traced across her mind, like a bright mote floating in the corner of her vision.

Today is the day my mother died.

Then the thought whisked away.

She holed up in a hotel room in Salvador, writing out the notes for her essay. She tried to wash her clothes in the sink, but the rinsewater retained the yellow color of the river even after two vigorous applications of Flocos LUX soap. When she was done with her notes, she called home. It was Mary who answered the phone.

The moment she heard Mary's voice, Elizabeth already knew what news she was going to deliver, more or less.

"You must return to Rio immediately," Mary said.

"What's happened?" Her own voice was flat, disembodied.

"Lota's father passed away suddenly, several days ago. I'm sorry to tell you that Lota has collapsed again."

·29·

THE WHITE HEN had met its end in the middle of West Fourth Street, directly in front of Nicola's market. The unfortunate fowl's wings were flattened thin as paper, outstretched on the pavement as if in its final moments it had attempted to take flight.

"A pigeon, I'd understand," Elizabeth said to her friends. She'd been standing on the sidewalk between the two men for some minutes, conjecturing about the chicken's origin. "Or a sparrow. But what's a chicken doing running across the road in Greenwich Village in the middle of the afternoon?"

"Obviously, she didn't quite make it to the other side," said Wheaton.

"Don't you think it's the strangest thing?"

"I've seen stranger in *this* neighborhood."

"An inglorious end to an inglorious bird," Harold pronounced sadly.

"I feel she should be memorialized somehow," Elizabeth said.

They walked around the corner to Perry Street. Approaching their houses, which stood facing one another on the same block, she felt the too-familiar anxiety of imminent separation. An extreme reaction to the circumstance, she knew that, but hardly any more extreme than any day out of the last five years. Throughout the summer, she'd passed her afternoons in Harold and Wheaton's garden, reading or writing letters while Harold pruned. They were dear friends who became dearer by the day. She didn't need talk or entertainment, just human company close by. It was impossible to be alone anymore. She'd lost the knack.

"I'm going to have to start wearing earrings dangling down to my bosom," Elizabeth said as they passed two young women in sheer cotton blouses with no bras, "and a guitar strapped to my back, if I'm going to fit in here. Lota won't even recognize me." Her nerves, she noticed, were breaking down the filter between what her eyes encountered and what her mouth found necessary to speak aloud. "Look," she said, as they arrived at the men's house, "here I am again, following you to your front door, as if I lived here too."

"But you *do* live here too," Harold said, drawing her up the steps.

They settled in the garden. Wheaton went inside to turn on the hi-fi. Elizabeth's logorrhea continued. "That Nicotiana looks very good here. It really works in this sooty soil. I'm so glad you took my advice. And doesn't it smell divine? I love how it smells in the evening. But oh my, that bamboo isn't exactly thriving, is it?"

Wheaton returned, and with a touch of urgency she asked, "Would you say it's five o'clock yet?"

"The usual?" Wheaton rose from the chair he'd just taken.

"Yes, please. A gin and tonic is the perfect drink for these sticky New York summers, don't you think?"

"What time does Lota come in?" Harold asked. He was never one for rambling along conversational side roads. He used his words sparely, and always directed them at the heart of the matter. It might be painful, but his bass voice was so soothing, his dark, deep-set eyes so calming, she didn't mind.

"Her flight arrives tomorrow afternoon," Elizabeth said. "I'm sure she'll be worn out after the trip, but maybe over the weekend you two would like to come for dinner? I want to make something special to celebrate."

"We'd love to," Harold said. His smile was beneficent, deeply kind; she wanted to kneel and kiss his hand.

SHE'D LEFT BRAZIL two months ago, with hardly twenty-four hours' notice. New York, in summer, she found abandoned by literate society. All her friends had gone elsewhere, to the Hamptons probably, or distributed themselves to the poles. Cal was in Maine. No doubt it was for the best, as she couldn't tolerate any company but Harold and Wheaton's across the street. Besides, she was still having headaches and dizziness from the concussion she'd received her last night in Rio. The only one still hanging around the city was Mary McCarthy, who kept calling to suggest lunch. What nerve! How she'd treated Lota in that nasty, vulgar book of hers was unforgivable. Elizabeth had been forced to pretend she hadn't read it.

In June, when she'd rushed home after the river trip, Elizabeth had entered the apartment to find shades pulled across every window. She'd never before seen it darkened in this way, with the world shut out. "She says the light hurts her eyes," Mary informed her, standing in the shadows like a ghoul. In the back room, Lota lay on the bed. A profound, or perhaps a drugged, stillness had taken hold of her body. Her breathing was hoarse, regular. Elizabeth sat beside the bed and leaned forward, pressing her palms to her eyes.

"Are you crying, Cookie? You shouldn't cry."

Lota had turned toward her, but in the darkness Elizabeth could not make out her face. It was her voice that was so chilling, all the emotion drained out of it but with an observing distance, as if mildly puzzled by its own lack of feeling.

"I thought you were asleep," Elizabeth said.

Lota did not answer. After a long while, she said, "My father always told me you could not trust Americans. They speak the right words, but they do not believe them. I don't know why I am always surprised when I see the truth in what he said."

"Lota, please. I've been so worried about you. I'm sorry I wasn't here when your father died. Has it been awful?"

"My father was old. It was only a matter of time. It is a pity, though, we did not have that lunch I asked you to make."

"I was waiting for you to tell me when you wanted it!"

"I'm not blaming you, Elizabeth. Though perhaps you might have suggested a menu. I would have liked to see my father one more time. He was a famous man, did you know that? For years he fought against the dictatorship. He was imprisoned by Vargas, and exiled. That's why we lived in Belgium. Did I ever show you the hat he was wearing when Vargas tried to have him killed, with the bullet hole through the brim?"

"Yes, Lota, you did. He was brave. Just as you are."

"Don't lie to me, Elizabeth. I'm nothing. There were many people at the funeral. All the men who knew and admired him. Carlos was there, and Burle Marx. Even Negrão came. They offered their sympathy, but it was strange how they all wore his face. They looked at me as though I were someone he could not be proud of. Not a valuable person, not beautiful. Just a woman who would never accomplish anything, who failed at everything she tried to do."

DECIO WAS NO help at all. He came to see Lota daily, but he deflected Elizabeth's questions. In the past he had been entirely forthcoming about Lota's condition; now he became secretive. Elizabeth lost her patience with him on more than one occasion, while Decio merely observed her with his cold analytical eye. Then there came the horrible night he requested that Elizabeth come to his house, where he told her firmly that for Lota's sake she must leave the country. Ouro Preto was not far enough, he insisted. Her presence was too damaging to Lota's health, she must go very far away for it not to be disruptive. Despair prevented Elizabeth from mounting any sort of defense. But it wasn't her *fault*, she wanted to say. Would no one be their champion? Would no one advise her to not give up fighting, after all these years? But no, the entire peanut gallery seemed to think she and Lota were better off apart—Decio, Mary, Lota's friends, even Cal.

Decio urged her not to delay but to leave Brazil at the earliest opportunity, tomorrow, if possible. Lota's very existence hung in the balance. He stood too close, bearing down on her. Elizabeth tried to back away, and the edge of the coffee table caught her behind the knee. Her leg buckled. She collapsed like a rag doll, hitting her head on the table edge. Then the comically perverse attentions of Decio as the doctor, the rush to get ice, the attempt to stop her nosebleed.

Elizabeth accepted banishment. She left the next day.

BUT OF COURSE the break wasn't clean. It never was. Lota's letters followed as soon as she arrived in New York, plea after plea to allow her to join Elizabeth there. Some were reasonable, written in good spirits, others obviously not composed in a coherent state of mind. Sick with worry, Elizabeth did not know what to believe or do. If she could only get through to someone objective, but there was no such person, everyone had their own agenda. Decio did not return her calls. Contacting Mary was of course out of the question. Six weeks after Elizabeth left, Lota sent a string of cables, increasingly urgent. Decio had given his blessing for the trip, she said; now she only needed Elizabeth's.

Three times, Elizabeth tried to confirm with the psychiatrist, but again she received no response. She couldn't bear the pitiful tone of Lota's begging. She wanted to be with Lota again. She wanted the chance to show Lota that she was valuable, that she was beautiful, that she was someone to be proud of. *Yes*, Elizabeth cabled back, *come to New York*. Come live with me and be my love.

THE FLIGHT WAS three hours late. The instant she saw Lota, so feeble that a stewardess had to help her down the stairs from the aircraft, Elizabeth knew that her judgment had been poor, the latest instance in a long history of poor judgments dating back to the dawn of her consciousness. She would call Decio again in the morning. How dare he have allowed Lota to leave Brazil in such a state? And Mary, couldn't she have dissuaded her somehow? Then Lota was coming through the gate, and Elizabeth stepped forward to greet her.

Lota was confused about where she'd actually arrived. "Will we stay with Lilli," she asked once they'd retrieved her luggage, "or is your new house ready?"

"No, dear, we're not in Ouro Preto, we're in New York," Elizabeth said gently. She refused to succumb to hopelessness; no doubt it was the long flight that had momentarily disoriented Lota. "We're staying at my friend Loren's apartment on Perry Street."

"Of course," Lota snapped. "I knew that."

As exhausted as she appeared, once they got to the apartment Lota insisted on unpacking. She hauled a heavy duffel up the stairs to the kitchen and removed twelve kilo bags of coffee, setting them in a row on the counter. "It helps me to wake up," she said when she saw Elizabeth's surprise.

Then Lota removed her clothes from the suitcase and meticulously refolded them, putting them away in the dresser while Elizabeth observed from the doorway.

"There is no need to follow me into every room like a puppy dog," Lota said as she brushed past Elizabeth on her way to the bathroom.

THEIR LAST HOURS together, Elizabeth will write to friends, were peaceful and affectionate. They had no quarrel.

"Would you like to go on a walk?" she suggested after Lota had settled in.

Lota turned an impassive face to her. She said neither yes nor no.

"I thought that after such a long trip, some air and some life might brighten you up."

At last, a smile. "Yes, we could both use some brightening."

On the street, however, Lota was very weak. She shuffled along, and Elizabeth took her arm, helping her into a chair at the first café.

"Would you like something to eat?"

"Not particularly."

Elizabeth ordered her a salad. Lota gazed at the passersby as Elizabeth reported on her New York summer. She shied from asking any question about Brazil. Lota's job, Decio, Mary, Carlos—each and every topic felt equally perilous. "I had lunch with Susan Sontag the other day," she said. "Her brain is way too big for me, that's certain. But I've hardly seen anyone while I've been here. I can't say I'm crazy about being back. I don't really feel American anymore. This isn't home. I thought perhaps next summer you and I might go somewhere else, together. What would you think of getting an apartment in Venice for a month or two?"

Lota picked at the food on her plate. "That's a beautiful idea, Cookie."

"The salad's not very good, is it? I'm sorry to have brought you here. Tomorrow I promise to cook something very special. Would you like to see Wheaton and Harold? I've invited them over. They've been such a godsend to me."

"They're nice," Lota said. "They're nice, and I'm glad they're your friends."

Elizabeth's mind began to grasp at any little thing to say, any bright, shiny thing. "Yesterday we actually saw a chicken run over in the road!"

Lota looked up. Her eyes regained their focus. "A chicken?"

"None of us could believe it. What would a chicken be doing in the city?"

"Hen or cock?" Lota demanded.

"It was a hen. Why do you ask?"

"It reminds me of something I recently read." Lota was smiling at her. "'The hen is a being. It's true, she couldn't be counted on for anything. She herself couldn't count on herself—the way a rooster believes in his comb.'"

"I'm sorry?"

"It's from one of Clarice Lispector's stories you translated."

"I know what it is, but how on earth do you remember that?"

"You do know Portuguese after all, Elizabeth."

"Or course I know Portuguese. I'm just embarrassed to speak it. My accent is so terrible."

"You ask how I remember. I remember everything you've written, every single poem. I was reading them again on the plane." Lota began to recite another. "*You helpless, foolish man, I love you all I can, I think. Or do I?* That was supposed to be me speaking, wasn't it? You were happy when you wrote that. I think you were very happy."

"Please stop quoting my poems, Lota. It makes me self-conscious."

"But were you very happy, once, with me?"

"I was very happy for a very long time. You know I was. And I will be again."

"Elizabeth, I've watched you struggle for so many years, working so hard to create beautiful things. I've admired how you never give up. You are not a dilettante like me. Promise me you will doubt yourself no longer. You are a wonderful poet. A *great* poet."

"You've admired me?" Elizabeth said.

Lota nodded.

"And you don't doubt me?"

Lota placed her hand over Elizabeth's. "I don't doubt you."

"Thank you, Lota. That is very kind of you to say."

"It is not kind, merely a fact." Lota seemed to be studying every detail of Elizabeth's face. Then she signaled to the waitress. "I think I will have an espresso. It will brighten me up."

WHEN ELIZABETH CAME to bed, she found Lota gripping a pillow in both arms. She was not asleep. Her eyes were open wide, her thoughts turned inward.

Elizabeth lay beside her and tugged on the pillow.

"I need to hold on to something," Lota said, hugging the pillow more tightly.

"You can hold on to me."

She watched Lota deliberating before she let loose of the pillow and scooted close. Instead of the grudging embrace Elizabeth expected, Lota pressed tightly against her, kissing the back of her neck with an intensity that might have been mistaken for passion. It was lovely to be held again, to be touched. And a surprise, in the midst of all this, to feel the light gathering of desire. Elizabeth imagined turning and pressing her lips to Lota's, but instead she remained still. She would make no demands.

She felt safe in the circle of Lota's arms as sleep overtook her. Elizabeth began to sink into a dream—no, it was something else, very vivid, half dream, half memory. Years ago, after the New Year's party they'd thrown in Copacabana, Lota's arms were around her. They stood in the ocean, at midnight.

As the fireworks exploded over the beach, Lota rounded up all the guests in the apartment, insisting they join the celebrants below. In their excitement, they did not wait for the elevator but rushed down the stairwell in a stream, down all eleven stories, and burst out into the night. Elizabeth slipped off her shoes and left them by the door.

Across the expanse of sand, thousands of candles illuminated many more thousands of people dressed in white. They were singing and drinking, and some were dancing to drumbeats, growing frenzied and falling to the ground in convulsions, as if possessed by spirits. Others waded into the ocean to set adrift their offerings to Yemanja, little blue sailboats full of fruit and bread, their luminous white skirts billowing and swirling in the water. Lota pulled Elizabeth into the waves and wrapped her arms around her. On the surface of the sea all around them floated white roses, gladioli, lilies, gardenias, a vast white carpet of flowers.

Elizabeth woke at early light. Lota was no longer beside her.

Where am I? Lota thought.

She had started from sleep in a strange bed. She was embracing Elizabeth, but she did not know where she lay. Then she remembered.

She'd taken a plane, a very long flight. Mary had driven her to the airport, her mouth so tight with barely contained sadness that she'd hardly spoken. I hope you have a good trip, she'd said in farewell as she dropped Lota off at the curb, refusing to come inside to send her off properly. Lota, too, was saddened that she could not tell Mary why she had to come to New York. That she had to be with Elizabeth, as selfish as that might be, to let Elizabeth know that she did not blame her.

That she loved her.

That she regretted how things had come to be between them.

She watched Elizabeth sleeping.

After her father died, there had been a flare of rage that she thought would incinerate her, but the rage burned off and then there was nothing and Lota could not prevent herself from sinking further and further into this cold nothingness. Decio talked with her almost every day, urging her to fight her way back to feeling. But Lota did not want to fight any longer. All the fight had gone out of her.

She left the bedroom and wandered into the apartment. It was a nice apartment, but very dusty! Maybe Elizabeth would be happy here after it got a good cleaning.

There'd been the hope, of course, that once she saw Elizabeth again she'd change her mind. A distant hope.

In the bathroom, Lota unzipped her toiletries bag, her fingers searching out the vial.

She was in the kitchen, staring at the row of coffee bags—how odd that she'd brought so much—when she heard Elizabeth calling her name. Dawn light seeped through the curtains. Lota stood at the top of a short staircase, hardly a staircase at all, only three stairs, which struck her as an odd architectural gesture. The pills had begun to take effect. Her hand, she discovered, still gripped the vial. Elizabeth appeared on the landing below, but at first she didn't see Lota in the shadows. Her voice was muffled, as if it traveled through water. Then she turned and looked up at Lota, watching her for some moments before her face began to crease with worry. Elizabeth came quickly up the stairs. Lota smiled at her as she fell forward.

She felt her body slipping, slippery, through Elizabeth's embrace, and then she went under the surface. It was quiet now. Weightless, Lota was free to drift. Elizabeth was above, in the air, and Lota could feel the pressure of Elizabeth's hand holding her own.

We're swimming, my love, you and I. I see you up there, in the shimmering blue. You're reaching down to me, but you won't reach me. This time you won't reach me.

Elizabeth was shouting, but Lota could hardly hear her through the water. What was in the vial? That's what she wanted to know.

It doesn't matter, Elizabeth. It's all right. I don't have to struggle anymore. I have come to the end. But I had to be with you. That's why I came here, to be with you.

Elizabeth wanted to pull her back up, she was trying to pull her into the air.

Let me go, Elizabeth. My love for you kept me fighting this long. But I don't want to fight any longer. Especially not with you, though, yes, we had our battles. You are very stubborn, and you drink too much. Do not deny it. You know it's true.

I'm swimming, and you're there! My love! You're holding my hand. Don't try to draw me up. But it's all right. You're there. I see you. Now you have to let me go. You have to let me go.

She tried to wrest her hand free, but Elizabeth's grip was fierce.

We loved the best we could, and that is more than most people ever have. Now let me go.

·30·

There is beginning, middle, and end, that is a fact.
The end of things is not a moral act.

THE NOTES WERE in her own hand, but Elizabeth had no recollection of having put them to paper. They were strange to her. She will experience the same feeling in another handful of years when she discovers letters she'd once written in Portuguese that she can no longer read.

Unpacking her things in the new apartment, she'd come across these scraps of writing among the loose papers she must have swept off her desk in Samambaia. She'd returned there briefly a month after shipping Lota's body back for the funeral. To meet with the lawyers who would settle her affairs, and to say goodbye to what friends remained. They were even fewer than she'd imagined. Nearly everyone blamed her, including those who knew better. They had to explain Lota's self-destruction somehow, she supposed, even if it meant sacrificing Elizabeth to their confused anger and grief. Her last visit to Samambaia had been disastrous, ending in a screaming match with Mary, who had already rifled through everything in the house, even private things, taken paintings that did not belong to her, and, worse, the absolute worst, *burned* Elizabeth's letters to Lota, for God's sake. Dumb to the world, Elizabeth had thrown what had not been ravaged into boxes and fled as quickly as possible.

A week ago, she'd caught a cab to the airport. Only the maid accompanied her. Lucia was from the north of Brazil, a superior human being. She held Elizabeth's hand as they passed through the Copacabana tunnel, sped along Lota's park. There was the puppet theatre, the gardens, the model airplane field, the playgrounds, the beach, the soccer fields, the modern art museum, all of them full of people.

"She worked so *hard*," Elizabeth said softly. Lucia squeezed her hand.

Elizabeth crossed back into her own hemisphere, in a plane high above the continents, north and south. She lived in San Francisco now. It was New Year's Day, 1968.

THE YOUNG WOMAN had found the apartment. She was very good at practical things like finding an apartment and organizing the kitchen shelves and leaving her husband. The flat was pretty in a Victorian, frosted-cake sort of way. Lota would have loathed it. Cold blue light filtered through every window, and though the sun was constantly shining, there was a chill in the rooms that penetrated to Elizabeth's bones, forcing her to wear wool sweaters indoors and even to sleep in them. That was, if she slept at all. Living with a child again was certainly something to get used to. The child was delightful, as children were, but its skin was so pale Elizabeth sometimes wondered if it were not malnourished. That morning the young woman had gone to the Haight-Ashbury to show off her baby to some friends who, if Elizabeth had heard correctly, were living in the park under a tree. Who was she to judge? She'd watched from the window until the young woman disappeared over a hill, then she'd changed her clothes and left the apartment as well.

No one paid her any mind on the tram. It was a city of youth, a tide of youth pushing the country into a social revolution, and she was merely an elderly lady who'd already had her day. Dressed all in white, her arms full of white flowers—even so, she attracted little notice. San Francisco was the capitol of flower power, after all. As the tram traveled away from the city center, past all the quaint gingerbread houses, up and down the hills, the other passengers, singly or in groups, disembarked. She was alone in the car when the train crested a last hill and there lay the Pacific Ocean spread before her, dark and glittering like mica. In the distance, two little peaked islands punctured the horizon.

Another city, another ocean. A child's small hand taking hold of her finger. Another way, perhaps, to say *beginning*.

At the end of the line, two strapping young men put their shoulders to the back of the tram and pushed, rotating the car in a circle to head back the way it had come. They were surprised to see her emerge through the doors. Elizabeth bade them good day and crossed the road. The beach was very wide and gray, not at all like Copacabana, backed by dunes and scrub, deserted, with a cold wildness to it. The ocean was rough, forbidding.

Elizabeth removed her shoes and walked across the sand.

A mutt ran past, scouting the beach. He looked up at her hopefully and hesitated in case she might throw a morsel, then trotted on. Elizabeth came around a dune and nearly stumbled over two lovers who lay entangled on the slope. The lady in white did not distract them from one another. The wind was brisk. At the water's edge it blew a cold spray into her face from the crests of breaking waves.

Tying the white skirt in a knot at her waist, Elizabeth waded into the water, so shockingly cold her feet were numb in seconds. Up to her knees, no farther. The undercurrent was very strong, threatening her balance. The retreating waves pulled at her and rapidly drew the sand from beneath her heels, like Yemanja's clutch.

But Elizabeth did not rush her ritual. One by one she dropped the flowers into the water—lilies, hydrangeas, peonies, roses, even some daisies. She'd bought all the white flowers she could find in her neighborhood, from three different florists. As many as her arms could carry, though now, in the vastness of the sea, they appeared a paltry collection.

She would never know why. She would never know if there was anything she might have done to prevent it. Maybe Lota had planned it all; or else it could as easily have been an impulsive act. Maybe she'd actually had trouble getting to sleep that night and lost count of how many sleeping pills she'd taken from the vial. Or maybe, as Elizabeth suspected, she'd simply grown bored with her own fallibility, murderously bored. Lota had always been impatient. Finally, perhaps, too impatient to live.

The white flowers lay on a bed of foam. A wave rolled over them and nearly pulled Elizabeth under as well. But she braced herself and remained standing as the flowers began to resurface all around her. Then the current caught them and swept them swiftly toward the south.

ACKNOWLEDGMENTS

While working on this novel, I found Elizabeth Bishop's own writings to be an endless source of instruction and delight. In particular, her collected letters served as a constant guide to her life and work during her years in Brazil. I wish to acknowledge that in several instances I have used phrases from her letters, journals, and drafts in the text.

A number of other books also proved invaluable, among them: *Remembering Elizabeth Bishop, An Oral Biography*, by Gary Fountain and Peter Brazeau; *When Brazil Was Modern, Guide to Architecture 1928-1960*, by Lauro Cavalcanti; *Rare and Commonplace Flowers, The Story of Elizabeth Bishop and Lota de Macedo Soares*, by Carmen Oliveira; *Conversations with Elizabeth Bishop*, edited by George Monteiro; *Elizabeth Bishop, Life and the Memory of It*, by Brett C. Miller; and *Carlos Lacerda, Brazilian Crusader, Volumes I and II*, by John W.F. Dulles.

I am very grateful for the advice and encouragement of Carrie Avery, Jeanne Carstensen, Lisa Conrad, Bernard Cooper, Helen Humphreys, Julie Leavitt, Dean Rogers at Vassar's Special Collections Library, and Sandra Vivanco for her insights on Lina Bo Bardi and Brazilian modernism. Many thanks also to Annie Tucker and Laura Mazer at Counterpoint.

Muito obrigado to the Brazilians: Ricardo Bandeira, Maria Teresa Camargo, Fernando Campana, Humberto Campana, Luiz Eduardo Mihich, Gustavo Motta, Rodrigo Murat, and Ayla Tiago de Melo.

I also wish to thank The Yaddo Corporation and The Escape to Create program in Seaside, Florida, where parts of this book were written.